Pious

By Mark Barber

ZMOK
BOOKS

Pious by Mark Barber
Cover by Mantic Games
This edition published in 2020

Zmok Books is an imprint of

Winged Hussar Publishing, LLC
1525 Hulse Rd, Unit 1
Point Pleasant, NJ 08742

Published under license with Mantic Games

Bibliographical References and Index
1. Fantasy. 2. Naval Warfare. 3. Adventure

Winged Hussar Publishing, LLC All rights reserved
For more information
visit us at www.wingedhussarpublishing.com

Twitter: WingHusPubLLC
Facebook: Winged Hussar Publishing LLC

'For Lydia - I hope you enjoy this story when you are old enough, because little girls can grow up to fight pirates, too!'

Pious

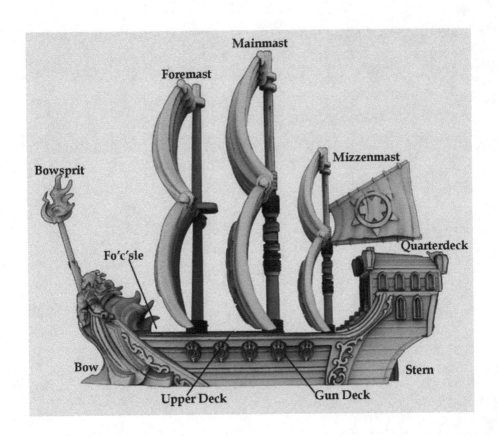

Elohi-Class Frigate (Batch Two) – Basilean Navy

Chapter One

"They're signaling, Captain!" Lieutenant Ganto grimaced as he leaned further over the wooden taff rail of the quarterdeck, his telescope pressed to one eye. "Looks like the signals are for us!"

Exhaling through gritted teeth, Captain Charn Ferrus lowered his own telescope and looked contemptuously across at where his ship's third lieutenant lunged across the quarterdeck, his exaggerated stance completely at odds with the rather mild state of the waters as the thirty-six-gun frigate pitched gently in the moderate waves of the Infant Sea. The young officer continued to stare out at the sloop to the south, clearly oblivious to the withering glare issued in his direction from his captain.

"Mister Ganto," Charn said calmly through a thin, insincere smile, "I was educated in interpreting signal flags as a boy sailor at the age of ten. That was, I believe, before you were born. Now, be a good fellow and confine your ill-educated ramblings to your juniors."

The young officer quickly lowered his telescope and turned to face Charn, his face paling as he opened and closed his mouth a few times in an unsuccessful attempt to formulate an appropriate response, before settling for the time-honored and completely correct reply to paternal advice from a captain of the Basilean Navy.

"Aye aye, sir."

Tutting to himself as he contemplated the idiocy displayed on a near daily basis by some of his ship's officers – in stark contrast to the utter professionalism demonstrated by his veteran ratings – Charn returned to his telescope and looked out toward the southern horizon. A sloop, single-masted and lateen-rigged, cut across the sun-kissed, turquoise waves on an easterly heading. Just visible behind it were another two ships of identical profiles, a shape he was more than familiar with. A squadron of sloops of the Basilean Navy, the closest of which was requesting assistance via a series of colored pennants trailing neatly from her outer halyards.

Charn snapped his telescope shut and turned to face Thaddeus Just; the ship's master, responsible for the frigate's navigation and sail setting. The white-haired warrant officer stood taller and straighter as soon as the captain's gaze fell upon him.

"Mister Just," Charn said, "make best speed to position us to windward of that closest sloop."

"Aye, sir," the wrinkled sailor nodded before turning to face the young sailor who clutched the ship's wheel at the center of the tall quarterdeck. "Helmsman! Port your helm, hard a-weather! And…

thus!"

A faint smile tugged at Charn's lips. The wooden deck heaved beneath him in response to the helmsman's input as the agile frigate altered course to head off toward the nearest of the sloops to the south. The master paced forth to yell out orders to ensure the sails were trimmed to maximize the benefit of the wind now off the port quarter. Sailors clambered precariously across the yards of the frigate's three masts, letting the white sails out to catch the warm wind and push the Hegemon's Warship *Pious* southward.

The frigate sailed majestically through the clear water of the northern Infant Sea, as nobly as if she owned the oceans herself. To the north lay Basilea, the chosen nation of the Shining Ones above, and the pillar of all that was good and righteous in Pannithor. The Infant Sea continued to sprawl out hundreds of leagues to the west, separating the Kingdoms of Men to the north from the deserts of Ophidia and the lush plains and forests of Elvenholme to the south, before eventually opening out into the forbidding Endless Sea.

Thaddeus paced over to stand by Charn, his eyes flitting between checking on the work of his sailors up in the rigging and assessing the situation to the south.

"What do you think they're after, Captain?" he asked gruffly. "We're close to the Sand Lane, it could be a merchantman in trouble."

"Could be," Charn mumbled, also wondering what possible problem a squadron of three sloops could have encountered that would necessitate them signaling a frigate for help. "I don't think I'm expecting too much of a courtesy by hoping they'll signal with a little more clarity in the near future."

Charn raised his telescope to one eye again and surveyed the blurred horizon, the extent of his vision still impended by the final remnants of a bank of early morning mist that the rising sun had still failed to burn off entirely. The three sloops were clear enough, and for a moment, Charn thought he saw a fourth ship in the distance; but years at sea had taught him that it was never worth jumping to conclusions based on a momentary blur that might have been seen on the horizon. However, after he blinked and returned the telescope, he saw a small, jagged outline that could never have been made by nature, his suspicions escalating rapidly.

"Mister Ganto," Charn called across to his third lieutenant, "look out to the horizon, perhaps two points south of southwest. What do you see?"

The young officer raised his telescope.

"I do not see... Wait... Yes, sir, there's a fourth ship, I believe."

The sloops had now all altered course to head south, their sheets taunt to haul in their sails and clutch on to every last gasp of wind as the fast ships raced toward the horizon. The very fact that three armed sloops had requested assistance from him and then turned away to dash for the south told Charn all he needed to know. He turned his head to bellow an order down to the upper deck below.

"Beat to quarters!"

***

Jaymes Ellias let out a low groan as he opened one eye, positively certain in his mind that he had been asleep for precisely one second when he was forced to awaken. The staccato beating of drums rippled down the passageway outside his cabin, reverberating off the wooden bulkheads of the frigate. Jaymes's eyes shot wide open. Beat to quarters. The ship was going to battle. Indistinguishable yells of command could be heard from the upper deck above him as he swung out of his fold-out, canvas cot bed. He quickly dragged on his blue uniform trousers and white shirt before hauling his boots on; not the footwear of an officer as he had been condescendingly reminded on many occasions by fellow lieutenants. After tying his dark hair back in a short ponytail, he completed his apparel by pulling on his jacket, dark blue and lined with gold lace at the collar and around the rank insignia on his cuffs.

Jaymes grabbed his black, bicorn hat from the wooden locker underneath his cot and took the two paces to the door at the end of his minuscule cabin, the majority of which was taken up by his bed and washing basin. Outside his cabin, in the narrow passageway running directly beneath the upper deck at the after end of the frigate, he grabbed his sword and scabbard from where it hung outside the handful of tiny, officer's cabins. The morning sunlight was blinding as he scrambled up the wooden ladder leading to the center of the upper deck, only a few wisps of cloud breaking up the otherwise flawless light blue of the spring sky above. Jaymes pulled his hat on atop his dark hair, worn front-to-back in the style of the Basilean Navy, rather than the side-to-side fashion employed by most navies of the Successor Kingdoms. He buckled his sword belt around his waist as a procession of sailors filed quickly out of the forward hatchway to line the upper deck, the center of which was exposed to the elements while the forward and aft ends were hidden beneath the fo'c'sle and quarterdeck respectively. The ratings – the sailors of the frigate whose ranks were not determined by a commission from the Hegemon appointing them as officers – were unique among human navies in that they, too, wore

3

uniforms; simple trousers and shirts of blue, with red bandannas tied over the top of their heads, tails flowing down the backs of their necks.

Jaymes was intercepted at the foot of the quarterdeck by Gregori Corbes, the *Pious's* first lieutenant. Gregori was in his late twenties, a couple of years Jaymes senior, and to the casual bystander would appear identically dressed; yet to the experienced sailor, the subtle differences in their uniform spoke volumes about the very differing fortunes of their careers. The gold adorning Gregori's long uniform jacket was of infinitely higher quality; a cockade ornamented his bicorn hat, and he wore a stylish neck cloth of black silk inside his shirt collar, despite the stifling heat of the Infant Sea in springtime. His blond ponytail tied back in a bow of black ribbon, Gregori wore expensive shoes decorated with large, polished buckles to compliment the thick, white stockings that covered his lower legs. All of these details spoke of a more affluent lieutenant, an officer whose career had seen a far greater degree of action and the share of prize money that came with the capture of enemy vessels.

"Morning, Mister Ellias!" Gregori shot him a friendly smile. "Only three days out of port and action already!"

"Morning, shipmate," Jaymes suppressed a yawn and wiped at his bleary eyes. "Has Walt mistaken a fishing buoy for a kraken again?"

"Nothing of the sort!" Gregori smiled again, but he lowered his brow in irritation at the accusation Jaymes had leveled at the competence of Walt Ganto, the third lieutenant. "Actually, the captain is already on deck and issued the order for beat to quarters."

Jaymes followed Gregori up onto the quarterdeck, happy for a blast of sea air across the back of his neck as the ship continued to increase speed. The sails from the trio of tall masts above him billowed out as the master barked up orders to the scores of sailors who moved precariously across the yards and through the rigging to make the adjustments necessary to harness every last benefit from the morning breeze. Captain Charn Ferrus looked across as the two lieutenants approached, his face twisting into a scowl as his dark eyes surveyed Jaymes from head to foot.

"Good morning, Mister Ellias!" he snapped. "Nice of you to join us at last. I do hope my ship being called to quarters has not interrupted your slumber too much?"

"Good morning, sir," Jaymes replied. "Apologies for my tardiness, I had only just closed my eyes after taking the entire night watch and handing over to…"

"Spare me the alibis, sir!" the captain growled before handing his brass telescope across to Gregori. "Mister Corbes! Cast your eye just to the sou' of southwest and tell me what you see?"

"Aye, sir," Gregori took the telescope and brought it to his eye.

The frigate's first lieutenant stared off to the distant horizon for some moments in silence. Jaymes looked ahead and saw two, no, three Basilean sloops pitching gently in the turquoise waters as they made best speed toward the south. They were not far from the Sand Lane; that much he knew from the watch handover only half an hour before when he had passed on his duties as officer of the watch to Walt Ganto. The Sand Lane was one of the busiest shipping routes to the south of the City of the Golden Horn, one of the wealthiest cities in any nation of Pannithor and the very center of sea trade for all of Basilea. Three sloops dashing toward the extremities of the Sand Lane followed by the order to beat to quarters could logically mean only one thing.

"I see her," Gregori murmured to himself. "Well, not a 'her', more of an 'it'. I wouldn't extend the courtesy of a feminine pronoun to that vessel."

"What do you mean?" the captain demanded, snatching back his telescope.

"The vessel to the south of our sloops, sir," Gregori replied, "looks orcish to me. And a large one at that."

"Orcs?" Walt exclaimed. "Here? We're barely out of sight of Keretia!"

The captain let out a grunt; a noise that Jaymes knew could mean that he was either in deep concentration or annoyed by the conversation around him. Either way, the three lieutenants silently and unanimously decided together to take it as a sign for them to cease conversing.

"By the Ones," Charn grimaced, "I think you're right."

He turned to face his trio of lieutenants.

"Mister Corbes, remain on the quarterdeck with me, for now. Mister Ellias, take charge of the upper deck aft. Mister Ganto, you have the upper deck for'ard. Mister Just, clear for action."

"Aye, sir," Jaymes acknowledged his order and turned to make his way quickly back to the steps leading down to the grim, continuous line of black cannons awaiting on the upper deck, Walt following him closely behind.

***

The scene materializing before Charn's eyes over the next half hour changed his appreciation of the dynamic situation unfolding before him. As the mist burnt away and visibility improved, he realized that the four Basilean warships were not closing with a single orc warship, but a pair. The smaller of the two ships was a twin masted affair of slightly smaller dimensions than the *Pious*, but not nearly as well-constructed or, from Charn's experience of fighting similar vessels in the past, not as well-armed either. The second ship caused him far more concern.

The larger orc ship was a brutal affair that almost looked as though it had been cobbled together out of ill-fitting parts of other ships, and then with some jagged, metal decorations bolted on as a macabre afterthought. The larger of the two vessels, a 'smasher' in orc parlance, according to reports from the Basilean Admiralty, boasted two full gun decks as well as additional weapons on its quarterdeck and fo'c'sle, giving it nearly double the punch of Charn's Batch Two Elohi-class frigate. It's brutal, course hull, while undoubtedly slower, looked significantly more solid; perhaps as much so as a Basilean third-rate ship of the line. Charn swore under his breath as he surveyed the enemy ship, now perhaps only six thousand yards away and closing, noting the battery of heavy cannons on the fo'c'sle that were pointing directly at the nearest sloop. He snapped his telescope shut and turned to his first lieutenant.

"There's a couple of merchant cutters heading north along the Sand Lane," he remarked dryly, "I think that's what those two orc ships were going for. We appear to have their attention now."

"Not like them to tussle with us, sir," Gregori winced as he brought his telescope to his eye again. "They normally know better."

"You are crediting orcs with thinking long term, Mister Corbes," Charn replied. "The fact that angering Basilea will undoubtedly result in their demise simply does not figure on their agenda. What does, is that their smasher could give *two* fifth-rate frigates like this a run for their money, and their captain is no doubt also aware that three piddling sloops are far from the equal of a frigate. Even without that second ship to support him, he has us at a distinct advantage."

"Aye, sir," Gregori nodded, "but we have the wind on our quarter and are sailing large, which gives us the initiative. And we have the gods on our side."

If those words had been uttered by nearly anybody onboard the *Pious*, Charn would have verbally torn them asunder. But not Gregori. One of the few sailors onboard he genuinely trusted and respected, Charn thanked the Shining Ones above that he had such a competent and capable officer as his first. He looked forward across the sleek, sweeping lines of his warship, past the quarterdeck and the open center of the upper deck below it, past the fo'c'sle and to the bowsprit; an elegantly fashioned beam of wood carved into the image of a torch, held by the beautiful effigy of an Elohi that clung gracefully to the bow of the ship to form a figurehead. The torch remained extinguished. He winced at the thought.

"Well," Gregori said as he returned to his telescope, "they've certainly made their intentions clear now."

Charn looked through his own telescope and saw puffs of smoke blossom up across the fo'c'sle of the orc smasher as the iron-clad, heavy bows heaved into the waves beneath the ship's blood-red sails. Seconds later, a quartet of great pillars of water sprouted up around one of the sloops from the cannonballs fired by the orc warship's heavy bow chaser cannons. Charn shook his head. He doubted the sloops would last long but knew they were doing their duty in trying to keep the orc ships away from the trade lanes so as to protect the merchantmen. He just wondered whether such an act was worth dying for. Regardless, the challenge to his honor had been issued, and there was no way he could back down from a battle now, not after spending his entire life fighting for the chance to captain a frigate. If he ran from a fight, the Admiralty would wrench him from a post-command and into an administrative job so fast it would make his head spin.

"Mister Just!" he shouted across to the ship's master. "Get me starboard side to alongside that big orc bastard! Eight hundred yards! Keep us out of range of their close quarter guns!"

"Aye, Captain!" the veteran master acknowledged before translating his thoughts into an order for the helmsman. "Helmsman! Starboard your helm, two points!"

The forward facing guns of the orc smasher spoke again perhaps two minutes later, giving Charn an idea of the experience of their crew based on the mediocre time taken to reload their guns. Great towers of water again shot up around the little sloop, closer, but not close enough to provoke a response. Meanwhile, the second orc ship – a blood runner – tacked away to head toward the third of the three sloops, the smaller guns on its own fo'c'sle awaiting for their targets to fall within range.

"Mister Corbes," Charn looked across at his first lieutenant, "go and take charge of the fo'c'sle guns. Load with round shot and hit that smasher with everything you can until we are within range of bar shot. And be so good as to educate the young gentleman in command of the guns on what you are doing, if you could. Good opportunity for the fellow to learn something if he lives through this."

"Aye, sir," Gregori touched two fingers to the brim of his bicorn hat in salute before making his way quickly forward toward the fo'c'sle.

***

Only a few feet below the gently heaving quarterdeck, Jaymes paced along the after end of the upper deck, between the lines of cannons secured to both sides of the frigate. The gun ports were open and the cannons were already loaded and run out, their stubby mouths protruding from both sides of the upper deck. The order had not been passed down yet to Jaymes to inform him which side of the frigate the captain intended to bring to bear on the enemy, so the lines of guns along both sides were each crewed with six men; once he knew which side would be firing, he would order the men from the idle side of the ship across to assist the active guns.

Jaymes made his way over to the center of the upper deck, the only part left open to the elements between the coverings of the quarterdeck behind and the fo'c'sle in front, and he leaned across the side of the ship to look out ahead at the unfolding scene of action. He was greeted with a refreshing blast of air, warm and laden with the scent of salt, and he saw two sloops bounding away from the frigate toward a hulking orc ship directly ahead. He muttered a brief prayer for the crews of the sloops, men he knew would not stand a chance against a proper orc ship of battle. His affinity to the sloop crews was perhaps more so than any other man onboard; Jaymes had only been with the *Pious* for three months and before that had never set foot on a frigate in his life. His early career, initially much to his chagrin, was one spent on sloops very similar to those he now watched, but confined to coastal duties to the west of the City of the Golden Horn.

They were fantastic years. Initially, as an ambitious midshipman in his adolescence, he yearned to be onboard a bigger ship sailing farther afield and facing deadlier foes. But, as the years went by, he grew to love the life of a coastal sloop officer. Days spent venturing out to sea only so far as to remain visual with the breathtaking scenery of the southern coastline of Basilea; perhaps lending assistance to troubled fishermen, once in a while intercepting smugglers and even then barely ever seeing any resistance. Then it was back ashore in time to watch the sunset in one of dozens of coastal village taverns, with a good bottle of wine and a pretty girl to share it with. The life of a coastal sloop officer was perhaps the best kept secret in the Basilean Navy. But that was a life Jaymes had now lost, although there was at least a girl now in his life who he hoped he could impress.

Jaymes's mind was brought back to the present as a low rumble, not dissimilar to thunder, issued from the south. He looked out again and saw blue-gray clouds waft up from the bows of the orc smasher; moments later, another four pillars of seawater rose up around one of the sloops as the cannonballs from the orc warship bracketed the sea around her, still not close enough to cause damage but certainly closer than the last volley. The lighter bow chasers on the first of the Basilean sloops now spoke in response, a normally admirable enough punch to the noise they created, but now decidedly meager in comparison to the orc warship bearing down upon them.

A hushed conversation drifted across from one of the starboard guns at the after end of the frigate, the tone of the gunners discernibly nervous, even if the actual words were not. Jaymes considered ordering them to keep silent but decided against it; they were just as entitled to be nervous about the approaching confrontation as he was. He made his way back to stand by the aft guns, just as the heavy bow cannons of the orc smasher thundered out again.

***

Charn let out an audible groan as the cannonballs smashed into the lead sloop. The little warship seemed to jolt with the impact of the shot, but from this range, Charn could neither see nor hear the effect of the damage. The sloop bravely sailed on, its own guns barking out a few seconds later. The second sloop supported the lead with its own weight of shot, blasting out a volley from its fo'c'sle guns and scoring a hit on the lumbering orc warship. The shots pelted against the ugly, iron snout of the smasher, causing no discernible damage that Charn could detect, even with the benefit of his telescope. He assessed the range of his own vessel from the smasher and reckoned it to be about at the limits of his own bow chaser cannons.

As if anticipating the thought, he heard a yell of an order from the frigate's fo'c'sle and the battery of light cannons at the bow blasted into life. Charn smiled in satisfaction as the bow of his frigate sunk back down a little; Gregori had ordered the bow guns to fire at the very top of a wave, with the sea itself angling the frigate's bows up a little and adding to their reach. Charn raised his telescope and saw plumes of water forced up just to port of the smasher; not a bad effort for a ranging shot, but battles were not won with good will alone – they needed to hit the bastard. If it had been any other officer, Charn would have been yelling corrective instructions across, but he was more than content that Gregori would apply the necessary corrections to his gunners. The smell of burnt gunpowder drifted back to the quarterdeck from the bow guns as their crews hurriedly sponged them out and reloaded them.

Off to the southeast, the third sloop was now engaged in exchanging fire with the orc blood runner; the smaller orc vessel was still substantial enough to cause a Basilean frigate concern, so it was certainly large enough to take on a trio of sloops without assistance. The twin masted orc warship loomed closer to the valiant sloop, the ludicrous looking metal drill on the prow of the vessel now turning as it cut through the clear waters of the Infant Sea. A superb display of gunnery from the sloop sent cannonballs pounding against the blood runner's wooden hull, again too far away for Charn to determine whether any significant damage had been caused. He raised his telescope to his eye and brought his attention back to the orc smasher that lay directly ahead, quickly counting what he could make out of the guns along the smasher's twin gun decks. Be it head to head or alongside each other, firing with broadsides, the orc ship had him slightly outgunned. Charn swore under his breath. He needed to turn and get his main guns lined up. He looked across to the ship's master.

"Mister Just, fighting sail."

"Aye, sir," Thaddeus replied before turning to bellow the order up to the sailors clinging to the yards and ratlines. "All hands! Fighting sail!"

***

Jaymes heard the order roared out from the deck above, followed by the shrilling of 'bosun's call' whistles to relay the order to the sailors in the rigging above. Fighting sail, an order that would set sails to best combine a compromise of speed and agility to allow freedom to maneuver in the fight, as well as free up more men to descend back to the deck and assist in manning the guns. The frigate swung about to port, the deck listing beneath Jaymes's feet as the entire vessel rolled to the right, leaning out of the turn. Francis Turnio, a young midshipman, appeared at the steps leading down from the quarterdeck to the upper deck.

"Mister Ellias, sir!" the adolescent called down. "The captain sends his compliments and commands that the upper deck is configured for action, starboard side to the enemy!"

"Gun crews! Action! Starboard side to!" Jaymes yelled.

The gun crews along the port side of the ship immediately dashed over to join their comrades on the starboard side, doubling the manpower at each gun. Jaymes looked up at the dark-haired midshipman.

"Francis!" he called up, stopping the young messenger before he returned to the captain. "We haven't got time for formalities, shipmate! Don't worry about rank and sending compliments, you just shout down the order as it is, got it?"

"Aye, sir!" Francis swallowed, his face pale.

Jaymes flashed him an encouraging smile before dashing over to the starboard waist of the ship. The frigate continued to swing around to port, the fore and main sails momentarily falling slack as the ship passed through the wind directly astern, before the great sails billowed out again with the wind off the port quarter. Jaymes looked across at the ugly orc warship off the starboard bow, the guns of the *Pious* drawing ever closer to lining up on the enemy. Having never laid eyes on an orc warship before, he could only estimate its size based on its masts and guns; and with that estimation, he could then provide a half-decent approximation of the range.

"Gun captains!" he shouted out across the upper deck. "Enemy to starboard! Fourteen hundred yards!"

"Enemy to starboard! Fourteen hundred yards!" Walt Ganto repeated from the forward end of the upper deck, passing on the order to his own gun crews. Each gun crew captain, the rating in charge of the team of sailors crewing each cannon, yelled at their men to drive metal hand spikes beneath the back of each cannon before prizing the rear of the guns clear of their wooden carriages. This allowed each gun captain to then set the gun's quoin; the wooden wedge that the captains hurriedly shoved into place to hold the cannon at the correct angle to fire at the range Jaymes had estimated.

The *Pious* centered her rudder and came onto an easterly course, cutting through the waves perpendicular to the two advancing orc warships. The guns were nearly lined up on the smasher; the crews were able to swivel them very slightly in place, but it was a laborious exercise and far quicker to turn the entire ship.

"Come on," Jaymes exhaled, sweat rolling down his neck as he stared across at the looming enemy warship, "give me the order... come on..."

Midshipman Turnio appeared at the edge of the quarterdeck again, his eyes wide with excitement as he stared down at Jaymes.

"F... fire," he stammered quietly.

Jaymes turned to relay the order to the upper deck.

"Fire!"

Chapter Two

The stench of ignited gunpowder from the deck below was overpowering; clouds of smoke wafted up from the gun ports along the starboard side of the frigate as the shouts of gun crew captains on the deck below echoed up to the quarterdeck. The orc smasher had altered course to starboard, clearly intent on bringing its thunderous broadside to bear on the *Pious,* but still not quite able to do so. The faster Basilean ship managed to stay ahead in the turn, its metal-encased bows cutting in toward the enemy ship to keep its guns lined up for another broadside as the brutal looking smasher edged its guns closer to shoot. Vicious little goblins were now visible in its rigging as they unfurled crude, patched sails seemingly at random in an attempt to catch more wind on one side of the ship to tighten the turn.

"I've left Mister Dernis with the fo'c'sle guns, sir," Gregori reported to Charn as he stepped back on the quarterdeck. "If you are happy for me to resume position here."

"Yes, content," Charn replied, looking forward to see if there was much chance of the bow guns lining up on the smaller of the two orc ships.

The blood runner had made an attempt to ram the crude, rotating drill on its bow into one of the sloops but had failed to catch the faster, more maneuverable ship by a considerable margin. However, with the sloop only being armed with forward facing guns, it was unable to fire on the blood runner as it turned away, narrowly avoiding a full broadside from the orc ship at a range that would have been catastrophic.

An order was barked out from the deck below, and the *Pious's* broadside fired again. The ship rumbled underfoot from the ear-splitting roar of the eleven heavy cannons facing starboard, supported by three light guns on the fo'c'sle. Only the larger-bore, close quarter guns on the quarterdeck remained out of range. Charn let out a short laugh as he saw the round shot from his broadside slam into the side of the orc ship, some shots thunking uselessly against its stout flank while others tore across the weather deck. The cannonballs smashed through the taff rails in a shower of wooden splinters and tore through the massed ranks of green-skinned crews mustered on the deck. Having moved onto the starboard side of the large orc vessel, one of the sloops opened fire with its own bow guns to pelt the stern, sending a salvo of shot smashing through the windows directly beneath the ship's quarterdeck. The gun crews waiting by the quarterdeck cannons cheered in unison.

"Shut up," Charn yelled, "or by the Shining Ones above, I'll keelhaul every one of you!"

His jaw clenched, he brought up his telescope and returned to surveying the orc ship. Their captain was clearly no fool; the smasher headed toward the *Pious*, unable to close the gap with speed alone but setting his sails to turn as tightly as possible to bring his more powerful broadside to bear. As the smoke from the most recent salvo of firing from the Basilean frigate began to clear, Charn saw the ugly muzzles of the orc ship drawing closer. With a great roar, the smasher's broadside erupted from its two gun decks, the shots falling in the *Pious's* wake and creating a storm of water as perhaps twenty projectiles plowed into the seas behind the frigate.

"Stupid bastard!" Gregori grinned. "He wasn't even lined up with us!"

"He knows that full well," Charn breathed, snapping shut his telescope. "That was a ranging shot. When he lines up with us in the next two minutes, he'll have us."

***

His eyes streaming from the acrid smoke of the guns, trapped below the ceiling of the quarterdeck above, Jaymes gasped for breath in the stifling heat. He quickly peeled off his heavy, blue jacket and tossed it across to an empty space between two of the unmanned cannons on the port side before turning back to watch the guns crews as they hurriedly reloaded. The crews were, by and large, highly experienced men with years of time spent on frigates, but a handful were landsmen – men who were yet to complete their first year at sea.

"Load with cartridge!" Jaymes called out to the gun crews.

His cry was repeated up forward by Walt Ganto, and the crews of the eleven starboard facing cannons on the upper deck hurriedly set about loading the powder charge into each weapon and ramming it down to the rear of the gun.

"Home!" each gun captain called in turn to confirm this stage of the reloading was complete. All except for the aftermost gun – cannon number twenty-two.

Jaymes watched as the gun captain of the rearmost cannon suddenly dashed forward to shout out a corrective command to one his loaders who was attempting to handle a round shot into the muzzle of the gun before the wad had been placed in, a full step ahead of the process. At the same time, a young crewman at the back of the cannon threw his handspike to one side and leaned in to pry his fingers underneath the cannon in a desperate attempt to lift it so as to reposition the wooden quoin.

"Stop!" Jaymes yelled above the din of gun captains shouting their orders, pointing at the offending crewmember. "Cannon twenty-two! *Stop!*"

"Avast!" screamed the crew's gun captain, translating the command into the correct nautical terminology.

Jaymes dashed across as other gunners momentarily turned to see what the commotion was about before their own respective captains barked at them to resume work on their own tasks. Jaymes looked down at the terrified landsman, a wide-eyed adolescent of perhaps sixteen years of age. Jaymes had never been good at issuing reprimands, even in the calmest of situations. He scrambled down beneath the gun and recovered the discarded iron handspike before handing it back to the young gunner.

"Don't use your hands, shipmate!" he issued an encouraging smile. "Use the spike – if that gun falls, you will lose every last finger! Now come on, you're doing a fine job! Back to it!"

The gun captain, a veteran, gray-haired sailor, having returned from the confusion at the muzzle end of the gun, looked at his young crewman with raging abhorrence.

"Janni!" he screamed. "Use the bloody spike or I'll shove it up your arse!" He then turned to face Jaymes. "Apologies, sir."

Jaymes looked forward and saw Lieutenant Ganto stood by the forward guns, barely visible through the still lingering smoke from the last salvo of gunfire, one hand raised to signal that his crews were all ready. Jaymes looked along the after half of the deck and saw that it was only the one gun that was now still loading. Walt had seized the initiative and continued with the loading commands for the rest of the deck, regardless of the problems faced by one crew. There was no time to waste waiting on a single gun.

"Fire!"

The frigate's gun boomed into life again, filling the upper deck with noxious, gray smoke and leaving Jaymes's ears ringing from the blast. Each gun leapt back from the recoil, nearly three tons of brass jumping some eight feet until held taunt by restraining ropes. Looking out over the starboard waist, he saw the round shot salvo tear into the smasher again, some of the projectiles tearing through rigging and sails, others carving a bloody path through the deck, while others still bounced off the hull or fell short entirely. There were no cheers, no shouts of elation for the crews finding their mark.

"Sponge your guns!" Jaymes bellowed, preparing the deck to fire again.

***

The starboard guns of the smasher exploded into life, an ill-disciplined ripple of cannon fire blasting haphazardly from the far side of the orc ship. A mere second later, the sloop exploded, the beautiful lines of the small ship replaced in an instant by a fireball of black, tinged with yellows and oranges, blossoming up toward the clear sky and spitting out twirling shards of broken timber. Charn screwed his eyes tightly shut and hung his head, as if that would somehow undo the horrific display of firepower he had just witnessed snuff out the lives of some fifty Basilean sailors.

Even from half a mile away, he could hear the guttural chanting, rhythmic banging, and cheering from the orc vessel off *Pious's* starboard waist. He opened his eyes again; he looked down at the gun crews visible in the middle of the upper deck and all the way forward on the fo'c'sle. The experienced sailors continued loading their guns regardless, while a handful of the landsmen stared in disbelief at the blazing wreck a mile to starboard before their gun captains screamed them back to action.

"It hit their powder magazine," Gregori muttered quietly to Francis Turnio, the young midshipman assigned to the quarterdeck as the captain's runner when cleared for action. "Poor bastards."

"They got too close!" Charn snapped. "And we may suffer a similar fate if we do the same!"

"Sir?" Gregori asked. "Should we load bar shot? Rip up their rigging and leave them floundering?"

"Have you heard a damned word I just said, sir?" Charn exploded. "Those bastards have still got a deck full of close in cannons that we are still yet to see fire! And it wasn't those that took out that sloop; it was their heavy guns the deck below! So no, Mister Corbes, I am not closing range with that vessel so that I can fire bar shot and he can demonstrate his entire broadside, rather than the mere half we are seeing at this range!"

Charn immediately regretted his aggressive outburst at his most trusted subordinate, who had merely offered him a tactical choice. He regretted that outburst infinitely more just a moment later when the orc smasher's port broadside opened fire.

The side of the orc warship momentarily disappeared in a cloud of black smoke as the heavy guns fired; not the precise combined shot of a Basilean warship, but an almost random series of explosions as the guns spat out their lethal shots. A series of dull whooshes followed the blasts for the merest fraction of a moment until the entire quarterdeck shook violently, knocking Charn off his feet. Splinters of wood the size of limbs twirled through the air around him, a body flew past somewhere in his peripheral vision, and the screams of wounded men surrounded him from seemingly every direction.

Mortified at the thought of being seen prone on the quarterdeck of his own warship, Charn fought through the dizziness and nausea and leapt back to his feet, checking around him to assess the extent of the damage. *Pious's* starboard quarter was torn open; the wooden deck smashed and two of the cannons knocked off their shattered gun carriages. One had fallen onto two sailors who were now trapped screaming below the three ton weapon; another poor soul who had evidently directly taken the impact of a cannonball now lay in two halves, his blood and entrails scattered across the splintered deck. Another half-dozen sailors lay dead or wounded. Midshipman Turnio stood frozen in place, transfixed as he stared at the corpse of the sailor torn in half at the waist. Behind him, Lieutenant Corbes lay crumpled on the deck in a pool of blood, rapidly expanding to soak up the sawdust that had been scattered across the deck before the battle commenced.

Charn opened his mouth to bark out a command but was overruled by his own guns as a colossal broadside spewed forth from the deck beneath, firing another salvo of round shot into the towering orc ship to starboard.

"Mister Just!" Charn yelled over the din of screaming men as the gun crews on the quarterdeck struggled to lift the cannon that had trapped two of their shipmates. "Keep station on that orc bastard! Don't let him close the gap!"

"Aye, Captain!" Thaddeus yelled in response from the far side of the quarterdeck.

"You there!" Charn pointed at a young rating standing by the nearest gun on the quarterdeck. "Take Mister Corbes below! Get him to the surgeon! Quickly!"

The young sailor dashed across to the wounded lieutenant and slipped an arm around his waist, struggling to raise him to his feet. Charn saw Gregori's legs move slightly in response as he attempted to assist his own helper, slowly struggling up to one knee. One arm was wrapped around his waist, but even with the heavy sleeve of dark blue intervening, Charn could see the vivid extent of blood that stained his white shirt and blue breeches. The pale-faced officer looked up at his captain as he slowly struggled to his feet. He knew.

16

"Get him to the surgeon!" Charn yelled again. "Fast!"

A second sailor rushed over and took Gregori's other arm around his shoulders. As soon as both of the wounded officer's arms were taken clear of his abdomen, Charn's suspicions of the severity of his wounds were confirmed. He paced across to his first lieutenant and looked him in the eyes.

"You did your duty admirably, sir," Charn said with sincerity. "Admirably."

"A pleasure… to serve the Hegemony… sir…" Gregori forced a smile.

Charn watched briefly as the lieutenant was carried forward toward the edge of the quarterdeck. He could tell by the slump of his head that he was dead before he even reached the steps to the upper deck. He turned and saw his young midshipman still staring in horror at the torn corpse of the sailor by the edge of the deck.

"Mister Turnio!" Charn thundered. "Get that body off my quarterdeck!"

Francis Turnio turned slowly to face him, his eyes unfocused as if intoxicated.

"Sir?"

"Over the side, man!" Charn pointed at the two bloody halves of the sailor. "Throw him over the side!"

Francis staggered forward, knelt by the lower half of the body, vomited helplessly, and then carried out his orders. Charn grunted in approval. If the boy was still alive in ten years, he would look back on this day and thank Charn for that order. He surveyed his quarterdeck and exhaled in momentary relief as he saw a semblance of order returning. The trapped sailors had been freed; the worst of the corpses had been ditched overboard and the wounded had been taken below to the surgeon. Thaddeus shouted out orders to the helmsmen to keep a constant distance from the smasher as below the gun crews quickly and efficiently reloaded the starboard cannons. They were still in the fight. Then the smasher fired again, and Charn watched in horror as his frigate's mainmast split at the base, collapsed, and tumbled down over the port waist.

***

The whole ship seemed to lift up out of the water and skip a few feet to port as the salvo of cannonballs slammed into her. Jaymes rocked on his feet, reaching out frantically to grab at the thick base of the mizzenmast for balance in the hot, dense smoke of the after upper deck. He heard a great, high-pitched cry that for a moment sounded like the death-throes of some great sea creature, or even the very ship herself, before the pitch of the screech changed to a squeal followed by a crash of splintering timber. He looked forward and saw, for what appeared to be for the first second or two, his eyes deceiving him as the mainmast itself snapped at the base and slowly lurched over to port. Sailors caught up in the yards above cried out in fright as the entire mast fell to the side, ropes snapping with bangs like pistol shots as they tried and failed to hold the heavy timber in place.

The main topsail fell into the water and immediately acted like the brake on a mine cart, dragging through the waves and hauling the ship about to port. Jaymes felt the very deck slow beneath him as he held on to the mizzenmast for support. He felt a nausea deep in his gut as he realized with terror that not only had they lost one of their three masts, they were also being slowed dramatically by the drag the debris was causing.

"Hatchets!" Jaymes roared over the din. "All hands! Grab hatchets and cut the mast away!"

Jaymes scrambled around in the smoke to find one of the chests by the mast, hauling it open to recover a hatchet before he staggered on to the mast and set about hacking away at the few ropes that still tenaciously clung to the heavy wooden anchor that would spell their doom at the hands of the orcs. Top men – skilled sailors from the mast above – were already crawling back up the felled mast, as agile as monkeys, scrambling to safety before grabbing hatchets to join in the effort of cutting away the debris. Ropes snapped as sailors frantically cut away with their blades, the mast shifting and rolling a little every few seconds until finally, with another creak of splintering wood, it fell away and rolled overboard. Coughing in the smoke, Jaymes stumbled over to the port waist and leaned over to watch the mast float away, relieved to see that not a single sailor had been caught out and left trapped in its torn rigging.

"Back to the guns!" he shouted. "Man the guns! Reload, starboard side! Shot your guns!"

***

Charn watched in near disbelief as his mainmast bobbed on the turquoise waves and floated past the port quarter of his mauled frigate. The jeers, grunts, and banging from the orc ship were louder now; whether it was because they had increased in ferocity due to their successes or because they were closer, he was not sure. He took a moment to estimate their range – perhaps a touch less than a thousand yards now. They were closing. Charn swore. Orc ships were notorious for the size of their crews and their savagery in boarding actions, and he now found his ship outgunned, partially crippled, and with a larger warship with nearly twice as many crew bearing down on him.

He had lost the fight. It was time to swallow pride and act so that he could get his men and his ship safely home. The two ships were on a southeasterly course now, with the wind having veered a little to a couple of points west of south. That was his only chance. He needed to exploit the superior seamanship skills of his crew to harness that wind and get away. But with one of his three masts lost, so was much of his speed. The orc captain would catch him. Unless he redressed the balance.

Charn ran over to the forward edge of the quarterdeck and yelled down a command into the smoke filled upper deck below.

"Load bar shot!"

The command was instantly repeated by his two lieutenants hidden in the gray smoke, both men no doubt unaware that they had just been promoted by virtue of their only competent brother officer falling in battle moments before.

"Mister Ellias!" Charn bellowed out.

"Sir!" a response came from beneath the quarterdeck, and Jaymes appeared at the foot of the wooden stairs below Charn.

The dark-haired man's eyes and nose were streaming from the fumes; his trousers and shirt were stained with sweat and smoke, and his knuckles were torn and bloodied where one hand was clasped around a hatchet. Charn glowered down at him. He was improperly dressed.

"Standards, man!" Charn thundered. "Where is your jacket? You are a commissioned officer in the Basilean Navy, and this is battle! I expect you to be properly dressed!"

"Aye, sir!"

"Listen here! We're coming hard to starboard, across that bastard's bows, and close! You'll get one shot at her rigging, so you bloody well make it count! Order the guns to fire as they bear, and high! Make a mess of her sails, understood?"

"Aye, sir!"

Charn rushed back to the center of the quarterdeck as another salvo from the orc ship boomed out, this time falling short of the crippled Basilean frigate as, by either their gunners overestimating the range or by the mercy of the very Elohi above, a moment of providence fell in favor of the *Pious*.

"Mister Just!" Charn called across to the frigate's master. "Come to starboard and bring us in closer! Put us near her port bow, but do not let us drift back into the line of that broadside!"

"Aye, sir!" Thaddeus confirmed. "And then what?"

"On my command, you'll come hard a starboard, cut straight across her bow! We'll hit her with everything we've got and then come about westward to retreat!"

"That'll take us straight across her bow chasers and into the starboard guns, sir!" the old master cried incredulously.

"I'll take the risk of four bow chasers!" Charn growled. "I'm willing to bet this entire ship that their crews are all manning the port guns, and by the time those sods have scuttled off to starboard, we'll be clear of them!"

"You *are* betting this entire ship, sir!" Thaddeus urged under his breath, just loud enough for the captain to hear but out of earshot of the other sailors on the quarterdeck. "And her entire crew! They'll either board us or blow us out of the water with those close in heavy guns!"

"You have a better idea? Now is the time! I'm all ears, Mister Just!"

The aging sailor remained silent.

"I thought not! Come to starboard and bring us in closer!"

Thaddeus shouted out commands to the helmsman and the few top men who still clung tenaciously to the yards on the foremast and mizzenmast as Charn stomped back over toward the upper deck.

"Mister Ellias!"

"Sir!" Jaymes appeared again at the foot of the stairs.

"As soon as those guns are loaded, send every man you have up top to man the yards! And no landsman! I need our best up there on the sails!"

"Aye, sir!"

"And put that bloody jacket on, man! The next time I see you without your uniform worn properly, I'll make you eat it!"

"Sir!"

Pacing back toward the helm, Charn stared out across the *Pious's* starboard quarter at where the orc smasher continued to surge through the waves toward them. The *Pious's* guns were lined up on her well enough, and the Basilean frigate lay in that sweet spot in between the enemy's port broadside and bow chasers, but the orc captain seemed perfectly content with sailing directly toward the frigate. He wanted to board.

Jaymes looked across the length of the upper deck as the gun crews completed loading the bar shot; projectiles consisting of two half-cannon balls held together by a rigid iron bar, designed to cause devastation against masts, sails, and rigging. The starboard cannons were now all loaded, and each weapon's captain shouted out commands to his crew to reset the quoins for higher elevation on the guns.

"Top men!" Jaymes shouted about the din as he paced up and down in the smoke of the upper deck. "As soon as you're finished, get back up top!"

The top men were generally the most experienced and capable of a warship's non-commissioned sailors, skilled and able to carry out the stomach-churning job of setting the sails from their precarious positions high up on the masts as well as doubling up to assist manning the guns when the ship closed up to battle. Men were cleared away from their guns in twos and threes, hurriedly scrambling up the forward and aft steps to the fo'c'sle and quarterdeck respectively to then nimbly climb up the rigging lines to their places on the two surviving masts.

The deck lurched underfoot as the *Pious* swung about to starboard toward the orc smasher, initially rolling into the turn before then stabilizing and leaning back out again, the starboard side of the frigate now pointing up well above the horizon. Jaymes rushed to the forward end of the deck to address the first gunners whose cannons would be lined up on the hulking enemy ship.

"Fire as she bears!" Jaymes yelled. "As soon as you've got a clear shot on her rigging, you nail the bastard! Gun captains, on your own initiative! Fire as she bears!"

Jaymes's order was replied to with a series of acknowledging shouts from the gun captains of the eleven brass cannons facing starboard, each loaded and ready with bar shot. Jaymes looked out over the starboard waist of the frigate and saw the larger orc vessel surging through the waves directly toward them, now barely five hundred yards away. Realizing the implications of what would happen if the captain's plan failed, Jaymes instinctively brought his right hand to his side and clasped it around the white, sharkskin handle of his saber.

***

"Helmsman! Steady there!" Thaddeus called out. "Steady as she goes!"

Pious

The wounded frigate's rudder centralized, and the warship rolled back to an even keel, plowing through the mild waves to cut across the smasher's bows. With only a couple of hundred yards between them, Charn now found himself looking up at the orc vessel's quarterdeck, towering above his own. While his fifth-rate frigate was far from the largest type of ship in the Basilean Navy, given his duties, he was certainly unused to the feeling of belittlement created by looking up at a larger hostile vessel as they drew closer.

Then he saw his opposite number. Raising his telescope, Charn tutted in disgust at the crowded quarterdeck of the looming orc ship; evidence of a captain who had no regard for the sanctity of the quarterdeck as the right of officers and dutymen only. One figure on that quarterdeck loomed above the others; amid the throng of hulking, green-skinned orcs clutching viciously curved cutlasses and pistols was one creature who clearly held command. Wearing a greatcoat of blood red embellished with epaulettes and tassels of glittering gold, his piggish features half hidden beneath a feathered, tricorn hat, the orc captain stared directly at Charn through his own brass telescope.

The fleeting moment of contact between the two captains was abruptly brought to an end when the bow chasers of the orc smasher boomed into life, their projectiles whooshing audibly across *Pious's* bows but mercifully failing to find their mark. That was the last threat between *Pious* and the one salvo Charn needed to strike home.

The grunting and chanting of the orcs grew louder as the two ships closed together, the screeching cries of malicious goblins festooned across the smasher's sails and rigging now joining the deep bellows of their orc cousins.

"Turn in when you can, Mister Just," Charn ordered. "Give the gunners a little more elevation to hit those sails."

"Aye, sir!"

The rusted, metal bows of the smasher cleaved through the clear waters, close enough now for Charn to make out the dents and bangs from previous ramming attacks. It was now or never.

"Helmsman! Port your helm! Hard to port!" Thaddeus commanded.

The frigate's rudder came hard to port, and the bow responded beautifully, slicing through the waves to steer starboard and straight across the smasher's path. The frigate leaned into the turn for a moment and then listed away again, her starboard waist tilting up to point the guns higher as the carved effigy of the Elohi on the *Pious's* bow seemed to lead the ship across the front of the enemy vessel, the angelic figure's torch held proudly aloft. An order was yelled out from the upper deck, and the first gun fired.

Charn saw only the blast of fire and smoke from the forward most gun on the frigate's starboard side, and then a hole tore through the smasher's billowing forecourse sail before carrying on to rip through the maintop sail hanging from the mainmast behind. The second shot blasted out a moment later, and Charn looked up to see a goblin sailor in the rigging transformed into a splattering of soggy flesh and blood, the remains a darker red against the scarlet sails that Charn only now noticed appeared to be made out of bed sheets stitched together.

Then came the third shot from the *Pious*, whooshing up into the smasher's sails and blasting the foremast yard clean off the foremast itself. The lowest of the sails on the foremast crumpled down onto the smasher's fo'c'sle, covering the deck in red cloth. As the frigate arced around the smasher's bows, the guns continued to ripple into life, shredding the sails, rigging, yards, and the goblin top men clinging to them. By the time the final Basilean cannon had fired, the smasher's course and top sails were torn to shreds, in some places hanging limply on pulverized rigging, and in others trailing uselessly behind their yards in the wind. Charn allowed himself a brief smile.

The *Pious* continued to turn to starboard, past the bows of the smasher to then run past her starboard side. Orcs and goblins alike jeered and screamed insults down at the smaller warship as their own, crude vessel slowed in the water with its sails shredded, what passed for officers on the deck yelling out orders to the terror-stricken goblins who clung desperately to the damaged masts above. Orders from the *Pious's* master were relayed up to her own top men via the shrill whistles of the bosun's calls, and sails were spread on the two surviving masts.

Charn looked straight across into the twin gun decks of the orc warship as they swept past. This was the moment he had gambled on, that the orc crew would not be professional enough to have measures in place to quickly crew the guns of the starboard side if the ebb and flow of battle rapidly changed. The gamble paid off. Shouts and jeers continued from the orc ship, but the guns remained silent.

A few of Charn's own sailors risked cheers of their own as the frigate sailed past the smasher to leave it in her wake; Charn permitted the brief display of relief. He looked back and saw the orc captain lumber to the rear of his own quarterdeck, two powerful hands gripping the taff rail. He leaned over and yelled in anger and frustration as his own crippled ship attempted to turn to pursue the Basilean frigate. Charn could not make out a single word the orc shouted out after him; if it had been a worthy and honorable foe, he would have considered saluting his opposite number, but for a thuggish orc, he managed only a patronizing wave of one hand before turning his back and looking north toward his route of escape.

Casting his eyes across the vast expanse of the sparkling seascape around him, he saw the orc blood runner turning to pursue him from the west. Not far from the blood runner, he saw the sad remains of one of the sloops, broken in half at the waist and sinking beneath the waves amid a circle of its own wreckage and survivors. The third sloop had already turned to run and was some way to the north, the fastest ship in the confrontation and well clear of danger.

Charn looked sorrowfully across at the sinking sloop and momentarily considered turning back to recover any survivors, but he knew that to do so would be to condemn his entire ship's company to a certain doom at the hands of the orcs. The blood runner did not pursue them for long; the smasher's captain clearly had enough sea-sense about him to order his smaller vessel to break off the chase as a Basilean frigate without a mainmast was still a frigate, with enough firepower to sink a blood runner twice over.

"Thatraskos, Mister Just," Charn nodded to the ship's master, "plot a course for Thatraskos. Let's go and get ourselves a new mast, and their Lordships of the Admiralty can tell us where to go from there."

Chapter Three

The creaking of the wooden boards as the *Pious* drifted across the evening waves was the only sound that accompanied the billowing of the sails above. The sun had set less than an hour ago, but a clear night sky lit by a half moon and twinkling with stars allowed Jaymes to see the waves clearly from the quarterdeck. The inky blackness of a sea beneath an overcast sky was something completely different; a void of unknown surrounding the meager lights of a quarterdeck where one false trip or slip would cast an unwary sailor into the abyss, swallowed up by the darkness of the night long before the sea itself claimed him.

But not on a night such as this. The evening breeze was still warm; the dark blue waves gently rocked the ship as if in maternal love, and dim lights on the horizon showed where the Sand Lane cut in from the east. The lights were from the fairly steady flow of merchant-men to and from the City of the Golden Horn to the north; Basilea's capital and Jaymes's home. He smiled fondly at the thought of that home and his future plans, of how close he was to shedding the uniform jacket he now wore and settling down for a life free of turmoil.

Jaymes looked back off the after end of the quarterdeck and saw the solitary light of the surviving sloop from the morning's battle against the orcs. Just as the sloop had signaled her intentions some hours ago, she had now altered course and was heading back south. Clearly confident enough that the two orc warships were well clear of the area, the sloop's captain was heading back to search for survivors from the two lost ships of the squadron.

Jaymes was already certain that nobody could have survived the magazine explosion from the first sloop; the second certainly would have seen many sailors clear the wreckage as she sank. However, even though the proportion of Basilean sailors on each ship that actually knew how to swim seemed to be increasing year by year, and those competent enough were now clinging to life in warm, calm waters, their odds of survival remained slim at best. Finding a man in the water was difficult enough; finding a floating head at night – even with a half moon and stars above – would require an act of the Shining Ones themselves.

A sniff from the other side of the helm alerted Jaymes to Francis Turnio, the midshipman who shared the watch with him. Jaymes made his way quietly across the quarterdeck, flashing a friendly smile to the silent helmsman as he passed by the ship's wheel. He looked across at Francis and his suspicions were confirmed. The constant blast of air across the deck of a ship often triggered the nose to run, but Francis's red-rimmed eyes betrayed the cause of his sniveling.

"You alright, shipmate?" Jaymes asked gently.

Francis sprang to attention as his eyes fell on Jaymes.

"Yes, sir! Sorry, sir, I..."

"Jaymes," Jaymes correctly quietly. "You'll be passing your exams for lieutenancy soon enough, so don't worry about standing on ceremony. Jaymes is fine. Just not in front of any of the others, especially the captain, or I'll be in more trouble than you."

"Right." Francis forced a weak smile.

At fourteen years of age, Francis had most likely spent at least three of them serving on warships. Jaymes had not spoken to him much during his three month tenure aboard the *Pious*, mainly as a result of them both being on different watches for most of the time, but he seemed a pleasant and capable enough sort.

"Was that your first time experiencing enemy fire today?" Jaymes asked.

"N... no." Francis shook his head. "I've seen a few battles. Not many. A handful. But I've never seen anything like what that orc ship did to us this morning."

In truth, neither had Jaymes. Not directly, at least. In his seventeen years of naval service, the majority of gunfire he had ever seen had come in these last three months onboard a frigate. As a sloop man, he had seen terrible damage inflicted on other ships when they came alongside in the capital; he even remembered a first-rate battleship – one of the gargantuan Dictator-classes – limping in tatters back in to port, sat low in the water due to her floods and with her artisan woodwork smashed to a pulp. Yes, he had seen other ships suffer, but even as mild as the *Pious's* damage was that morning, it was the most Jaymes had ever experienced.

"It wasn't so much the ferocity of their fire," Francis continued. "It was... a man was hit. A gunner on the quarterdeck. The captain told me to throw him overboard. I... I did it in two goes because..."

Jaymes patted the adolescent on one shoulder warmly. Receiving gunfire was something he had very little experience of. As a coastal sloop officer, primarily responsible for the safety of small, coastal ships, often in ferocious water, dealing with the dead was something he was well-accustomed to.

"Yes," he exhaled, "that's a tough job to contend with. Good on you, Francis, for having the stomach to see it through. I know it seems callous to deal with it in such a way, but with shot and splinters flying everywhere, the decks need to be clear. That was something important you did. Well done for having the courage."

"I didn't even know his name," Francis continued in a whisper. "That somehow makes it unbearable. I knew his face, what with only a couple hundred of us onboard, but I didn't know his name. I feel terrible for that. I was the last living thing to have contact with him before he was thrown overboard like a scrap of bad meat, and I didn't even know his name. I thought about asking his friends, but I think that would make them angry."

"I don't think so," Jaymes said honestly, "I think they'll be more than sympathetic to what you had to do today. Just... keep it quick. If the captain catches you fraternizing with the ratings, there'll be hell to pay."

Francis's response was cut off as a slim figure appeared at the forward end of the quarterdeck. Clambering up the steps from the upper deck, Walt Ganto pulled his bicorn hat on and made his way briskly over to Jaymes and Francis.

"Evening, Mister Ellias," Walt nodded, "Mister Turnio."

"Hello, shippers," Jaymes replied. "What are you doing up here? You've got the middle watch, you should be asleep."

"Captain wants to see you."

"Oh. How bad?"

"He's calling people 'sir' again. It must be pretty bad."

Jaymes let out a long sigh.

"Right oh. I'll see you later."

Walt cleared his throat as Jaymes moved to leave.

"What?"

"I'm taking on the duties of officer of the watch from you. A proper handover, if you please."

Jaymes looked incredulously around at the empty seas and fantastic visibility.

"Really?"

"I didn't make the rules, Mister Ellias."

Jaymes sighed again and stretched out his back before turning to face Walt.

"Mister Ganto," he began, "the ship is making way to the north. Winds have slackened, so we are currently only making about five knots. Sea state is slight. There is a half moon – it's there, directly above you, you can't miss it – so visibility is epic. One might even say worthy of a poem. There is no significant shipping, only the merchantmen on the Sand Lane, over that way. Are you content?"

"Content, Mister Ellias. I have the conn."

"You have the bloody conn," Jaymes tutted before dragging his feet off toward the steps leading down from the quarterdeck. He made his way to the upper deck before proceeding aft, past the guns he had commanded only hours before, and to the door leading to the captain's grand cabin at the after end of the frigate. He stopped by the door, took a moment to straighten his collar and smooth back his hair, and then knocked on the door.

"Yes!"

Jaymes entered the cabin and found the captain sat behind his desk, the moonlight pouring through the row of small, tombstone shaped windows running along the after end of the ship. The cabin, or cabins to be more precise, were plush; sheer luxury in comparison to Jaymes's cabin, and certainly when compared to the simple hammocks strung up between the cannons that the majority of sailors onboard could call their home. A richly woven rug covered the wooden deck while an ornately carved couch lay against the starboard bulkhead, its cushions matching the rug.

A short passageway, only a few feet in length, led to the captain's day cabin at the very after end of the ship, while doors to either side led to the captain's sleeping cabin and dining cabin. A dining cabin was one of the captain's privileges of rank; it was customary for a warship's captain to request permission to dine with his officers in the gunroom below, should that captain be so inclined toward socializing with his officers. Charn Ferrus was not such a captain.

Jaymes brought himself to attention before the desk.

"Lieutenant Ellias reporting as ordered, sir."

The captain continued to scratch away at a parchment with a quill pen; most likely transcribing his account of the action earlier that day. He would, no doubt, be required to justify why he was limping back to harbor without his mainmast and an expensive repair bill to send on to the Admiralty. After a few seconds, he returned the pen to a small jar of ink and looked up.

"At ease, Mister Ellias."

Jaymes slid his right foot out by a pace and clasped his hands at the small of his back. He would much rather have been invited to sit down on the couch, but he thought that perhaps he should consider himself fortunate for the small mercy of being allowed to relax from standing to attention. As if to emphasize the point that the hospitality of a simple chair had not been offered to Jaymes, Charn walked over to a small cabinet on the starboard side of the cabin, retrieved a bottle of wine, and poured out a single glass. He took a sip and turned back to Jaymes.

"Now that Mister Corbes is dead, you're the first lieutenant. Effective as of tomorrow. You'll need to complete your watch this evening, first."

"Aye, sir," Jaymes replied.

Charn paused, staring across at the younger officer as if to gauge a reaction, before taking another sample of his wine.

"You seem underwhelmed."

"Not at all, sir," Jaymes replied, rather dishonestly. "I shall do my level best to live up to the example set by Mister Corbes. He was a fine officer."

"And if those words were spoken by any other man on this ship, I would have believed them," Charn replied grimly, "but not from you. Not you."

Jaymes glanced across at his captain. Charn's dark eyes bored into his own, the lines on the man's weathered face visibly added another decade to his actual age.

"Yes, sir," Jaymes offered vaguely.

"'*Yes, sir*'," Charn repeated quietly, pouring himself another glass of wine, "'*Yes, sir*'. I'm an honest man, Mister Ellias. I believe that to be the most core value of a naval officer, despite what our Hegemon might say. Honesty, integrity, the quality of our people, it is what makes our navy superior. So with that honesty first and foremost, I believe it right to tell you to your face that I don't like you. Personally and professionally. I think you are a poor officer and an unlikable man."

Jaymes mulled over the words. He knew himself to be a relatively thin-skinned sort; having had years of self-reflection after various altercations, he knew himself well enough to know he took offense more easily than most. Yet here, confronted with a truth he had known for some time, he found himself without a care.

"Yes, sir," he replied wearily.

"And there's the problem!" Charn snapped, slamming an open palm against the top of his desk. "Any officer worth his salt would protest! Would defend himself! Would stand up for his principles and show some grit and self-respect! But not you! You're quite content to stand there sloppily, moments after being informed that you have been promoted to second-in-command of a fifth rate warship, *my* warship, and shrug off both the genuine honor I have bestowed upon you, and my honesty in assessing your character! Your... flaws."

Jaymes considered delivering the same response yet again, but he elected to remain silent. He stared across the cabin at the windows on the after end, noticing for the first time the subtle but exquisite craftsmanship that must have gone into the intricate woodwork that framed the panes of glass. He wondered how long such a painstaking job would take for an artisan.

"Still nothing to say?" Charn spat. "You are second-in-command of this ship, if you won't be open and frank with me, then who will?"

Jaymes looked across at him.

"You don't want me to be honest and frank, sir," he said evenly.

"I'll bloody well decide what I want, sir!" Charn roared. "And I want you to be honest! And frank!"

Jaymes exhaled quietly, formulating his response, running through options and outcomes in his head as he decided just how honest to be. How frank.

"Four days, sir," Jaymes said, "perhaps five if the weather turns. That's how long it is to Keretia, and that's how long it will be until you find another lieutenant to properly replace Gregori. And then I'll be your second lieutenant again, possibly even your third if you find two officers with enough experience. So I honestly, frankly, don't believe you have bestowed any honor onto me. I believe that you require a first lieutenant and it was between me and Walt Ganto. As Walt has held his lieutenancy for about half a dog watch, I was chosen as the best one out of one option available. Sir."

Jaymes found himself instinctively bracing for the inevitable explosion of temper that was bound to follow. It never came.

"Well, that is honest," Charn said calmly, almost reasonably as he drank another mouthful of wine, "and you are entirely correct. I'll replace you the minute that option is made available to me. But until such a time – and in my experience of these things, it may well be considerably longer than five days – you are my first. If I drop dead, you command this ship. And what utterly perplexes me, what truly baffles my brain, is that you genuinely don't seem to give a shit. Fifth rate warship, Elohi-class frigate. And a Batch Two at that! You are the first lieutenant. How old are you? Twenty-five?"

"Twenty-six, sir."

"Twenty-six. And what, my ship isn't good enough for you? You expect more than first lieutenant on a thirty-six-gunner at your age?"

Jaymes paused again. The conversation was not flowing in the direction he expected. Not by any stretch of the margin.

"It's not my age, sir, it's how long I've been doing this for. I joined young. I've been in the navy since I was nine years old. Seventeen years of this. And after seventeen years, all I've got to show is one passed exam. And I passed that first time, and young. I've been a lieutenant for nearly a decade. I spent years of my life giving all I've got, living and breathing this navy, volunteering for everything I could, asking to be drafted to a battleship to see what war really is."

Jaymes paused for breath. Again the outburst did not come. He continued.

"And with passing exams young and early and volunteering for everything I could, I stand before you here as a nine-year lieutenant without any experience of command or any hope of advancement. Today was only the third time I've ever commanded a gun deck in anger. So no, I don't expect any more at my age. But I should. If this navy rewarded hard work. I'm not prepared to waste any more of my life in a vocation where blind luck or knowing the right people gets you further than hard work and ability."

Charn's eyes narrowed in anger. He planted his hands on his desk and leaned across to stare at Jaymes.

"You've spent most of your life sunning yourself on the deck of a sodding sloop appointed to coastal defense in some of the calmest and most peaceful waters in the world, and you want to lecture me on hard work?"

"I didn't choose what ships I served on!" Jaymes snapped, surprising himself at the ferocity of his own response. "I asked again, and again, and again to be sent to a fighting ship! Yes, for the last few years I've not bothered! I gave up hope! And then finally, two years ago, their Lordships send me a letter to tell me that my time on sloops is over! But do you know where they sent me instead? To the capital for an administrative job working as a liaison officer with a ship building company who is developing plans for a new third-rate warship! I'm a sloop officer! What the hell do I know about big warships? But they sent me anyway! And I've spent two whole years of my life telling confused and disappointed looking ship builders that I have no idea what they are asking me! So yes, I've given up! Next chance I get, I'm out! I'm done with this! Vice Admiral Horton has already assured me that he will accept my resignation next month."

"You've given up," Charn muttered in disgust, "that's your response to adversity. Just give up! That's the measure of Jaymes Ellias. The great hero who put up with shit to a point, and then just rolled over. Is that what we should have done this morning?"

"We did do that this morning!" Jaymes exclaimed. "We ran away!"

"We retreated, still fighting, still shooting," Charn said coolly. "If we'd had it your way, we would have just surrendered. That's what giving up is. And that's why I don't like you. Now Walt Ganto, he's a different fellow altogether. Walt Ganto is an idiot! Isn't he?"

Charn paused, his brow raised and his palms held up passively as he awaited a response. Jaymes remained silent.

"An idiot," he repeated, "and that's why I like him. Because I don't expect too much from him. He'll mature in time, and he'll be perfectly adequate, even perhaps competent. A poor officer but a good man who tries his best. I like Walt. But you? You're frustrating. I received a letter from your previous captain. He describes you as having great promise, great potential. He says you have a gift with a saber and that his crew admired you. You were always his first choice in leading boarding parties. Yet I see none of that. I see a petulant brat who thinks the world owes him a living, and that at the grand old age of twenty-six, life hasn't gone exactly the way he wanted it to, so he's not playing anymore. Packing up his toys and going home. That's why I don't like you. Because you could be good at this, truly noteworthy, if you would just grow up, stop sulking, and do your job."

Jaymes remained silent. This time he was actually at a loss for words. Somehow, in some way, Charn had twisted the situation and manipulated words to leave him actually questioning whether he was right or not. Wondering if he was being over-entitled. Petulant.

"Mister Ellias," Charn said formally, announcing in no uncertain terms that the honest and frank conversation was now over and he was once again being addressed by his captain, "go back to the quarterdeck and resume the watch. Think on what I've said. I'm thirty-eight years old, I know nobody of importance or influence who has affected my career, and I'll never advance from being a frigate captain. I have a friend commanding a first-rater, and another who is an admiral. But this is good enough for me, and I thank the Shining Ones for it. Go on. Sod off."

Jaymes stood to attention and walked briskly toward the cabin door.

"Ellias," Charn called out after him.

He stopped at the door and turned back.

"I'm sorry about Gregori. I know he was your friend."

Jaymes nodded and left the cabin.

***

A bead of sweat rolled slowly down the middle of Karnon Senne's back as he stood rigidly on the sun-drenched jetty. His helmet seemed to attract the entire focus of the morning sun, heating up unbearably and burning the back of his neck when he shifted uncomfortably in place to alleviate the pressure of standing still for over an hour. Exotic birds tweeted and chirped from the lush palm trees to his right, adding a cheery music to the hustle and bustle of the daily activity of the port of Thatraskos.

The wooden jetty was one of twenty; and that was just in the southern berth of the port. The bay itself cut in northwest from the coast, with the white-walled, terracotta-roofed buildings of the city stretching out across the yawning coastline to connect the two great forts that defended the bay's mouth, like jagged teeth at the front of two open jaws. The bay converged tightly to form the mouth of the River Thatras, the sparkling waterway that then continued northeast through the foothills of the island to the mountainous north coast, some thirty leagues away. The northern end of the harbor was home to trade fleets from all over Pannithor; the boxy, sturdy ships of the Genezan trade fleets stood out even to Karnon's eyes from their anchorages and berths next to their slimmer, sleeker Basilean counterparts.

The southern end of the bay was home to the naval port and accompanying dockyard. The deep water port, from what Karnon had been told, was second only to the City of the Golden Horn in its capacity to accept ships of gargantuan sizes; it was even deep enough to allow the towering Dictator-class first-rate ships alongside, although it was far more common for them to remain at anchor in the deeper waters of the bay itself. As it was, Thatraskos was home to the Keretian Fleet, primarily made up of sloops and frigates used to patrol the shipping lanes, while the huge warships of the Basilean Battle Fleet operated from the capital, nearly one hundred leagues to the north, on the mainland.

Perhaps two dozen Basilean warships lay alongside their jetties on the southern berth, most of them were small, single-masted sloops, although there were also a smattering of the larger, two mast frigates and even a couple of Gur Panthers; warships crewed by the stern women of the Basilean Sisterhood. This time last year, Karnon would have seen them merely as 'ships' and 'slightly bigger ships'; the intricacies of nautical terminology had played no part in his life other than acting as a method with which to ferry him and his soldiers to foreign wars, but now in his new role, he had taken an active interest in learning more about this confusing, new world.

For the second time in the last few minutes, the thunder of cannons sounded from the southwest, just out of view and around the corner of the towering Naval Administration building, complete with its marble pillars and light house.

"What is that?" Sergeant Porphio Aeli murmured under his breath from a pace back and right of where Karnon stood.

"Saluting," Karnon whispered back, "the warships are saluting each other on passing."

"They salute by shooting at each other?"

"Do you think they might do so with just powder, and without actually loading shot, Sergeant?"

Karnon was glad to see that Porphio picked up on his disapproving tone and decided against any further conversation. The forty soldiers had been stood out on the jetty in rank and file for over an hour now, awaiting the return of the warship they had been assigned to. Each soldier wore the ubiquitous white tabard, commonly employed as standard uniform in most of Basilean's legion. Karnon had his assembled troops wearing their helmets and boots but was practical enough to order them to wear shirts and blue leggings rather than their normal, heavy armor, given the stifling heat. However, he had still insisted on an impeccable turn out. As a freshly promoted, acting captain in the Basilean legion in a military role that the Duma had only given final approval to a week before, Karnon knew well that first impressions counted.

With eight years of campaigning under his belt, he was well-accustomed to the harsh realities of soldiering, and every bone in his body protested at the idiocy of standing his men in rank in the baking sun for over an hour while sailors and dock workers wandered idly past, giving them nothing more than a cursory, confused glance at best. But he was also well aware of the Basilean Navy's reputation for standing on ceremony at the most bizarre and impractical of times, and it was imperative that he create a first impression that was right and proper.

A frigate drifted slowly into view from around the corner of the stunning Naval Administration building, sailing serenely through the warm, turquoise waters and past the neatly maintained line of palm trees that ran along the coast line. At least, Karnon thought it was a frigate. He narrowed his eyes in confusion as he realized it had two masts but seemed somehow too long for a vessel rigged in such a way. Then, as it drew closer, he realized that it was because the central mast was missing, snapped off near where it met the upper deck. His eyes widened again as he wondered how much force it must have taken to blast such a sturdy construct clean off a warship.

A series of shrill whistles sounded as the frigate neared the jetty; men clambered along the yards of the two masts and busied themselves changing how much sail was suspended below them. To what purpose, Karnon had no idea. He watched as minutes ticked by and the warship drifted closer to the jetty with agonizing deliberation, finally moving close enough for a rope to be thrown across to the jetty where it was recovered by a sailor and tied loosely around a sturdy wooden beam.

"Come on!" Porphio whispered to himself in frustration as the job of bringing the frigate to the jetty continued to advance at a snail's pace. "How hard can it be?"

"Enough," Karnon whispered sternly.

A second rope was thrown from the back of the ship to the jetty as a small skiff was rowed to the far side of the ship where, under the yelled commands of one of the sailors on the boat, it set about nudging the warship closer to the jetty in a particularly ungraceful manner. More minutes passed by. More whistles sounded from the frigate and enormous amounts of human effort were expended to slowly edge the ship closer to the dock, inch by inch. Finally, the ship's side banged gently against the wooden jetty and more of the incessant whistles and shouts coordinated ropes being tied to hard points. A soldier from the ranks behind let out a stifled, sarcastic cheer before Erria, the second of Karnon's two sergeants, hissed out a particularly offensive threat to ensure silence resumed.

With the frigate safely alongside and secured to the jetty, the orders and unremitting whistling continued as sailors secured sails to the yards, and the intricate maze of endless bits of rope on deck were wrapped around seemingly anything that could accommodate them. More minutes passed. Karnon glanced up to the back of the ship and saw two men, formally attired in blue coats and black hats, glancing down at him.

"Company! Attention!" he yelled.

As one, the forty soldiers brought their feet together with a crunch of boots slamming down on the wooden planks beneath them and brought their arms smartly down to their sides. From his restricted field of view, his eyes facing directly ahead, Karnon could just about make out a few curious glances from sailors from the frigate who now ambled around the jetty, checking the security of ropes with mild disinterest. The ship fell relatively quiet, with a few orders called across the deck at a more reasonable volume. The warm waters lapped against the hull of the warship. Sea birds cawed overheard while the more colorful birds in the palm trees continued to sing merrily. The sun rose higher in the sky, the stifling heat continued to grow in ferocity. Still nobody came. Suppressing a curse under his breath, Karnon turned smartly to the right to signify he was falling out of the parade before he walked briskly over to one of the sailors milling about on the jetty.

The sailor was perhaps thirty years of age, wearing loose fitting trousers and a simple shirt, both of blue; his feet were bare and his long hair was tied back in a rough ponytail beneath an overhead bandanna of faded red.

"Who are you?" Karnon inquired as he paced over, removing his helmet and running a hand through the short locks of his chesnut, sweat-soaked hair.

"Gill," the sailor replied with a sneer. "Who are you?"

"Captain Karnon Senne, Company Commander, Hegemon's Warship *Pious* Detachment, 5th Maritime Legion of Foot."

The sailor's eyes widened as he stood bolt upright.

"Sorry, sir! Had no idea! How can I help you, sir?"

"Go and tell your captain that his detachment of marines is on the jetty, awaiting his inspection," Karnon replied.

"I... I couldn't do that, sir. I mean... I wouldn't. It might be more appropriate if you were to come and see him yourself, sir. Not trying to be awkward, but sailors don't really go bothering the captain, not directly. I could go and tell the bosun's mate. He'd tell the bosun, who'd then tell the first lieutenant. And then he could tell the captain. But it might just be quicker if you come onboard and see the captain yourself. I'm sure that would be fine, given your rank, sir."

"Are you taking the piss, sailor?" Karnon asked.

"No, sir, not at all, sir. There's a way things are done on warships. Sailors don't go bothering captains. If you'd like to come with me, sir. Oh... once you're onboard, stand to attention and salute, if you would. It's the Hegemon's ship and we're flying his ensign, it would be an insult if you didn't."

Shaking his head in exasperation, Karnon followed the sailor up the wooden gangway and across the starboard waist of the ship. He followed the sailor's lead and stood to attention and saluted as soon as his feet hit the deck.

"The captain's day cabin is aft, sir," the sailor pointed below the highest deck on the back of the ship, "just behind the steps to the quarterdeck. You can't miss it."

Perhaps a dozen sailors were still on deck, washing down the wooden planks underfoot or polishing the brass work at various points across the ship. To a man, they all glanced across at him with clear curiosity as he made his way to the door he had been directed to. He knocked loudly, waited for an affirmatory grunt from inside, and then entered. After pacing through a short corridor, he emerged in a large cabin, spanning the width of the ship, with bright sunlight pouring through a series of windows on the back end of the ship. The captain

– instantly recognizable by his garb if not the fact that he was the sole occupant of the day cabin – was a man in his late thirties, with graying hairs overtaking the brown at his temples, and a wrinkled face. He looked up from his seat behind a desk facing the front of the ship, a pair of dark eyes regarding Karnon from beneath heavy eyebrows. Karnon stood to attention.

"Sir. I'm Captain Senne of the 5th Maritime Legion of Foot."

"So?"

Karnon looked down at the older officer's dismissive sneer and instantly made up his mind that he disliked him.

"My men have been waiting on that jetty for nearly two hours, sir. For you to inspect them."

"Why in the world would I want to do that?"

Greeted with an apparent complete lack of respect, Karnon made the decision that he would repay in turn. Relaxing from being at attention to a more natural stance, he reached inside his pocket and produced his letter of authorization, which he then casually tossed onto the captain's desk.

"Because we're here to join your ship," he smiled, without warmth.

The captain snatched up the letter and stood as he tore the binding ribbon off the rolled parchment. His features darkened as his eyes flicked along the lines of neatly written narrative. He then looked back up at Karnon.

"How many of you are there?"

"Forty."

"There isn't room for you. I've already got over two hundred men aboard."

"That last signature on there is from the Admiral of the Keretian Fleet. I don't know much about the navy, but I know enough to work out that if an admiral says something is going to happen, a captain bloody well does it."

"Don't you bloody well tell me how the navy works, you insubordinate little shit!" the captain suddenly yelled with a ferocity that surprised, but did not intimidate, Karnon. "You don't come prancing on to *my* ship and tell *me* how I shall conduct her affairs! On a Basilean warship, the captain is king! Do you understand me?"

"What I understand, sir," Karnon grimaced as he leaned in, "is that this ship is one of the first in the entire navy to be blessed with its own compliment of marines. Professional soldiers, specially trained to fight at sea, all volunteers and drawn from the ranks of some of the most experienced men in the entire legion. Those forty men stood in the sun outside there aren't sodding boy sailors for you to take the piss out of; they're the legion's finest. Now, I've come here with an open mind and a willingness to learn, and on this ship I will follow your orders to the letter. The bloody letter. But respect is a twin edged blade, and you *will* respect my men."

The captain cast his eyes over the letter again before looking back across at Karnon, his eyes now more curious than angry.

"How long have you been a soldier for? You look like you're not even old enough to drink."

"Nine years, sir," Karnon replied. "Nine years of pretty much constant campaigns. If you've heard of it, I've probably killed it."

"Nine years isn't particularly long," the captain raised his brow, "certainly not a vast amount of experience for a captain."

"Then I must be quite good at my job to get promoted quickly," Karnon sighed irritably, well-accustomed to the now tedious routine of 'the grumpy senior officer' – a performance he had seen too many times already. "And the Duma has decreed that, given the amount of time taken to rise to the rank of naval captain compared to that of a legion captain, legion captains are to be considered the equivalent to naval lieutenants."

"Then who holds seniority between them?"

"At sea, a naval lieutenant holds seniority. On land, it is the legion captain."

"So what our politicians have decided," the captain summarized, "is that a naval captain is considered higher at all times than a legion captain, who is considered higher than a naval lieutenant on land, but that a naval lieutenant is a higher rank at sea? Well, I'd imagine that will only be a temporary state of affairs. That's just bloody silly and will lead to no end of confusion. One would hope they'll get this straightened out in the next few weeks; Shining Ones forbid this should go on for centuries. Well, tell your men to get themselves onboard and sling their hammocks on the lower deck. They'd better not be expecting luxury."

"I guarantee they've all seen worse, sir," Karnon sniffed. "Now, are you going to come and inspect the men, or shall I give them the afternoon off to go and get drunk?"

The captain quickly suppressed a smile, a wicked glint in his eyes betraying his humor at the verbal exchange. He walked over to a series of pegs on the back of his door and retrieved a jacket of dark blue and a black, bicorn hat.

"Alright, let's go and see these marines of yours," he cleared his throat. "So... how long have you been operational as a unit? I've heard rumors of specialized marines for the past five years now, but nothing has ever come to fruition."

"The 5th Maritime Legion of Foot was commissioned less than a month ago, sir," Karnon said, following the captain to the cabin door, "at the academy at Spartha. We were among the first five hundred men to complete the training."

"Then I shall expect great things from you and your men," the captain smiled bitterly. He stopped abruptly after taking one pace outside his cabin. "Oh, one more thing. Captain Senne, wasn't it?"

"Yes, sir."

"Do you know what 'keel hauling' is?"

"No, sir."

"Well then. If you ever speak to me like that again, you'll bloody well find out, officer or not. That was your one free pass. I'm extending that courtesy to you because you've made a good first impression. I need officers with some balls and a no-bullshit attitude. But you just remember, you're on a warship, and you don't have the first sodding clue how things work around here. And as far as you're concerned, once you set foot on my deck, I am the very Duma personified. Understood?"

"Understood, sir."

Chapter Four

The rust-flecked, iron-encrusted bows of the smasher momentarily came to a rest against the crumpled jetty. The stylized metal lump at the front of the ship cleaved into the pillars and boards to slowly plow a path through them until the ship ground to a halt amid a small pile of splintered wood. With the front of the ship just slightly run aground, but not enough that dragging it clear again later would be much of a problem, Ghurak nodded to himself and grinned at a job well done. A successful berthing. The cheers, grunts, and roars let out by his crew stopped momentarily as the entire ship suddenly listed to the right with a great creaking and squealing of wood, but that to came to a halt as the *Green Hammer* settled on the shallow sand bank at an acceptable angle. The cheering resumed again.

The bright moon shone down through a few, wispy layers of cloud above as the warm breeze continued to billow out the sails from the *Green Hammer's* hastily repaired three masts; goblin sailors scuttled down from their perches across the rigging as the entire crew – somewhere between five and eight hundred orcs and goblins; Ghurak did not know how many, nor did he care – lumbered up from ladders leading to the decks below or pried their way through holes from old battle damage to cram onto the top deck. Even above the general cacophony and chaos of several hundred rowdy, green-skinned sailors eagerly looking forward to stepping ashore for the first time in some two weeks, Ghurak could hear the shouts, roars, and occasional gunshots drifting across the warm, night air from The Ankorage; the small town set up on Axe Island by the orc and goblin pirates.

"Shud'up!" roared Drika, Ghurak's gargantuan first mate. "Shackle the cackle! The lot of you!"

Drika's order was relayed from orc officers down to their sailors via a series of yells and thumps, cascading down to the goblin sailors through more shouting and audible clips around the back of bald heads, before a hushed silence finally fell across the upper deck of the *Green Hammer*. Drika turned to face Ghurak, his scarred face as grim as ever as he brought up one hand in a three-fingered salute.

He was, aside from Ghurak, the very picture of everything an orc pirate should be; his eye patch actually covered an empty socket left by a bitter clash with salamander corsairs, rather than the show patches modeled by some orcs. His broad, muscular shoulders were partially hidden beneath a sleeveless greatcoat of dark blue, beneath which a curved cutlass hung from a broad belt. The look was complet-

40

ed by a broad-rimmed, tricorn hat of black, adorned with a gold skull.

"Admrul!" Drika reported. "Crew is ready for your orders."

Ghurak paced forward to the front of the tilted quarterdeck, his heavy boots thumping on the dry, wooden planks underfoot. He adjusted the collar of his blood red greatcoat as he cast his eyes across his crew, the hundreds of them crammed across the upper deck, squeezed in around the cannons, masts, and the mass of ropes that Ghurak mostly understood; a level of understanding far in excess of the majority of his crew but certainly still leaving him dependent on a handful of his brighter goblin specialists.

He briefly thought about addressing his crew for a few moments, trying to explain to them why this voyage had been something of a failure. In their eyes, they had sunk a merchant ship and then sunk two Basilean warships, as well as forcing one of the larger ones to flee. That was a victory to most orcs. But not to Ghurak. Ghurak was a krudger; an orc at the top of the violent tree that was about as close to a society as the orc race had bothered with, a status that he had achieved ostensibly through sheer, brute force and strength.

But the truth was a little more complex than that. Ghurak was smart. Not elf smart; not even human smart. But smart enough to know that outward shows of force could get you far in an orc clan, but not nearly as far as combining a bloody-mindedness and fighting ability with a bit of thinking and an ability to plan ahead. That was why he knew that sinking enemy ships was not enough; he needed to capture them, so he had something to trade with. Because trade was what made the world work for the weaker races, and while he was building his strength to crush his foes underfoot, he needed the ability to trade to get the ships and guns that he needed.

"You did well!" he shouted out to his crew.

They did not need to hear much more. The cheering started again before Ghurak held up a hand to silence it again.

"You did well enough! Most of you, anyway. Those who didn't do well, I know who you are! I'm watching you, you skiving, lead swinging bastards! I'm watching you. But for now, go to town! Drink, fight, get drunk, kill each other a bit! And I'll see who's left when I call you to sail again!"

An ear-splitting roar of approval went up in unison from his crew before the mass of green bodies before him surged and jostled for the two rope ladders that were thrown down to the sand bank below. The joy and joviality of a night of drinking and fighting almost instantly turned violent when a group of goblins at the front rope ladder began pushing and squabbling among themselves, the pathetic slaps and punches resulting in one runty goblin being pushed into the back of an orc. The orc let out a roar of anger and picked the goblin up by his neck, bashing the goblin's head into the front mast until his skull caved in. Ghurak shrugged. That was how the crew weeded out the weak.

Ghurak watched his crew disembark, clambering down to the shattered jetty and sand banks before trudging off through the crooked palm trees lining the sandy beaches, chanting and jeering as they made their way in a ragged line toward The Ankorage.

"You coming, Admrul?" Drika asked.

"No."

"You're not staying here?"

"No. I'm going to go to Vanata."

Ghurak just about made out a low grumble of disapproval as Drika's remaining eye narrowed.

"What you going there for?"

Ghurak turned to square up to Drika, stepping quickly forward and leaning in to stare into the younger orc's eye. Drika was the taller of the two – barely – but in terms of muscle and sheer bloody-mindedness, Ghurak was more than content that he had the edge.

"You listen here!" Ghurak spat. "We've been through this before! I do the thinking, you enforce! I make the plan, you make sure it happens! Now, you and me, we go back. I haven't forgot the way things used to be, and I haven't forgot where we came from. But that, Drika, that is the only reason I haven't ripped your sodding throat out of your arse for questioning me like that! You got it?"

Drika's fists clenched and his shoulders hunched up, just momentarily, before he thought better of it and looked away.

"Yeah, Admrul," he said hoarsely, "yeah. I got it. But every time you go and talk to those humans, the warriors here, they talk about it. They're not impressed…"

"Then let them talk!" Ghurak exploded, slamming a fist into Drika's shoulder which knocked the towering orc back a half pace. "If they've got a problem, bring them to me! Their job is to drive the boat and fire the guns! They don't think! I do the thinking! Look around you! Where do you think these guns came from? The good ones at least! Where do you think I learned how to fire them so I could teach you stupid bastards? Where do you think the sails came from? Lines of goblins, sat round chatting while they do some knitting? No! These boats don't run on plundered bits alone! So, again, you piss off and leave the thinking to me!"

Drika took a step back, his head tilted a little to one side in an action that was about as close to a submissive gesture as a hulking orc of his stature could manage, before turning to barge his way to the front of the shoving and punching queues leading to the rope ladders dangling from the side of the *Green Hammer*. Swearing to himself, Ghurak removed his tricorn hat and adjusted the ragged curls of his white, powdered wig before shoving his hat back atop his head. The stupid thing itched as much as ever – he only really noticed when events around him slowed down enough for an irritable scalp to matter – but most of the famous human admirals and pirates seemed to favor them, so Ghurak was willing to endure the itching for apparel that commanded respect.

Of course, Drika and the warriors had a point; dealing with humans ran against the grain; the thought of striking a bargain with those soft bastards rather than just killing them and taking what he wanted seemed completely unnatural. But, as humans went, Cerri and his pirates were about as close to orcs as they could be; vicious, cutthroat bastards who lived to fight, plunder, drink, and pillage. They were not so bad. And without them and their help, Ghurak was nothing more than a double-hard bastard who could fight better than anybody else. With them, he was a double-hard bastard with a fleet of warships and the supplies he needed to keep them running. And he was an orc with a plan; a plan that revolved around just such a fleet.

Ghurak paused. The sound of revelry from the lines of orcs heading toward The Ankorage caused him to reconsider his night for a few, pensive moments. He let out a thoughtful grumble. The progress of that plan of his could wait for one more night.

***

His feet echoing around the cavernous main hall of the port's Naval Administration building, Charn followed the spiral staircase up around the outside of the room toward the second floor. The ceaseless sunlight plunged through the tall windows built around the outside of the circular main hall, casting pillars of bright light down onto the speckled, marble slabs that made up the ground floor. Charn reached the second floor and left the stairs, his footfall silenced as he moved onto the broad corridor leading to the admiral's office, the thick, blue carpet contrasting the carved wood-paneled walls.

The walls were decorated with paintings of every class of Basilean warship imaginable from the past two centuries – including one of the *Pious's* sister ships, the *Virtuous* – which added some life to the otherwise empty hall and corridor. The *Virtuous* was the first of the Batch Two Elohi-class frigates; incorporating an elongated hull to accommodate three masts and an increase in firepower, compared to the standard two masts of the Batch One Elohi-class frigates. *Pious* was the second of the trio of Batch Two frigates on operational trials, before a decision would be made as to whether the Batch Two would replace the older Batch One. In the interim, the shipyards of Basilea continued to churn out the Batch Ones as fast as ever.

Aside from the two marines guarding the main entrance – soldiers who wore the same white tabbards that Charn had first seen on the marines who had paraded on the jetty for his arrival – he was yet to see anybody in the building.

After the City of the Golden Horn, Thatraskos was the Basilean Navy's largest naval base, and as such, was an establishment that Charn was well used to navigating his way around. The base itself was run by Admiral Sir Jerris Pattia, himself an ex frigate-man, with the infamous Vice Admiral Horton - who was fortunately away at the capital - acting as his deputy. Charn followed the wood-paneled corridors around to the building's west wing, looking down through the windows at where his battered frigate lay alongside the jetty on the far side of the naval yard as he approached the admiral's outer offices. Charn barged his way past a young midshipman before reaching the office, knocking before letting himself in.

A rotund flag-lieutenant in his mid-twenties stood from behind his desk as Charn entered the office. A balcony window behind him looked out over the yard and the sunlit bay, again with the *Pious* and her missing mast in the very center of the frame as if the subject of a purposefully ordered painting to cement Charn's humiliation at limping into port.

"Captain Ferrus, sir," the admiral's aide smiled uncomfortably, "the admiral's previous appointment finished early. You may go straight in."

Charn grunted an acknowledgment and paced across the outer office before rapping his knuckles on the admiral's door and letting himself into the next room. The admiral's office was twice the size of the outer office, not including the extensive balcony that looked out over the sunlit bay and lush jungles sweeping inland to the northeast. The same array of nautical paintings adorned the walls, but these were interspersed with display cabinets of scale model ships; not the beautiful but functionless models built by rich folk with an abundance of time to spare, but historic models used by actual ship builders during the design process of some of Basilea's most – and least – successful warship designs.

Admiral Sir Jerris Pattia was a short, lean man in his mid-forties, his bulbous features at odds with his wiry frame. His blue, uniform jacket was trimmed with gold at the sleeves and lapels, and a series of medals and honors accompanied the heavy, gold epaulettes draping from his shoulders. Upon seeing Charn enter the office, the admiral smiled and sprang up from his desk, walking over to extend his hand.

"Charn! Thank you for stopping by! And glad you brought your ship back safely after that nasty surprise!"

Charn shook the admiral's hand and found himself already deeply analyzing the senior officer's words. Was that a genuine effort to put Charn at ease? Was it overly patronizing for a man of his experience? Was everybody across the frigate fleet already laughing at him running from a fight with a mast left bobbing on the waves behind him?

Jerris walked over to a drinks cabinet by the far wall and proceeded to pour out two glasses of a deep, treacle-colored drink.

"Bit early for that, isn't it, sir?" Charn ventured.

"The sun's always high over a yardarm somewhere in the Hegemon's fleet," Jerris smiled slyly.

"Fair enough," Charn shrugged in acceptance of the old nautical expression about drinking and accepted the glass before following the admiral's direction to sit down in the plush chair on the near side of his desk.

"We received your message from the *Sprinter*," Jerris said as he sat in his own chair. "She came in a day before you did. Said you signaled to her that you ran into orcs! Orcs?! Attacking Basilean warships? That is a rarity to put it mildly, this close to the mainland."

"That's what happened," Charn said, already feeling his cheeks warming with redness. "We were signaled by one of our sloops. One of three that we ran into not far off the Sand Lane, four days south of here. We followed them in and found two orc warships; a smasher and a blood runner. We went head to head with the smasher after she sank one of the sloops, and we shot some chunks out of each other. The blood runner took down a second sloop, and I'd lost my mainmast. I'm afraid that I elected to get my ship and her crew to port rather than lose the *Pious* in some foolish display of stubbornness."

"Quite right, Charn, quite right. Leave the suicidal bravado for the bard's tales. No, that makes perfect sense. What was more thought provoking to me was your logic behind coming straight back in to port, rather than doubling back to look for survivors once those orcs had gone."

Charn's eyes widened. He opened his mouth to speak but found only an awkward and incriminating silence as he frantically thought through just how the admiral could have come into possession of so many facts already.

"The *Heaven's Tearer* got in shortly after the *Sprinter*," Jerris explained as if reading Charn's mind. "She was the one sloop that survived the encounter. Her captain told me what he saw; that you swung around the smasher's bow and gave her what for, tearing her for'ard sails to shreds, and then you pelted for home. He'd already got clear – a fair decision in a sloop – but then doubled back. They rescued thirty-eight men from the water. Thirty-eight! We shouldn't be leaving sailors behind, Charn. Why didn't you go back?"

"I'd lost my mainmast, sir!" Charn protested earnestly. "A sloop is the fastest ship in the fleet! They can come and go as they please – if they'd seen an orc, they could have turned around and been gone again before the orcs even knew they were there! For me in a frigate, they'd see me miles off, and some of their ships can keep up with me, and that's before I've lost a mast! If I'd taken *Pious* back and they'd seen me, the *Heaven's Tearer* would be fishing *my* crew out of the water alongside the others!"

The admiral leaned back in his chair and pressed the tips of his fingers together, his eyes fixed humorlessly on Charn's for several long, silent moments before he spoke again.

"Fair enough," he cleared his throat, "I see your point. No point in escaping only to jump straight back into a fight you couldn't win. You understand, Charn, one has to ask these questions. The Admiralty doesn't just give you a ship without the accountability that comes with it. But anyhow, that still leaves us with a smasher and a blood runner operating near our trade routes. And what's worse, captained by an orc stupid enough to declare war on the Basilean Navy. It won't do, Charn. No. It won't do."

Charn breathed out slowly, relieved that the conversation had moved on from the accusations against his actions and decisions.

"So what now, sir?"

"Well, you'll go back out there, find that orc, and blow his balls off with an effective broadside," the admiral said nonchalantly as he sampled the pungent liquor in his glass.

Charn leaned forward in his seat.

"Sorry?"

"After your repairs are complete, naturally," Jerris smiled.

"It… it's a smasher, sir. As much as my heart glows with patriotic fervor for the Hegemony and pride in the fine minds that design our frigates, it's a smasher. It'll tear the *Pious* in half!"

"I didn't say I would send you out alone."

Charn paused again, his eyes narrowing suspiciously.

"By the time you've got a new mast sprouting out of your midships, I'll have the *Vigil* and the *Veneration* alongside, back from their patrols. Three Elohi-class frigates, Charn. With you as the lead captain. Reckon you can take the bastard out with that?"

After his early, somewhat facetious comment regarding his patriotic fervor, Charn genuinely did feel his heart glow as he jumped to his feet.

"I'll have him, alright!" he sneered. "Nothing the very Abyss itself could spew out would stand up to the broadsides of three frigates! I'll find the bastard, and I'll break his ship's spine!"

"Good," Jerris took another mouthful from his glass. "Good. Don't celebrate too soon. This isn't a gift; this is a responsibility that you need to get done. And quickly. But I'm sure you're the right man for the job. Now, those marines. How's that coming along?"

Feeling only partially deflated at the reminder of his new, somewhat awkward passengers, Charn sank back into his seat.

"The lower deck is somewhat crowded, sir. Not as bad as it could be with the men on different watches at all hours. And while I'd be the last man to question the fighting prowess of the Duma's legions, I do wonder how easy they will find it transferring those skills into the maritime environment. Soldiers are landsmen, after all."

"Not these ones – at least, that is the aspiration. It will take time, but each journey begins with a single step, and this is that first step. The 5th Maritime Legion of Foot was re-roled into this to ensure our ships are just as effective in boarding and with shore parties as they are at sailing and gunnery. These men are all volunteers, have all passed rigorous selection tests, and have all carried out weeks of additional training in fighting at sea. I think you'll be pleasantly surprised with them, if any green-skins decide to board your frigate."

Charn sucked through his teeth.

"You disagree?"

"I hope you're right, sir," he said, "but our sailors have a good enough history with close quarter fighting at sea, and I'd rather have another forty sailors who can work around the clock in any position on the ship than forty swordsmen who I'll only use once a month, at best."

"But if that encounter that crops up once a month goes sour?"

Charn nodded as he thought through the countless examples of ships lost to boarding actions.

"Point well made, sir," he conceded.

"Good," Jerris drained the rest of his glass and then stood up, his mannerisms hinting that Charn's time in the admiral's office had now expired. "When's your old mast coming out?"

"They start work this afternoon, sir," Charn said, finishing his own glass and standing. "My purser tells me that stores here have everything we need to get a new mast put in in very short order."

"Well, you know where to send the bill," the admiral reached across to shake Charn's hand warmly again. "Good to see you again, Charn. Make sure you drop in again after your repairs are complete, and I'll have your orders signed and authority to lead this frigate squadron we spoke of. Any thing else I can help you with?"

"A lieutenant?" Charn chanced. "I lost my first in the encounter. A very good man; a credit to the service. He'll be tough to replace."

"I'll see what I can do," Jerris nodded sympathetically. "I doubt I'll be able to magic up a lieutenant with enough experience to take on the role of a first, but I shall see who I can find. Nearly forgot – how is your wife?"

"Don't ask," Charn grunted, his mood immediately deflating at the thought. "Thank you for your time today, sir, much appreciated. Goodbye."

He turned to leave, closing the door behind him gently before striding straight past the admiral's flag lieutenant. His mood quickly lifted again as he paced down the corridor, until he found himself beaming from ear to ear at the prospect of leading a squadron of frigates in a hunt for the bastard who had crippled his ship and sent him in flight from their last encounter.

***

The small boat nudged against the sandy beach with a scrape and a thud before coming to rest. The base of the tree line only a few yards ahead was partially hidden by a thin layer of mist, the white strands of moisture swirling out from the swamp hidden just over the lip of the ground. Nocturnal insects warbled and rattled from the trees, a cluster of them buzzed and swarmed around two torches that had been thrust into the sand near the water line.

"Wait here," Ghurak ordered his quartet of goblin rowers. "Don't go wandering off. The humans are more vicious bastards than you think; they'll slit your throats as soon as look at you."

Ghurak stomped over to the front of the boat and stepped ashore, his feet sinking into the wet sand up to his ankles until he took a few paces up the moonlit beach and began making his way across to the settlement. The beach led around to the south to a steep incline that in turn sloped up to a rocky cliff looming some hundred feet over a lagoon. Ghurak followed the cliff path for about ten minutes until he reached a sharp turn.

The settlement of Red Skull revealed itself as Ghurak rounded the final corner of the path. Perhaps a dozen ships, although it was impossible to tell now given their woeful material state, lay crunched and crumpled up on the beach, extra huts and wooden buildings built upon them and around them with a myriad of bridges and stairs interlinking them. The pirate town was named after the first ship that crashed upon the shore; the old Genezan caravel, *Red Skull*, formed the very center of the settlement, age and the elements having long ago broken her spine and left the huge ship in two near equal halves at the top of the beach.

Music and laughter drifted across from Red Skull's multiple taverns, while occasionally a pistol shot cracked out from somewhere in the town. Lights illuminated the entire, sprawling graveyard of wrecked ships, showing where small groups of pirates staggered drunkenly from tavern to tavern. Swearing to himself, Ghurak paced back down the incline toward Red Skull, one hand firmly clasped on the handle of his cutlass. He reached the edge of the town, where a solitary human pirate sat on the edge of a capsized boat hull, idly picking away on a stringed instrument as he watched the approaching orc with mild curiosity. While the island of Vanata – and the town of Red Skull on its southern shore – was occupied in the vast majority by humans, there was a smattering of buccaneers and corsairs from other races, but certainly no orcs. Orc pirates habited the neighboring Axe Island. That was the way it was.

Ghurak sneered at the musical pirate as he stomped past, the rough, dry planks of wood beneath his boots creaking with every heavy footstep. He made his way past a trio of staggering, laughing buccaneers who immediately fell silent as they saw him, the stench of alcohol that wafted along with them was noticeable even to Ghurak and his underdeveloped, orcish sense of smell. Following the maze of stairs, rickety bridges, and rope ladders leading across the town of wrecked ships, Ghurak finally arrived at the doors of the 'Final Grapeshot', one of five taverns in Red Skull. He heard the sounds of music, merriment, smashing glass, and animated conversation as he planted his hands on the doors and flung them both open.

Perhaps fifty people were in the tavern; mainly human but with a handful of elves, dwarfs, and salamanders breaking up the monotony. The majority of inhabitants were sailors, but a dozen or so women were interspersed among them, following the age old and almost uniquely human custom of exchanging carnal favors for money. The dimly lit, low-roofed tavern did not so much fall completely silent on Ghurak's entry as it did hush temporarily a little, but he was content to see that he was greeted with looks of fear and respect from the crowd of drunken pirates. The last time he had visited the Final Grapeshot, a bunch of them had laughed at his wig. He had beat four of them to death with his bare hands to emphasize the point that his wig was no laughing matter. The groups stood by the bar and sat around the scruffy, circular tables all returned to their foaming tankards and bawdy conversations.

Ghurak walked forward. The crowds parted respectfully to allow him past as he made his way across the middle of the tavern, beneath the flickering candles attached to the improvised helm wheel chandeliers dangling from the crooked ceiling, past the bar, and over to the balcony windows at the far end of the room. There, as predictably as ever, he found Cerri Denayo.

Cerri was a tall, lithe man in his mid-thirties with black hair slicked into a neat ponytail and a thin, fastidiously maintained moustache. His trousers, boots, and long coat were all black, with only his white shirt breaking up the darkness of his attire. With a tankard in one hand and a young woman sat on each knee, he looked up at Ghurak as the orc approached.

"I'm surprised to see you again," Cerri admitted. "I told you not to go near the Sand Lane."

"Then you're no expert on reading an orc's face," Ghurak sneered, his tone a guttural growl next to the comparative high pitch of the human, "because I'm not back here to tell you that you were right. In fact, I'd say my little trip went well."

Cerri's dark eyes glinted a little as they narrowed.

"How well?"

"Three sunken ships well," Ghurak grunted, "two of them were navy."

Cerri's eyes opened wide in alarm.

"Whose navy?"

"Basilea."

Cerri looked across at the two scantily clad girls sat on his lap.

"Go," he ordered curtly.

Ghurak watched the human women leave. He had learned what it was that a human defined as beauty, not because he had any interest himself; but because he knew that a beautiful woman, much like a physically strong captive, could be sold into slavery for a higher price. Little things like that marked him out above his fellow orcs. It was why he captained a smasher with two full gun decks – he knew how to make money as well as simply how to wage war and kill.

"Come with me," Cerri addressed Ghurak with the same tone as he barged past him.

Ghurak grabbed the slim pirate by one arm and leaned closer in.

"Who the hell do you think you're talking to?" he growled.

Cerri looked up at him without a shred of fear.

"You can come in here and kill a pirate or two without causing much of a stir," Cerri hissed, his voice low, "but you seem to forget that there are three men who run this island, and I'm one of them. So let me be more direct with you. Speak in your language. Follow me out of this room, or I'll take the pistol that's in my belt, shove it in your ugly mouth, and blow your brains out over the wall behind you."

Ghurak's fist instinctively clenched in anger around the scrawny human's arm. He lifted the man up until he teetered pathetically on his tip toes, his teeth clenched as a hiss of pain escaped from between them. Ghurak looked down, wide-eyed, at the squirming human as he thought through the most bloody and painful way he could tear him apart with his bare hands. But he needed him. Cerri knew that. Ghurak's fang-jawed mouth broke out into a grin. A guttural laugh followed soon after as he released his iron grip.

"I knew there was a reason I liked you. Come on, then."

Cerri's pace at leaving the tavern betrayed his anxiety, even to Ghurak. The hulking orc followed the lithe pirate out into the hot night and up across a series of wooden steps nailed across the hull of an ancient trading barque until they found a secluded area, overlooking the swampy jungles to the west.

"Listen here," Cerri brandished an extended finger at the huge orc, "I know you're a big fellow, but you're not bright. That's why I'm praying to the Ones above that you don't know your arse from your elbow when it comes to recognizing an ensign."

"A what?"

"A flag, you idiot! The flags on the back of those ships you sunk! What colors were they?"

Ghurak's initial reaction to finding himself on the receiving end of an insult at the hands of a wiry human was one of fury; certainly not prone to bouts of creativity, Ghurak nonetheless found himself visualizing just how easy it would be to kill Cerri in a hundred ways, right there on the wooden platform overlooking the jungle below. But he was in Cerri's world now. As important as Ghurak was – especially as one of the trio of recent krudger-turned-pirate chiefs on Axe Island – he was now addressing his opposite number on Vanata; one of the three human pirate chiefs. If Ghurak laid a finger on Cerri, he would have several hundred armed men to deal with. Violence – always the first and best response – was not an option in this case. Ridicule would have to do.

"Ha!" Ghurak cackled. "What's wrong? You all worried I trod on a snake's tail? Yes, Cerri, I know a Basilean flag. I sunk two of their little ships, and I blew the mast off one of the bigger ones! What of it? I'm still here! They're not! They ran! Like cowards! I'm not worried! You shouldn't be, either! Show some spine!"

"Show some brains!" Cerri yelled. "Do you know what you've done? The Basilean Navy? They'll come looking for you! And when they do, it won't be with a couple of skiffs! Basilea is the most powerful nation in the world! Or at least one of them! We're pirates! We go pick at the scraps, we tangle with isolated merchantmen who we know we can take down, and we leave no witnesses! We don't go shooting at warships! You think this is some crappy bard's song? This is real life! We operate at the edge; we don't go blundering in and wage war! Do you know what you've brought against us? You haven't trodden on a snake, you've kicked a dragon square in the nuts!"

Ghurak processed the human's words, slowly, shaking his head in disgust at the man's overt lack of courage. He fished his pipe out of the pocket of his red greatcoat, thumbed a wad of tobacco into the bowl, and held it over one of the torches illuminating the platform to light the pungent leaves.

"Let me explain this to you," he grunted at Cerri. "You see, the way I see you is the way you see an elf. You look at those prissy little pricks as clever but wet. Whinny little shits, but with good brains. Good ideas. No good in a straight punching match, though. That's how orcs see your lot. You're bright, but no good in a fight. Understand?"

Cerri looked up incredulously at the towering orc as Ghurak sucked in a lungful of flavored fumes from his pipe.

"No!" Cerri spat. "Not at all! If you've got a point to make, then make it!"

"Humans can't fight!" Ghurak explained, slowly and loudly, leaning in for emphasis. "You stick to your bright ideas! Your lot is good at that! But fighting? No! So your friends in the Basilean Navy can come after me all they want, because I've got the ships, the guns, and the warriors to hit them harder!"

"This big ship you hit," Cerri interjected, "the one that ran away. What was it?"

"I don't know."

"How many masts?"

"Three."

"Square-rigged or fore and aft?"

"What?"

"Were the sails square or triangles?!"

Ghurak stopped to remember the encounter. "Squares."

"How many gun decks?"

"One. But with a few more guns on the top. And there was some wooden woman carved into the front of the boat."

Cerri swore out loud and turned his back, spreading his arms wide in exasperation before he turned back to stare venomously up at the orc again.

"A frigate! An Elohi frigate! One of the new ones with three masts! You shot up an Elohi and let it crawl back home!"

"So what?" Ghurak sneered. "Let it come back out and fight again! I'll shoot its other masts off!"

Cerri let out an agonized cry and sank his head into his hands.

"Let me spell it out for you!" he growled. "You've insulted the most powerful military in the world! They won't stand for that! They'll be coming for you! And that means they'll find us, too! Vanata is less than two leagues from your Axe Island! This affects all of us! They're coming, and when they do, they'll be sending a whole squadron of frigates, if not something bigger! Have you ever seen a Dictator-class battleship?"

"It doesn't matter! They're not going to find us! We're in the middle of the sea, a big sea at that! I'm not so clever, but I can read a map! They're never going to find us, so stop shitting yourself over nothing! How many islands of this size are there out here? A hundred? Be a man, little Cerri! This is nothing!"

The mustached corsair took a step back and fell silent for a few moments, his breathing slowing slightly as he stared out over the swamps. He finally turned back to Ghurak.

"So what is it you want? You came here to find me for a reason."

Ghurak flashed a jaw full of sharp, yellowed fangs.

"I need more guns."

"What kind?"

"As big as you can get. I had a smasher and a blood runner crewed up and running. Two good ships, as well as a few of the crappy little ones. That's why I'm an admrul now and not just a captin. But the lads, they've put together another blood runner. So now I've got three good ships, as well as the crappy little ones. I'm getting another crew together for the new blood runner, but I haven't got the guns for it. You need to get some for me. Then maybe I'll keep these Basileans away from you."

"I've got guns. What have you got for me?"

"What?"

"What are you giving to me in exchange for me providing your new ship with very valuable and pricey cannons?"

Ghurak's smile slowly faded.

"Wait here, Cerri. We're going out to the Sand Lane again. Leaving in the morning. I'll bring something back for you."

Chapter Five

Jaymes sat on the chest at the end of his bed and looked uncomfortably around the cabin. He had told the captain as clearly and politely as he could that, given the very temporary nature of his promotion to the post of *Pious's* first lieutenant, he was more than content to remain living in the second lieutenant's cabin. Naturally, this had been met with the normal string of surly comments, roared at the upper extremities of volume, with the word 'sir' tacked on to the end of each accusatory sentence, the gist of which was that the captain believed it was the proper thing for Jaymes to move cabins. Even though it was likely for only a few days, and it was literally one cabin further aft from the second lieutenant's.

It was not so much the complete waste of time that upset Jaymes – after all, he had only a few possessions with him and it took minutes few to move them – it was the principle. This was Gregori's cabin. And, while Jaymes had not known him for long, and they were certainly very different men with very different outlooks on life, both personally and professionally, he had still been a friend. Shaking his head, Jaymes stood and opened his door to walk into the passageway outside.

A handful of the doors to the other officers' cabins were also ajar; some men were still at work while others were preparing to go ashore for the evening. Kennus, the ship's surgeon, and Artimio, the purser, could both be seen through their cabin doors sat perched on the end of their cot beds, hard at work with their record keeping as they leaned across makeshift desks atop their sea chests. Pannus, the ship's gunner, had already proceeded ashore.

Jaymes glanced toward the forward end of the ship and saw Karnon Senne, the new marine officer, step out of his own cabin dressed in a rather eye-catching – too much so, in Jaymes's opinion – pair of mustard-colored breeches, complimented with a jacket of dark green. A very different aesthetic to Jaymes's simple black trousers and white shirt.

"I take it you know Thatraskos well enough to know where is worth going for the evening?" Karnon asked Jaymes as he walked across.

"Yes," Jaymes replied. "As a rule of thumb, the further one can be bothered walking, the better. You'll only end up in a Duty Watch bar otherwise."

"And now in words a landsman can comprehend?" the stocky marine queried.

Jaymes let out a low murmur of disappointment in himself. He had always resented the sailor's tradition of using obscenely complex and incomprehensible slang and nautical terminology seemingly for the sole purpose of ostracizing those who could not understand it. And here he was, doing the very same without even realizing.

"Sorry, old habits seemingly die hard, no matter how much you want them to. Duty Watch bars are taverns full of sailors. Without generalizing the Basilean sailor into one oversimplified, generic being, the majority of our lads will go out into town with the sole aim of getting as blind drunk as quickly as possible. The theory being that time spent actually walking is time wasted that could be spent drinking, and thus our sailors don't stray very far. So, the further you walk from the harbor itself, the more civilized the drinking establishments become. I intend to walk for a good half hour."

That was partly true, at least. Jaymes knew exactly which tavern he intended to walk to and exactly who he was trusting to have a chance encounter with. He only hoped that sending a letter to her before they last sailed was not too forward. Jaymes's deliberations were interrupted as Walt Ganto emerged from the second lieutenant's cabin – Jaymes's previous abode. At first, Jaymes found himself confused to see that the young officer was still wearing his uniform, even though their last conversation had been very explicit in their shared desire to spend an evening ashore in a good tavern. However, on looking closer, Jaymes realized that Walt's uniform was freshly laundered and neatly pressed.

"You're going out tonight in rig?" he challenged.

"Yes," Walt declared defensively.

"You don't think that's a bit crass?"

"Not remotely. I've put my years in to earn the right to wear a lieutenant's uniform, and I'll be damned if I'm going to give up on the opportunity to impress the ladies by pretending I'm some... ordinary fellow!"

Jaymes glanced across at Karnon and was relieved to see the disdain evident on his face.

"Suit yourself," Jaymes shrugged with an exasperated sigh, "but where we're off to, it's the norm to attempt to impress the ladies with charming conversation rather than shiny buttons. You're choice, though."

"I rather thought I'd just throw some money at the problem to spare the time," Walt grinned. "I'm going to that place Gregori recommended to us last time we were here. The Bay View."

Jaymes's eyes opened in horror.

"The Bay View? You want to go to a brothel, wearing uniform?"

"It's not a brothel! It's…"

"From what Gregori told me," Jaymes interrupted the younger officer, "it's an establishment where you give money to a woman, and she takes you to a room for sex. That is literally what a brothel is."

"There's more to the place than that!" Walt protested, "There's…"

"Walt, I've only ever given a direct order to another lieutenant twice in my entire career," Jaymes stopped the flustered man a second time, "and now I'm making this the third time. You are *not*, under any circumstances, going to disgrace the Hegemon's uniform by going to a brothel in rig. Either come with us or, if you persist in following through on your little scheme, go to your cabin now and get changed out of rig and into civilian attire. This isn't open for discussion."

Jaw agape, Walt stared silently at Jaymes for a few moments before looking across to Karnon.

"You coming with me?" he asked the sullen-looking marine officer.

"I'm married."

"The question still stands," Walt risked a mischievous smile.

"Happily married," Karnon grunted, folding his thick arms across his chest. "I'm not going to a brothel with you. Now I strongly suggest you do what you're told, or you're likely to piss me off as well."

With the speed and drama of a petulant adolescent, Walt flung himself back into his cabin and slammed the door behind him. His temper still flared, Jaymes turned away and shook his head.

"Come on, leave him to it," Karnon shrugged. "Let's go find somewhere decent for some food."

The two men left the ship and made their way out of the naval dockyard toward the town itself. The sun was low in the sky and a handful of scattered clouds painted a few different colors across the azure heavens above. Conversation between Jaymes and Karnon was, from Jaymes's point of view at least, stifled and even a touch awkward in that customary way that happened when two very different strangers were forced together socially. Jaymes tried to generate some conversation by discussing his two keenest interests – reading and fencing – but was more than astute enough to realize that Karnon's curiosity was aroused by neither.

The two walked out of the archway at the northerly most point of the dockyard's perimeter wall and followed the steep streets up and away from the port district, toward the more affluent southwest quadrant of the town. The universal white houses with their terracotta roofs were still almost magical in their beauty to Jaymes; very different from the eclectic mixture of architecture he had grown up amid in the City of the Golden Horn. There was something wonderful even in the lack of color in the vegetation, as the summer heat had a nasty tendency of killing off any foreign flowers that more wealthy inhabitants might attempt to plant.

As they neared the top of the hill that ran parallel to the governance buildings, Jaymes felt his throat grow tight and his heart thump a little in his chest. The letter bothered him. He had only met Melenia four times, but he had enjoyed their conversation on each occasion and felt, perhaps hoped, that it was reciprocated. The letter he had left in her hand before they had last sailed seemed like a great idea at the time; an open and honest confession that he enjoyed her company, more than anything else. But there was one sentence he had written that he realized only later could be terribly misinterpreted. *'I would very much enjoy the chance to get to know you a little better'*. He had meant that quite literally; their was no implied, salacious pressure in his words but there was also no way she could know that. Perhaps he was overthinking it. He knew he had a tendency to do so.

"Here we are," Jaymes looked up at the entrance to the 'Sunset Inn' as they approached.

The Sunset Inn occupied two floors, with the upper floor being mainly outdoors to give a commanding view over the bay below, but with a thin roof giving protection from the very occasional shower of rain that the island experienced. While the prices were certainly well above the norm, it was a hidden gem in the town, with exquisite food and spirits imported from across Pannithor. Jaymes walked in through the front doors and looked across the tables that lay out before the bar.

Perhaps half the tables were taken, each by small groups engaged in polite conversation at reasonable volume, while serving staff brought out platters of food and glasses of spirits or exotic fruit juices. The setting sun cast long shadows through the windows at the far end of the building, but the highly polished wooden floors and immaculate white walls were well lit by candles dangling from simple but pleasing chandeliers above.

Jaymes's eyes fell on Melenia almost immediately. Wearing an elegant dress of red, her dark hair tied up and held in place via a gem-encrusted clip, she sat at the bar with a man in a black jacket, his back turned to the entrance. Melenia was laughing in delight at his words, leaning forward to rest a hand on his knee as she did so. Her eyes momentarily flickered across to Jaymes, then after a moment's recognition, they came back to meet his properly. She smiled awkwardly and shrugged in sympathy before turning back to face her partner and laugh again with him.

Jaymes froze in place. He felt his shoulders slump in rejection, the thumping in his chest intensifying as embarrassment and self-loathing immediately replaced the anxiety he had felt leading up to this moment. He turned to leave but realized how ludicrous that would look to Karnon; he had dragged the other man all the way to the top of town but now would give anything to be back on the ship, settling for a mediocre dinner before turning in for an early night. Karnon looked straight ahead at Melenia. He then looked back at Jaymes, then at the bar again, and then nodded.

"This place looks like a shithole," he shrugged. "I want to go somewhere else."

Jaymes let out a sigh of relief and felt a smile threaten to take hold.

"Thank you," he breathed in genuine appreciation as he followed Karnon back outside again.

"You known her long?" Karnon asked as he led the way further into town.

"No," Jaymes admitted, "there was no agreement between us. She's done nothing wrong."

"But she knew you liked her?"

"…Yes," Jaymes said truthfully after a pensive pause. "Yes, she did."

"Then sod her," Karnon said dourly. "Her loss. Come on, let's go find somewhere for some food."

***

"I don't like this skulking around in the dark!" Captin Kroock grunted.

From where he leaned over the chart table, sheltered in a little hut on top of the quarterdeck, Ghurak's eyes narrowed in anger. He stood up straight, as straight as any orc could manage, adjusted his wig and hat, and turned to stomp out onto the blood runner's quarterdeck. Kroock and his First Mate, Turug, looked up at the towering orc admrul as he paced past the trio of goblins struggling with the ship's wheel.

"What?" Ghurak demanded.

The blood runner, *Driller*, continued to sail on its northerly course, its third night at sea since leaving Axe Island, the clouds above now thickening and denying much of the moon and starlight that had made finding their way through the waves so easy on the previous nights. Ghurak had chosen the *Driller* over the much larger and more powerful *Green Hammer*, as it better fitted his plan; smaller, less obvious, perhaps even just a little faster. He was relatively happy with where they were on the chart; both in terms of being certain enough of their navigation and being confident in his bold plan. This was not the time for dissenters. A rabble of goblin rope handlers seemed to sense the rising tension in their orc overlords and quickly scuttled off the quarterdeck, leaving only the three orcs and the nervously mumbling goblin helmsmen.

"Sneaking around at night, Admrul!" repeated Kroock, the captin of the *Driller* and another tough, vicious orc who Ghurak had trusted in for years. "This isn't our way! This isn't how we do things!"

Ghurak clenched his fists as he stared down at his subordinate. Yes, a tough orc – his missing right ear that was lost in a fight with an ogre was testament enough to that – but not an orc with Ghurak's cunning. Not an orc with brains. Sure, he had brains enough to understand how the winds affected a ship, how to read a map, how many barrels of food and grog to take with him to keep his crew alive; but as with most orc sailors, the majority of his leadership fell down to taking advice from his legion of scrawny, scraggy goblins and then deciding how to act on that advice. Ghurak himself was just as guilty of that when it came to the finer aspects of seamanship, but with strategy? No. Ghurak had that all stitched up himself.

"Here's an idea," Ghurak said, his voice low and hoarse. "How about I be the admrul and I come up with the plans, and then you be one of my captins and you do what you are told with *my* ship, before I punch you in the face and break open your snout? How's that for a plan?"

"The captin's got a point, Admrul." Turug folded his arms. "Sneaking around a human shipping lane with no lights on. This ain't bringing war to 'em. This is acting like a bloody elf."

Ghurak looked down at Turug. Turug was not one of the original crowd. He had not escaped from slavery with Ghurak, Drika, Kroock and some of the others back in the dark days. He was good in a fight and had never run from an enemy, but it seemed to Ghurak that now he had advanced a little, now he was second-in-command of one of Ghurak's ships, he was a little too cocky. This was maybe a warning that Ghurak had left it too long since the last time he made an example out of somebody. But that was easily remedied.

With a roar of rage, Ghurak leapt forward and wrapped his immense hands around Turug's throat. The younger orc responded instantly, grabbing Ghurak's wrists with his own hands and trying to pry them free of his neck. Ghurak leaned in, impressed not only with the first mate's strength and fighting spirit, but also the aggression that boiled in his eyes as he stared up at the admrul. But overpower him, he could not.

Ghurak was again impressed by Turug when, on realizing that he could not drag the vice-like hands from his throat, the young orc instead clenched a fist and punched Ghurak full on in the face. The first blow smarted; the second one broke a bone somewhere in his snout with a sickening crunch. The third blow was soft. That was because by that point, Turug had collapsed to one knee as his eyes began to drift out of focus.

The muscular, trunk-like arms that only seconds before were propelling fists into Ghurak's face and drawing blood were now only capable of slapping pathetically against his assaulter's face and hands. The fire in Turug's eyes faded, replaced by fear and then outright panic, and finally a look of pleading that made Ghurak hate him even more. Saliva dripped from Ghurak's lipless mouth in eager anticipation of the final moments until Turug collapsed limply in his hands. Just to make sure, Ghurak dragged the lifeless orc over to the side of the quarterdeck, heaved him up onto the edge of the deck, and then threw him overboard to disappear beneath the black waves below. Chuckling grimly to himself as he snorted out a jet of blood from his broken snout, Ghurak paced back over to the helm.

"That clear?" he grinned to Kroock.

"You shouldn't have done that!" the blood runner's captin growled at his admrul.

"What?"

"That bastard owed me money! You should have checked his pockets before throwing him to the sharks!"

Ghurak nodded and shrugged as he thought over the captin's words.

"Alright, yeah. I'll give you that. But look, I'm the one with the plan. And the plan is to capture another ship. Sinking them all isn't going to get us what we need. So we carry on with the plan. We put this ship smack in the middle of a shipping lane. And we wait. We wait quietly, in the dark, with none of our lights on. Look around you! There're lights everywhere from all the others! We're surrounded by ships! When the sun comes up, we see who's about, and we see who is already got their sails sorted for going into wind, while we're all ready for going downwind. And then, being faster, we catch them up and we've got them. Got it?"

Kroock looked up at him while a handful of goblins carefully and theatrically tip-toed back to their stations on the quarterdeck.

"Yeah, I understand the plan, Admrul," Kroock said, "but the plan takes us just south of Spartha on the map! This ain't some shipping lane off the coast of the Successor Kingdoms, this is Basilea! I'm all for a fight, Admrul, you know me, but..."

"Enough!" Ghurak snapped. "Listen in! We are not just south of Basilea! We're days south! Leagues away! And even if we weren't, it wouldn't matter! Let them bring out all the ships they want! You saw how we did the other day! Let them come! I'll gun down every last one of the soft bastards!"

Ghurak's grin became a low chuckle as he eagerly stared off to the horizon, impatient for the sun to rise and the light to reveal his prey.

***

Clambering up the wooden steps from the upper deck to the quarterdeck, Captain Caithlin Viconti nodded curtly to her first mate as she made out his bulky frame silhouetted against her ship's stern lights, the pre-dawn glow behind him only now beginning to light up the western horizon. Glancing forward, she saw the stern lights of the *Wave Explorer* only perhaps five hundred yards ahead. This left her own vessel, the *Martolian Queen*, in the same place that it was before she had fallen asleep for the night; at the very back of the convoy of five merchant ships.

"Good morning, Captain," greeted X'And, her salamander first mate, as she paced across the deck to stand between him and her helmsman. "I trust you slept well?"

As much as Caithlin appreciated the reptilian sailor's attempts at pleasantries, she was far more interested in their progress.

"Good morning, X'And," she replied. "What progress have we made over night?"

"Still slow," the gray-skinned salamander smiled a fang-toothed but uncomfortable grin. "The easterly wind we had last night has backed a little, closer to northeasterly now. Perhaps fifteen knots. Progress is slow. We are still at least two days behind schedule."

Caithlin nodded silently and turned to look across the bows of her brig toward the east again. The route from Geneza to the City of the Golden Horn was simple enough but very much at the mercy of the legendarily erratic and unpredictable winds of the Infant Sea. Of course, as the most junior captain of all five merchants ships in the convoy, one could argue that it was not her problem and certainly not her fault; but if the cargo spoiled on the voyage, then it would have a direct effect on the payment for every sailor on all five ships.

"I'm sure our luck will turn soon," X'And smiled again, a warmth permeating the gravelly tone of the veteran salamander sailor's voice.

"Thank you, X'And," Caithlin murmured irritably as a blast of warm morning air swept through the darkness and across the *Martolian Queen's* upper deck, ruffling the short ponytail of her dark blonde hair.

Despite her irritation at the unfavorable winds delaying yet another day of what should have been a contemptuously simple voyage, she still immediately regretted her shortness with her first mate. The salamanders were known across all of Pannithor as one of the great, sea-faring races, and she was particularly fortunate to have a salamander first mate with two decades sailing experience. That put X'And's first voyage occurring when Caithlin was five or six years old; about the time her father had first taken her sailing in the small lakes of west Geneza. She felt a sudden burst of anxiety as she thought of her father and the amount of money he had invested in the family share of the *Martolian Queen*. She owed it to him to prove that the investment was wise, prudent beyond the mere love and support a father shows in a daughter's embryonic career as a merchant sea captain.

The deck heaved a little underfoot as the brig listed gently in the dark waves, the sails of the two masts billowing above in what little wind they could cling determinedly to. Caithlin mused over her options as she picked irritably at the lace cuffs of her white shirt, wondering whether it was worth discussing the financial implications of the now unavoidably tardy arrival at the Basilean capital city with Owynne.

Owynne was the South Mantica Trading Company's representative on the voyage, the keeper of the purse strings, and the final arbiter of how much the ships' pay would be docked upon their late arrival. He should, of course, have stationed himself on the *Blue Albatross* – the convoy's lead ship – but his rather unsubtle and growing infatuation with Caithlin had led to his decision to sail onboard the *Martolian Queen*. While she could not fault the man's tenacity – she was aware enough of her aesthetic appeal, although capitalizing upon it had always seemed rather crass – he was very much wasting his time. Caithlin's drive and ambition was directed solely toward expanding on the successes of her father's merchant shipping business, and even if the day came where she was in the market for returning the affections of an admirer, it would not be one who was twice her age and lacking any dynamism.

"Captain," X'And said warily, walking across to the port side of the quarterdeck, his eyes fixed to the northeast and into wind, "something is not right."

Caithlin walked over to his side and looked out in the same direction. The black skies were still slowly lightening to a dark blue, just about enough light to now reveal that the heavens above were still dominated by overcast clouds. The sea had a moderate swell but certainly nothing even close to concerning.

"What is it?" she asked.

"There's a ship, out there to the northeast," X'And pointed a clawed hand off toward the horizon. "She has no lights."

Caithlin looked out across the dark waves but saw nothing. A line of orange was now drawn across the horizon in anticipation of the rising sun, but the world remained dark. An entire battle fleet could have been hidden off her ship's port bow, and she would be none the wiser. But she knew X'And well, and she respected him. So she waited. And as the seconds passed by and her eyes adjusted to the darkness, slowly catching up with the salamander's superior vision, she saw it.

A twin-masted vessel; only marginally larger than her own, its crude lines and angular hull were completely unfamiliar to her. The ship had the wind almost directly behind it; not taking full advantage by placing it off the quarter, but certainly positioned well enough to pick up a good pace as it cut through the waves directly toward the convoy. Caithlin grabbed her telescope from her belt and brought it up to one eye, but the distortion of the lens made it impossible to make out any further details in the pre-dawn darkness.

"We need to get the guns ready," X'And said gravely.

Caithlin stared across at him incredulously.

"You think?" she frowned dubiously. "We're in Basilean waters and not far from the mainland. I hardly think any pirates would be stupid enough to risk attacking on a main trade route running from Spartha to the Golden Horn."

"I never said they weren't stupid," X'And growled, the concern in the veteran sailor's tone now beginning to unnerve Caithlin. "That's not just a pirate ship. That's orcs. We need to get the guns ready."

Caithlin's eyes widened in alarm. Orcs? Here? On only two occasions in twelve years of professional sailing had she ever encountered pirates, and both had resulted in something of an anti-climactic resolution. But orcs? Their presence on a main Basilean trade route was simply impossible – the Basilean Navy's patrols ensured that. Yet the ship bearing down on them was proof of the exact opposite. Somehow, the orc warship had even managed to position itself between the convoy and the Basilean coast, cutting off the most obvious route of retreat.

Caithlin looked across her ship at the meager firepower she had available; six light cannons – four on the upper deck at the waist, and two on the quarterdeck. A total broadside of three light guns, with nothing firing forward. And then there was her crew; thirty-five sailors, only six of which had any naval experience and had ever fired a cannon in anger. Her heart beating fast in her chest, she realized that they were in real trouble. She closed her eyes, took a calming breath, and then turned to address her crew.

"Ring the bell! Signal the convoy! Pirates, closing from the northwest! Load the guns and run them out!"

***

Ghurak lowered his telescope again and grinned viciously. The five ships he had made out in the meager light just before dawn were all forcing their way against the wind, meandering slowly eastward at a pathetic rate of knots as he positioned to the north of them, ready to turn back around and rush down toward them with the wind at his back. He felt the deck of the *Driller* heave and fall beneath his feet, goblins in the rigging above him chittering excitedly as they made adjustments to the sails that he only half understood how were increasing the ship's speed.

Four of the five ships were of mediocre size, with two masts and a small smattering of guns visible on their top decks. The lead ship was larger; a boxy looking thing with three masts. That would probably have the best cargo onboard, but it would also have the most guns and the biggest crew to overcome. Attacking that one would undoubtedly cause him the greatest losses, and right now he needed every last green-skin to crew that second blood runner that was so close to being ready to add to his fleet. No, better to plan for the long term. That meant going after the easy pickings.

"Kroock!" Ghurak yelled across the quarterdeck to the *Driller's* captin.

"Yeah, Admrul?"

"That little one at the back of the line," Ghurak pointed to the twin-masted ship at the trailing end of the merchant convoy, "that one! Point at him, smash him up a bit with the guns, and then get us next to him. I'll lead the warriors across."

"Right, Admrul," Kroock nodded obediently before turning to his second mate; a huge orc with dark green skin who Ghurak did not remember ever laying eyes on before.

"Front and back sails! Top and bottom! Lower 'em a bit!" Kroock commanded.

The second mate turned and shouted down from the quarterdeck to the mass of sailors waiting in the middle of the ship.

"Front and back sails! Top and bottom! Lower 'em a bit!"

The order was relayed from orc to orc, and then from goblin to goblin, each shout higher pitched than the last until it was practically screamed by the scraggy goblins clinging to the yards above. The patchwork red sails were let out a little and the ropes on deck hauled in tighter as the blood runner turned to head straight for the ship at the back of the convoy.

***

The orange rim of the morning sun was visible over the horizon now, adding just enough color to the world's palette to make out more details of the orc warship. The blood red sails, the ludicrously oversized metal drill on the bow; even the upper deck overcrowded with a horde of green-skins was visible through a telescope from this range. The severity of the situation had already been passed down below deck, and the remainder of the brig's sailors hurried up to the open air from below.

Caithlin snapped her telescope shut and turned to X'And.

"They're heading straight for us," she lowered her brow grimly. "They've singled us out."

"I think we should run," the salamander tilted his head, his serpentine facial features curiously human in the regret they conveyed. "Even if the entire convoy manages to hit them on their way in, it won't stop them. They'll board us, and then there is not a thing we can do."

Caithlin's thoughts were interrupted as Owynne walked up to the quarterdeck, pulling on his grand, green coat over his heavy frame as he did so.

"Good morning, all!" he beamed, placing his velvet, tricorn hat on, atop his graying hair. "Good morning, Captain! All seems serious already! We're not still behind schedule, are we?"

Caithlin looked across at her first mate for a moment, and then she turned to address the company purser.

"We're being attacked by pirates, Mister Wurrio," she said without humor. "Orcs, as it happens. If you look over your shoulder, you'll see them."

Owynne's face cracked into a smile that quickly became a mirthful laugh. He swatted a hand through the air as if to dismiss the jape, until he then looked over his shoulder, let out a cry of terror, and turned back to face Caithlin and X'And.

"Shoot them!" he cried. "Sink their ship! Do something, we have to do something!"

"Our guns are not lined up to take a shot, and if we alter course, we will be moving away from the rest of the convoy," Caithlin replied seriously. "And as for attempting to fight them, how many guns do you assess they're bringing to, X'And?"

The salamander sailor raised his telescope, took a moment to look at the orc ship, and then snapped it shut again.

"They've got bow chasers coming into range shortly, Captain. If they get alongside, they've got about triple the number of guns we have, and I'd guess they're probably twice the size."

Up ahead, the *Blue Albatross* opened fire with its port broadside, an uneven ripple of almost pathetic sounding gunfire from its light cannons that resulted only in a cascade of water splashes in a seemingly random pattern around the orc warship. Around, but certainly not close. The *Blue Albatross*, like the *Martolian Queen*, was crewed by competent, professional sailors who were highly skilled and experienced at their job. But their job was not to routinely operate weapons. The poor display of gunnery from the convoy's lead ship made Caithlin's mind up for her.

"Rudder to port," she ordered her helmsman, "take up a southerly heading. Full sail, fore and main. Give me everything we've got."

X'And nodded before rushing down to the upper deck, shouting out a series of commands to the sailors who scrambled up the rigging to take place on the yards and let out the sails. The *Martolian Queen* swung about, her bows digging into the waves as she turned to starboard.

"Wh... what are you doing?" Owynne demanded, his face white and his eyes wide. "You're leaving the convoy!"

"They seem fairly content for us to be picked off while they continue without their sacrificial lamb," Caithlin replied. "And as this ship belongs to me and the crew depend on me to make the right decisions to keep them safe, this is what I have elected to do."

A crackle of cannon fire sounded from the orc ship, and the tops of the bows disappeared in a great plume of black smoke. A dull whine of increasing intensity built rapidly up in the space of a second before pillars of sea water fountained up to either side of the *Martolian*

Queen's quarterdeck, falling down and soaking Caithlin, Owynne, and the ship's helmsman in cold, salt-laden seawater. X'And rushed back to the quarterdeck.

"A lucky shot," he grimaced, "but regardless, they have our range. It gets worse from here."

***

Stood at the very front of the quarterdeck, his immense green fists wrapped tightly around the wooden rail in front of him, Ghurak stared intently at the line of ships ahead. The first two had fired at him – the lack of both power and accuracy of their guns resulting in fits of laughter from the orc and goblin crew – but they continued stubbornly on against the wind at a snail's pace. The last ship had turned away in an act of cowardice that only made Ghurak want to board it even more. The merchant ship's sails had now dropped fully and it was picking up speed as it attempted to flee to the south, but it did not appear to be accelerating nearly quickly enough.

"How long on those guns?!" Ghurak yelled across the top deck to the gunners at the front of the ship, "Come on, you lazy dogs! Load! Load 'em up!"

The blood runner continued to bear down on the convoy, quickly closing the gap as the sun slowly rose.

"We're going straight past that fourth ship, Admrul!" Kroock called from his position near the map hut and the wheel. "Do you want to hit him up the arse with a broadside on the way past?"

"Yes!" Ghurak yelled back over his shoulder. "Yes! Give him something to remember us by!"

"D'you want us to fire up the drill?" Kroock asked hopefully.

"No!" Ghurak bellowed. "No! No! No! Do not fire up that sodding drill! We've come out here to capture a ship and take it back with us! I want to board it! I want a ship and slaves to sell! You are not starting up the drill, got it?"

Kroock nodded sullenly, looking forward wistfully at the immense drill on the front of his vessel.

Ghurak looked to the south again as the heavily laden merchant ship continued its pathetic attempt to escape from him. The noises from the front of the ship drifted back to him as they plunged through the water; the shrill, excited reports of goblins yelling to their orc gunners that the cannons were loaded and ready to go. A guttural command was roared out and Ghurak gritted his teeth in delight as the front guns boomed again, a cloud of black, deliciously sooty smoke washing back over the top deck of the blood runner. Ghurak did not see the fall of shot, his vision clouded by the noxious smoke from the guns, but the chants and cheers from the gunners told him all he needed to know. He grinned broadly. They had hit the merchant ship.

Chapter Six

Caithlin's faith in the care the Shining Ones placed over her was renewed a second after the first cannonball struck. The shot smashed against the starboard quarter of the merchant brig, causing the whole ship to shudder violently from the impact. Caithlin was thrown down to the deck; as she fell, the second shot smashed into the side of the quarterdeck, and she watched in morbid fascination as a twirling splinter of wood, the size of her arm and deadly sharp, span through the space where her head had been only a moment before.

She fell to her hands and knees with a thud, her heart hammering away in fear, but her mind curiously calm in the face of the first time in her life that she had survived being directly shot at. She heard screams and cries of wounded men; one somewhere behind her and one somewhere up above. Galvanized into action, she leapt back to her feet and looked around to take stock of the situation.

The quarterdeck was littered with shards of wood, the stern itself crumpled and bowed from the impact of one of the projectiles. Ghen, one of her newest sailors, lay screaming near one of the quarterdeck guns, splints of wood piercing one of his thighs as he rolled around in agony. Up above, the port main shrouds – the rigging ropes holding the mainmast in place from the sides – now hung loose and flapped in the wind while Torrin, an experienced top man, lay dangling from the surviving shrouds by one ankle, blood from a wound across his chest sprayed across the edge of the main sail.

"X'And!" she shouted above the chaos and confusion of the cries of the panicked and wounded. "Keep driving us south!"

Caithlin pulled her sailing knife out of her boot, jammed it between her teeth, and leapt up onto the black ropes of the port shrouds. Looking up ahead at Torrin, her whole world lurched back and forth in a familiar rhythm as the *Martolian Queen* listed from side to side in the waves, her displacement in space growing in magnitude with each few feet she continued to scramble up away from the deck and toward the yard arm above. Dozens of feet above the foamy waves, high enough above the deck that a fall would spell out her death, Caithlin continued to scramble acrobatically up over the ropes and lines that she had known for practically her whole life, undeterred by the stomach-wrenching height she ascended to.

"Captain…" Torrin called out weakly, his eyes blurred as he feebly attempted to right himself and reach up to free his trapped ankle.

"Hold still!" Caithlin removed the knife from her mouth momentarily to call out, climbing nimbly across to the wounded sailor.

It was only upon reaching him that she realized the flaw in her rescue plan. Only a touch over average height and slim of build, she had no idea how she would support the burly sailor's body weight once she had cut his ankles free of their entrapment. Looking across the tattered shrouds, she identified one of the ropes that was cut and now served no purpose. Grabbing her knife, she quickly cut away at another end of the rope and then, on freeing it from the damaged mast, used it to quickly tie around the wounded sailor's waist.

She ignored his screams of pain as she did so, as well as the blood that flowed over her hands, knowing that getting the man back on deck immediately was his only chance of survival. High up over the waves and splintered wood of the deck, Caithlin quickly tied a secure bowline knot around Torrin and then tied the other end to the sturdy wood of the yard above them. Then the orc warship's bow chasers thundered into life again.

Caithlin braced herself as she heard that same, terrible whine rip through the air, and then the sailcloth next to her tore open. She saw only a blur but felt as though a powerful gust of wind suddenly smashed into her, throwing her back to cling desperately to the rigging. Then it was gone, and there was no time to think over what had just happened. She looked down below at the quarterdeck and saw two of her sailors staring up at her.

"Below!" she yelled down over the whistling wind. "Wounded man, coming down!"

Wrapping her knees securely within the rope latticework, Caithlin let go of the rigging with both hands and leaned back to grab at the end of her wounded sailor's survival line. With her other hand, she reached across with her knife and sawed away at the shrouds that had caught his ankles until they parted. Torrin fell on a few inches until the rope around his waist caught him. Gritting her teeth, Caithlin paid out the rope, hand over hand, as she steadily lowered her injured sailor back down toward the deck. Hisses of exertion became audible yells as her arms burned with the toil of lowering the heavy sailor, until finally she saw his comrades on deck reach up and safely take him off the line.

A job successfully completed, but there was no time for self-congratulations. Caithlin looked around the damaged shrouds, quickly worked out what rigging could be quickly and easily repaired, and then set about tying off as many of the lines as she could in secure knots before descending dexterously back down to the quarterdeck. She looked across at the orc pirates as she neared the deck, her pulse quickening as she realized they were drawing closer. The *Martolian Queen* was simply not fast enough.

"Waisters!" she yelled across to her sailors working on the upper deck waists. "The guns! Ditch them! Throw them overboard! And up for'ard – the anchors! Cut the anchors loose!"

X'And was waiting for her as she hopped back down the last few feet onto the deck.

"How's Torrin?" she asked.

"Not sure," the salamander winced uneasily before glancing down and emptying a measure of black powder into his pistol.

"You planning on stopping an entire boarding party with your one shot?" Caithlin raised her brow, her arms still ablaze with exertion.

"It's not for the orcs," X'And said quietly, looking up at her sorrowfully. "You know my past. I've seen what will happen to a woman like you. This is the kindest thing I can do for you as my friend, if it comes to it."

Caithlin felt an unusual and powerful mixture of emotion, something between terror at her predicament and gratitude for her friend's difficult gesture, but then she resorted to her time-honored and successful method of dealing with all such things in life and quickly buried those emotions where they could not affect her.

"We're not there yet, X'And," she forced a slight smile, "not by a long shot. Now put those muscles to some good use and help the waisters. Get those cannons overboard."

"Aye, Captain," the salamander sailor issued a toothy grin before dashing down to the upper deck.

Caithlin wiped the blood from her shaking hands against the legs of her tan breeches and resumed her place by the helm of her ship. With a salamander and seven men behind it, the first cannon was pried off its carriage and thrown over the starboard waist.

"The guns!" Owynne yelled. "What in the seven circles are you doing with the guns?!"

"Mister Wurrio," Caithlin shot the company purser with a threatening glare, "this ship weighs some four hundred tons. At two tons a piece, losing those guns is rather a good start in slimming her down if we intend to run."

"Twelve tons out of four hundred?" Owynne exploded, his face reddening as he blurted out his words. "That's barely a dent!"

Caithlin stopped to ponder on his words for a second. Losing the anchors as well would shed a few more tons but still not enough. The man had a point.

"You are entirely correct," she agreed before turning to shout out another command to her thirty-five sailors, "All hands! All hands! After the guns and anchors are gone, get down below! Ditch the cargo! Throw our cargo overboard!"

"What?!" Owynne gasped. "You can't do that! That's not your cargo! That belongs to the company! Do you have any idea how much it costs?"

"No, but I do know precisely how much it weighs," Caithlin countered as she glanced back at the orc warship that was now close enough for her to hear the grunts and screams from its crew across the morning winds.

"That's enough!" Owynne screamed. "Enough! I'm taking command of this ship! You own only a one-fifth share in this vessel; the company owns two-fifths! I'm taking command!"

Repressing an unhelpful and unladylike string of obscenities that would, at least, have made it quite clear how she felt about Owynne, Caithlin forced another bitter smile.

"I only own one-fifth of the ship," she admitted as she watched another cannon fall overboard, "but my father owns two-fifths. So that is a family share of three-fifths, which is the majority. This ship belongs to my family, and I am supremely confident that my father would want to see his only child survive rather than this whole crew killed, in addition to the ship and her cargo falling into the hands of pirates. Now, be a good fellow and cease any form of communication with me until this is all over, lest I have *you* thrown overboard to save me another half ton."

Ignoring the purser's spluttering, Caithlin paced across to the helm of the brig.

"You get down below and help move the cargo," she ordered her helmsman as she placed a hand on the wooden wheel. "I'll take her from here."

***

Ghurak's words were drowned out as the row of guns on the port side of the blood runner exploded into life, belching out black smoke in the wake of their murderous cannonballs. Less than half the gunners hit the target; the back end of the rearmost of the four ships that still remained in the convoy trudging on stoically to the east. The shots smashed into the ship, just too low to plow across the deck but also too high to hit the rudder. Ghurak cursed at his luck; crippling the rudder would have been enough for him to change targets and shift focus to an even easier kill. As it was, he watched the convoy crawl away as the four human ship captains abandoned their fifth ship, leaving the vessel to the south alone and exposed as it continued in its attempts to flee the orcs. Ghurak laughed. The cowards were leaving their own behind to ensure their escape. Then again, he shrugged as he thought it through; he would be more than happy to do the same to a shipload of goblins. But he would never run from a fight.

Looking forward again, he raised his telescope and surveyed the lone merchant ship. It was actually picking up speed now – he could tell that by the length of its wake, something that Cerri had taught him – and the blood runner was now only creeping slowly forward in comparison as the gap between the two vessels closed only painfully slowly. Through his telescope, he saw something tumble from the back end of the ship. He grinned victoriously. The ship was falling to pieces. He only hoped it would remain intact long enough for him to board it, capture the crew, and then cobble together enough repairs to sail the thing back home to sell.

Something else fell from the back of the merchant ship. It was a box. A third one followed only seconds later. Ghurak's smile transformed into a scowl and he slammed a fist into the base of the blood runner's back mast.

"The bastards!" he yelled. "Those soddin' bastards! They're dumping the cargo! *My* cargo!"

The ship was expensive; slaves would also fetch a decent price, but whatever the cargo was, it was valuable enough to hire a small fleet of five ships to move it, and Ghurak could only watch helplessly as it was flung overboard by a chain of human sailors passing box to box from a hatch in the middle of the ship to the aft end. He swore again, several times. Some of the boxes smashed as soon as they hit the sea and sank away beneath the waves, while others floated serenely along in the wake of the merchant ship.

"We could fire up the drill!" Kroock offered. "Take out their rudder!"

"Shut up with the drill!" Ghurak boomed. "That's my ship, and I don't want it damaged! Aim high and take down its sails! Don't you let them escape from me!"

Kroock winced with one eye but loyally turned to holler out an order to the front of his ship.

"Keep shooting, lads!" he yelled. "Blow its sails off!"

***

Another salvo of cannonballs struck the stern of the *Marto-lian Queen*, sending a shudder of distress through her beams. Caithlin looked over her shoulder, her cool exterior eroding. She saw the orc ship continue to close from directly astern as its viciously pointed, metal bow cut through the waves and smashed the trail of discarded, wooden cargo boxes into splinters. She heard more cries of the wounded from the deck below, where she had set in place the chain of sailors who were passing boxes from the cargo hold to then dump unceremoniously from the stern windows.

With every one of her sailors engaged in the vital activity of shedding the load from the ship, Caithlin was left completely alone on deck at the helm. The plan seemed to be working; the *Queen* was slowly increasing speed and certainly seemed just a touch lighter to respond at the helm, but the orc pirates were still closing and their guns were still firing. Caithlin had even sent her top men down below to help off-load the cargo. With the sails set and no intention of changing course, they would only be needed to carry out hasty damage repair; and if that eventuality came to the fore, she would call for them. It was best for her to remain at the helm. If one person should remain in clear view of the orc gunners, it should be her. *'Test yourself,'* she remembered her father telling her with great severity in his tone, *'if you are to survive this world, test yourself. Every single chance you get.'*

She realized that it was the first time she was alone on deck since her teenaged years, escaping from her studies to take a skiff out on the calm waters near her home, delighting in the simplicity of sailing in far simpler times. Now, with the blood of one of her sailors spread across her clothes and her ship jolting periodically as it was struck by cannon fire, the realization that she would probably be dead within the hour began to sink in.

X'And appeared at the top of aft hatchway, scrambling up on deck before rushing over to the helm.

"That last hit went straight through the cargo handlers at the gallery windows."

"How are the men holding up?" Caithlin asked.

"Six dead, ten wounded."

"Six dead?" Caithlin exclaimed. "Six? Who is it?"

"Worry about that later, Captain," X'And advised gently.

In her years of sailing, she had seen sailors washed overboard to their deaths in storms, she had seen top men lose their grip and plummet to their doom, dashed on the deck below in front of their crew mates. But these things were relatively rare, perhaps a death per long voyage at most. Six dead sailors in the space of an hour was something that she had never seen, not on her ship. Other, less fortunate ships slipping beneath the waves on the horizon in the worst of storms, perhaps; but never on her ship.

"We have bought some time," X'And said, "but they are still closing. Unless we do something else, this can only end one way."

Her hands clinging to the wheel, her breaths now filling her lungs through sharp inhales, Caithlin's dark eyes dropped down to look at the pistol tucked into her salamander first mate's belt. She looked up at her friend and considered saying something hopeless, but she decided silence was best, lest she reveal that fear was overtaking her. The salamander patted the gun at his hip.

"We're not there yet!" his gravelly voice said kindly. "Not yet. I have another idea."

The salamander dropped to one knee and took a chart from his coat pocket, unfolding it across the splinter-strewn wooden deck.

"We're here," he said, stabbing a clawed finger into a point on the chart, "northwest of Ploutoria, right? Running east of us right now is the Eress Ridge. Ploutoria is the only part of that ridge that extends above sea level, but the rest of it is lurking right beneath the surface. Some of it is sandy shallows, other parts are jagged rocks. If we alter course to the east and head straight through it…"

"We'll be dashed apart," Caithlin whispered.

"No! Well, maybe… but looking below, the *Queen* is sitting about two feet higher in the water now. We're not dragging nearly as much of the keel, certainly not compared to those orcs behind us. If we head east, at worst we'll smash open our hull and we'll sink. I'd rather go down with the ship than face those orcs. But at best?"

"We'll glide right over the top and they'll be cut to ribbons behind us," Caithlin breathed, some hope blossoming in her heart again.

"I don't think we'll do any gliding," X'And admitted, "not if we pick something proper to trip up those orcs. We will scrape the keel, we will take damage, and we will take on water. But I think it's our only chance. She's your ship, Captain."

Caithlin did not hesitate. There really was no choice to be made.

"Get the top men back up on the yards. We're heading east."

***

"Come on! Come on!" Ghurak urged, saliva dribbling down his angular chin as he stared longingly at the merchant ship that edged ever so slowly closer, but never close enough.

They had altered course to the east; something that if Kroock had been quicker on the uptake would have allowed them to cut the corner and catch up. But, as it was, Kroock could merely scream at his rigging goblins to copy the sails set by the merchantman, given that neither he nor Ghurak truly understood how to best harness the full power of the wind. Ghurak had a goblin on the *Green Hammer*; Ratchit. He would have known what to do.

The bow guns continued to blast out, now somehow missing their target even though the range had barely changed.

"It's the wind," Kroock declared confidently, "same as the sails having to change, now the wind's not straight behind us. Those cannonballs are getting blown off course."

Ghurak looked across incredulously at his subordinate.

"I might not know much about boats and sails, Kroock," Ghurak grunted, "but I know my weapons. And you are talking shit! The wind doesn't blow cannonballs off course! They're too heavy! We're missing because this boat is sitting at a different angle in the water, and those useless bastards of yours firing the guns aren't adjusting their damn aim! So you go tell them to sort their aim out, or I'll be up there to sort it out for them! And they don't want that, I promise you!"

Kroock saluted and then stomped off down to the top deck, hurling orcs and goblins alike aside as he made his way up to the front deck to bark at his gunners. Ghurak swore and reached into his coat pocket for his pipe. Long minutes dragged by. The *Driller* was no longer gaining on the merchant ship. The gunners continued to miss with their shots. And up ahead, the water suddenly seemed noticeably choppier.

***

"Not far now!" X'And beamed. "Just keep her heading east!"

Caithlin looked down at the two compasses visible through their glass windows in the cabinet just forward of the helm, making small adjustments on the wheel to keep the *Martolian Queen* plunging on slowly against the northeasterly wind. She could see the disturbances in the water ahead; after another minute, she saw the first of the jagged rocks poking up through the green waters. Normally such a sight would fill her with concern, but for the first time, the dangers presented by those rocks were their only chance at escape.

"Pass the message down below," she said to X'And, "tell the men to prepare to repair flood damage."

X'And had taken only a few paces when the next wave of cannon fire struck the *Martolian Queen*, causing Caithlin to cry out loud as she was flung forward, left winded as her chest slammed against the wooden wheel. She looked up and let out a cry of anguish as she saw her salamander first mate crumpled at the foot of the ladder leading from the quarterdeck, covered in a layer of splintered wood.

"X'And!" she yelled, clinging frantically to the helm as she looked around for somebody to take the ship's steering from her. "X'And! Get up!"

The salamander stirred and slowly raised himself to one knee and then staggered up to his feet. He turned around and shot a groggy smile at Caithlin, blood seeping from wounds across his face, leg, and tail.

"X'And!" Caithlin called desperately again.

The salamander held up a hand.

"I am alright, Captain! I'm no hero! If I need aid, I assure you that I will tell you!"

Caithlin's relief was short lived. The ship lurched and rolled as it sailed into the disturbed water around the rocks, and Caithlin felt her heart sink in despair as she realized that her inputs into the helm wheel met with no resistance. She turned the wheel again, but it only confirmed her worst fear. The helm was completely free to spin. The last shot had disconnected the steering gear. They had no control over the rudder.

Sprinting to the back of the ship, Caithlin grabbed hold of the taff rail and leaned over to look down at the rudder below her. Finally, just one spot of luck. The rudder was jammed dead amidships. They were now constrained to plunging on straight ahead, no matter what. Embryonic plans for repairing the steering gear were only just beginning to formulate in Caithlin's head when, once again, the whole ship lurched and groaned, and she was forced to hold on to the rail to remain on her feet. Caithlin looked back at the pursuing orc ship but was confused by the lack of black smoke across her decks. They had not been shot. Then the source of the damage became apparent by a relayed series of alarmed shouts bellowed out from below deck.

"Flood! Flood! Flood in the cargo hold!"

***

The might of the *Green Hammer* would have cut through the rougher seas without even noticing; the smaller and lighter *Driller* began to pitch and roll more noticeably as the pursuit into the more turbulent waters continued. Ghurak pushed his feet out a little further to center his balance as he stared impatiently at the merchant ship eluding his grasp. Up ahead, the brig was also swinging just a little more uncomfortably in the unsettled seas, still doggedly clinging to its easterly course as if delaying the inevitable would somehow lessen the severity of her fate at Ghurak's hands. It would not; quite the opposite, given the frustration the ship was causing him.

"Can I lead the boarding crew across, Admrul?" Kroock asked hopefully, a vicious glint in his eyes.

"No," Ghurak replied as he stared out at his target. "I'll go. I'm taking that ship myself."

Ghurak's concentration was diverted across to a collection of small, lowly looking rocks protruding up through the foamy surface of the water, not far ahead of the *Driller*. His eyes narrowing, he stared at the rocks and thought through whether it should be of any concern; he estimated that the blood runner was narrow enough to fit between them, even without any particularly accurate steering, so it should not cause him any problems. But something still nagged away at the back of his mind, something preventing him from being wholly comfortable with his decision.

"Rocks!" a frantic cry was issued from a goblin clinging resolutely to the front mast. "Rocks! Both sides!"

"Yeah, I've seen them!" Ghurak shouted back.

Ghurak's arms were flung to either side as he staggered back, the whole ship jumping beneath him in time with a loud bang followed by a sickening scraping and screeching from the decks below. The *Driller* initially pitched bow up and then rolled a little to port, the orcs and goblins crowding the decks being thrown from side to side as two, then three ill-fated goblins fell screaming from the rigging above; two fell into the sea while the third plummeted into the deck with a sickening thud.

The screeching from below deck continued for another few seconds until the entire ship came to an abrupt halt. There was a moment's eerie silence until a series of muffled shouts and screams echoed from the decks below as guttural orcs and shrieking goblins yelled over the top of each other, preventing any coherent message from reaching the upper deck. Snarling in rage, Ghurak paced over to the hatchway leading below deck, flinging orc and goblin alike aside as he did so. Then, above the chaotic din below, Ghurak made out a single word above all others.

"Flood!"

Ghurak swore viciously and lashed out with a booted foot to punt a passing goblin into the back mast. He stared ahead in raging frustration as he saw the merchant ship he had spent every daylight minute chasing drifting away to the east, out of his clutches.

"Don't just whine about it!" he roared down the hatchway. "Get hammers! Get nails! And fix the sodding thing!"

Ghurak had never experienced firsthand what it was like to be trapped on a sinking ship, but he had seen enough go down around him to know how quickly it occurred. The *Driller* was trapped; stuck on the rocks below the water with holes in the hull, but not going anywhere anytime soon. They were safe enough.

"That's twice we've been outsailed by humans," Kroock grumbled. "That's twice we've been made to look stupid. Maybe it's time we stop relying on guns and axes, and we actually learn how to sail these things. Properly."

His jaw aching as his sharp teethed clamped together in rage, Ghurak turned around slowly to stare down at the *Driller's* captin. An orc he had personally picked to command the blood runner, based on his history of bloody brutality and their past together in slavery. He was aware of the concept of loyalty – not something he considered inherently orc-like, but a good enough idea nonetheless – and for a moment he saw his anger overriding that loyalty to one of his longest serving warriors. But he had already killed one orc with his bare hands on this voyage, so he did not need to remind the crew who was in control. And, perhaps more importantly, Kroock was right. He was actually right.

Ghurak was savvy enough to know that he still had a lot to learn about waging war from the sea. As a krudger, he was accustomed to fighting and accustomed to leading his band of warriors, but he only had a single year of experience at sea. One year of trying to learn too many ropes, and taking the war to other pirates to learn his new trade. That was easier. Pirates fought back instead of running. He could beat somebody who turned to fight him. Catching up with somebody running away was more difficult than he thought. He was a capable enough sailor to figure out how to move a boat in the right direction to get to a destination in one piece, and how to turn it to get his guns lined up on an enemy who was fighting back, but little more than that.

Ghurak had started this new venture directly as a captin, solely by virtue of being in charge of the group that took control of a ship of war and thought it would be good to use it to fight with. And, until he learned more about how to use a ship to get what he wanted, he thought it might be best to turn back to what he was good at. Simple, honest fighting and killing. He stomped over to where the map was pinned to the table inside the little hut by the steering wheel. If he could not yet use a ship to grab another ship successfully, he could at least use it to get his warriors somewhere on a map where he could do some damage.

"This ends here," Ghurak spat, "this messing around. Those bastards made me look like a fool! I'm no fool, Kroock! And I'm not messing around any more like some stupid jester! So you go down below, you make sure this boat gets fixed properly, and then when the seas rise up a bit, we carry on! And we are not going back without something to show for it! This messing around ends right now!"

Chapter Seven

The mid-morning sun beat down on the quarterdeck from a cloudless sky as Jaymes paced across the gleaming, wooden boards. The jetty that the *Pious* lay alongside for repairs was now all the more crowded after the frigate HW *Vigil* had arrived the previous evening. The *Vigil*, like the *Pious*, was an Elohi-class, but of the original Batch One design, with a shorter hull and only two masts. The jetty was a hive of activity as stores were brought onboard the *Vigil*; two long lines of sailors linked two huge piles of crates on the jetty to the ship itself, via her forward and aft gangways.

The sailors passed the crates from man to man to transport the seemingly endless stock of supplies up the wooden gangways and into the ship, where they would then be passed down the hatchways to eventually arrive at the orlop deck in the bowels of the ship. There, the various stocks of food, timbers, clothing, ammunition, and powder would be stored before the entire, tedious procedure would be repeated in reverse to remove the empty crates from the ship and back to the jetty.

Fortunately for the ship's company of the *Pious*, this procedure had been completed days previously. The stump of the shattered mast had been removed and, after an awkward day of the frigate looking somewhat ungainly with only two masts, the replacement arrived and the fitting commenced. Now, with the work all but complete, the ship would need to sail for trials to ensure the new mast was correctly fitted before she would be allowed to commence the hunt for the orc pirates. That was once the rigging was secured; the mountainous task of correctly attaching the stays and shrouds – the ropes holding the mast in place – was still to be completed. This all, at least, fitted in well enough with the planned timeline as the third frigate – the *Veneration* – was yet to return from her own patrol. Jaymes gazed up at the workers who set about securing the stays and shrouds to the mast until Karnon, his sole company on the quarterdeck, suddenly spoke.

"So," Karnon said from where he stood on the edge of the deck, his back to the sparkling sea as he stared up at the new mast, "talk me through the decks again, because this makes absolutely no sense."

Jaymes removed his hat momentarily to run one hand through his sweat-soaked hair before returning it and nodding to the marine officer. As much as the details were boring to Jaymes, he appreciated Karnon's attempt to understand and appreciate this new environment he now found himself in.

"Alright," Jaymes mused, "you're on the quarterdeck. This is where the ship is commanded from, and where the helm and compasses are located. The captain always has command of the ship, but he can't be here around the clock; so the 'conn' of the ship is delegated to the officer of the watch. This is either one of the lieutenants or one of the more experienced midshipman. Except for me. As the first lieutenant, I don't stand watches anymore, but don't worry about that."

"So," Karnon summarized, "the officer of the watch shouts the commands up to the men on the masts?"

"No, no, that's the master. For us, that's Thaddeus Just. He's a warrant officer, which means he isn't a *commissioned* officer like a lieutenant. The warrant officers onboard are the master, the gunner, the boatswains, the carpenter, and the surgeon. So, all the people who live with us in the single cabins at the after end of the gun deck. The only addition to that is the ship's chaplain, who is not a warrant officer, but the Admiralty can't currently spare us one of those, which is why you've got his cabin instead."

"I would have thought that pretty vital on a fighting ship, a priest skilled in healing magic."

"Sadly, magic users are rather few and far between in the fleet," Jaymes explained, "and while the healing of divinity magic wielded by priests would be fantastic in battle, I think most of us would choose a battle-mage skilled in aeromancy. Given that we are slaves to the direction of the wind, having a mage who can control and focus that wind would change everything, every day."

Jaymes paused, contemplating just how much everyday life would change with a mage harnessing such power onboard. He had heard of their exploits on the big, first-rate battleships but had never actually witnessed a display of such power with his own eyes.

"Alas," he continued, "either way, you'll only ever see chaplains and mages on the big ships, not frigates. Too few join the fleet so there are too few to be spared. My sister, Clera, married an aeromancer, you know. One of your lot, a legion battle mage. I thought about trying to persuade him to join the navy, but then I realized that I liked him too much to inflict that on him, so I didn't bother."

The look on Karnon's face told Jaymes that he was digressing from the point.

"Anyhow," Jaymes continued, "the warrant officers are highly specialized in what they do. Whereas a lieutenant might only be with a ship for a couple of years, the warrant officers often stay with her for their career."

"Alright," Karnon said slowly as he warily watched a seagull circling overhead the quarterdeck, "so why doesn't the officer of the watch give orders to the sailors on the masts for setting the sails right?"

"Well," Jaymes tilted his head a little to one side, "the master is the expert on sail setting and getting the best out of the ship in any given conditions. The officer of the watch *tells* the master *what* he wants from the ship; the master then translates that into orders for the top men to set the sails and for the helmsman to steer a course."

"Why not just train the officer of the watch to a higher standard so he can do that himself?"

"Because being officer of the watch is just one duty for the lieutenant or midshipman; they do other things. They need to know how to command guns, lead boarding actions, lead shore parties, look after the welfare of the men, write reports... all sorts of things. The master is the expert in navigation and ship handling."

"What about the captain?" Karnon persisted, his eyes still fixed warily on the persistent seagull hovering above them. "What happens when he is on the quarterdeck?"

"Depending on the experience of the captain, he might well know sail setting and navigation better than the master. He might not. Either way, the captain tells the officer of the watch what he wants to happen."

"Wait... wait..." Karnon held up one hand, his face furrowed in confusion. "You still have an officer of the watch on the quarterdeck even when the captain is there?"

"Yes..." Jaymes answered hesitantly.

"So... the captain gives an order, which the officer of the watch repeats, which the master expands on, and then the helmsman turns the wheel? Given that the captain is stood about ten feet from the helmsman, why doesn't he just tell the helmsman what to do himself?"

Jaymes opened his mouth to reply. Nothing came. He closed his mouth again. A sailor in the store ship line to the *Vigil* dropped a crate, which smashed, causing rapturous and sarcastic applause and jeers from his peers until an angry shout silenced the joviality. The seagull overhead cawed noisily.

"Well," Jaymes thought aloud, "it all sounds rather silly when you put it that way. TNB, I suppose."

"TNB?"

"Yes, TNB. Typical Naval Bullshit. You see, there's often a really efficient and pragmatic way of doing things, but we don't like that sort of thing in the navy. If we can add some more flags, bells, salutes, and whistles – especially the sodding whistles, we seem to love those bloody things – then by the Ones above, we'll do it. Efficiency be damned if we can make a bloody long-winded and overly complicated procedure out of it all instead. Anyhow, are you happy enough that you understand the intricacies of the quarterdeck and its function?"

"'Happy' isn't exactly the word I'd use," Karnon admitted, "but let's move on. What about that front deck?"

"The fo'c'sle," Jaymes corrected.

"Foke-sul," Karnon repeated phonetically.

"Yes. Used to be called a 'fore castle' in days gone by. Because it was at the front – the fore – of the ship, hence the front mast is the foremast, and it used to literally have a wooden castle-like structure there for fighting from. But the castle is long gone, and over the years, the word has been condensed to be pronounced 'fo'c'sle'."

"So there was an aft castle?"

"Yes!" Jaymes smiled enthusiastically, finding himself curiously happy that the marine was catching on. "Exactly right!"

"Then two questions leap to mind," Karnon said dryly. "First off; if the fore is the front, why is the back mast called the mizzenmast instead of the aft mast? Second, if you've clung to the term 'fore castle' or however you now choose to pronounce it, why is this bit we're stood on called a quarterdeck instead of an aftcastle or, better still, an a'c'sle?"

Jaymes fell silent again. The bell tower in the Naval Administration building chimed to signify a half hour. The seagull cawed again.

"TNB?" Jaymes sighed in resignation.

"But I'm just getting started," Karnon continued. "Why are there no guns on the gun deck, but there are on the upper deck, and why isn't the upper deck the upmost deck?"

"Oh, that's easy enough. The upper deck is the upper most *continuous* deck, and on a larger warship with multiple decks housing cannons, the gun deck would have guns. But on a frigate, which has only one deck fitted continuously with guns from stem to stern, they're on the upper deck *above* the gun deck – which on a larger ship would be the *second* deck with guns in addition to the upper deck – so convention calls for us to still call it a gun deck as it's the next one down from the upper deck. Even though it has no guns and the upper deck does."

Karnon stared across at Jaymes in abject silence, his face a picture of confusion and disgust.

"That makes absolutely no sense. No sense whatsoever. You've named the decks after what they do on a completely different type of ship?"

"I haven't personally named them, no, but..."

"But it makes no sense at all!" Karnon protested.

"Call it T…"

"TNB," Karnon interjected, "yes, I've got that much."

The debate between the two men was brought to an abrupt halt when Jaymes saw an officer walk across the jetty from the *Vigil* toward the *Pious's* aft gangway. The man was tall and lean, walking with a spring in his step that seemed somehow familiar to Jaymes. He wore an elaborate bicorn hat, adorned with a colorful rosette, and the single gold epaulette on the right shoulder of his blue jacket marked him out as a junior captain. The young frigate captain arrived at *Pious's* aft gangway where he was saluted by the two sailors who guarded it at the jetty. Jaymes turned to call down to the bosun's mate on the upper deck.

"Pipe visiting officer!" he called.

Benne, the tubby bosun, grabbed his whistle and raised it to his lips, blasting out the shrill tune that signaled to all on the *Pious* that a distinguished visitor had arrived. Jaymes and Karnon both stood to attention as the tall captain stepped off the gangway and onto the deck of the *Pious*, bringing his right hand up in a smart salute to acknowledge the Hegemon's flag that flew from the frigate.

Jaymes let out a doleful breath and closed his eyes as he saw the face of the captain. Alain Stryfus looked across at Jaymes, smiled from ear to ear to display his flawless teeth, and then strode up to the quarterdeck to meet him.

"Well, of all the people to bump into out here!" Alain beamed. "Jaymes Ellias! How long has it been? I haven't seen you since… well… when was it?"

"Hello, sir," Jaymes nodded respectfully, the acknowledgement of Alain's senior rank sticking in his throat. "About six or seven years now, I think. Suda Bay was the last time we crossed paths."

"Of course, Suda!" the tall captain grinned. "Well, what are you doing here? I'm absolutely astounded to see you still in the rig of a mere lieutenant! I thought a man of your ambition and confidence would be captain of a Dictator-class by now! Still, I suppose things don't always turn out the way we hope. You win some, you lose some, Jaymes."

Jaymes gritted his teeth bitterly as Alain turned to address Karnon.

"Hello! You must be one of these new marines I've heard so much about. I'm told that my own detachment arrives here for embarkation tomorrow."

"Captain Senne, sir," Karnon folded his arms, "and yes, I believe it's Captain Fetton who will be leading your detachment on the

Vigil."

Alain's response was interrupted as Charn walked up onto the quarterdeck. Alain turned and smiled a friendly greeting to the older captain.

"Captain Ferrus, I presume? I'm Captain Stryfus, of the *Vigil*. I thought it might be advantageous to make your acquaintance face to face at the earliest opportunity."

"Right," Charn said with a slight shrug, his face not betraying a single shred of emotion, "let's go and have a chat, shall we?"

Alain followed Charn back to the steps leading down to the upper deck. After a few paces he turned back to face Jaymes.

"Nice to see you again, Jaymes," he beamed. "Sorry again about how things all turned out for you. Maybe your luck will pick up."

Jaymes watched his comrade from years past disappear off in Charn's wake, his temper on a knife-edge after what he knew was clearly intended as malicious comments. Karnon uttered a single word under his breath, confirming that his thoughts about Alain were not at all dissimilar.

***

Charn hung his hat on one of the pegs inside the door leading to his cabins and gestured to Alain to do the same. He then walked across to his desk and sat down, pushing aside the stack of logistical reports left by Artimio, the ship's purser, to reveal the chart spread out beneath them. Alain paced over to the chair facing Charn's desk and sat down – without being invited to do so, Charn noted. He pondered on his sentiments over the minor transgression of etiquette but decided that as a fellow captain, he would let it pass. However, there were other issues on his mind, and Charn prided himself on being a man who spoke his mind.

"No, no," Charn said quickly, silencing Alain as soon as he opened his mouth to speak, "I shall start. Now, here you are as a frigate captain at the tender age of... what?"

"Twenty-six," Alain replied.

"Twenty-six. So I assume you've done a good amount of time at sea. Boy sailor, brief stint as a midshipman before passing your lieutenancy exams on the first attempt? Good, thought so. So, a veritable young thruster of a man with his own frigate at twenty-six."

"I've been a captain for nearly eighteen months now. So I actually achieved that at twenty-five," Alain explained.

Charn leaned across his desk and assessed the young officer for a moment in silence, in an attempt to ascertain whether he was deliberately trying to cause annoyance. He then continued.

"I was promoted to captain at the age of thirty-one. So in your eyes, even though I have over a decade's more experience than you and I have been a captain for nine years, I must be quite the failure. An embarrassment to work alongside, yet alone as a subordinate."

"No! Not at all! I…"

"In that case," Charn leaned forward aggressively, "given that Mister Ellias is in the same position in his career that I was when I was his age, can you explain to me precisely how you justify your deliberately provocative and malicious comments to him, while also sparing me the humiliation of surviving your withering judgment on what you consider to be an appropriate rate of career advancement?"

Alain leapt to his feet.

"Now look here!" he began. "I've come across here in perfectly good faith to converse with you as an equal, not be lectured like some petulant, young gentleman! I made no such criticism against the pace of professional advancement of you, or anybody else in your position! I made a well overdue observation regarding the less than stellar advancement of a man whom I knew well as a seventeen-year-old! A man who took himself far too seriously, was overly critical and judgmental of all others, and who was rather outspoken about his self-perception of his incredible potential to advance within the service!"

"Ah," Charn folded his arms, "that makes perfect sense. Judge the man and belittle him based upon his actions, no, *words*, as a boy, nearly a decade previously. Let us then agree to disagree on whether that is the appropriate way to speak to another captain's first lieutenant. But, moving on. You have by now received written orders placing your ship as part of a temporary squadron that I command. You are, therefore, by definition, my subordinate in this task. Yet you still think it fit to come skipping across the jetty and onto my ship without so much as an invitation or a letter to warn me off about your intentions?"

Alain planted his clenched fists on his narrow hips.

"As a lieutenant, I was perfectly at liberty to visit another ship alongside without the requirement to send a letter."

"But you're no longer a lieutenant, sir," Charn smiled venomously, "you've made that perfectly clear. And as such, your word now carries a lot more weight. What if my ship was in a poor state, hmm? What if the place was a shambles? Covered in filth and not scrubbed in days? What if the place was a veritable den of iniquity, stacked from stem to stern with whores and drunken fools? Captains do *not* simply prance onto another captain's ship without so much as the common courtesy of a warning that they intend to visit, sir. It's rude."

Alain planted his fists on Charn's desk and leaned forward.

"The state of a warship is a direct reflection of the captain. If this place was a shambles, then I would not think you worthy of the courtesy of a warning."

Charn narrowed his eyes and slowly raised himself to his feet. He was the first to admit to himself that the majority of his thunderous outbursts at his subordinates were for show; to emphasize a point and to maintain the illusion of unbridled ferocity that was so advantageous in keeping good order on a warship. But the man stood before had, in every sense, incurred his spite.

"Captain Stryfus, there are two types of captains in this navy. I shan't go into details, suffice to say that I am one type of captain and you are the other. I have no time and very little respect for the other. You've been promoted early which is, in my experience, due to exceptional ability, luck, or family ties. I'm content that it isn't the first of these, so you've either stumbled across some great prize ship to make your name, or an admiral is nailing your auntie. Either way, this is my ship and you have disrespected her. So don't say another word, take your fancy hat and piss off. Immediately."

Charn watched with no small amount of satisfaction as the young captain snatched his hat off the peg and stormed out of the cabin, slamming the door behind him. Content that he had dealt well with the situation, Charn decided to reward himself with a glass of something strong. Pouring out a plucky measure of brandy, he stared out of the stern windows of the *Pious* at the glorious, sparkling sea of the bay. It interested him that Jaymes was once a man of ambition and self-confidence. But fate had intervened to push him past his point of clinging to those virtues. As he took a sip of his brandy and sniggered at the ridiculous spectacle of the angry captain storming back across the jetty to the *Vigil*, Charn wondered if the loss of those virtues was something he could remedy.

***

After that disastrous morning, luck seemed to shine on the *Martolian Queen*. The damage to the hull was repaired and the majority of the water pumped out. The wounded sailors were patched up as best as was possible, given the limited medical expertise onboard, and the ship continued on eastward. Even the winds changed in their favor, which was not only of huge importance to their speed, but it also allowed them to steer using sails as, despite X'And's best efforts, the steering gear was wrecked beyond any repairs that could be carried out at sea.

Two days later, Caithlin stood on her battered quarterdeck as the brig drifted into the deep-water harbor of Thatraskos. The midday sun reflected off the idyllic, turquoise waters as the *Martolian Queen* limped toward the northern end of the bay. A port authority cutter sailed out to meet them from the picturesque northern shoreline. Thatraskos truly was a place of beauty – remarkably so, given its huge military presence – the neat houses, beautifully crafted administration buildings, and lush jungles all easily outstripped the negative influence of the grim, purposeful coastal forts guarding the jaws of the harbor.

The cutter maneuvered alongside the wounded cargo vessel, and one of its crew stood up at the aft of the little ship, raising a copper speaking cone to his lips.

"Hello there! *Martolian Queen*?"

X'And moved across to recover a speaking cone from the bosun's locker and then walked over to the starboard waist to shout out a reply.

"Aye, sir, we're the *Martolian Queen*."

Caithlin was glad at least that they were expected; upon reaching Star Point – the southwest corner of the island of Keretia – they had signaled to a lookout at a coastal defense position that they were damaged and their intentions were to continue on to Thatraskos.

"Can ye steer, sir?" the sailor on the coastal cutter yelled up to them.

"No, no steering. Gear is smashed and rudder is locked a'midships," X'And replied.

There was a brief conversation aboard the cutter until an order was shouted back.

"Come in north as far as ye can, sir, and then drop anchor. With your permission, we'll come alongside to take your captain ashore."

"No, no, sir!" X'And called back. "We've no anchors!"

There was another pause before the next direction was shouted up.

"Follow us, sir! We'll take you to a buoy and secure you there!"

Caithlin exhaled in frustration. They were alive, they had the Shining Ones above to thank for that. But now life carried on, and she was a captain with a ship she did not fully own, damage she could not afford to repair, harbor fees she could not pay, and a dumped cargo worth a quarter share of the ship to explain.

"I can supervise taking us to the buoy," X'And said quietly as he walked back across to Caithlin. "Perhaps it would be best if you headed down below and took a few moments to yourself."

Caithlin looked around at the rest of the harbor. To the north were trade ships of various sizes, alongside a few privately owned sailing vessels. To the south was the imposing Basilean Naval yard; dotted with sloops, brigs, and even a trio of frigates. One of the frigates was moving steadily eastward, setting sail for the open sea. She noted with mild interest that it was fitted with three masts rather than the normal two for a Basilean frigate, making it more similar to frigates of other navies. It would soon be passing by the *Martolian Queen's* stern.

"There's a Basilean warship coming," Caithlin said wearily. "Get ready to dip our ensign."

The salamander looked over at the warship and then back at his captain.

"Cathy, we're shot to shit!" he exclaimed. "I think even the Basilean Navy will understand that and not expect us to stand on formalities!"

"X'And, we are a Genezan registered trade ship in a foreign port with a naval presence. I will stand on ceremony, and I will be courteous. Please send one of the men to the ensign and bring it to the dip to salute that frigate as she passes."

"Aye, Captain. And the buoy?"

"I'll see to it."

Caithlin walked over to the fo'c'sle to take charge of the sailors who had assembled to cast the lines down to the cutter below. The tall, beautiful frigate sailed majestically over, perhaps a little closer than it needed to as if inspecting the *Martolian Queen's* damage out of morbid curiosity. As commanded, her sailor at the ensign dipped it halfway down its flagstaff to salute the warship as it passed. With a series of shouts and shrill whistles, the frigate dipped its own blue ensign in acknowledgment. Caithlin looked up enviously at the mighty frigate as it passed.

She recalled her father taking her to Lake Gehr to teach her how to sail as a child; they would stop for dinner afterward at the same shore side tavern every time. The tavern allowed a vendor to trade there; a skilled old sailor who carved wooden model and toy ships. It was always the naval vessels that sold; wide-eyed children were fascinated with the sleek warships bristling with guns more so than the stocky, functional cargo ships. Caithlin herself had three model warships on her windowsill at home – one of them a frigate.

Pious

Three Basilean naval officers – distinct in their heavy coats and black hats – looked down at her from the quarterdeck of the frigate. Two then returned to their duties, but one continued to survey the damage on the battered Genezan brig. He raised one hand in a slow wave, his poise somehow conveying his sympathy even from the distance between them. Caithlin returned the wave gratefully before bringing her attentions back to coordinating her crew's efforts with the buoy. The frigate carried on, the splendid craftsmanship of its stern in full display as it altered course for the open sea. The name of the frigate was carved in the wood of her stern in stylized letters, each the height of a man. *'Pious'*.

Within half an hour, the *Martolian Queen* was successfully secured to the buoy, not far from the northern trade jetties, with four sailors positioned in the orlop deck to continuously keep pumping out the sea water that seeped in past the makeshift repairs on the hull. The cutter bumped gently alongside the brig, and lines were thrown across to secure the vessels together so that Caithlin could safely make her way across.

Owynne made his appearance on the deck, two sailors struggling to carry his heavy, wooden chest behind him. He walked straight across to the port waist and made to grab at the rope ladder that led down to the deck of the cutter.

"Where are you going?" X'And demanded.

"My business here is done," Owynne sniffed dismissively. "You have lost our cargo, and with it, your payment. I am going ashore to negotiate how much the Viconti Shipping Company now owes the South Mantica Trading Company, which will no doubt include the surrender of the three-fifths share of this ship as a minimum. With that in mind, I'll also need to find a new captain. Excuse me."

"You're still on Captain Viconti's ship!" X'And yelled. "So stand aside and let the captain off her own deck first, as is right and proper!"

The Trading Company official barked out a derisive laugh and swung a leg over the waist of the ship. With a growl of rage and fists clenched, X'And made to dash forward until Caithlin rested a hand on his shoulder to stop him.

"Leave it be," she said, "it is not worth it."

Owynne disappeared below to stumble and slip down the ladder to the cutter. Caithlin turned to address the sailors assembled on the *Martolian Queen's* deck; twenty or so, over half of her surviving sailors. The men ceased their work and turned to look at her from their various stations.

"Rest assured," she told them, "I will use every last coin I have to pay you your wages first, before I even consider repairing this ship or repaying my debts. Honoring my commitment to you all is my first priority."

Caithlin felt her hands shaking uncontrollably as she saw a few of the men turn to mumble quietly to each other, glancing back at her as they did so. She clasped her hands tightly together at the small of her back to hide the display of emotion. Benj, one of her oldest and most experienced top men, stepped forward from a small group stood at the foot of the mainmast.

"We saw what you did for Torrin, Captain," the ageing mariner grunted. "He'd be dead if it weren't for you. Don't worry about rushing to pay us, Captain. We know you're good for it."

Caithlin felt a sickness rise to her throat as a wave of emotion swept over her. Physically and mentally exhausted from two days and two nights of fighting to escape pirates and keeping her battered ship afloat, she teetered on the very precipice of an emotional breakdown, triggered by this act of kindness and faith from her crew. That would not do. Steeling herself, she clenched her fists behind her back and stood up straighter.

"Thank you," she said coolly to Benj and turned to make her way down the ladder to the awaiting cutter.

***

It felt almost wayward to Caithlin, felonious even, to be sat on the lush chair of dark red velvet in her bloodstained and frayed clothing that stank of sea-water and sweat. The chair was one of several in the dark corridor outside the harbormaster's office; several other rooms sprouted off the main corridor, most of which resonated with conversation or laughter from within. Caithlin felt her eyes drifting shut, her body still swayed rhythmically from days at sea, at odds with the world suddenly returning to a steady state of no motion. Now, in the relative silence of the dark wood-paneled corridor, illuminated only by the midday sunlight shining in through a solitary, tall window near the top of the staircase leading up to the first floor, Caithlin was left alone with her thoughts about the future.

Her father had worked so hard to establish the family company and had invested so much faith in her to build on the family name and success. He owned two-fifths of the ship and she one-fifth, but given how much money she now owed the South Mantica Trading Company, it mattered little. She would have to sell the ship. Even if she could afford the repairs – which she definitely could not – and even if she could afford to replace the guns, the price of the cargo alone was crippling. She did not even have enough money to secure a passage home to Geneza; not after trying to pay her sailors something for their toil.

The door to the harbormaster's office opened to reveal a short, stern-looking woman who was nearly twice Caithlin's age, her severely scrapped back gray hair adding to her unyielding aesthetic. Owynne walked out of the office and briskly past Caithlin, refusing to even grace her with an acknowledgment of her presence as he passed.

"Come on in, Captain," she sighed as she held the door open.

Caithlin walked into the small, neat office, obediently sitting down in another of the red-velvet cushioned chairs in front of the harbormaster's desk, as she was directed to by the older woman. The harbormaster sat on the far side of the desk, the light pouring into the office through two wide windows doing an unmerciful job of highlighting the wrinkles in the older woman's face. The harbormaster spread out a roll of parchment and took a quill pen from a bottle of ink.

"Name and ship?" she demanded, the clipped tones of her Basilean accent sounding almost harsh when compared to the inflections Caithlin was more accustomed to.

"Caithlin Viconti. I'm the captain of the *Martolian Queen*. A medium brig registered in Geneza."

The harbormaster scratched away on the parchment with her pen.

"And you were attacked by pirates?"

"Yes. My first mate believed them to be orcs. I'm afraid I can't recall positively seeing their crew on deck, even when they were close. It's all a bit of a blur."

The stern woman looked up from her writing and across the desk at Caithlin. Her features softened for a brief moment.

"What damage has your ship suffered?"

"Six dead sailors. We buried them at sea. Ten wounded. My steering gear is broken, my hull breached below the waterline, and structural damage to the after end of the ship. Oh… and I had to jettison my cargo and cannons to make good our escape."

"Sails good?"

"We repaired them. They're fine."

The harbormaster passed across a small nautical chart to Caithlin.

"Can you confirm that the spot marked on the chart is where you were attacked?"

Caithlin looked down in surprise at the chart, noting the accuracy of the position of the life-changing incident only two days before.

"How… how did you know…"

"The rest of your convoy arrived in Hymenirkos yesterday. They sent a message here, just in case you did arrive. From what the letter says, they turned back and recovered about half of the cargo you threw overboard."

Caithlin's eyes opened wide in hope.

"They've recovered half of it?" she exclaimed, half standing out of her chair. "Then that's half the debt they will charge my father's company gone?"

"I'm afraid not," the harbormaster shook her head, her features showing a hint of remorse and sympathy. "They can legitimately claim that you failed to transport the cargo as agreed, forcing them to double their efforts. They could even claim that the moment you dumped the cargo overboard it became legal plunder in open seas, and so they were merely profiting on opportunity. Either way, the letter says that if you were to arrive here, that you are to be informed of what you owe them."

Caithlin sat down slowly again and took in a deep breath.

"Go on," she swallowed.

The harbormaster passed across the letter. Caithlin glanced over the cold, legal phrasing of the accusations, her heart thumping sickeningly as another bout of reality hit her in the gut. Then she saw the monetary figure quoted and found herself gasping for breath. The short harbormaster shot to her feet and walked around to stand by her, stopping and looking down awkwardly at the pathetic, broken sea captain.

"I can't afford this," Caithlin whispered, "I can't afford to repair the ship. I can't afford to pay the crew. I can't even afford your harbor fees. What do I do?"

The harbormaster perched on the end of her desk and smiled uncomfortably.

"Under the terms of the Ekhos Trade Accord, you were in a shipping lane which falls under the responsibility of the Basilean Navy to provide security for. I believe that is enough mitigation for me to wave your harbor fees for one month, as our navy has sadly failed to provide that protection which was assured to you. That gives you some breathing room. I can point you in the direction of some companies here who can repair your ship, but I'm afraid I can't help you with payment for them. The only other thing I can offer you is some clean clothes. You are about the same size as my daughter. Be back here at six bells and you can be my guest this evening. You'll be able to think a little straighter after a wash, some food, and a good night's sleep."

Caithlin felt another wave of unwelcome emotion threatening to engulf her. She took a few deep, steadying breaths before looking up at the harbormaster, her only avenue of help in the darkest hour in her entire life.

"Why are you extending such kindness to me?" she ventured hesitantly.

The harbormaster smiled again, this time with some genuine, overt warmth.

"This is Basilea. The chosen land of the Shining Ones themselves. Charity is a fundamental pillar of our way. And on a personal note, I know what it is like to be a young woman in a foreign land, caught out with real problems and not a coin to address them with. I'll help you as best I can, just as somebody once did for me. But I fear your best option might be to sell that ship."

Caithlin nodded and stood, her limbs weary and her eyes heavy.

"I know," she said, "and thank you. I will go back to the ship to inform my crew of where we stand. I will be back here this evening to accept your kind offer of hospitality."

The harbormaster stood, too, and offered her hand.

"Kassia Rhil," she introduced herself.

Caithlin took her hand and shook it.

"Thank you again, Missus Rhil," she sighed in exhaustion.

"I'll see you in a few hours," Kassia nodded. "You and your ship aren't sunk yet. We'll think of something."

Afraid of sounding insincere by repeating her gratitude yet again, Caithlin forced a smile and turned to leave. She closed the door behind her, her hands shaking again, before dragging her weary feet toward the port authority building entrance to head back to her ship and face the next stage in living with the consequences of her actions.

Chapter Eight

Peering over the starboard waist of the *Pious*, Karnon watched the thin smear of land on the northern horizon disappear from view as the trio of warships plunged through the waves on a southerly course, away from Thatraskos. The trial for the new mast had been a mere afternoon's work just south of the harbor; this was now Karnon's first voyage as a member of a ship's company and, as his luck would have it, the sky was littered with towering clouds of white and gray, generating a stiff wind and specks of rain in the humid skies as the waves continued to grow in ferocity around the three frigates.

The bows of the *Pious* plunged down and cut into the green waves, the sea splitting to either side of the warship as water sprayed up the metal clad bows. With a sickening lurch and a creak of wood, the bows pitched up again, and Karnon felt a momentary sensation of near weightlessness, his fists clinging tightly to the wood of the taff rail running along the waist of the frigate. Again, the ship pitched down, and Karnon felt his core and limbs grow heavy before the pitch of the ship reversed.

They had been clear of the harbor for less than an hour, and already he felt as sick as a dog. Every minute that passed by seemed to require the most gargantuan of efforts to endure, and the plan was for them to spend a full week on patrol. At that moment, Karnon would have given anything to exchange the vicious waves of the sea for the mortal dangers of a battlefield. A battlefield that at least stayed still.

Footsteps thumped on the wooden steps behind him as Jaymes dashed down from the quarterdeck to the upper deck. He made his way over to Karnon, his gait as steady as if taking an evening perambulation across a calm hillside.

"Not enjoying this?" he asked, his voice hushed to keep the exchange of words private from nearby sailors, his expression sympathetic.

"I'm fine," Karnon replied tersely.

"It's normal, don't worry," Jaymes said quietly, "it's all about balance. Your body gets used to it. Until it does, you just see it through."

"Don't patronize me!" Karnon snapped, his throat dry and nauseous, his head pounding and his whole body sweating. "I've seen more battles than you have storms, I can cope!"

"Fair enough," Jaymes shrugged. "You want to throw your temper about? I'll put it in different terms. You see the tops of the waves are white? And you see that the seas are calm enough for the other two frigates to be launching sea boats to send their captains over to us? This sea is what we'd call 'light to moderate' in its state. After moderate comes heavy. Then severe. You're expected to do your job in all of that, so best you stop your tantrums and get your shit together."

Jaymes turned to walk away.

"Alright, alright," Karnon called after him, "sorry. I'm just finding this more difficult that I thought. Except for that trial yesterday, the only time I've ever been at sea is in a cargo ship full of troops, and those things are steady as a rock."

Jaymes's face softened again.

"Alright, there's a few different ways to crack this, but different things work for different people. The ship moves more at its extremities, so standing right in the middle will give you the least movement. But we're already not far from there and that's not working."

"So what's next?" Karnon gasped desperately.

"Come with me," Jaymes replied.

Karnon followed the naval officer forward, past the mainmast and toward the steps leading up to the fo'c'sle. Jaymes walked straight past a pair of waisters – sailors stationed at the ship's waist – casting them a warning glare as they momentarily smiled wickedly at Karnon's misfortune as he struggled forward, practically rebounding off each cannon along the starboard waist. Sweat pouring off his brow, Karnon planted one foot on the lowest step and then summoned up his determination to follow the sailor up to the fo'c'sle above. As soon as his head emerged above the steps, he was hit in the face by a blast of salt-laden air.

"How the hell does this help?" Karnon gasped, staggering forward past two of the fo'c'sle men to wrap an arm around the base of the foremast. "You said the ship moved a lot more at the front!"

Jaymes turned to face him and nodded, his feet spread apart a little more than normal for balance, but still as unaffected by the moving deck as any other man in the crew.

"Yes, it moves more here," Jaymes admitted, "but you've got fresh air going into your lungs, and you can see what's coming. Look dead ahead. Look at the horizon. Focus on that. That way, your eyes are telling your brain what's coming before your sense of balance does. Take deep breaths and look ahead."

Karnon bit back on a vicious retort on how ridiculous that notion sounded, knowing full well that his temper was frayed due to the headache and nausea, and knowing Jaymes for long enough to be fairly sure this was a genuine attempt to help and not a practical joke. He took in a deep breath of the salty air and stared ahead, focusing on the jumping line of the horizon as the deck rose and fell beneath his feet, alternating the sensation of heaviness and floating with each passing moment.

"This isn't much, is it?" he asked Jaymes.

"It's... choppy," Jaymes replied. "We're moving a bit. It's worse because we've slowed right down for the sea boat transfer, otherwise those rowers would never catch us up. That's the other two frigates sending their captains across to us for a meeting. But it's not so much how much we move that makes people sick, it's the rhythm. You get used to it. Don't worry about this, I once saw a man throw up on a sloop that was tied up alongside to a jetty. It all affects us in different ways to begin with."

Karnon stared ahead. Long minutes passed. He squatted a little and stood up straight in time with the waves as the *Pious* crashed through them. Jaymes walked off to converse briefly with two of the sailors who were inspecting the securing ropes of the fo'c'sle cannons. Slowly, but surely, Karnon's headache began to ease. He stood a little straighter, one hand planted against the foremast instead of clinging to it desperately.

The two sea boats from the accompanying frigates closed the gap to the *Pious*, their sailors heaving against the choppy waves as they approached the wooden wall of the frigate. Karnon could only clearly see the sea boat from the *Vigil*; its captain stood up at the very front of the boat, one foot planted dramatically on the bow and his fists planted against his hips as he stood as steady as a rock in the turbulent sea.

"You feeling any better?" Jaymes asked as he walked back over.

"A little. Thank you. Honestly."

"Quite alright," Jaymes smiled. "Did they not give you some sea time during your training as specialized maritime soldiers?"

"We were supposed to," Karnon forced an uncomfortable smile, "but apparently it would have cost a lot of money to file us all through. They cut costs by conducting our boarding action training on ships at anchor in Spartha Bay."

"The navy and the legion sacrifice quality of training to save a few coins, what a shocker," Jaymes rolled his eyes. "Anyhow, when you feel up to it, go take in some water from the scuttlebutt. Don't take big gulps, just slow sips. That'll help."

"The scuttlebutt?" Karnon asked.

Jaymes turned and pointed to a large bucket of water aft of the base of the mainmast.

"Why not just call it a bucket?" Karnon exhaled in frustration, shaking his aching head wearily.

"TNB," Jaymes beamed before turning to head back toward the quarterdeck.

***

"I think we got off on the wrong foot," Alain smiled awkwardly as he entered the day cabin at the after end of the upper deck. "I brought this by way of an apology."

The young captain revealed a bottle from within the folds of his dark boat cloak and handed it across to Charn. Charn accepted the green, glass bottle and cast his eyes over the label. Twenty-year vintage, from the famous Karathos vineyards. Both rare and expensive. As much as Charn wished to remain angry with the impertinent young captain of the *Vigil*, the bottle of wine was simply too good to refuse.

"Perhaps we were both hasty with our words," Charn flashed a brief smile. "Thank you for the kind gift. Gentlemen, please."

Charn gestured to the chairs set out by the table in the day cabin. Samus, his steward, had already laid the table out with an embroidered cloth and a pot of spiced herb tea to go with a plate of dry biscuits, all of which tenaciously clung to their scant hold on the table top in the meandering sea.

"Samus!" Charn called out to where his steward waited outside the cabin. "Come and get rid of this tea. And get some glasses."

He turned back to address the other two frigate captains as the three men took their seats.

"What better time to drink this excellent wine then now, at the beginning of our first patrol together."

Charn's doleful steward ambled over to remove the steaming pot and cups, returning moments later with the glasses Charn had demanded. Charn looked across at the other two captains. Alain Stryfus leaned forward over the table, his chiseled chin resting on one fist pensively as if about to plan the most cunning operation in nautical history. Opposite him sat Captain Marcellus Dio of the HW *Veneration*, a broad-shouldered but relatively rotund man in his early thirties, with a heavily receding hairline and pale eyes.

Charn poured the wine and passed the glasses over to his guests before raising his own.

"To a willing foe, and good sea room to defeat him."

The two captains repeated the traditional toast before drinking from their glasses. Charn returned his own to the table, holding it cautiously in place with one hand in case the sea state did pick up any further and threaten to spill the precious liquid. It was every bit an excellent wine. With his other hand, he pointed to the chart that had already been fixed to the table.

"You gentlemen don't need me to emphasize to you the importance of the security of the Sand Lane. We were just west of the Sand Lane – about here – when we ran into the orcs. Hopefully you've both already read the report. One smasher and supported by a blood runner. We lost two sloops and did very little damage in return. The blood runner doesn't concern me in the least, but that smasher does. We then have the second attack, well off northwest of the first, closer in fact to the Primovantor Route."

"Assuming it's the same bunch," Marcellus cleared his throat, "and I do think it safe to make that assumption at this point, those two points in such a short space of time would narrow down the base of operations quite significantly. To attack both of those shipping lanes in such a short space of time, I'd bet them to be running out of the Infantosian Islands, off to the south. They've been a nest for pirates for decades now."

"True," Alain nodded, "but if that is the case, even the might of three frigates would be ill-advised to prowl around there. Larger forces have attempted to clear pirates off those islands without success. Furthermore, while I agree that it is most likely that these two attacks have originated from the same crowd of pirates, there is every chance that they possess more than two vessels, and that the second attack came from a third vessel, not one of the two you ran into."

Charn grunted in agreement. It was, alas, unwise to assume the playing pieces to be set out so simplistically. His response was cut off as the ship jolted with the booming of guns from the fo'c'sle. Charn smiled to the other officers.

"Gunnery practice," he explained. "I'm making use of my new marines by training them to operate the guns. That'll free more of my proper sailors to remain up top in action."

"I saw your marine captain as I stepped onboard," Alain grinned. "Poor fellow looked rather green around the gills."

"We all have to start somewhere," Marcellus admonished, taking another sample of the wine.

Charn agreed with the statement but did not see the need to show any sympathy to the marines who were struggling with seasickness. As hardened men of war, he expected them to deal with it and overcome it quickly.

"The question remains," Charn continued, "what is our long term strategy? Our route is already decided for this patrol, but what of the future? I am ruling out separating this squadron, before either of you even suggest it. If we encounter that smasher again, we will need all three frigates to bring her down. So we stay together."

"The Sand Lane is the life blood to the Hegemony from the south," Marcellus said. "We would not be wrong by patrolling that route."

"My counter to that," Alain suggested, "is that the Sand Lane already has regular patrols, and we have been assembled to send this bastard one thousand fathoms down. We're here for vengeance for our lost men, and the insult to the Hegemon in attacking our ships. I think we need to do more than a show of force along the shipping lanes. They attacked the Primovantor Route. They're willing to strike within spitting distance of our mainland, and that's embarrassing."

Charn grunted again. Being given command of a squadron of three frigates was indeed a wondrous thing. Even glancing over his shoulder through the stern windows at the perfect station keeping of the *Vigil* and the *Veneration* as they slid elegantly across the waters off *Pious*'s port and starboard quarters respectfully, Charn felt a warm glow of pride. But the task ahead was less than simple, and every attack that took place along the sea routes Basilea was sworn to protect was, exactly as Alain had phrased it, embarrassing.

"It is but two attacks," Charn said. "We do not have much to go on. Until more of a pattern is set, we must be thankful that we are out here in force, in a timely manner, only days after that first attack. We patrol the Sand Lane. If luck is with us, we'll find them and send them to the bottom. If not, we wait. We wait for them to strike and seal their own bloody fate."

***

Grunting in satisfaction as the first salvo of cannonballs plunged into the water well short of his ship, Ghurak lowered his telescope from his eye. The small, hilltop fort was certainly taking them seriously as a threat now. The sun was low in the sky, nearly touching the horizon and casting a long, shimmering field of orange across the calm surface of the water. At the foot of the hill, below the wooden fort, Ghurak could see the huts of the little colony by the sandy beach that lay dead ahead of the blood runner.

"And you don't want us to shoot back, Admrul?" Kroock stared across incredulously at Ghurak from where he stood next to the goblins hanging from the ship's wheel.

"No," Ghurak shrugged, "you'll never get the guns high enough to shoot up there. I'm not bothered. Reckon there's only, what, four or five guns up there? If they hit us, we'll patch up the holes and keep going."

Ghurak looked forward across the top deck of the *Driller* – eighty orc warriors were packed into the middle of the ship, their axes held ready and their scarred, green faces lit up with vicious grins in anticipation of the upcoming fight. Half of the orcs were Ghurak's greataxes – his biggest, oldest, and most vicious warriors. Goblins chittered to each other as they nimbly scrambled across the rigging lines above, setting the sails at the commands of the trio of senior goblin sailors who paced the deck beneath them. Ghurak still had not bothered to learn the names of those three.

"The fight, I get," Kroock admitted as the fort's guns fired again, their whooshing cannonballs still not making the range to threaten the *Driller*, "but running the boat up onto the beach? We'll get stuck – again – and then shot to hell, Admrul!"

"No," Ghurak spat, patting one of the battered books next to the map he looked over. "I've been doing some reading, Kroock. That's why we're here. It's low tide. The water's low on the beach. In a few hours, it'll be high tide. So, we can run straight over, ram the *Driller* up onto that nice soft beach where we won't tear its arse open this time, and then we can jump down and get straight into the fight. We're too low down for that fort to shoot at us, and then when we're done, we jump back on the boat and wait for the tide to pick us up, and then we sod off again."

Of course, Ghurak had not read the book. That would be decidedly un-orc like. He had told one of his goblins to read the book and then explain the pertinent points to him, slowly and clearly. Regardless, Kroock looked up at the larger orc, failing to hide the confusion that still clearly wracked his brain.

"We'll be facing the wrong way, Admrul!" he squinted. "It'll be a bloody pain turning the boat around, and then they'll shoot us on the way out, when we're moving against the wind, all slow!"

"No," Ghurak shook his head, "you're doing it again! Leave the thinking to me! They're not going to shoot us! You've got to think like a human. We'll have a boat full of prisoners, a whole load of their lot. They're not going to risk sinking us when we've taken a load of prisoners. That's not how they think. They won't shoot us. And that's assuming there's any of them left to fire their guns."

The third salvo of cannonballs shot over from the wooden fort, this time plunging into the clear waters to straddle the *Driller* and send columns of water fountaining up and crashing down over the ship's deck. The growing danger of the accuracy of the shots caused excited chatter from the axe-wielding orcs near the mainmast and a few bellows of laughter. Ghurak looked up and saw the granite cliff beneath the fort looming closer. The settlement at the top of the beach looked disgustingly neat; the wooden huts all arranged in perfect rows with their pristine, timber walls and palm leaf roofs. He would have that remedied soon enough. He stomped over to the middle of the top deck.

"Listen in, you bunch o'bastards!" Ghurak yelled. "Listen up! We're hitting the beach soon! As soon as we do, you get off the boat! Greataxes, get on this side, you're following me! The rest of you, you do what Captin Kroock tells you! Remember! We're here for prisoners! Any of this lot who fight you, you kill them! You rip them apart! Any of them who run? You go get them, and you bring them back here! Every one of them you bring back is money, got it? So kill the ones that fight, grab the ones that don't! That simple!"

The disgruntled murmurs and snorts from his assembled warriors were less than enough to convince Ghurak that his plan was readily accepted and would be followed. He let out a growl and stared down at them, his sharp teeth clenched.

"Let me spell it out for you!" he sneered. "I want prisoners! And you lot are going to get them for me! You are not going to cut them up, you are not going to bite their heads off! Whatever you do to my prisoners, I'll do to you! You bite their arms off, I'll bite your arms off! Don't believe me, you just test me and see! You kill the ones that fight, and you bring back the rest as prisoners here for us to sell, or I'll snap your necks and pull them out of your arses! Got it? I asked if you've got it?!"

The second round of responses from his warriors was good enough to assure Ghurak of their compliance, for now. He could not blame them. They wanted a fight. They wanted to kill, and they had not had enough killing for too long. But dead humans would not bring him the money he needed to equip his second blood runner, or pay his crew.

Ghurak raised his telescope again to look up at the colony. He saw a flag on top of the fort – one he roughly recognized as the flag of Geneza – as well as a larger wooden building with a tower. At the top of the beach, he could now see the colony's inhabitants scrambling out of their huts, ushering their young together in panicked groups before rushing off to the far end of the colony and up the hill.

"Listen in!" Ghurak yelled again. "They're already running! They'll either run to that fort, or into the jungle! Either way, we follow them! Captin Kroock, your lot'll head to that big building with the tower! It's one of their churches, and it's where they keep gold, so you grab it all and get it back here! My lot, we'll go up to the fort!"

As the *Driller* swept across the waves and through the shallow bay toward the beach, the fort's guns fired again. A cannonball swept over the *Driller*'s masts, plowing straight through the crow's nest on top of the middle mast and smashing it into pieces of fluttering wooden splints and goblin limbs that twirled down into the sea. Ghurak could not help but laugh at the sight of the bits of goblin plunking into the water.

"That was a good shot!" Kroock barked out a short laugh. "Fair play to 'em!"

With the wind almost directly behind the two masts of billowing, patchwork red sails, the *Driller* ran straight as an arrow through the shallow waters.

"Get ready!" Ghurak yelled, unsheathing his broad-bladed cutlass.

With a thump that resonated throughout the entire ship and a crash of splintering wood, the *Driller*'s metal bows shunted through the surf and into the soft sand of the beach. The front of the ship jolted up, and half of the orcs and goblins on the deck were knocked to their feet from the force of the impact.

"Get off!" Ghurak yelled. "Over the side, you scurvy bastards!"

"Flood!" a panicked shout drifted up from the hatchway leading below deck. "Flood at the front!"

"Not again!" Ghurak scowled after swearing viciously, before shoving his head into the hatchway to yell a response. "Get it fixed! Now!"

His heavy feet pounding on the wooden boards as he ran up the tilted deck toward the front of the blood runner, Ghurak looked up and saw his orcs piled up ahead of him, shouts and roars of delight as they hurled themselves over the edge of the deck to plunge down into the shallow waters below.

"Out the way! Out the way!" Ghurak yelled, shoving dense orc bodies to either side as he made his way to his rightful place at the front of the mass of warriors.

Planting one fist on the wooden rail jutting around the front of the ship, Ghurak hurled himself over the side of the *Driller* and felt a rush of hot air and brief moment of weightlessness before he plummeted into the warm sea up to his waist. Dragging his heavy feet up and free of the viscous sand that clung to his ankles, Ghurak followed the line of axe-wielding orcs who made their way up onto the beach. He was surprised to see the dead body of one of his warriors float past him, leaking blood into the clear water from a wound in the chest where an arrow protruded up toward the sky above.

He heard a thud as another arrow slammed into the front of the ship, jutting out of the wood just above the great, metal drill. Looking forward, Ghurak saw a line of perhaps ten archers at the top of the beach hurriedly shooting deadly projectiles down into the orcs wading through the water. As the warriors behind him continued to jump off the sides of the ship and into the water, the first orc reached the beach and sprinted up the dry sand with his axe held high, screaming gutturally from the depths of his lungs. An arrow slammed into his gut and then a second into his head, and he dropped down dead to the sand.

"Get in your groups!" Ghurak yelled over the excited grunts and roars of his warriors. "Get on that beach and get into your fighting groups!"

As long as there was armed resistance to his plan, there was no scope for idiots running amok and charging blindly into enemy soldiers. Ghurak could not afford to lose orcs that way. The first few orcs assembled on the beach, their round shields raised as they obediently awaited the arrival of their fellow warriors. Ghurak heard the ringing of bells from the top of the church tower and saw the small exodus of human women and children continue from the top of the settlement toward the hilltop fort, as their men ran down with spears to bolster the beach defenses.

Reaching the beach, Ghurak hurried over to the line of axe-wielding warriors, noting with dissatisfaction that another two of his warriors lay dead in the white sand.

"Axes! This side!" he yelled to the staggered lines of orcs reaching the beach from the shallow water. "Greataxes! You lot get on this side! Two groups of each!"

Ghurak felt a flare of pain shoot up to his neck from his shoulder, and he looked down to see an arrow protruding from the top of his arm. Swearing and staring up through narrowed eyes at the human archers, he yanked the arrow out and threw it aside.

"Come on!" he boomed at Kroock as the orc captin finally dragged himself up onto the beach. "They're your two groups! Take the first lot up and kill those sods with the bows!"

"You heard him!" Kroock yelled, grabbing his two axes from his belt and holding the first aloft. "You lot, with me! Let's go!"

Ghurak grunted his approval as he watched Kroock lead the twenty screaming orcs in a charge up the beach; the amateur ship's captin now replaced with the battle-hardened, bloodthirsty and competent warrior Ghurak knew from old. Ghurak grinned as he looked down at the blood leaking out from the wound in his shoulder. It was great to be back on dry land and in a proper fight. He turned to look down at his greataxes assembling to his left, raising his massive, notched cutlass as he did so.

The sight of the hulking mass of greataxes broadened Ghurak's vicious grin. Clad in thick plates of black armor, the battle-scarred orcs carried hefty, two-handed axes with a cruel assortment of extra blades and spikes at the heads and hafts of the weapons. A few had embraced their new, nautical direction and had painted crude emblems of deadly sea creatures on their armor. The front rank of the first group looked up at him expectantly, their thick fists clenched around their weapons and their eyes glinting in anticipation of the fight ahead.

"Up the beach and into them!" Ghurak hollered. "Any of them who stand and fight, you rip them in half! Kill 'em! Kill 'em all!"

With a roar, Ghurak raised his cutlass over his head and ran up the beach. The combined scream of nearly forty orc warriors dominated the beach, with another twenty guttural voices added as the final orcs from Kroock's second group joined the charge. A line of soldiers, or something closely approximating soldiers at least, appeared at the top of the beach. Two ranks of men in red tabards, wearing light armor and clutching short spears, moved out from the line of the wooden huts to face the advancing orcs. To the right, Kroock's warriors had caught up with the first few of the fleeing human archers and were brutally hacking them down, cutting the men asunder as they attempted to flee from the screaming wall of green muscle.

With a shout of command from their leader, the human spearmen charged down the shallow incline of the beach to meet the advancing orcs. They were outnumbered probably two-to-one and outmatching in a fair fight anyway; they had guts, Ghurak conceded, he had to give them that. Off to the left, a second group of humans appeared at the edge of the beach. Similar in numbers but without the uniformity of the red tabards, the haggled ranks of men carried makeshift weapons made up of tools and farming implements. Ghurak grimaced. He would be surprised if they even stood and faced the charge.

He looked across as he continued to run, noting that his second group of greataxes had already shifted their focus to the makeshift warriors. Then, very much against his plan, a wave of arrows pelted down from the jungle to the west of the beach and tore through the left flank of the greataxes, felling two of them. No time to worry about that now.

Ghurak looked ahead and saw the twin lines of human spearman bearing down toward him and his warriors. Their deadly spears held forward, the men let out a combined cry as they ran, high-pitched to Ghurak's ears and almost comically goblin in its tone. He picked out a man in the center of the front rank, a thin, snarling soldier with a dark moustache. He would be Ghurak's first target.

With a thunderous roar, the two walls of warriors met with a crash atop the white sand. Ghurak batted aside the thin human's spear and brought his heavy cutlass down to hack open the man's chest, easily cleaving through the meager armor and spattering the sands in blood. A second blow hacked straight through the thin, sinewy human flesh to cleave the man from shoulder to midriff, cutting off his head and one arm savagely.

The second rank of spearmen were already in the fight, their weapons thrusting through the gaps of the first rank to attack the orcs. Yelling a ferocious war cry, Ghurak barged forward to force his way into that second rank, lashing out with his cutlass again to lop off a terrified looking soldier's hand and then slice open his neck, sending him staggering down to the sand in a spurt of blood to be trampled underfoot. A third human warrior turned to face Ghurak as he recovered his cutlass, looked up at the snarling, blood-soaked orc krudger, and then thought better of it. He turned and ran, and the cascade began.

With cries of panic, the rear rank of spearman broke and followed the soldier fleeing from Ghurak. The gargantuan orc turned in place and thrust his cutlass through the back of one of the spearman still fighting on the front rank. The hole that opened up allowed his greataxes to pour through and envelop the human soldiers who had stood their ground to fight, bloodily hacking them down. To the left, the pathetic group of makeshift defenders had already bolted, and they were sprinting headlong through the huts of the settlement toward the path leading up to the fort. On the right side of the beach, Kroock led his orcs off toward the church.

"Come on!" Ghurak bellowed, "Chase them down! Get me my prisoners!"

Ghurak led the charge through the wooden buildings, shouting and swearing viciously at any orc who stopped to consider looting a house rather than staying with the group. The path on the far side of the buildings curved around left to head up to the small cliff top on the southwest corner of the island, where Ghurak could see the flimsy defenses of the hastily constructed fort. The fortifications were centered on a single, circular wall made of wooden posts driven into the ground. The rooftops of two buildings were just visible, peering over the palisade wall.

As Ghurak led the screaming, thunderous charge up the hill, the doors to the fort slammed shut as the last human survivors from the battle on the beach dashed through. Seconds later, a line of perhaps a dozen archers appeared atop the wall, and arrows whistled down into the advancing orcs, thudding into green flesh to either side of Ghurak and felling two more of his warriors.

"Get off the road!" Ghurak decided quickly. "Follow me!"

Ghurak sprinted down to the right-hand side of the path, where the ground sloped away to form a natural embankment. Arrows continued to harry the orcs as they trampled through the long grass to the cover of the embankment before crashing to a halt in the comparative safety of the shallow ravine. Ghurak extended a finger to point at his greataxes, quickly counting roughly how many remained. A little over thirty. He had actually lost about ten veteran orcs to this hasty, pathetic ambush centered around the cowardly actions of skulking, human archers. The ravine fell silent, the only noise now being the deep breathing of his warriors and the cacophony of whistles and calls from the exotic birds hidden away in the dense jungle that sprawled out to the northeast.

"Listen in!" Ghurak yelled to his grunting, rage-filled warriors. "We're taking that fort! I'll bet everything that those scum have lined up their cannons on the doors, waiting for us to charge straight through! So instead, we'll take the whole wall down! We charge straight up, spread out along the wall, and hack it down!"

A series of enthusiastic roars and growls echoed from the orcs as they moved around to prepare to face the archers for the sprint up the road. Ghurak looked up at the fort. He had not counted on losing so many of his orcs, and even when he returned to Axe, being stuck on an island in the middle of the ocean was not the best recruiting ground for replacements. At least he would leave here with four new cannons and a string of prisoners to sell. He nodded in satisfaction. The plan was simple enough. With a roar and a string of obscenities, he led the charge back up the hill.

Chapter Nine

The juddering and rocking of the horse-drawn carriage seemed abrasive, even crass in comparison to the smooth, elegant pitch and roll of a frigate. Even after only a few days at sea, Charn's sense of balance struggled to cope with the sudden transition to dry, firm land as the carriage came to a halt. The polished, wooden door to the plush carriage was gently opened by the coachman, who bowed his head respectfully as Charn stepped out and onto the gravel path.

He was immediately awestruck by the magnificence of the governor's mansion – a truly vast construct of smooth, white stone whose lines roughly followed that of a four tower castle, but with all the harshness of a defensive building replaced with the elegance and refinement associated with his office. Clinically cut, rectangular hedgerows ran along the front of the mansion, each sparkling in the night air with delicate candles fitted on small plates to the top of the hedges. The sound of music drifted through the grand, double doors of the house as two coaches pulled away from the entrance, their horses' hooves crunching on the gravel as another coach arrived.

"I'd forgotten how grand this place is," Marcellus Dio commented as he stepped down behind Charn, pulling his hat on and clasping his sword to his waist. "I don't think I've been here in a couple of years."

"I remember playing in these gardens as a child," Alain Stryfus said, the last passenger to alight from the carriage. "My father was stationed on Keretia briefly in a diplomatic role. There's some fantastic fountains around the back."

The three naval captains, resplendent in their dress uniforms of dark blue and white, walked up the smooth, white steps to the grand entrance of the mansion. It had come as something of a pleasant surprise to find a letter from the admiral awaiting each of them upon coming alongside in the harbor that afternoon, inviting them to the governor's Thatraskos mansion. It was not a grand or formal affair – merely one of the governor's periodic displays of good will to influential individuals on the island of Keretia – but a very welcome invitation nonetheless. His more extravagant affairs were held at his main home on the island's capital of Koronai, nearly twenty leagues to the southwest.

The captains were met by two servants; young men in grand jackets of gold-trimmed orange that rivaled the richness of the captain's own uniform coats. Charn handed over his hat to one of the servants and took the small glass of sienna-colored liquid that was offered in

110

its place. He led the way into the mansion, his polished boots echoing across the cream, marble floor as he walked into the cavernous main hall.

A magnificent hanging chandelier of crystal illuminated the huge hallway, the natural light of the moon denied by thick curtains of red velvet that hung from the long windows. The hall was decorated with statues of both human and elven origin, with impressive family portraits in thick, brass frames hanging from the smooth walls. The trio of captains were ushered through a door and into the mansion's ballroom, where a quartet of musicians plucked away melodically on their strings by the entrance.

Light marble floors and white walls, with one wall being made up entirely of mirrors to add to the open, airy feel, again characterized the ballroom itself. The opposite wall had a long table laid against it, generously filled with exotic fruits, platters of cheeses, and a selection of spirits and fine wines. The gathering itself was fairly intimate, no more than thirty guests, the low buzz of conversation rising above the gentle music from the musicians seated by the entrance.

Charn scanned his eyes quickly across the assembled guests. He vaguely recognized a handful and was properly acquainted with even less. Most were state officials of high standing, interspersed with a smattering of notable locals, either important men and women in business and commerce or landed nobility. He quickly glanced across the assembled men and women to see if any wore the vestments or symbols of magic users, just in case the opportunity to charm an aeromancer into joining his crew might present itself. Charn recognized the governor himself, Lord Gectus Ecclio, locked in an animated conversation with Admiral Sir Jerris Pattia in the near corner of the room. The admiral looked up as the trio of captains entered the ballroom and beckoned them over.

Muttering under his breath, Charn forced a half-smile and navigated his way carefully past a pair of elven diplomats conversing with an uncomfortable looking dwarf emissary.

"Here we go," Marcellus said quietly, "let's see how the admiral wants to dress up this one."

"Good evening, my lord," Charn bowed his head respectfully as the governor turned to face him. "Good evening, Admiral, sir."

"Captain Ferrus, is it?" the governor smiled. "The admiral was just telling me all about your latest endeavor."

The governor himself was a tall man in his fifties, with a flamboyant wig of gray curls extending down past his shoulders. He wore a tunic of light blue trimmed in white which, while intricate and exquisite, seemed almost subtle and pedestrian when compared to the attire of some of the room's occupants.

"That is good to hear, my lord," Charn said. "May I present Captain Marcellus Dio of the *Veneration*, and Captain Alain Stryfus of the *Vigil*."

The appropriate exchanges of formalities were briefly conducted before the governor returned to their initial conversation.

"I hear you came alongside only this afternoon, gentlemen?"

"That is correct, my lord," Charn replied, "we have been out for five days, hunting for ships from a small fleet of orc pirates that have taken their operations to this area."

"So I hear, so I hear," the governor continued to smile, although the subtlest tone of irritation crept into his words, "but you did not find anything on this latest patrol?"

"Sadly not, my lord," Marcellus chimed in, rescuing Charn from bearing the brunt of the polite inquisition alone, "but this was merely a quick run to show force in the local area and brush the cobwebs off our crews a little. As frigate men, we are used to working alone, so it was well worth getting out for a few days to practice working together as a squadron before we properly take the battle to these orcs."

"A show of force," the admiral nodded, "good, good. The very fact that three frigates are out there, showing any and all that these sea lanes are guarded by the Hegemon's finest, that'll keep any orc from daring to stray too close. If we can't find them just yet, we can scare them away, at least."

Lord Gectus winced a little at the words, opening his mouth to speak, deciding against it, and then reversing that decision to fire a query across to the naval officers.

"Can a frigate stay at sea for longer than five days?"

"Absolutely, my lord," Admiral Jerris said, "significantly longer than that."

"Then why did you come back here if the orcs are still out there?"

Charn exchanged an uncomfortable look with Marcellus. Alain stared over the two older captains at the far corner of the room, clearly uninterested in the entire conversation.

"Supplies, my lord," Charn explained to the governor. "While our ships can hold supplies for significantly longer than five days, not everything we needed was ready for us. We made the decision to get out there and commence the hunt immediately, even if only for a few days, rather than waste time alongside in port."

"Fantastic!" the governor smiled genuinely. "I'm very glad to hear that such fighting spirit is alive and well in the Hegemon's navy! Besides, you couldn't have stayed out for any longer, or you would have missed my party this evening!"

Charn and Marcellus joined the admiral in a brief, polite laugh. Alain, his attention drawn back to his immediate surroundings, barked out a much louder laugh in what Charn believed to be an over-zealous, ambitious support of the governor's sense of humor. A 'career laugh' that Charn had seen exhibited by many a driven, striving officer. The governor smiled politely at the young captain.

"Captain Stryfus. I know your uncle very well. How is he?"

"Bearing up well in his retirement, my lord," Alain beamed. "I think his most troubling challenge is working out what vintage to crack open with each evening meal."

The governor gave a short laugh, but again Charn saw Alain's concentration drift over to the far side of the room.

"You seem rather distracted this evening, Captain," the governor remarked.

Charn looked over his shoulder to see what the fuss was about. In the far corner of the ballroom, a small semi-circle of dignitaries had gathered around two women. The first, Charn recognized from previous dealings: Kassia Rhil, the harbormaster of Thatraskos' northern port; a competent and well-respected woman whose husband was known for his myriad of business dealings. The individual with her, Charn did not recognize. A woman in her mid-twenties, of jaw-dropping beauty, standing a little above average height with sandy, blonde hair pulled back in a ponytail. She wore a long gown of vivid yellow that left her tanned armed and shoulders exposed, the gathering of material at the waist showing that the ill-fitting dress was borrowed from a slightly larger woman.

"Ah, what a coincidence," the governor smiled. "Your eye appears to have fallen on one of my guests. Would you like me to ask her to join us?"

"Quite alright, my lord," Alain grinned. "Where I'm from, any man worth his salt can talk to a beautiful woman himself, without the need for an introduction."

"And what, precisely, marks you above the rest of us as the ideal candidate for bringing her over here?" Charn heard himself blurt out.

"Well, that's simple enough," Alain scoffed, "I'm the only one here who isn't married and who isn't old enough to be her father. Excuse me for a moment."

Charn watched in annoyance as Alain glided confidently across the marble floor to effortlessly interpose himself into the conversation next to the beautiful woman. Judging by his facial expression, the governor shared Charn's distaste. Admiral Jerris burst out laughing.

"That, gentlemen, is a frigate captain if ever I saw one! Keel bursting open with confidence, charisma, swagger… that is precisely the kind of young man who should be driving the Hegemon's frigates! Good, good!"

Charn felt decidedly unwell after absorbing the words. He remembered a time when he was reliably informed by others that he was attractive to ladies, able to strut across ballrooms and turn heads in his wake. A decade flew by so quickly and could make such a difference. Now, approaching forty, he felt past his prime and as wrinkled as a prune, accompanied only in life by old injuries that hurt more now than they did when he first suffered them, and a failing marriage to a wife who made little secret about looking elsewhere for companionship whenever he went to sea.

Alain soon returned with the two women by his side. He cast a dashing smile as he stood back to allow them both to join the governor and the naval officers.

"My lord, Admiral sir, gentlemen," Alain said, "may I present Missus Kassia Rhil and Caithlin Viconti."

Charn stepped forward to carefully take Caithlin's fingers, bowing to kiss her hand.

"Missus Viconti, or miss?" he asked.

The young woman took his hand and shook it firmly to deny him the kiss, pressing a hardened, scratched palm against his own that felt more like a sailor's hand than a lady's, calloused by long years of working with ropes and sails.

"Captain," Caithlin corrected without humor.

"Captain Viconti is a recent acquaintance of mine, via Missus Rhil," the governor nodded at the harbormaster. "She is captain of the *Martolian Queen*, the Genezan merchant ship that rather skillfully made a narrow escape a week ago from those orc pirates you are hunting. Perhaps the three of you could explain to her the successes you were just telling me of with your… what was it… show of force? I am not a military man, so my opinion carries only limited validity, but I still remain confused as to how spending five days at sea without firing a single shot can be seen as a success."

Charn felt his heart skip a beat. He remembered seeing the *Martolian Queen* at in the bay, battered and bruised, when he had slipped out of port a few days before to trial his new mast. He looked across desperately at the admiral for help. The admiral's stern, wide-eyed stare made it clear that the onus was completely on Charn to dig himself out of this embarrassing mess he had suddenly found himself in before the governor.

"We... we have a comprehensive plan to scour the area until we find him, my lord," Charn explained, "but for now, every day we are at sea without occurrence is a day that our very presence has scared the threat away."

"I'd argue that every day you spend at sea without occurrence is a day that you've been looking in the wrong place, Captain," Caithlin countered coolly, her sing-song accent revealing her to be of Genezan upbringing. "And what is the crew of a frigate? Two hundred men?"

"Closer to three hundred on an Elohi-class!" Alain nodded enthusiastically. "What, now we've got these new marines onboard!"

"Three hundred," Caithlin winced, "so between the three of you, that's nearly a thousand men on three fifth-rate warships that you are using to do nothing more than fly your flag every day. I'm not a military woman, I'm merely a trader; but to an outsider, that sounds cripplingly expensive and rather like a waste of resources."

"Well, I..."

Charn's response was cut off when Jerris took him by one arm.

"Would you excuse us for a moment, please?" he asked gently. "My lord, ladies."

The admiral practically dragged Charn off to one side, out of earshot and away from the incessant droning of the quartet of musicians.

"What the hell was that?" Jerris demanded.

"What, sir?"

"You're making us look like jesters in front of the governor! You're a frigate captain, man, I don't expect some simple merchant captain to defeat you in a war of words just because she's batted her eyelids at you!"

"She's got a point, Admiral."

"I know that! I know! Look, the dwarfs are playing up to the east, and we've sent most of our frigates that way to show them that we mean business! I've got third-raters – *third-raters!* – on patrol way south because the Ophidians aren't keeping these ghost fleets in check in their own back yard! I've promised more ships to the Duma to act as escorts for troop ships heading west! Three frigates is a significant commitment in this day and age, Charn! We are stretched thin! Now get back over there and get that point across! Stop making me look like a damn idiot in front of the governor! Go on, go!"

***

Caithlin turned away, feeling color rushing to her cheeks. The stifling climate of Keretia in springtime did little to help her growing feeling of unease. She was not accustomed to mansions, high society, heavy ball gowns, and expensive perfumes. She almost immediately regretted the harsh words she had snapped at the terrified looking Basilean frigate captain, but after another moment's contemplation, she realized that she had merely said what she felt, and that several of her sailors now lay at the bottom of the Infant Sea because the Basilean Navy had not done what it had promised it could and would do: provide security.

She looked over to where the admiral was reprimanding the senior of his three frigate captains – too far away to hear the words, but the body language and facial expressions told her all she needed to know. After another wave of the hand, the other two captains were summoned over, away from the governor.

"Caithlin," Kassia sighed as soon as the four naval officers were out of earshot, "that was perhaps a little unkind. Those men are only trying to do their jobs to the best of their ability."

"Respectfully, I disagree," the governor said as a servant rushed over to replenish his wine glass. "Those men are being paid a generous amount of money to keep the shores and shipping lanes of the Hegemony safe. They are failing to do so. The Duma has not commissioned them and given them each a warship to simply cruise across the Infant Sea and then dash back here in time for parties. No, they must do better. But never mind that now, what about you, young lady? I received Missus Rhil's letter, explaining your situation."

Caithlin looked up at the tall governor. While she had certainly witnessed a small show of temper from him, he had a kindly, avuncular face she found herself trusting.

"My ship is damaged beyond my means to fund repairs," Caithlin explained, her cheeks again burning in shame of asking a stranger for charity. "I owe money to the South Mantica Trading Company."

"Quite a lot of money, I hear," the governor said quietly.

Caithlin briefly toyed with the idea of making a joke to lighten the situation, but the knots in her stomach prevented her from accessing her rarely utilized sense of humor. She managed to muster a slight smile and a shrug. The governor returned the smile and clasped his hands at the small of his back.

"Look, you know as well as I that the only way to fix this problem is to take on a loan to repair your ship, get her working again, and then work to pay off your debts. The loan, I can help you with. But the problem with that is that for you to work off that loan, I am rather limited in the work I can offer. I am an official of the Basilean Duma, I have no viable connections with trade and commerce. If you are happy to accept a loan that ultimately will be paid by the Basilean Duma, you would have to be willing to work your vessel in a rather... new environment."

Caithlin glanced across at Kassia. The older woman, her only true ally so far from home, offered an encouraging smile. Caithlin looked back at the aging governor suspiciously.

"What new environment, my lord?"

"You heard yourself that we have problems with orcs and the like. How would you feel about us both signing a letter of reprisal?"

Caithlin's eyes widened.

"You want me to become a pirate?"

"A privateer."

"Same thing, my lord!" Caithlin exclaimed. "'Privateer' is something of a dirty word among professional, respectable sailors! You're asking me to kill for money!"

"I'm offering you the chance to pay off your debts by converting your merchant brig to a ship of war, take on a temporary acting commission as an officer in the Basilean Naval Auxiliary, and use your skills to help clear these waters of murderous scum so that other crews won't suffer the pain and torment that you and your men were forced to endure."

Caithlin stopped and stared ahead, her eyes focusing on her own reflection in the mirrored panels running along the far wall. The music continued, the conversation and laughter carried on, every other guest at the gathering completely oblivious to the momentous crossroad Caithlin had just reached in her life. The losses she had incurred to save the ship and the lives of everybody onboard had left her with a very real chance of a prison sentence and utter financial ruin for her father. Of course she did not want to become a privateer! But right now, she could not see any other option. She looked back at the governor, whose smile now suddenly appeared wholly more predatory in the wake of his devilish offer to her.

"How would I pay off my debt?" Caithlin folded her arms. "Privateers make money by capturing enemy ships. I have neither the skills nor the ship with which to capture another vessel."

"You would have to discuss the finer particulars of monies with Admiral Pettia," the governor gestured to the admiral, who slowly made his way back across with his trio of chastened frigate captains. "He would be able to give you more details."

Caithlin felt her heart pounding again as she saw the predatory quartet of naval officers drift back across, like sharks moving in to surround a sinking ship.

***

"How much use could you make of a brig, Admiral?" Lord Gectus greeted as the four officers moved back to the conversation.

"In what capacity, my lord?" Jerris asked.

"That's what I'm asking you, Jerris."

"How big a brig are we talking about?" the admiral enquired cautiously.

"Four hundred tons, unladed," Caithlin answered.

By the entrance to the ballroom, the musical quartet finished their seemingly endless song with a flurry, and the gathering paused momentarily for a polite round of applause. Charn returned his gaze to the admiral and the captivating merchant captain, wondering where this would all go as the musicians began again.

"That's a fairly large brig," Jerris said to the young Genezan captain. "Are you thinking of using her to ship supplies here from the capital?"

"No," the governor interjected, "I'm thinking of offering this young lady a letter of reprisal."

"Oh!" Jerris exclaimed after a pause. "Oh. How many guns are you carrying?"

"None," Caithlin replied, "we pushed them overboard to lighten our load to escape the orcs. I did have six."

"Four hundred ton brig," Jerris mused. "What say you, Charn? D'you think we could squeeze more guns on her than six?"

"Triple it, sir," Charn responded without hesitation. "Nine a side, without a problem."

The Genezan woman's face shifted through a range of emotions in the few seconds of awkward silence that followed. Charn saw hope, despair, anger, and finally a resolute determination wash across her lightly freckled features.

"No," she said at last, "thank you, but no. I'm not a fighter. I neither understand warfare, nor do I wish to. My father would not want to see me or his brig put to war. I thank you for your kind offer, but a military life holds no purchase on me. I... I am simply not an aggressive person. I don't want rigid discipline in my life, and I doubt my crew will either. I... excuse me, sirs, please."

Charn watched as the distressed young woman made her way toward the exit, Kassia rushing after her. The governor took the opportunity to conveniently recognize an elven diplomat in the next circle of conversation and drift over to join in with his discourse.

"What do you think?" Jerris asked, turning to address his three captains. "Worth pursuing?"

"Definitely!" Alain declared excitedly. "Did you see the size of her..."

"The brig, Captain," the admiral growled, "I meant the brig. Is it of any use to us?"

"It's just a brig, sir," Marcellus said. "Three frigates are enough for the job in hand, and a single brig won't add much."

"I disagree," Charn said. "I want to keep the frigates together, but having a brig with us – assuming you would be happy to attach the vessel to my squadron, sir – would give me another ship with which to hunt. That widens our net considerably. And, if we do shove eighteen guns in her, she'll be able to go toe-to-toe with a blood runner and possibly even win. That leaves us to concentrate on this smasher that it still at large. I think a brig would be incredibly useful, sir."

"If we needed a brig," Alain chipped in, "why didn't we get one in the first place? The northern harbor is full of them!"

"Because nobody wants to do it!" Charn growled with a conscious effort to keep his voice low. "It's a shit job! Have you never stopped to wonder why every time a merchant vessel comes alongside, there is a queue of skilled sailors waiting for the opportunity to join her crew? And every time a warship comes alongside, we need to station guards to stop the crew deserting, and then we need to send gangs ashore to impress men into our crews against their will! We pay our sailors less for more danger and worse living conditions, man! And here we have a ship and crew who are so desperate, they could be bolstering our force!"

"Alright, enough!" Jerris raised a hand to silence the captains. "I don't need some heart-melting social commentary on the poor conditions my crews are forced to endure, thank you, Captain!"

"Quite, sir," Charn nodded.

He had, of course, meant the statement merely as just that; a statement of fact rather than a criticism or complaint. But it was a fact, and a well-known one at that. Keeping the crew of a warship happy was a nearly impossible job. There was a reason why naval crews had such a notable ratio of unskilled landsmen among them. The skilled men ran at the first chance they had.

"I've made my mind up," Jerris declared. "I want that brig. And I think we can get her. You saw her captain. She was teetering, there, for a moment. She can be convinced."

"Then I'm the man for the job, sir!" Alain volunteered. "You leave that to me! I..."

"Oh, shut up, you tit!" Charn scowled. "Did you hear a single word the poor woman said? She's not aggressive and not of a military mindset! You are the very last man we should be using to try to convince her!"

"Charn's right, Alain," Jerris smiled sympathetically. "You stand down on this one. We need a different approach entirely."

Charn's eyes widened. He took a contemplative step back as the embryo of a cunning plan germinated within his mind.

"What I think we need, sir," he said slowly, "is somebody far less threatening. A bone idle, easy-going, pretty boy pacifist who can charm her into thinking this whole thing is far more romantic and adventurous than it actually is."

"That could work," the admiral shrugged thoughtfully.

"I'll see you at your office first thing in the morning, sir," Charn beamed. "I have just the man for the job."

***

Standing to Charn's right, Jaymes followed suit and slid his heel across to stand to attention before the admiral's desk, his saber tucked in firmly at his hip. The admiral looked up from his desk, blinding rays of morning sun pouring into the office through the open balcony doors.

"Oh, don't bother with that!" Jerris smiled. "Nobody's in trouble! Take a seat, we've got a lot to talk about!"

Reticent to do *anything* in an admiral's office, Jaymes waited until Charn had sat down before he, too, allowed himself the small luxury of lowering himself into a chair. The admiral hurriedly set about emptying a decanter of dark rum into three crystal glasses before passing two over to his visitors. Jaymes glanced across incredulously at his captain; it had only just passed eight bells in the morning. Charn replied with a warning glare and picked up his glass.

"Thank you, sir, most kind. To the Hegemon's health."

Both senior officers drained their glasses in one gulp. Jaymes downed his own rum, pleasantly surprised to find the high quality of the drink made it far more palatable than he was expecting. Jaymes opened his eyes in surprise as the admiral filled all three glasses again. He sat down and leaned back in his grand chair.

"So, Charn, this is the young fellow you were telling me about?"

"Yes, sir," Charn replied. "Lieutenant Ellias, first of the *Pious*."

"You have a first name?" the admiral asked.

"Jaymes, sir."

"And has Captain Ferrus told you why you are here?"

Jaymes glanced across at his formidable captain.

"No… not really, sir. Merely that I had been specially selected for an important assignment."

The admiral exchanged a smirk with Charn and then shot to his feet, pacing around the desk as he addressed Jaymes.

"Jaymes. I need you to take a beautiful woman out to dinner. It needs to be in the single most expensive and extravagant hotel in Thatraskos. And the Admiralty will be paying the bill."

Jaymes turned slowly in his chair to regard the admiral. He looked across at Charn, waiting for a bitter, grim laugh but saw none.

"Sir?" Jaymes stammered.

"The *Martolian Queen*," Jerris continued, "a relatively sizable brig that escaped from the orcs not so long ago. She limped in here and was towed to the northern port a couple of days ago, where she is currently alongside with a shattered steering gear and a leaking hull. I want you to take her captain out to dinner, give her this letter that I have written, and use all of your charm to persuade her that it would be wise for her to accept our kind offer of commissioning her and her vessel as a privateer."

Jaymes somehow found himself even more confused by the situation the more the admiral explained it.

"You want me to persuade a woman to become a pirate, sir?"

"*Privateer*, Lieutenant. There is a substantially significant difference. As long as that courageous and noble privateer is flying Basilean colors, naturally. Otherwise yes, those bastards are all pirates."

Jaymes recalled staring sympathetically down from the quarterdeck of the *Pious* as they sailed out to trial the new mast, looking at the wrecked brig as the crew attempted to maneuver her across to a buoy in the harbor.

"Why me?" he asked quietly.

"She's… something of an opinionated young lady," the admiral continued, "rather set against the idea of embracing the military lifestyle. Your captain here tells me that you're of a similar mindset."

Jaymes slowly placed his glass down on the polished desk in front of him. A fresh, morning breeze swept through the office from the open balcony, and Jaymes heard the familiar clanging of halyards against their flagpoles outside.

"I'm not sure I'm comfortable with this, sir," Jaymes said carefully. "Perhaps it is best if this captain is left to make her own mind up."

"By the Ones, Lieutenant!" Charn snapped. "You're being asked to take a stunning filly out to dinner and have their lordships pay for your privilege! No, not asked, *told!* Your duties as a naval officer don't suddenly cease as soon as you set foot on dry land, man! You've been given an order!"

"Charn," Jerris held a hand up, "please."

The admiral moved back around to the side of Jaymes's chair before squatting down next to him and placing a paternal arm around his shoulders, looking out of the balcony and across the sparkling seas.

"Jaymes, Jaymes. Don't think of this as a task! Think of it as an opportunity! Charn, how many times in your career have you been paid to take a woman out for the evening?"

"None, sir."

"None, sir!" the admiral repeated gleefully. "You see? Fortune is smiling on you, young fellow! How many experienced sea captains do you think I currently have on my list who have requested duties to serve in my fleet as a privateer?"

"None, sir?" Jaymes ventured a guess.

"None, sir!" the admiral beamed, patting him on the shoulder. "Because it's a bloody awful job! It's dangerous and unpredictable! Most privateers barely make enough money to exist! So look – you go and take her out. Think of where this could lead! A dashing young fellow such as yourself, a beautiful woman like her… a year from now you could be famous as a heroic frigate captain, romantically embroiled with a notorious and beautiful pirate captain!"

Jaymes turned his head slowly to stare in bewilderment at the delusional admiral.

"In a year, sir, my intention is to be outside the navy. I hope to leave imminently, sir."

The admiral stood up again and let out a long, good-hearted but deeply patronizing laugh. He clapped a hand on Jaymes's shoulder again.

"We've all been through that!" he grinned. "We all get disheartened at some point – normally as a senior lieutenant – but you won't leave! You'll still be here in a year, I promise you! Anyhow, here's the letter, and my flag lieutenant has a bag of coins for you for this evening. Bring back what you don't spend. Any questions?"

Jaymes looked up helplessly at the admiral, but no words sprang to mind.

"Good!" Jerris smiled. "Now, Charn, you said you had another matter to discuss?"

"Yes, sir," Charn said. "There's still the matter of the lieutenant you promised me. I'm relying on midshipmen on the quarterdeck more than I am comfortable with."

The admiral drained his second glass, glanced across at the decanter, clearly thought better of it, and left the glass empty before casting a toothy grin at Charn.

"Already done, old boy. Lieutenant Innes. He'll be across with you by midday."

Jaymes saw the rare delight of a genuine smile emerge across his captain's craggy face.

"Fantastic, sir!" Charn said enthusiastically. "How long in is he? I need good officers with a good grasp of their business."

"He passed his lieutenancy board yesterday," Jerris nodded, "very promising young man! I sat on the board myself! Only eighteen, but I see a great career ahead of him!"

Charn was still swearing long after they had left the admiral's office, recovered the money from the flag-lieutenant, retrieved their hats, and were striding back to the *Pious*.

"Eighteen!" he exclaimed again after a string of profanities, ignoring the salutes from the marines at the entrance of the administration building. "What in blazes do I want some eighteen-year-old lieutenant who has barely seen half a dog watch? Well, Mister Ellias, this is clearly your lucky day. The admiral is paying for your dinner, and now it would appear that your promotion to first lieutenant of a frigate is permanent. Congratulations."

"Thank you, sir," Jaymes mumbled, his gratitude to his captain as equally insincere as the felicitations he had just received.

Chapter Ten

A few conversations stopped and most heads turned to look over the two orcs as they walked into the Final Grapeshot tavern, but the music and general activity carried on regardless. Ghurak walked into the dingy tavern, the top of his black hat all but scrapping against the low ceiling as he did. Twenty or so pirates and their ever-present women were packed into the room, some singing and drinking, others playing cards in the darker corners around tables piled with coins. Ghurak walked over to the bar and stopped to grimace down at a pair of human pirates, who silently moved aside to let him through.

"Any point getting a drink?" Kroock grunted from his side.

"Don't bother," Ghurak growled, "their stuff all tastes like piss water to the likes of us. Don't waste your time."

A corpulent, bald human looked up from behind the bar, trying for a moment to meet Ghurak's stony stare and failing almost instantly.

"You after Cerri?" he asked.

"Yes," Ghurak glowered, "go and tell him that Admrul Ghurak is here."

"It's alright, Dernt," a familiar voice spoke up from behind the orcs. "I know they're here. Pretty hard to miss, really."

The orc pirate turned and looked down to see Cerri, the human sailor, holding onto a foaming tankard of some alcoholic drink that was so tame, Ghurak could not even smell it. Cerri looked up. He did manage to meet Ghurak's stare.

"Word travels fast, Admiral," he raised his brow. "You and your boys have been busy. We'd better go have another talk."

Ghurak looked across at Kroock.

"Wait here," he ordered, "and if any of these maggots try their hand... well, just don't kill them."

"Aye, Admrul," Kroock hissed, folding his enormous arms across his barrel chest and staring around at the pathetic cast of wiry human sailors.

Ghurak followed Cerri past a pair of the hushed, improvised gambling tables and took a seat in the furthest corner of the tavern, in an isolated booth that the orc barely managed to squeeze himself into.

"So," Cerri said, leaning forward over the battered table, "what have you got for me?"

Ghurak paused for a moment. In as much as it was possible for an orc to calm and center himself, he managed. Talking across a table to some skinny, wiry, cocksure human ran against everything that defined him, everything that made him an orc. Orcs killed humans; that was the natural order. But this orc needed this human's help. For now. And so it fell onto him to walk and talk like a human, or at least close enough, and deal in goods and money rather than deeds and blood.

"Slaves," Ghurak replied, "I've got a hundred slaves."

"You went out to capture a ship."

"I know what I went out for!" Ghurak growled, leaning over the table, "but I have returned with slaves. And you will exchange them for guns."

"You took slaves from the colonies? From the Eleccian Isles, I take it? You know there is a Basilean gold mine tucked right in on those islands you've just sailed through?"

Ghurak's eyes widened at the thought. A gold mine. He had just proven beyond doubt that his warriors were well capable of fighting and winning on land, and a gold mine would be a profitable target. But his own goal was to master the sea, and that goal did not appear to be drawing any closer.

"A gold mine," Ghurak mused. "I thought you made it clear that you were upset about me killing Basileans?"

"Doesn't look like I can stop you," Cerri shrugged, leaning back in his chair, "so I might as well be neighborly and help guide you in the right direction."

"The gold mine can wait," Ghurak waved a hand irritably to one side. "I've brought back slaves. And you are going to take them and give me guns for my second blood runner, just as we said."

"I might," Cerri met his glare without flinching, "but you never told me you were bringing slaves. That's more difficult for me to shift."

Ghurak slammed a fist into the table, hard enough for the impact to finally elicit a fearful reaction from Cerri.

"Don't bullshit me, Cerri! Don't you dare bullshit me! I never told you what I would bring back! You never told me what you wanted for those guns, only that you had them and you were willing to give them to me! You say there is honor among pirates, so you prove it! You start twisting your words now like some sort of weasely elf, and we have a problem!"

"Alright, alright!" Cerri held his hands up. "Just... what slaves have you brought back?"

"About half the colony," Ghurak replied. "It was all we could fit in the ship. I took all the men and there was a bit more room, so we packed in some of the women and children as well."

Cerri's eyes narrowed and his lips twisted into a vicious sneer.

"No. No! Absolutely not! I'm not selling women and children into slavery!"

Ghurak smiled slowly. His grin grew into a low laugh. The human instinct toward feeling protective of their weak was truly pathetic. He had somehow expected better from a pirate, even a human one.

"So we agree you'll sell the men." Ghurak nodded. "That's good! You can leave the women and children with me and my boys, if you like. That's fine by me."

The human pirate looked away for a moment. Laughter from one of the tables briefly drowned out the music provided by an old sailor with some sort of squeezebox. Cerri looked back.

"I'll take them. I'll take them all."

"Good," Ghurak grunted, "wise choice, Cerri. It keeps me happy and is probably better for those children. Better a slave then a meal. Where are you taking them?"

"Ophidia," Cerri answered quietly, "I'll send them across with my next shipment in a few days. I'll take them off you tomorrow morning."

"Again, wise," Ghurak smiled maliciously. "The boys might get hungry soon. And as for my guns, you bring them across and put them on my second blood runner. Tomorrow."

The sound of glass smashing snatched Ghurak's attention away from the conversation. He looked back to the bar and saw Kroock slowly turning in place to face three human pirates, one of them holding the remains of a broken bottle. Kroock shook his shoulders, and shards of broken glass fell to the floor. With a great roar, he clenched a huge fist and brought it smashing up into the closest pirate's face, snapping his head back and sending him staggering over to collapse into a table behind him. The other two pirates darted forward to smash their fists into Kroock's face.

Ghurak grinned.

"No!" Cerri snapped as Ghurak leapt to his feet. "Don't you…"

Ghurak stomped over to the fight as a tall, bald-headed pirate smashed a wooden chair over Kroock's back. Kroock had a younger pirate held firm in a headlock, while he pounded the man's face repetitively with his free hand. He certainly seemed to notice the chair smash against him but did not react. Then, an enormous human pirate with a graying beard and scars on his face that any orc would envy charged over and slammed a fist into Kroock's snout, knocking him to the floor.

"Get up and fight, you scurvy dog!" the human growled hoarsely.

The tavern erupted into anarchy; half of the assembled pirates leapt to the aid of their human brethren while the remaining corsairs – including all of the non-humans, Ghurak noticed with interest – quickly darted for the doors and out into the night. A lithe-looking pirate with a blue bandanna and a short beard made the unwise decision to attempt to bar Ghurak from joining the fight. Ghurak smashed a fist into the side of the man's head to knock him half senseless and then picked him up before throwing him at the wall by the main doors. He let out a grunt of satisfaction as the pirate plunged straight through the wooden walls with a crash of splintered boards, but he also noticed with some grudging respect that the man was straight back up to his feet and rushing to join the fight again.

Another two unkempt pirates flung themselves into an attack against Ghurak. The first sailor - a tall, broad-shouldered man - punched him in the face while the second, shorter man grabbed a metal tankard in each hand and aimed a flurry of blows at the orc, using the tankards as impromptu knuckle dusters. Grinning broadly, Ghurak soaked up a few of the blows before lashing out with a fist at the taller pirate. The buccaneer ducked beneath Ghurak's attack and slammed a fist into the orc's belly, just as his accomplice smashed one of the tankards across Ghurak's face.

Ghurak's head jolted back and he felt a hot flare across his snout as blood was drawn. Grunting a series of expletives, he brought the heel of a clenched fist smashing down on top of the shorter pirate's head, connecting with a crunch and knocking the man out cold. His second and third punches were again ducked and dodged by the tall pirate, but the fourth struck with a straight fist to the center of the face. Letting out a cry of pain as his nose was broken, the man staggered back with his arms flailing out to each side. Ghurak let out a battle cry and flung himself forward, planting his shoulder into the man and charging.

The pair crashed through the bar, smashing the wood into splinters as they tumbled to the dirty floor in an ungainly heap. Barking out a short laugh, Ghurak staggered back to his feet and turned to assess the fight. Kroock was locked in a fairly even fistfight with the enormous human, while around them were perhaps seven or eight men who had remained for the brawl in the trashed tavern. Leaning across to swing a heavy punch into the closest pirate, Ghurak send him flying out of his way before he then swung his left arm in to plant a fist into the head of the blue-bandanned pirate who had just rejoined the fight, propelling him across the room to smash into one of the tables.

Pious

Exploiting his opening, Ghurak leapt at the huge human who faced Kroock, grabbing him by the collars of his jacket and swinging a hefty headbutt into the man's forehead. The human's head snapped back, his forehead split open by the blow, but Ghurak was surprised when the man retaliated in turn with a headbutt of his own, knocking off Ghurak's hat and wig. Ghurak brought up a knee into the huge man's groin and was rewarded with a high-pitched shriek of pain as the lumbering pirate doubled over; he followed up with an elbow to the side of the man's head to knock him sprawling to the floor.

"I haven't killed any of them," Kroock grinned across to Ghurak, "just like you said!"

Ghurak's response was cut off as the pirate with the blue bandanna appeared yet again, slamming a fist into Kroock's belly and then swinging an uppercut into the orc's chin to knock him back. Ghurak moved over to fight side-by-side with his brother orc, but his way was barred as the massive pirate he had just felled dragged himself back up to his feet, blood dripping down his face from the wound across his forehead. The huge human and colossal orc faced each other for a moment as the tavern fight raged on around them. Ghurak laughed. His evening was just getting started.

***

Feeling decidedly underdressed in his simple trousers and white shirt, Jaymes walked into the foyer of the Dominion Yacht Club. The entrance to the grand building was brightly lit, with a thick carpet of purple running along the center of the pale tiled floor. An almost perfect looking concierge of a similar age to Jaymes glanced across at him with barely hidden distaste. The club itself was a very new development, following on from the recent trend for extravagantly wealthy men and women to invest in small vessels that existed almost solely for pleasure sailing and as a status symbol – yachts. Feeling that perhaps it would have been better to attend the meeting in uniform, Jaymes approached the concierge.

"Can I help you, sir?" the slim man issued a thin smile, displaying his perfect teeth.

Jaymes doubted that the man wanted to help him in any way at all.

"I have a table booked for eight bells," Jaymes replied.

The concierge maintained his smile, but the moment's hesitation betrayed his doubt over Jaymes's honesty.

"Your name, sir?"

128

"It was booked by the flag-lieutenant of Admiral Sir Jerris Pattia."

There was a pause.

"This way, please," the concierge winced.

Jaymes was ushered into the club's dining area. Everything about the club house screamed ostentatiousness; the single room was tall enough to house two large floors, yet consisted of only one, while each of the dozen seating areas had enough space around them to easily accommodate an entire party. Two walls of the building were made around long windows, looking out over the tranquil waters of the bay and the gently drooping leaves of the lines of palm trees.

Taking a seat at his reserved table by one of these windows, Jaymes took a moment to stare out across the bay. At the far side of the harbor he saw *Pious* alongside the Admiralty jetty, next to the *Vigil* and the *Veneration*. The ships to the north were mainly cargo vessels, interspersed with the occasional small passenger ship that would make the journey between Keretia and the mainland. The sun was still a good hour off setting, but the evening sky was beginning to darken, casting long shadows from the tall sails of the ships in the bay as the waters were momentarily disturbed by a trio of small dolphins jumping a few feet into the air.

Sighing as he contemplated buying a ludicrously expensive drink from the pocketful of heavy, gold coins he had been issued for the evening, Jaymes watched the playful dolphins wistfully. He could never afford to frequent a club such as this. The feeling did not leave him counting his lucky stars at the evening's opportunity, so much as leaving him feeling like an imposter, that every pair of eyes in the room was judging him by his simple clothes and assessing him as unworthy to share that room with them. He looked across at some of the other tables and saw titled lords and ladies, wealthy elven dignitaries, all the sorts of people that were well above his path in life. The sooner he could resign his commission, leave the navy, and go home to join his friends in their new business endeavor, the better.

The concierge appeared back by his side and cleared his throat.

"Sir? Your guest has arrived."

Jaymes looked up. He had heard enough about Captain Caithlin Viconti's appearance but still found himself staring at a vision that he somehow had not expected. Standing a little over average height in a dress of turquoise that matched the waters of the bay and emphasized her femininity, she looked down at him coolly from her dark, enchanting eyes. Her sandy hair was held back in a bow tied in a sailor's knot, a few loose locks of hair framing her perfect face.

"Captain Viconti?" Jaymes shot to his feet, moving around the table to offer a chair to her.

The concierge was quicker, pulling a chair out from the table with a dramatic flourish to allow the woman to sit down, while simultaneously leaving Jaymes looking awkward and useless by her side. He moved back around to sit opposite her.

"Good evening, Captain," he risked a slight smile, "my name is Jaymes Ellias. I was sent here to host you for the evening. May I offer you a drink? A glass of wine, perhaps?"

"I don't drink alcohol, Mister Ellias," the captain said sternly, her thick accent betraying her Genezan origins. "I shall take a water. You may drink as much wine as you wish."

Jaymes looked up at the concierge and smiled awkwardly.

"A pitcher of water, with two glasses, please."

He looked back at Caithlin and found her staring at him impassively, as if assessing him in the same way that he had only moments before imagined the other patrons were doing. He realized that he had rather expected to find a broken woman; battered and bruised after a narrow escape from pirates to now find herself destitute and facing a prison cell. Instead, he found an unerringly confident ship captain who emanated the same poise and gravitas as that idiot Alain Stryfus from the *Vigil*.

"The weather is holding out," Jaymes said. "I haven't spent a great deal of time in this area in spring, but this is..."

"I'm not here to discuss the weather with you," Caithlin interrupted, placing the tips of her fingers against each other as she leaned forward over the table. "I am here to discuss whether it is worth my while to accept payment from your Admiralty to convert my vessel into a ship of war."

"Yes," Jaymes said quietly, producing the admiral's letter from his pocket and passing it over, "of course."

Caithlin took the letter but kept her eyes focused on his.

"Have you read this letter?" she demanded.

"I was ordered to," Jaymes replied.

"So you are here to negotiate the terms?"

"No, ma'am," Jaymes said, "I am here to clarify the terms. I do not have the authority to negotiate any changes."

"Why not? What are you, exactly? An Admiralty administrator?"

"No, ma'am. I'm a lieutenant from one of our frigates."

"Then why have they sent you?" Caithlin frowned. "As you say, you have no authority to negotiate. I must confess to being rather offended if your admiral believes me to be so shallow as to sign across my ship and crew purely because he sent across his most handsome officer to smile at me over a glass of wine at sunset. I'm afraid I'm made of rather sterner stuff than that."

"I... well..." Jaymes stammered in confusion.

He was rescued as one of the club's staff brought over their pitcher of water and poured out two glasses before leaving the two sailors alone again by the spectacular view over the bay. Only then did Caithlin look down at the letter. Jaymes stared out over the bay again, scanning the waters for the dolphins he had seen before as he awaited a comment from the merchant captain.

"Ten years," Caithlin finally said.

"Sorry, ma'am?"

"Ten years," she repeated, "if one works through the numbers on this letter, it equates to ten years service as a privateer in the Basilean Navy before the debt is paid off. A decade. Mostly because of the preposterous level of interest. That is not acceptable. Not for what I am offering."

Jaymes paused. Was she bluffing? Surely she knew that all she was offering was a damaged brig with no guns and a minimal crew? Yes, a brig was a fine vessel in the right hands and offered a splendid compromise between speed and agility, and the capacity for cargo or a decent broadside, but she was acting as if she had brought a first-rate battleship to the negotiating table. Then again, given how long it took to build any warship, let alone crew her and find a competent captain, the instant addition of an armed brig to the fleet at Keretia was a significant event. If indeed it did happen.

"Ten years would be worst case, ma'am," Jaymes explained carefully. "If you accept a temporary commission as an acting captain in the Basilean Naval Auxiliary, your terms as a privateer would allow you to attack any enemy of the Hegemony. That extends not only to any state we are at war with but also covers pirates. So, you would be rewarded for removing any threat from Basilean waters and would also have the prize money from any vessel you capture, minus the one-tenth share owed to the Admiralty as stipulated in the terms of your commission."

"So," Caithlin exhaled, "my ten years is reduced significantly based upon how aggressive my actions are, and how successful I am in taking other people's ships."

"Yes, ma'am. Otherwise you are paid a salary based upon your patrolling of Basilean sea lanes and providing a part of our standing security fleet actions. Which does not pay nearly as well as prize money, just the same as it does for fully commissioned warships of the Basilean Navy. And that would take roughly ten years to pay off the combined debt of your repair fees, outfitting fees, eighteen cannons, and the Admiralty paying off your entire debt to the South Mantica Trading Company for your lost cargo and a two-fifths share in your vessel. And... the interest."

For a moment, just a brief moment, Jaymes saw the façade break. The young woman's stern exterior gave way to the quickest flash of utter despair and loneliness. Jaymes felt his heart grow heavier in sympathy for her predicament as he remembered gazing down from the quarterdeck of the *Pious* as they sailed past Caithlin's battered brig.

"And you think these terms are favorable?" Caithlin demanded.

"Are you asking me personally or professionally, ma'am?" Jaymes asked.

"Both."

"Well, my duty to the Admiralty dictates that I emphasize to you that these terms are more than reasonable, that the interest on your losses has not been capitalized by their lordships, and that ten years service as a privateer is significantly more favorable than even half that amount of time in a prison cell. Professionally speaking. However, I've always prided myself on being a good man first - an honest man - and a naval officer second. Those two don't always go hand in hand. So, as an honest man, speaking personally, no. I wouldn't accept this offer. No."

Jaymes saw another flash of emotion in the brig captain, a hint of surprise and genuine interest in his words.

"You would not accept this offer?" she asked.

"No!" Jaymes said honestly. "Privateer work is dangerous! If you sign for that commission, there is a very real chance that you will be killed! No amount of money is worth that! I'm certainly not advocating a term in prison, but money isn't worth any of this! Just sell the ship. Sell the ship to the company to pay off your debts and go home. Go home healthy and alive, and start again. If you're asking me for my opinion, that's what I would do. I'm looking to leave this all behind as soon as I can, and when I go home, I'll only just have enough money to buy into a company with some old friends to start again myself. If I were you, I would sell the ship."

"I can't do that, Jaymes," Caithlin said, her voice suddenly completely different, as if confiding in a friend. "It's my father's ship. I can't let him down. If I sell that ship, it will sink his entire company. I can't do that to my father."

"If your father is anything like mine, then I would bet it is what he would want," Jaymes risked. "Certainly, my father is a rather distant sort at the best of times, but he has always been there for me, and he would lose it all if it meant keeping me and my sister safe. Any parent worth their salt would do that for their children. I certainly don't mean to intrude in your affairs, and I truly hope I am not coming across as rude or prying, but you have asked for my opinion and I give it to you honestly and impartially. Sell the ship and go home to your family."

The two fell silent as they looked at each other across the table. The scent of something exotic and delicious wafted over from the far side of the room as platters of food were brought out to another party of wealthy yacht owners. Jaymes watched with growing sympathy as seemingly a thousand thoughts raced across the mind of the young woman sat before him. Then, slowly, her very human vulnerability re-hardened and molded back into her original cold, distant form.

"What is this outfitting charge that is mentioned in the letter?" she asked coolly.

Jaymes glanced out of the window for a brief moment. She had made her mind up. He had not arrived at the yacht club with any ulterior motive, but following his heart in the last few moments, he had found that he suddenly wanted to help guide her toward the right decision, and he had seemingly failed.

"Outfitting refers to both your vessel, and to you personally," he explained. "Your brig will need work to ensure she can be fitted with eighteen guns. There will also be conversions required to accommodate the increased size of crew. The repairs also involve a more modern, lighter steerage gear. For you personally, while you will not hold the rank and privileges of a commissioned captain in the Bailsean Navy, you will hold acting captain's rank in a temporary capacity and so would be expected to dress accordingly. Blue jacket with gold lace, black hat, officer's sword, and the likes."

"Increased crew," Caithlin mused, "it says here that you would expect my brig to be crewed by… approximately one hundred and twenty sailors. I currently have thirty-five sailors listed on my books. Explain that one to me."

"Well," Jaymes began, "the admiral has negotiated the loan of fifteen sailors from each of the three frigates in Captain Ferrus's squadron. That gives you another forty-five sailors to bring your crew to eighty, on the proviso that you sail alongside Captain Ferrus and follow his orders while attached to the squadron. One hundred and twenty is more an ideal rather than a requirement, and your outfitting stipend also covers the hiring of additional crewmembers."

"As long as I follow his orders?" Caithlin queried. "Do I even have a choice?"

"Yes, ma'am," Jaymes nodded. "As a privateer captain, your ship is very much yours to do with as you please. While you are not entitled to the privileges of Basilean naval rank, you are also not constrained by our rules and regulations, only the maritime law of sailing under a generic Basilean flag. You are not required to obey the orders of a Basilean naval captain. Unless you accept the loan of those forty-five sailors, of course."

The merchant captain fell silent and stared out the window across the bay. At the far side of the room, one of the club's waiting staff opened the grand, veranda doors to allow in a cool evening breeze. With it came the sounds of the bay as sunset approached; the gentle lapping of the waves on the sandy beach below the doors, and the soothing rattling of the nocturnal insects hidden away in the palm trees and colorful tropical flowers that surrounded them.

Jaymes realized that the silence descending between him and Caithlin had now gone on for quite some time, yet she seemed content to be lost in thought, certainly more comfortable in the silence than he was. He glanced across at her momentarily, her expression confirming that she was indeed working through several things in her troubled mind.

"Are you sure that I can't buy you something to drink, ma'am?" Jaymes offered. "I've been sent across with a good deal of money, and it would be a shame to hand it all back over. I suppose there is at least a very positive message in there somewhere; if they have given me this purse full of money, clearly they are taking you very seriously and have a good deal of respect for your skills and experience."

The blonde woman shifted her cool gaze from the bay back across to him. She regarded him in silence for a few moments, her stony stare still lacking any hint of warmth or emotion.

"Why do you keep calling me 'ma'am'?" she finally asked. "You have already explained that even if I accept this offer, I am not truly a part of the Basilean Navy, and therefore not entitled to the privilege of being addressed as your senior."

"I know," Jaymes shrugged, "but that's purely a personal thing again. You command your own ship, and that's something I've never managed to do, and I doubt I ever will. Showing you the respect that you are due as a ship's captain, irrespective of the role of the ship, is the very least I can do."

"Why would you never command your own ship?" Caithlin asked, her eyes narrowing suspiciously.

Jaymes paused for a moment, unsure how much he thought it was appropriate to divulge to the icy merchant captain.

"As I mentioned, I'm leaving the navy, and soon. This just is not the life for me. When I go home, I don't have any plans on sailing on anything larger than a small skiff. But... that has nothing to do with why we're here."

Caithlin turned to look out pensively across the bay again for another protracted moment of uncomfortable silence. She did not turn to face him when she spoke again.

"I shall deliver my response to the admiral, in writing, first thing in the morning. I have extra terms I wish to be addressed. If they are addressed, I will accept a commission as a privateer."

Jaymes swallowed, somehow disappointed that she had made that decision. But it was not his life to lead and not his mistake to make. He had at least been completely honest with her, and that was the right thing to do.

"Aye, ma'am," he said quietly.

"I think I shall have that expensive drink now, Lieutenant," Caithlin said, still staring off into the distance. "But just the one. I have a feeling that tomorrow will be a long day, and an early night would do me the world of good."

***

Charn placed his pen down on his desk and looked up as the young officer brought his feet together to stand to attention. The low angle of the sun focused its beams directly through the stern windows of the *Pious* and into the young lieutenant's face, making him squint uncomfortably in the orange glow. His discomfort pleased Charn greatly.

"Lieutenant Kaeso Innes, sir," the boy reported, handing across the rolled parchment of his orders for Charn's inspection, "previously of the *Ark Dominion*."

Charn glanced through his new lieutenant's orders without interest, failing to see anything out of the ordinary in the wording of the document. He looked up and cast a critical eye over Kaeso. Thin, of average height, with tousled, dark hair and a pale face periodically punctuated with red pimples.

"So, you're a battleship man?"

"Aye, sir." Kaeso squinted.

"Are you disappointed to be leaving the big ships behind to come to a frigate?" Charn demanded.

"No, sir. Not at all. I requested frigates specifically. It is why I was sent here to sit my lieutenancy exams, sir."

"And why, may I ask?" Charn continued his interrogation.

"With less officers onboard a frigate than a big ship of the line, those fewer officers get real responsibility far quicker. I thought it a better opportunity to prove myself, sir."

Charn leaned back in his chair and smiled grimly. Good. Good lad. He liked that answer very much.

"Then welcome aboard the *Pious*, Mister Innes," Charn said gruffly, taking care not to exhibit any signs of being pleased in his new subordinate. "As of this moment, you are this ship's third lieutenant. You will report to Mister Ellias, who will inform you of your duties in the watch and your division. Now, did the admiral send you onboard with a letter for me? I was rather expecting some correspondence from his lordship."

Kaeso's eyes widened, and he quickly reached one hand around to his pocket, from which he produced a bundle of bound envelopes. He handed them across to Charn, who took his letter opener, a slim, brass blade given to him by his wife on the occasion of his thirtieth birthday, and opened the first letter. Skim reading the few lines instantly soured his mood.

"*...on this morning... commissioned as the Hegemon's Warship* Martolian Queen... *privateer warship attached to the Keretian Fleet... as previously agreed, fifteen sailors from each frigate are to be temporarily detached to her... in addition, at the request of her captain, Lieutenant Jaymes Ellias is also to be loaned from the HW* Pious *to the HW* Martolian Queen...*"

Charn swore under his breath. He distinctly recalled Jaymes returning onboard shortly after sunset the previous evening, as sober as a paladin and not in particularly high spirits, merely two hours after he had stepped ashore to meet with the *Martolian Queen's* captain. What on earth had he said or done in such a short space of time to impress her that much? Charn swore again. Bastard. He folded the letter and turned his attention to the next in the pile. His eyes opened wide. The second letter bore a red Admiralty seal. He looked up at Kaeso.

"Did you see this seal?" he demanded angrily.

"N-no sir, I..."

"An Admiralty seal! These are orders to sail, man!"

Charn quickly tore the letter open and again cast his eyes quickly over the content.

"*...received reports of piratical activity in the vicinity of the Genezan colony of Baudethra... given the nature of this attack, their lordships have significant concern for the security of the mines at Antegia Keys... you are to sail immediately and make haste to Antegia Keys, where you will ensure the defenses of the mines are bolstered by a detachment of marines taken from the ship's companies of Pious, Vigil, and Veneration...*"

Charn shot to his feet.

"If you want an opportunity to prove yourself, Mister Innes, then I suggest that next time you are sent aboard a warship with orders for her to sail immediately on urgent business, you prioritize handing those orders to her bloody captain!"

Leaving the gaping-mouthed officer looking around helplessly, Charn barged his way out of his day cabin and onto the upper deck.

"Bosun," he shouted, "muster all hands-on deck! Prepare to slip and proceed!"

"Aye, sir!"

The captain's orders were translated into a series of shrill whistles and the frigate burst into life as Charn made his way down to the gun deck before proceeding aft to the gunroom. He found practically all of his ship's officers – his lieutenants, marine captain, and warrant officers – all still engaged in polite conversation over a leisurely breakfast. The gunroom fell silent as the captain barged in.

"We've been given orders to sail, immediately!" Charn announced. "Those orcs have raided a Genezan colony in the Eleccian Isles! We've got a gold mine right near there, and we've been given orders to ship our marines across to bolster the defenses! Captain Senne?"

"Sir," Karnon replied stiffly, standing as he did so.

"Do we have all we need onboard to provide support for a land-based defensive position?"

"At a pinch, sir, but as we are right next to the main naval stores, we would be far better placed if we spent an hour getting more supplies onboard."

"You've got half an hour, so make it count," Charn barked.

The marine captain dashed out of the gunroom to see to his orders. Charn turned back to his other officers.

"Mister Ganto, run across to the *Vigil* and the *Veneration* and tell their captains that we are setting sail for the Eleccians, immediately! The rest of you, get up there and make sure this ship is ready in all respects to sail as soon as possible. Not you, Mister Ellias, you stand fast."

Jaymes looked across expectantly at the captain as the other officers rushed to their positions.

"Mister Ellias, I have no idea what you did last night, but it would appear that this morning's commissioning of the *Martolian Queen* as a Basilean privateer is based upon you being loaned across to her. You clearly made an impression."

Jaymes's face was a picture of confusion.

"Aye, sir," he managed.

"So get your kit and sod off! I'm leaving you behind. I'll see you when we return. Don't do anything stupid while I'm gone!"

"Aye, sir. Oh… sir… regarding Mister Ganto running across to the other two ships to inform them of our sailing orders; I believe the *Vigil* is intending to store ship early this afternoon. They might not be ready to set sail with us. With you. Sir."

Charn swore again and looked around for something to kick.

"Right! Right! Get off my ship, Mister Ellias! Go to the *Vigil*, tell their captain to catch us up as soon as he is ready! Oh, and while he is at it, tell him to send his most senior lieutenant across to me so he can replace you while you're off making pirate queens swoon on that damned brig!"

"Aye, sir."

Charn stopped again as another thought entered his mind.

"In addition! Tell him he can also send forty-five sailors to the *Martolian Queen*. If he can't be bothered to store his ship in a timely fashion, he can provide all of the promised sailors to those privateers rather than spreading the burden across those frigates who can be arsed to store their ship in a timely manner!"

Jaymes failed to suppress his malicious grin as he departed to pass Charn's orders on to his old rival. Content that he had a plan beginning to form, Charn rushed back to the quarterdeck to coordinate a timely departure from Thatraskos. The war was coming to the orcs, and they did not even know it.

Chapter Eleven

Karnon glanced over his shoulder and saw the pair of anchored frigates ever so slowly grow smaller as the rowing boat drew closer to the shore. All six of the boats from the two frigates were being used to transport the marines ashore, each boat's sides lined with sailors at the oars while the center housed Karnon's marines and their equipment. Up ahead was the Basilean island of Kios, a relatively small landmass of only perhaps half a dozen leagues across, mainly consisting of jungle. But as the boats were rowed steadily into the bay, Karnon could see evidence of a settlement amid the trees, complete with two tall pump houses.

From nowhere, an unwelcome and unwanted thought about his wife, Sabine, forced itself to the fore of Karnon's mind. Just before sailing from Thatraskos, he had received a letter from her. Their engagement had been short, but he had known her long enough to read between the lines of her writing and appreciate that her brave words hid real pain. It was what had concerned him for some time now. Marrying a soldier was marrying into a very unique lifestyle and one that a spouse could never truly appreciate and fully understand until that soldier went away on duty. Days would be long and lonely, nights even longer. Help with even the smallest of things would at best come from sympathetic men and women in similar situations, at worst it simply would not be there at all. Counting the days down to some semblance of normality was a painful process, and all of that depended on a soldier surviving to return home intact – sadly, that was never a foregone conclusion.

But all of that would have to wait. Right now, Karnon had a job to do, and the woes of his home fires were not a part of that. The six boats approached the shore; a long, sandy beach secluded within a shallow bay at the western end of the island. There were four men waiting at the beach, no doubt alerted by warships going to anchor and disgorging boats not far from their shore. The half-dozen white boats gently nudged up against the sandy beaches in turn. Karnon hopped out of his own boat, immediately stepping into warm waters that extended up to his knees, washing over his leather boots to fill them. Commands were shouted by the marines' leaders – Captain Berso, the commander of the detachment of marines from the HW *Veneration*, and his two sergeants, joined Karnon's own sergeants in quickly yelling out orders to assemble the marines in their units on the beach.

Content that his soldiers were being effectively cajoled into their respective units, Karnon paced over to the four men waiting near the top of the beach. He noted as he approached that all four were armed, but their weapons remained sheathed. The tallest of the figures, a broad, middle-aged man with a head of white stubble and a weathered face, stepped out to meet him. The man wore a simple tunic of pale blue, crossed with a broad, white stripe, his bare arms displaying a numbered tattoo on his shoulder. An ex-legion man.

"Captain Vell," the man announced his name gruffly. "My men are contracted by the Capital Mining Company to defend this site."

Karnon exhaled. Mercenaries. They could prove to be useful, depending on their attitude to the arrival of the marines.

"Captain Senne, 5th Maritime Legion of Foot," Karnon introduced himself. "We have been sent here at the orders of the Keretian Fleet, following reports of pirate activity in these isles."

"Not here," Vell folded his thick arms defensively. "We would have sorted it out, alright. It's our whole purpose in being here. From what we've heard, that happened down to the south, at one of the Genezan colonies."

"That may be," Karnon said, glancing over his shoulder to see the eighty marines already setting about organizing their equipment, "but if they're in this area, there's a good chance they're coming back, and this site is the most valuable Basilean target. We're here to defend it."

"No," Vell gave a single shake of his head, "this is a private site, owned by the Capital Mining Company. Its defense has been entrusted to me."

Karnon narrowed his eyes. That answered his question regarding cooperation.

"The island belongs to the Hegemon, and the settlement is made up of his people. The Duma's authority on his behalf in commanding the legion is significantly more so than your mining company. So I will be taking command of the defenses here. Do we have a problem?"

Vell looked past Karnon at the four units of marines on the beach behind him.

"No. No problem."

"Good," Karnon said. "Now, what have you heard about pirate attacks in this island chain?"

Vell looked over his shoulder at his trio of mercenaries and then back at Karnon.

"Not much. A single ship full of orcs. They landed at Baudethra. They ransacked the settlement and the church and then left with every body they could pack onto their ship. Women and children, too. They took over half the colony. We took a boat across as soon as we could to see if we could help. Just found some burnt buildings and dead bodies. Man and orc. There were a few survivors. Not too many."

"What'll they do with the slaves?" Karnon asked.

Vell's face twisted in a grim frown.

"They'll take them south. Nowhere else to go. They'll take them to Claw or Mos-Luxa most likely."

Karnon nodded. Attacking a colony was one thing; abducting women and children to sell as slaves was another. That colony might not have been Basilean, but it was innocent nonetheless. And protecting the innocent was the Basilean way. Karnon turned to face his soldiers.

"Sergeant Erria!" he shouted out.

Erria, the more experienced of his two sergeants, sprinted across the yellow-white sand to his captain.

"Sir!"

"I need to get back onboard the *Pious*," Karnon explained to the veteran soldier. "I have news that Captain Ferrus will want to hear. While I'm gone, you are in command of the *Pious* marine detachment. Support Captain Berso and his men in establishing the defenses until I get back."

"Understood, sir," Erria said, casting a suspicious glance at Vell before jogging back over to his marines to continue bellowing orders out to them.

Karnon looked up at Vell.

"How many men do you have here?" he asked.

"Twenty-five."

"How many did they have defending the colony at Baudethra?"

"About the same," Vell frowned.

"How d'you figure you would be able to defend these mines from the orcs, then?"

Vell looked back at his men and exchanged a gruff smirk.

"'Cause we're better soldiers. We're ex-legion. Every one of us."

"Can't argue there," Karnon issued a brief smile, "but now you're eighty legion soldiers better off. I need to pass this all on to the captain of that ship before they go. As soon as I'm back, we'll get this place ready for war, because when those orcs find out about these mines, that's exactly what they'll bring here."

***

Pacing along the deck of the newly completed ship with his hands clasped behind his back, Ghurak nodded in satisfaction. The blood runner – a ship he named the *Blood Skull* after a few moments' thought – now gave him more power to play with. Tied up alongside a rickety jetty on the east coast of Axe Island, the *Blood Skull* sat opposite the *Driller* and alongside the *Green Hammer*, the three ships forming the core of his growing fleet. Driven up on the beach to the south was a small, eclectic flotilla of single mast warships – common 'rabble' ships that were captained by ambitious goblins who Ghurak had neither the time nor inclination to meet. The rabbles waxed and waned in size but gravitated to Ghurak and the *Green Hammer*, and the other pirate adm-ruls of the island, in an attempt to cling on to their growing successes. It did not bother him. It was a few more guns that could prove useful.

Ghurak stomped over to the back of the *Blood Skull* and watched as the three-mast barque sent over by Cerri departed to the south. The exchange had gone on without any problems; Ghurak's guns were de-livered just as promised, and the captured slaves were dragged off to the human pirate barque to sail for Mos-Luxa. That process had been noteworthy to Ghurak; he had always thought of himself at the top of the ladder of beings that induced fear, or at least close to it, but was sur-prised to see the human women screaming in terror and attempting to escape as they were handed over from the orcs to pirates of their own kind. Perhaps there was a fate worse than being eaten by orcs. Ghurak did not give it much thought. He had kept all of the humans he had captured in good condition, good enough to fetch a fair price, and now he had the guns he wanted to continue to wage the fight he wanted. Whatever happened to those slaves now was of no interest to him.

"What do you think of it, Admrul?" Kroock asked as he walked across the rear deck of the new warship.

Ghurak looked across his new ship again. The high rear deck gave a commanding view, bristling with guns along both sides. Two masts were ready with new sails – dyed blood red, as with the rest of his fleet – and the front of the ship boasted a newly constructed ram fashioned to look like a minotaur's skull, complete with horns jutting out forward. The ship was crewed largely by goblins, as were his oth-er two warships, bolstered by a smattering of orcs to take command and lead the boarding parties. Ghurak had not bothered to count how many; his trickle of successes had ensured a steady stream of volun-teers from the rabble ships, so crewing was becoming less of a problem. However, his reputation was based largely on his successes before he opted for a life at sea, a fact he knew would soon hamper him if he did not succeed on the waves.

"It's good," Ghurak grunted, "it'll do. We need to get this thing out on the water and in a fight. And soon."

Drika, Ghurak's long serving second-in-command, folded his huge arms and looked down at the hive of activity on the upper deck below. Goblins secured ropes, orcs hefted crates of shot to the magazine below, halfling cooks supervised the chain of goblins passing food crates down to the galley.

"Who will be the captin of this one, Admrul?" Drika asked.

Ghurak paused to think the query through. He had an abundance of good warriors; good fighters who could not only tear their opponents apart, but also lead a charge in some semblance of order. What he did not have was any orcs with any real, useable knowledge of sailing a ship of war against an enemy vessel. He would have to make do with what he had, as he always did.

"Shargol," Ghurak decided after another few moments. "Shargol can be captin."

"What?" Drika growled. "Admrul! I've been working for you for years! Since we were knee high as slaves, I've stood by you! This should be my ship! I've earned it!"

Kroock looked across at Drika, his fellow ex-slave and sometime rival for Ghurak's approval. His scarred face twisted in disgust and his fists clenched. Ghurak stared down at the two orcs and folded his arms. He could see Drika's point. Loyalty was something of a human concept, something a bit soft; but as much as it pained Ghurak to admit it, there was something in that concept. Drika had stood by him, axe in hand, since they escaped from their chains as adolescents. But there were two obvious problems with giving Drika command of the *Blood Skull*. One was that Ghurak would lose his highly capable second-in-command on the *Green Hammer*. The other was perhaps even more crucial.

"Drika," Ghurak grunted, "if you had this ship and there was another ship you wanted to board and capture, if you could attack from any direction, where would you put the wind?"

"Right behind me, Admrul!" Drika answered with a confident sneer. "I'd get the wind right up our back and hit them hard!"

Ghurak shook his head. Admittedly, the entire concept of placing the wind on the quarter was something that he had only learned from Cerri the previous evening, but he was not going to let his subordinates know that.

"If you put the wind right behind you, your back mast would get it," Ghurak grunted, "but what about your front mast? The wind can't get through the back one, or around it. No, Drika. You put the wind behind you but slightly to one side, on the quarter. That way, both masts get the wind and you go fast."

Drika's face twisted again in something between confusion and disappointment. His gaze lowered.

"You can kill with an axe as good as any orc I've ever seen," Ghurak continued, "you can lead a charge, you never need to prove that to me again. But you can only just about command a gun crew, because you only half know how. And you can only just about position a ship for the same reason. I don't doubt your arm, Drika. I doubt your brain."

Kroock's yellow-fanged mouth cracked into an amused sneer.

"But... that's not our way!" Drika protested. "I'm no damn elf! I face my foe and I hack them down! Same as any real orc!"

"But how are you going to face your foe if there's a sea between you and him?!" Ghurak yelled, shoving Drika back with both hands. "You can't walk on water! You need to use the ship! You need to sail properly and then shoot properly! *Then*, you can cut them down! But you don't know how to sail and you can barely shoot! You can't captin a ship!"

A flash of rage illuminated Drika's dark eyes as Ghurak shoved him back a pace with every accusation. The huge orc looked up at his leader but did not retaliate. He waited until Ghurak had finished and then stood up straight, his face stoic and resolute.

"Got it, Admrul."

Ghurak took in a few long breaths, his urge to fight and kill fading just a little. He looked at his second-in-command, obedient and unyielding as ever. No, using intellect was never part of the traditional orc plan. But blind and calm obedience was not either, yet Drika displayed that quality in every fight and it always worked out as a result. Ghurak nodded and turned away.

"Go find a book on sailing," he grunted at Drika, "and read it. Or at least find some little runt who can read it to you. I know it isn't the orc way. But it's the only way we can take these ships and use them as weapons of war. We need to understand them. We sail tomorrow at dawn, all of us. All three ships. If you can come back to me before then and tell me something I didn't know about sailing a ship of war that you've learned from a book, something that will allow us to close with our enemies so we can cut the bastards down, then this ship is yours. If not, Shargol gets it. Understood?"

A hint of a smile tugged at Drika's uneven mouth.

"Understood, Admrul."

***

Caithlin would have preferred not being able to see the *Martolian Queen* from the window at the port authority office. The ship sat unhappily in dry dock, her hull being scraped clean as part of the agreement she had haggled with Admiral Pattia, while her steering gear was improved with a lighter, more responsive, and ultimately more expensive fit. It was a load off her mind that her father's ship was now being repaired and improved, but it would, perhaps, have been better if the brig was out of sight and out of mind.

Deprived of her sleeping quarters onboard for the duration of the refit, Caithlin had again been forced to look to Kassia, the harbormaster, for help. After finally spending a morning purchasing all of the accruements required for her to transform herself into an acting captain of the Basilean Navy, she now found herself crammed into a tiny room behind the harbormaster's office, looking out over her wounded ship as she changed into her new uniform.

Uniform was perhaps an overstatement. Caithlin had observed that Basilean Naval ratings wore dark blue, while officers wore blue breeches or trousers with a white shirt. Given that she was neither, she had opted for white breeches and a matching white shirt, accompanied by black boots and a sword belt. She buttoned up her shirt, tied her blue neck scarf inside the open collar, and pulled on her heavy jacket of dark blue trimmed with gold lace. She then attached her newly purchased saber and scabbard to her belt and grabbed her black, tricorn hat. Glancing up at herself in the reflection of the window, she let out a long breath at the sight of the formal, militarized stranger who looked back. Deciding against moping, she clutched her sword uncomfortably to her side and opened the door into the harbormaster's office.

Kassia looked up at her from behind her desk. Caithlin hoped she would not pass comment on her new, enforced aesthetic but failed to see how the older woman could ignore it.

"Don't take any crap from them, Cathy," Kassia said seriously. "The navy needs you and your brig as much as you need them right now."

Caithlin reached into the pocket of her jacket and produced a purse containing the last of the unspent money given to her for accepting her commission. She placed it onto Kassia's desk. The older woman looked down and shook her head.

"Take it," Caithlin interrupted her before she could speak, "please. You and your daughter have done so much for me. Let me at least have this one."

"It's a noble gesture," the harbormaster said with a hint of a smile, "but the harsh reality is that you still need money. You are not out of the storm yet. There will be plenty of opportunities to repay charity in the future."

Kassia tossed the small bag of coins over to Caithlin.

"Buy me a drink this evening," she smiled to the privateer captain. "I'm sure you'll have a lot to say about your first day as a pirate."

The walk around the harbor wall from the northern dock to the naval docks at the south of the bay was uncomfortable, to put it mildly. The physical discomfort of breaking in brand new leather boots and wearing a heavy jacket in the blazing morning sun was only part of the issue. The second part of her rising discomfort was not so kindly provided by the looks and hushed comments she received from the merchant sailors and dockyard workers as she traversed her way along the path at the water's edge. Female sailors were relatively uncommon outside of the Basilean sisterhood; female ship captains were rare, but certainly not unheard of. But being a young woman dressed in the uniform of a Basilean Naval privateer, complete with pseudo-captain's rank on her shoulders and an officer's saber at her hip, she would not be surprised if she was alone in holding that status in the entire Infant Sea.

Caithlin could hear the cannons booming away from the naval dockyard well before she arrived there. She made her way into the naval facility, her commissioning certificate being enough to grant her admission but not sufficient to earn a salute from the marine guards. After asking directions around the sprawling dockyard, she finally found her sailors assembled on a long, stone mole jutting out into the bay. Ten cannons on their wooden carriages, secured to hard points via thick ropes, lined the mole and pointed out to sea. Each gun was crewed by six men; some wearing the blue of the Basilean Navy, others garbed in the attire of civilian sailors. Her sailors.

"Fire!" came a yell of command from a single figure at the end of the line of guns.

Each gun captain held their smoldering slow match over the touchholes at the back of their cannons, and with a ripple of deafening booms, the weapons ignited, belching out plumes of black smoke around a brief flash of red flame. The guns jumped back, held firm by their ropes.

"Stop your vents!" the voice of command yelled out, recognizable as Lieutenant Ellias now that Caithlin climbed the stone steps up to the mole. She emerged at the top of the stairs and saw the gun captains lean over to secure their vent-pieces into the smoking touchholes on the guns.

"Sponge your guns!" Jaymes shouted out. "Roundly! Roundly! Seconds matter, so make it fast!"

A single man in each gun crew leaned over the muzzle of his gun, swabbing out the bore of the gun in preparation for the next shot. The mole stank of burnt powder, the vile smell drifting across in the warm, morning breeze. Jaymes noticed Caithlin approaching and turned quickly to address the sixty sailors.

"Captain on deck! Gunners, by your guns!"

Each of the uniformed sailors quickly dashed over to line up at attention in front of their guns. The merchant seamen of Caithlin's crew ambled over into lines, confusedly copying the example set by their military brethren. One sailor hidden amid the crews let out a loud wolf whistle as Caithlin approached.

"Stop that!" Jaymes bellowed. "The next man who fails to show the captain the correct marks of respect will be flogged! Don't believe me, you feel free to try me!"

The lines fell silent. Jaymes placed his bicorn hat atop his head and walked over to Caithlin. He stopped in front of her and raised his arm smartly in salute.

"Captain," he greeted formally, "port watch gunnery training is in progress. The men are ready for your inspection, ma'am."

Caithlin looked up at the young officer with some confusion, his handsome features hidden beneath the black smears of gun smoke.

"You should return my salute, ma'am," he whispered quietly, "just to acknowledge it."

Caithlin raised her hand to the brim of her hat.

"You don't need to salute me," she said.

"I know I don't need to, ma'am. But I think it's proper, given that I am temporarily one of your crew."

Caithlin looked along the lines of sailors stood by their guns. Her guns, once the repairs were complete and they were fitted to her ship. She was not surprised by the wolf whistle as she approached, it had certainly followed the trend of her treatment as she made her way across the dockyard, but she did at least appreciate Jaymes's defense of her.

"You don't need to call me ma'am, either," she said quietly, "that's not how I run my ship."

"I think it better if I do, ma'am," Jaymes replied formally. "I should be setting an example to the men. They need to know that your authority is absolute, just as it is for a captain on a frigate."

Again, Caithlin appreciated the support. She was glad of her decision to insist on Jaymes being part of the crew while they settled in to their new role and their new lives, but she was also aware that she was yet to speak to him about that. It would certainly be more honest for her to let him know that he was there upon her insistence.

"Very well," Caithlin nodded, "tell them to continue. I'd like a word, if I may."

Jaymes turned to the nearest gun crew.

"Harker!" he shouted out to the shaven-headed gun captain.

"Sir!" the man stepped forward.

"Take charge of gunnery practice. Continue with wads and prime only, do not load shot yet. Keep a close eye on the less experienced gunners."

"Aye, sir!"

Caithlin paced upwind away from the guns as Harker turned around to yell orders out at the sailors to resume gunnery training. She waited until she was a good distance away from the guns before turning to address Jaymes.

"When we get onboard, I think it best that your sailors dress in civilian attire," she said. "I won't have my men in uniform, and I'd rather break down the boundaries between the two groups. I think they'll work better together without any 'us' and 'them' approach."

"Aye, ma'am, sounds sensible," Jaymes agreed.

She looked up at the Basilean lieutenant. It seemed like a good time to level with him. She opened her mouth to speak but found easier words than the ones she had planned coming out.

"I appreciate the formality in front of the men, Jaymes. But if I'm honest, I don't like being called 'ma'am'. I don't stand on formality."

"Yes, Miss Viconti."

"Cathy," Caithlin said, "my friends call me Cathy."

The stern looking sailor's features warmed a little.

"Cathy it is, then."

Caithlin turned to look out south, past the stone breakwater and at the sparkling Infant Sea as it flowed off toward the horizon. A smattering of bulbous clouds broke up the clear sky, and an assortment of sails punctuated the clear waters.

"We need to get to sea as quickly as possible. I can't stand pacing around here dressed up like some sort of war hero when I haven't fired a shot. The moment my ship is ready, we are setting sail."

"Right," Jaymes said, "I'll make sure everybody is ready for that. She'll be a grand vessel, after the repairs and changes. She'll be lighter and faster than she ever was. Ready for battle."

Caithlin looked to the north of the bay where her father's ship suffered under the hands of the naval carpenters. She then looked back at Jaymes.

"She'll be ready. But I won't. Jaymes… I don't even know how to load a pistol. I've never held a sword in my life, let alone fought with one. Can you teach me?"

Jaymes wiped a grimy hand across his blackened brow.

"I'm not sure I'm the best for it," he admitted. "I'm a good enough fencer, but there's a huge difference between fencing and actually fighting."

"But you have fought with a sword? You have… killed enemies?" she asked hesitantly.

The Basilean officer narrowed his eyes slightly.

"Once or twice. I really haven't seen much fighting."

"Once or twice is infinitely more than I have. This afternoon, if you would. If we're going off hunting real pirates, I'd like to stand a chance of surviving a fight when I actually meet them."

Chapter Twelve

The *Pious's* bows delved down into the foamy water, the wooden Elohi carved beneath her bowsprit seeming to reach down from the heavens to touch the waves before thinking better of it and soaring up again as the fo'c'sle heaved up again. His feet well apart for balance, Charn stared through his telescope at the lone ship less than a league ahead as they fought with a beam wind to try to close the gap. Behind him, the *Veneration* and the *Vigil* were staggered back in line astern as the three frigates sailed south, the low evening sun now an orange smear across the hazy horizon beneath a clear sky.

The ship sailing away from them was swift enough; three masts, with the foremast and mainmast being square rigged, while the mizzenmast was fore and aft; a barque, often used for cargo but sometimes as a fast transport for important individuals. She was flying the colors of Valentica; a powerful nation to be sure, but one that relied on its army far more than its miniscule fleet, and one that had little business in displaying a presence in the east Infant Sea.

Closing his telescope, Charn made his way back across the heaving upper deck and up to the quarterdeck, where Lieutenant Kaeso Innes was on duty as officer of the watch.

"Valentican, Mister Innes," Charn grimaced, "if you believe that."

"Seems a touch unlikely, sir," the freshly promoted third lieutenant agreed.

Charn barked out a short, bitter laugh. This would be the fourth vessel the *Pious* had challenged since receiving word of the orc attack on the Genezan colony in the Eleccian Isles, all of which were able to prove their legitimacy in these waters, and none of which had seen any suspicious activity. With the three ships boarded by the *Vigil* and *Veneration*, that amounted to seven uneventful boardings between the frigates of the squadron.

"Mister Just!" Charn yelled across the quarterdeck to the ship's master. "Can you get any more out of her?"

"No, sir," Thaddeus shouted in response, "any change to the rigging or course now, and she'll start losing knots, not gaining them."

Charn swore quietly and stared ahead. The Valentican barque was fast, but not as fast as a Basilean frigate. They were gaining. They would be close enough soon.

"Mister Turnio!" Charn shouted. "Signal that barque! Tell her to haul in her sails!"

"Aye, sir!" Francis shouted before rushing over to the signals locker and setting about linking up his pennants to hoist up to signal the order to the barque. Charn narrowed his eyes. The other ships they had boarded had all been trivial affairs, easily done. But this? The barque had picked up speed as soon as the frigate turned to intercept her, and her Valentican colors simply made no sense. Charn had spent more than enough years at sea to trust his instinct, and every fiber of it was telling him that the barque's captain had seen him and was trying to open the distance between them.

"Mister Innes," Charn called across to Kaeso, "be good enough to head down below to the gun room. Send my compliments to Mister Blake and tell him to prepare a boarding party."

"Aye, sir."

Charn stomped back across the upper deck to the fo'c'sle. Lieutenant Blake was the officer he had poached from the *Vigil* after he had been ordered to surrender Lieutenant Ellias to the *Martolian Queen*. Tobias Blake had very quickly impressed him; an officer with nearly a decade under his belt as a lieutenant, primed and ready to take command of his own vessel at the next opportunity. There had been a chance to send Blake back across to the *Vigil* when she had caught up with the *Pious*; Charn deliberately did not capitalize on that opportunity.

"Fo'c'sle men!" he called up to his sailors in the rigging and yards of the foremast. "On deck! Load the bow chasers with bar shot!"

A dozen of his sailors nimbly scrambled down to the deck and quickly set about preparing the forward facing cannons for action. Charn looked over his shoulder and saw the signal pennants hoisted up on the frigate's outer halyards. He brought his telescope up again to examine the barque. There was no response. Charn grunted. The sun was out on the starboard bow, gifting the crew of the barque with a clear view of the *Pious*. They could see the signals, alright. Charn was sure enough of that.

He looked across the bows, estimating the range to now be a little under a mile. They were rapidly closing to the outer range of cannons, although now with the cumbersome bar shot loaded. His hands clasped at the small of his back, Charn stomped angrily back to the quarterdeck, spitting out a trail of curses as he did so. Shortly after he arrived, Kaeso returned to his station, accompanied by Tobias Blake. The temporary first lieutenant brought his right hand to his cap in salute as he saw Charn. Charn noticed the officer was already wearing his sword and had a pistol tucked into his belt.

"Good evening, sir," the short man said hoarsely. "Mister Innes has passed on your orders. The boarding party is preparing for action as we speak. Are we beating to quarters, sir?"

"No, Mister Blake," Charn winced, staring out at the Valentican barque again, "not yet."

A few minutes passed in silence. Then, quite without warning, a low rumble issued from the speeding barque and wisps of gray smoke puffed up over its stern. A second later, the unmistakable whine of flying round shot sounded across the evening air, and two great columns of water shot up from the sea a few dozen yards ahead of the *Pious*.

"Beat to quarters!" Charn thundered.

The drums hammered out and the sound of shouts and yells from below deck announced all off-watch sailors rapidly preparing themselves for action. Samus, Charn's steward, was up on the quarterdeck in seconds, handing across sabers to the captain and the third lieutenant. Charn raised his telescope again and regarded the barque – he watched as the Valentican flag was hauled down from the mainmast and quickly replaced with a black flag, adorned with an inverted skull superimposed over a bleeding heart.

"Bastards," Charn breathed.

"That's them, then," Tobias muttered as he peered through his own telescope. "Pirates, but I don't recognize their ensign. Probably some unimportant minion of the pirate leaders running out of the Infantosian Islands."

"Agreed," Charn said, "I'm more than content that those are the bastards we are looking for."

"Should we be loading round shot in the bow chasers, sir?" Kaeso ventured.

Charn slowly turned his head to stare across at his third lieutenant.

"What advantage does round shot give over the bar shot I have ordered to be loaded in the guns, Mister Innes?"

"Better at penetrating the hull, sir. And longer range."

"What advantage does bar shot present?"

"Better at damaging the sails and rigging, sir," Kaeso replied hesitantly, as if unsure where the conversation was leading, given how elementary the questions were.

"Why are we chasing that ship down, Mister Innes?"

"Because it... ah... apologies, sir. Because it is potentially full of captured colonists that we are rescuing from slavery. So... shooting up the hull rather than the sails would be a terrible idea. Sir."

Charn exchanged a disapproving look with Tobias, glad that he finally had an officer onboard who knew his business beyond ensuring that the ship was pointed in the right direction and probably would not collide with something in a shipping lane. Since losing Gregori Corbes, he had missed that comfort of having at least one officer he could rely upon to run the ship while he slept.

The barque's stern guns erupted again, but this time the shots fell even wider than the first salvo.

"How long, Mister Innes?" Charn demanded.

"Sir?"

"How long between shots? You've been keeping an eye on the timings, I would hope."

The silence that greeted Charn's query was answer enough.

"Mister Blake?" he turned to the senior lieutenant.

"About three minutes, sir," Tobias replied coolly.

"About three minutes," Charn repeated. "You need to keep an eye on this sort of thing, Mister Innes. It gives us our first indication of the levels of skill and expertise we are facing in an enemy crew. Three minutes is decidedly mediocre to reload and fire a medium weight cannon. Mediocre at best."

"But why, sir?" Kaeso ventured. "They're in a barque which is clearly outmatched by a frigate, and they are being chased down by three. What do they hope to achieve by antagonizing us?"

Charn turned to Tobias.

"Mister Blake?" he asked pointedly.

The short lieutenant turned to face his junior.

"They know we are chasing them down, Mister Innes," Tobias explained, "and they know we are faster, too. Their only hope is to lose us once the sun sets, but at this rate of closure, that won't happen. All they can hope to do is foul our sails and rigging and slow us down enough to make good their escape in the night. But with two more frigates at the close trail behind us, they don't have many options."

"Right again, Mister Blake," Charn issued a thin smile, "and how many men do you reckon it would take to crew a barque of that size?"

Tobias looked over the pirate barque and contemplated his answer for a brief moment.

"Minimum of twenty or so, sir. If she were a merchant vessel, I'd guess thirty to be more likely. However, given the colors she is flying, I'd expect a pirate vessel of that size to be crammed with over a hundred of the sods to make boarding actions more likely to succeed and to allow the redundancy of dispatching a crew to sail any prize ships they capture."

Charn smiled again. He liked Tobias. It was a shame he could not keep him on as the *Pious's* first lieutenant permanently. In his day, as an eighteen-year-old lieutenant of Kaeso Innes's standing, that level of knowledge would be expected of any junior officer. Now, it seemed, freshly promoted lieutenants were expected to achieve a notably lower standard at their promotion board.

"That'll do for now, Mister Blake. Go and prepare your men for the boarding action. We're not far from the bastards now."

"Aye, sir."

The gap between the two vessels continued to close as the sun dipped to touch the horizon, casting long shadows across the green waves. Another few shots barked out from the pirate vessel but only succeeded in one shot hitting the *Pious* on her bow with nothing more than cosmetic damage to show. With a range of now well less than a thousand yards, Charn was happy to return the compliment.

"Bow chasers!" he shouted across the upper deck to the fo'c'sle gunners. "Bar shot! Enemy vessel's rigging! Fire!"

The order was repeated by the gun captains, and the *Pious*'s forward facing guns blasted into life, sending a plume of black smoke washing back over the upper deck to drown out the salty stench of the sea with the bitter smell of burnt powder. Charn allowed himself a brief grin as the shots straddled the barque; not a hit, but close enough that his gunners knew their ranging was correct. The gun captains wasted no time in yelling out orders to have their guns swabbed out and re-loaded.

"Captain, sir!" Thaddeus shouted across from the forward end of the quarterdeck, looking back over the frigate's stern. "The *Vigil* is signaling! Looks like she wants an update on the situation."

"Not now!" Charn scowled, finding his temper erupting at seemingly everything that Captain Alain Stryfus did these days. "The bloody fool should be able to see what is going on and act under his own initiative!"

The gap closed. Through his telescope, Charn could make out figures on the barque's deck – exactly as predicted, it was a busy upper deck crammed with sailors. Part of him regretted sending his marines ashore at the gold mine at Kios, but probably outnumbering the pirates by two-to-one, he still fancied his chances.

The *Pious* continued to bear down on the barque, the distance closing with each passing minute and allowing Charn to make out more details on the stern of the enemy vessel. He had not quite expected the bloody boarding action that now appeared to be a grim inevitability, thinking it more likely that if the slaver ship were discovered, the captain would elect to surrender to the might of three frigates. Still, the opportunity was there for him to continue the education of his juniors and inferiors.

"Mister Innes," Charn barked at his third lieutenant, "what d'ye think the barque's captain is likely to do?"

Kaeso flinched as the stern guns of the barque erupted again, sending a pair of cannon balls zipping past the port side of the quarterdeck.

"He'll keep running, I think, sir," Kaeso ventured. "He'll try to delay our coming alongside and boarding him until nightfall, when he'll hope to slip away. But it already looks far too late for that."

"So," Charn continued impatiently, "what will he do instead? He knows we will be alongside him in moments! Well, man, speak! What would you do?"

P... prepare to repel boarders, sir?" Kaeso stammered.

"How?!"

The answer was correct, but Charn was after the detail, where traditionally the demons lay. No answer was forthcoming, so Charn turned to bellow his orders down to the sailors on the upper deck.

"Gunners, port side!" he yelled. "Load grapeshot!"

The order was repeated, and dozens of sailors dashed across to prepare the port side guns with their deadly ammunition; canvas bags filled with small, metal shot that lacked range and punch but spread out upon firing; it was devastating against the exposed crews on the upper deck of a warship.

Charn frowned. He fully expected his opposite number aboard the barque to be ordering his own gunners to load the same deadly ammunition for when the *Pious* drew close alongside to board.

Up forward on the fo'c'sle, *Pious's* bow chasers blasted out another salvo of bar shot. The heavy, twirling projectiles sliced through the air and into the rigging of the barque, sending the top half of the vessel's mizzenmast crumpling down into her deck. The Basilean gunners let out a brief cheer before one of their petty officers screamed out a tirade of expletives to silence them; just a moment quicker than Charn, who was about to do the same. Deprived of half of one of its three masts, the barque began to slow almost instantly. Charn narrowed his eyes and smiled venomously.

The frigate plunged on through the heaving sea, quickly closing the gap to only a couple of hundred yards. Then, quite without warning, the barque suddenly altered course to port, slowing rapidly in the water and presenting its side to the rapidly approaching Basilean warship.

"Helmsman! Starboard your helm!" Charn yelled, bypassing the normal routine of sending his instructions via the ship's master.

"Helm hard a'starboard! Gunners, load grapeshot! Starboard guns!"

The gunners on the upper deck rapidly abandoned their positions on the port side of the frigate and dashed over to load the starboard guns as the *Pious* lurched uncomfortably to port, under full rudder from the helmsman. The barque's captain had clearly seen the frigate's crew preparing the port guns and so cleverly took the initiative to turn hard to port to force the frigate to follow, lest they sail straight past the barque, or turn and plough headlong into her – an event the pirate captain clearly knew that Charn did not want to risk.

The frigate turned nimbly inside the smaller vessel, drifting close enough now for Charn to be able to make out the faces on the packed upper deck of the barque staring up the frigate. It was the perfect opportunity to fire, and again Charn's instinct gleaned of years of battling at sea kicked in.

"Down!" he yelled. "Everybody down!"

The port side of the barque rippled with cannon fire. With a sound like a million hail stones blasting through a forest, the barque's broadside of lethal grapeshot cut up into the frigate. Splinters of planks flew back in a storm of wood from the impact point on the starboard bow, tearing across the fo'c'sle and upper deck. Screams of pain mingled with the commanding yells of gun captains. Charn clambered back up to his feet and looked forward, seeing the starboard side of the fo'c'sle littered with dead and dying sailors, the boards awash with blood. He looked down at the barque as his own guns lined up on the smaller ship.

"Starboard guns!" he yelled. "Fire as she bears!"

The order to fire was repeated by Walt Ganto on the upper deck to relay to the gunners before it was then taken up by the first gun on the fo'c'sle's starboard side. The first cannon's deadly hail of grapeshot spewed out into the packed deck of the barque. At one-second intervals as the *Pious* continued to swing about to port, each gun lining up in turn, the gun captains yelled out the order to fire. Black smoke billowed out of the starboard side of the frigate as Charn stared down in satisfaction from his vantage point on the quarterdeck, his fists clenched and his jaw set. The rippling broadside cut into the barque, the blasts of iron shot cutting bloody swathes through the packed sailors. The stench of powder drifted back to the quarterdeck, and Charn's hearing was replaced with a high-pitched whine as the quarterdeck cannons fired down into the barque. He only just made out the shout from Thaddeus.

"Boarding, sir?!" the master yelled.

"Aye, Mister Just!" Charn replied.

"Helmsman! Port your helm! Hard a'port!"

The agile frigate responded instantly, reversing her turn to bring her slender bow sweeping to the right. A moment later, the *Pious* clattered into the barque with a crunching of protesting wood and tearing of sailcloth as the rigging of the two vessels intertwined.

"Boarding party," Charn thundered, "away!"

"Boarders," Tobias Blake screamed from his position at the starboard waist, his saber held aloft, "on me!"

It would be the gallant officer's last words. As he planted a foot on the side of the *Pious's* upper deck and prepared to jump down to the barque, a pistol shot erupted from below, and Tobias crumpled to the deck, a bullet hole planted in the center of his forehead. One of the ship's petty officers leapt forward to take charge of the boarding action, a crude cutlass held in one hand as he leapt down screaming onto the deck of the barque. Dozens of Basilean sailors followed him, yelling from the bottom of their lungs as they brandished a deadly assortment of boarding pikes, cutlasses, and cudgels.

Charn let out a sigh of despair at seeing such a promising officer cut down, and then he turned to stare down at his third lieutenant.

"Mister Innes, go and take charge of that boarding action!"

"Aye, sir!" Kaeso shouted with a spirit that pleasantly surprised Charn, before rushing over to the starboard waist of the *Pious*, drawing his saber, and leaping down into the swirling melee that was developed on the deck of the barque.

Samus again appeared at Charn's side, taking a moment to salute before offering his captain a loaded pistol.

"Just in case, sir."

"Thank you, steward," Charn replied, taking the pistol and tucking it into his belt.

He made his way over to the starboard side of the quarterdeck and looked down at the frantic, bloody fighting on the barque below. His own sailors had driven a wedge into the center of the upper deck, fanning out to advance forward and aft against the packed deck of pirates. The noble crowd of Basilean naval blue, speckled with red bandannas, cut through the ill-disciplined but ferocious mass of pirates as cutlasses clashed together, pistols fired, and men yelled out in agony as they were ran through with boarding pikes. More pirates clawed their way to the upper deck through the hatchways from below deck, dashing up to join the fight. Dozens of Charn's sailors, still at their positions on the starboard guns, looked back expectantly at their captain as they awaited permission to jump down into the fray.

"Not yet!" Charn shouted, eager not to hinder his own sailors with a fresh wave of bodies smashing into them from above. "Wait for my command!"

Kaeso Innes had fought his way to the aft end of the barque, bleeding from wounds to his head and one arm, but still bravely facing the snarling mob of some two dozen pirates that were crammed onto the barque's quarterdeck. Charn saw one of the pirates wore a grand hat embellished with a colorful rosette that complimented his long, green coat. No doubt the captain. Charn took his pistol, cocked the hammer, and looked down into the fray to await an opportunity to shoot at his opposite number. Seeing that it was very unlikely that such an opportunity would present itself in the vicious fight, he settled for shooting down into the mass of pirates, blowing a bloody hole in the back of one of the buccaneers.

"Steward!" Charn called, holding his smoking pistol to one side. "Reload, if you please!"

He glanced forward and saw Walt Ganto had taken charge of the sailors still on *Pious's* upper deck, organizing them into waves of armed boarders ready to join the fray. Charn looked down at the barque and saw his men had the upper hand in the fight that raged over the blood-drenched deck as blades continued to clatter and shots were fired. He assessed that there was now enough of a gap for his men to maneuver.

"Mister Ganto!" he shouted to his second lieutenant. "Take twenty men! Get in there!"

Unsheathing his gold-hilted saber, Walt led the next wave over the side of the *Pious* and into the fight. Some of Charn's sailors were now scrambling up the rigging of the barque, blades clamped between their teeth as they set about advancing on the handful of sharpshooters that fired down from the barque's yard arms. The shouts and screams began to die down in intensity. Up forward, on the barque's fo'c'sle, the last few pirates threw down their weapons and surrendered to Charn's victorious sailors. The pirates on the quarterdeck, however, continued to fight on for a few more minutes until a trio of Charn's sailors managed to surround the pirate captain, who was quickly run through with a boarding pike and then brutally hacked down with bloody cutlasses. With their leader gone, more pockets of enemy sailors gave up the one-sided fight, until finally the commotion of battle was replaced with the victorious cheers of Charn's sailors.

Smiling in contentment, Charn took the opportunity to make his way down to the *Pious's* upper deck and then across to the barque as the *Vigil* and *Veneration* caught up with them from the north. Walt

Ganto had already set about commanding his sailors to shove the surviving pirates off to the starboard side of the barque's upper deck. Charn made his way toward his second lieutenant but was intercepted by the blood-covered figure of Kaeso Innes. The young lieutenant saluted.

"Enemy ship, secure, sir. The hold is full of slaves. About a hundred."

"Very good, Mister Innes," Charn said, genuinely impressed with the fighting spirit of the latest addition to his ship's company. "Get the surgeon across here to take care of the prisoners. Mister Ganto! Separate these scum into two groups; one to be caged up here in the slaves' pens, the other to be secured in the *Pious's* brig."

"Aye, sir!" Walt nodded.

Charn turned back to Kaeso and gave the boy a genuine smile of pride.

"Well done, lad. Well done. Pick thirty men for your prize crew. You have command of this barque for the return to Keretia."

***

Pulling the cork of the green bottle out with his teeth, Karnon took another few paces away from the freshly dug trench and sat on the dry stone wall running around the perimeter of the mining settlement. He took a few mouthfuls of the cheap wine, perfectly satisfied with the low quality of the beverage as he looked across the shallow waters of the bay and into the sunset. The defenses were all but complete; enough trenches dug for the marines and Captain Vell's mercenary guard force for if the orcs attempted to bombard them from the sea, as well as a series of natural looking obstacles such as steep slopes and dense foliage that would force any attacker to take a narrow, winding path that was overlooked by several ideal positions to shoot crossbows from above.

Having decent crossbowmen was something that he did not have to worry about, not like his early days in command in the legion. The legion marines were all volunteers and had all served a minimum of two years soldiering. As well as passing a grueling physical selection process, each soldier had to be fully proficient with spear, sword, and crossbow; whereas in the regular legion, a soldier could complete a term of service having only mastered one of those weapons. They were physically fit, independent thinkers who were all well able to take command of a small unit if necessary and skilled with a variety of weapons – both on land and in the maritime environment. Karnon genuinely hoped that orcs would show up. His men needed to fight; months of specialized training and then no fighting was bad for the soul.

Dripping with sweat from hours of digging, Karnon watched as the last of his marines put the final touches on the construction of the trenches, ensuring the steps leading down to them were wide enough for armored men to dash down in a hurry. Sergeant Castus Erria walked over from the fortifications to sit next to Karnon.

"This is as good as it'll get, sir," the aging sergeant offered.

"Agreed," Karnon replied, passing over the bottle of wine. "Stand the men down for the evening. One drink each, if they choose to head off to the miner's tavern. They need to be fresh as a daisy every moment we're here, just in case the orcs do decide to pay us a visit."

"Hopefully none of them are stupid enough to let themselves go while on the job, sir," Castus winced, looking out across the darkening waters of the bay as the waves rolled gently up the shallow beach.

Karnon continued to stare down, his eyes picking out a trio of large turtles who slowly limped across the beach, using their paddle-like flippers to carefully massage mounds of pale sand over the top of their precious eggs. Staring at the water's edge, Karnon thought over their specialized training for this new maritime role. For not the first time, he wondered if learning to swim would have been a good prerequisite for his soldiers in their new environment. Then again, they were still expected to wear armor during boarding actions, so if any of them did fall overboard, all of the swimming proficiency in the world would not save them.

"Looks like your admirer is back," Castus nodded over to the edge of the miners' huts, where a tall, thin girl with dark hair who was barely out of her adolescent years was strolling back from the well, looking over at Karnon as she struggled with two heavy buckets of water.

Karnon had already forgotten her name. A pleasant enough young woman, one of the miner's daughters, but too forward for his liking. Especially given that he had already dropped his marital status and his wife's name into conversation with her on several occasions, seemingly with no impact on her intentions. Karnon raised a hand to his pocket again, feeling the carefully folded letter from Sabine still safely where he had left it. Every time he read the letter, he found a new sentence or phrase that hinted at her sadness without him and her possible resentment at the reality of the challenges she faced alone. Things had been so much simpler when she was simply the girl back home and not his wife.

Karnon raised himself to his feet and pushed the cork back into the top of the bottle of wine.

"Fall them out," he instructed his sergeant, "but send tonight's sentries over to me. They need to know the importance of staying alert out here. We're in a new environment, and once this place gets dark, I'd imagine a whole boat-load of orcs could row ashore right under our noses if we aren't paying attention."

Castus looked up at the darkening skies.

"At least there's a full moon," he pondered, "that'll help the sentries. I'll send them across to you directly, sir."

Karnon nodded, heading over to where his tent was pitched in the center of the marines' encampment. He still had his doubts over whether the orcs would attempt to attack the gold mine, or if they were even aware of its existence. But if they did appear, his soldiers would be ready for them.

Chapter Thirteen

Ghurak smiled as he lowered his telescope, the bows of the *Green Hammer* pointing eastward toward the busy sea lane. The morning sun rose into a sky of low, broken cloud spreading over a fair to rough sea, causing even the towering, mighty *Green Hammer* to lurch and list a little. The masts of perhaps a dozen vessels dotted the horizon, varying in size from small sloops, ketches, and cutters up to larger merchant vessels. Ghurak guessed that some of the sloops were likely to be naval rather than trade, but given his last encounter with a frigate had ended in the Basileans fleeing, not even the mildest of concerns entered his mind. He had found a rich vein of shipping that had been left all but unguarded. This was his chance.

"Ratchit!" Ghurak shouted down to his most seasoned goblin, who lurked at the foot of the mainmast. "I want us alongside the biggest cargo ship we find! What are my options?"

Ratchit scuttled up the mainmast as Ghurak resumed his stare off to the east, picking out a wide, three-mast vessel that towered over the tiny fleet of single and double-masted ships moving along the sea lane. Satisfied to be back in command of his smasher, Ghurak only hoped that the two orcs he had trusted as captins of his blood runners were capable and reliable enough to carry out his orders. He would soon find out.

Ratchit returned to the upper deck after a few moments and scrambled off to present himself to Ghurak, raising a hand in salute as he approached. A line of gold earrings pierced one of his long, green ears and a scraggy, blue bandanna covered his bald head, giving him a faintly ridiculous appearance. But he knew and understood sails, and that made him a rarity in Ghurak's crew.

"Wind's from the northwest, Admrul," he reported, his voice shrill and weedy in comparison to the orcs of the crew, "good for our current course. As soon as we get in the shipping lane, we'd want to turn starboard, toward the south. If we turn north and go against the wind, those human ships will weather it better and we'll slow quicker. We want one that is heading south, Admrul."

Ghurak grinned from ear to torn ear.

"That big one," he sneered, "the one with the three masts and the wide sides. That's heading close enough to south."

"Aye, Admrul," Ratchit chipped in. "She's a cat-rigged barque. With a waist like that, she'll be full of cargo."

Having little interest in Ratchit's display of terminological knowledge, Ghurak stomped over to the group of goblins operating the *Green Hammer's* wheel.

"See that ship over there?" He pointed a stubby finger at the large barque. "Point us in front of it. Keep us aiming about a ship's length ahead of it."

Minutes passed. Many of the vessels had already altered course, no doubt terrified by the towering, red-sailed pirate ship bearing down upon them from the west. Some turned to take full advantage of the wind and flee in whatever direction they could; others altered course to head to the north, clearly savvy enough to know that the lumbering orc smasher would not sail well with a heavy, into-wind component to its course. Ghurak let out a low laugh. He was outfoxing them. They would all be transfixed by him, the terrified human sailors on their defenseless cargo ships, staring across at his huge ship as it sailed in from the west. None of them were thinking to look eastward, where his two blood runners lurked in the glare of the rising sun.

"One of them is coming right at us, Admrul," said Irukk, his newly promoted first mate, "one of the little ones."

Ghurak looked across in the direction his first mate's telescope was pointing and saw a sleek, single mast ship cutting through the waves as it headed toward them, its triangular sail turned against the mast to harness what little it could of the wind as it headed westward.

"Ignore it!" Ghurak spat. "It's just a sloop! It can't scratch us! Carry on for the barque!"

The barque had turned directly away now, heading eastward with the wind off its port quarter, the same as Ghurak's warship. With every visible ship scattering to the four winds, only the single sloop grew larger as it closed with the *Green Hammer*, the blue ensign of the Basilean Navy flying from its flagpole.

"Front guns! Load round shot!" Ghurak bellowed across the upper deck to the front of the ship.

The sloop may have presented no credible threat to him, but he might as well blast it to pieces as he passed it on the way to the real prize ahead.

"Round shot, both sides!" Ghurak added, just in case the sloop swept past.

He begrudgingly admitted that he admired the bravery of the little Basilean warship as it closed. Shoving his way through the crowded deck of the *Green Hammer*, barging past orcs and goblins, he repositioned himself on the front of the ship and raised his telescope again. They were certainly gaining on the large cargo ship, and the sloop heading straight at them was probably within a thousand yards now. But it was a small target, and he had seen now on several occasions that human gunners were both more accurate than his own crews and quicker to load their guns.

"Wait for it!" he warned his green-skinned gunners.

The pair of guns on the front of the sloop fired, a staccato crack that was barely audible from upwind. Only a second later, Ghurak heard the whizz of the cannonballs, but both splashed harmlessly off the smasher's starboard waist.

"Wait for it!" he said again.

The sloop seemed to leap and dive over the green waves as it approached, a senseless gesture in Ghurak's opinion, as there was nothing the ship could do to stop him from attacking the merchantmen. He briefly wondered what he would do if their roles were reversed, but then decided that he would never be stupid enough to be caught facing a smasher from a sloop in the first place. He peered through his telescope again to estimate the range. Less than eight hundred yards. Close enough.

"Front guns! Fire!"

A billow of black smoke washed back over the *Green Hammer* as the forward firing cannons barked in quick succession. Stomping forward through the dark clouds, Ghurak emerged into the clear air at the prow of his ship just in time to see four plumes of foaming seawater cascade down around the enemy sloop, certainly close enough to cause concern to its crew but not having inflicted any damage. Ghurak swore and turned to face his gunners.

"They'll come around one side or the other! Be ready for my command to fire!"

The sloop swung about rapidly and altered course to head south, the wind billowing in its single sail as it darted across the waves away from the lumbering orc warship. No matter. When a wolf chases down a deer, it cares not for an insolent mouse yipping away at his heels, Ghurak mused. He raised his telescope again and smiled grimly as he saw the distance between the *Green Hammer* and the bloated trading barque continue to draw closer. He looked down at his front gun crews to bellow an order to reload but found himself nodding in satisfaction as they had already taken the initiative and were swabbing out the cannons, ready for the next shot.

"Chain shot," he commanded the gun crews, "we'll take their sails!"

The turbulent seas continued to clear, the myriad of trading vessels scattering to each point of the compass. Up ahead, Ghurak saw two sets of blood red sails on the eastern horizon. His smile grew broader. His captins had positioned their ships well. The trading barque, clearly unsure whether to turn into wind and risk slowing down in the face of the advancing smasher, decided instead to continue to plough on to the east in an attempt to speed past the two waiting blood runners.

"He's coming back around again, Admrul!" Irukk shouted from the back of the ship, pointing to the south where the small sloop had repositioned off the smasher's starboard quarter and was now approaching with a beam wind. The cannons on the front of the sloop cracked out again, this time their shots tearing through the sails and rigging of Ghurak's flagship. A great rend was ripped through the largest of the sails on the rear mast, and following a brief, pathetic scream, a pair of bloodied green legs fell down to the deck with a sickening thunk, the other half of the unfortunate goblin sailor scattered to either side of the ship in a bloody mist.

Ghurak let out an angry yell. The impertinent little bastard would not give up! He stomped back to the rear of the ship, next to the wheel.

"Back guns! Load round shot! Riggers! Get up there and patch that sail up!" Ghurak boomed.

Goblins scurried around the rigging lines in response to his command as the rear gun crews quickly set about loading the aft facing cannons. His anger rising, his fists clenched in frustration at the pathetic little ship that was threatening his capture of the prize, Ghurak made a decision.

"Bring us around to the south!" he yelled. "Get the starboard guns lined up on that little bastard! Now!"

Ghurak looked across at his new first mate. Irukk, clearly having heard about the fate of subordinates who questioned the wisdom of their admrul, turned to face the goblins at the wheel.

"You heard him!" the young orc screamed. "Hard to the right!"

The deck lurched beneath Ghurak's feet as the *Green Hammer* lurched across to starboard, leaning into the turn initially and then up and away. The Basilean naval sloop responded almost immediately, turning hard to starboard to face south again. But it was not quick enough. With the momentum already gathered in its little sail, it drifted into range of Ghurak's guns as it attempted to turn and flee.

"Starboard guns," Ghurak thundered, "fire!"

With no pattern or order, each of the guns across the smasher's two gun decks fired in turn as their gun captains repeated their admrul's order. The whole ship rumbled and tremored with each shot as the black cannons jumped back against their restraining ropes, spewing out fire and dark smoke in turn. Two shots, then a third and a fourth, splashed harmlessly around the sloop in an ineffectual bracket. Then a shot struck home. And then another. The sloop seemed to lean away from the orc smasher as round shot pelted its hull, too far away for Ghurak to see what damage was being caused. Then, seemingly in slow motion, the little warship's mast teetered and fell, completely detached at the base. The mast and sail plummeted down across the back of the ship, leaving it helpless and completely at the will of the tide. Cheers erupted across the upper deck and echoed from the gun deck down below.

"Hard to port!" Ghurak shouted above the din at the wheel goblins. "Left! Come left! Point back at the barque!"

There was no time for celebration. There was certainly no time to waste in charging down and eliminating a miniscule, insignificant sloop. The prize was ahead, and Ghurak had wasted precious time in turning out of wind and allowing the barque to slip away from him. He stared through his telescope to assess the position of his two blood runners; one continued to charge straight toward the trade barque while the other had changed course and was chasing down a twin-masted ship to the south. Ghurak was content enough with that outcome; he only needed one other ship to squeeze the barque into his trap.

The blood runner ahead of the barque – now just about close enough to identify as the *Blood Skull*, under the command of the newly promoted Captin Drika – fought against the head wind to close with the bloated trading vessel as Ghurak's *Green Hammer* closed from astern again. The barque came about slightly to starboard, attempting to slip past the advancing blood runner. Drika's ship reacted quickly, turning to head it off and prevent its escape.

"Come right!" Ghurak shouted to his wheel goblins. "Come right a bit! Cut the corner and get me closer!"

As the barque's towering, corpulent rear end pointed toward the *Green Hammer*, two puffs of smoke appeared behind its rearmost mast as cannons were fired back at the smasher. One flew wild while the other shot – a lucky one, no doubt – smashed against the rusted metal prow of the hulking orc pirate ship with a loud, resounding clang.

"Front guns, fire!" Ghurak yelled.

The guns barked in response, and the familiar, pleasing stench of burnt powder wafted back across the *Green Hammer's* upper deck in billows of dark, noxious fumes. Goblins scrabbled along the centerline of the upper deck with clanking buckets of water for the guns, threading their way between jeering orc gunners and lumbering warriors, stood impatiently with their axes as they waited for a boarding action.

"Reload!" Ghurak commanded. "Front guns! Reload! Chain shot!"

The forward firing guns from Drika's new command fired with a dull crump, and Ghurak saw splints of wood blossom up from the barque's deck only a moment later. His rapidly expanding grin grew into a low, guttural cackle of delight. He had her. The barque could not escape now. Both the front and rear facing guns of the trade ship – only two of each, no doubt quickly dragged around from the waist – blasted out a paltry response to the advancing orcs, succeeding in scoring a single hit on the front of Drika's blood runner. Up forward, the four gun crews of Ghurak's forward firing cannon completed their load as they drew closer to the barque.

"Aim high! At the sails! Front guns, fire!"

The cannons blasted again, flames billowing out of their stubby muzzles as they spewed their deadly projectiles out across the foamy waves. The shots tore through the barque's rigging, blowing off half of a yard arm from the rear mast and sending its sail tearing down to the deck below. Only moments later, with the two orc vessels closed to only a couple of hundred yards ahead and astern, the barque's flag was quickly hauled down from its pole at the back of the ship.

"They've struck their colors," Ghurak sneered.

"Admrul?" Irukk queried.

Ghurak looked over at the young orc.

"They've brought their flag down," he explained with contempt. "It means they've surrendered."

Irukk stared at the trade ship is bewilderment.

"But... they've still got guns," he stammered. "They can still fight!"

"I know," Ghurak spat in disgust.

The human sailors knew they had no chance. They clearly expected mercy. They would receive none.

"Gunners, port and starboard!" Ghurak shouted, "load grapeshot! Greataxes! Assemble your warriors! Prepare for boarding!"

Ghurak glanced across the starboard waist to the south and allowed himself a brief smirk of satisfaction as he saw Kroock's blood runner catch up with the trade ship it was pursuing. The day was going well. He was about to capture two ships and their cargo in a single battle. And, he pondered as his attention was brought back to the lumbering barque ahead of him, he was also about to cut down a few dozen cowardly sailors for good measure. That would be good for the morale of his warriors. Ghurak nodded in satisfaction as he lit his pipe and then unsheathed his cutlass. The day had gone well.

***

The wind picked up as the *Martolian Queen* rounded the edge of the breakwater, exposed to the elements of the open sea. The refreshing breeze provided some relief to Caithlin as she stood awkwardly to attention on the quarterdeck of her own brig, still in sight of the Naval Administration Building and its imposing, ornate tower. Her crew of some eighty sailors lined the upper deck, the naval men resplendent in their blue uniform; the civilians-turned-privateers wearing what blue they could cobble together at short notice.

Stood rigidly along the starboard waist was her new contingent of salamander corsairs; a quartet of veteran sailors brought onboard by X'And, under the command of a salamander sailor of some repute by the name of Obtess. The vicious, scarred, pistol-wielding salamanders would no doubt make a fine addition to her crew when the shots began to fire and cutlasses clashed during boarding actions.

Caithlin was not one to stand on ceremony, but this was the first time the *Martolian Queen* had ever set sail under a Basilean flag; and in full view of the office of the admiral who had paid for her repairs, she was eager to show the requisite marks of respect. An involuntary smile broke out across her lips as the bows of her brig dug into the waves, the sails billowing out above her in a fair breeze. Only days before, she had wondered if the battered ship would ever sail again; and if it would, she saw no way it would ever be under her command. Yet here, even with the gnawing in her gut that had not left her since the severity of her debts had truly sunk in, she allowed herself the briefest moment of happiness as she took her father's ship back out to sea, repaired and seaworthy once more.

"Bosun," she ordered from her position by the ship's helm, "pipe the carry on."

The bosun raised his bosun's call to his lips and blew a two-tone blast from the metal whistle. The sailors assembled on the upper deck turned as one, some dashing up the rigging lines to return to their duties across the masts and yards; others disappearing below decks to attend to the myriad of tasks that required attention as the ship headed south away from Keretia. Satisfied that she was out of visual range of the admiral's tower, Caithlin removed her heavy greatcoat and folded it neatly over one arm. She felt immediately relieved as the sea breeze cut through the slits in the sleeves of her silk shirt; a decidedly piratical garment of billowing white with slits from shoulder to cuff to leave her arms bare in the tropical heat. She removed her hat and turned to face Jaymes, surprised to see him also doffing his heavy coat and hat.

"Just following my captain's lead, ma'am," he issued a slight smile.

"I think I can captain a ship well enough without a frock coat, Jaymes," she said, returning the smile more broadly and for longer than perhaps she should have.

She was rewarded with a warmth inside when the Basilean lieutenant returned her lingering glance and conspiratory smirk. She turned away after a few moments and saw X'And staring across from the fore end of the quarterdeck, his reptillian eyes narrowed in disapproval.

"The wind is on the port quarter, Captain," her salamander first mate reported, "ready for full sail."

"Good," Caithlin replied, "set full sail."

She turned to address her helmsman.

"I'll take her for a while."

Committing herself to the decidedly un-captainly act of taking the wheel of her own ship, Caithlin smiled broadly as she felt the response of the brig in her hands. With its new steering gear and its hull freshly scraped, the vessel felt lighter and more responsive than she ever remembered. It reminded her of those first magical days of learning to sail with her father, back home on Lake Gehr. The thought cast a dark despair over her as it reminded her of the letter she had dispatched to her father the previous day, updating him on her predicament. Telling him that she had done the unthinkable and accepted a commission as a privateer in a foreign navy. That she was going to battle against deadly pirates. She knew he would despair, that he would suffer from sleepless nights of worry, but she had to tell him the truth. There was no other way.

Caithlin watched her sailors working on the upper deck and climbing nimbly across the rigging to set the sails. The integration between her original crewmembers, the sudden and massive influx of Basilean sailors on temporary loan, and now a few new individuals attracted to the idea of working on a privateer ship had presented some interesting challenges. Her sailors were all professionals, well-trained and experienced. A good number of the Basilean naval men were still landsmen – having less than a year's experience at sea – or were barely qualified beyond that point. Yet, with that typical military arrogance, they assumed they were better at their job than their civilian counterparts, which had caused a good deal of friction.

This was not helped by her own sailors suddenly having to adjust to their living spaces being crammed with four times as many bodies. Living, eating, and sleeping onboard a ship at sea was difficult at the best of times, but now even that basic quality of life had been eroded for her sailors. Even with the touching display of loyalty her original sailors had displayed toward her in remaining on the ship in its new role, she knew that the realities would already be overriding sentimentality and a self-imposed sense of duty. Most of them would probably leave next time they came alongside at port. And then Charn Ferrus would want his own men back, and that would leave her back in serious trouble. But if there was one thing she had learned from the calamitous changes in her fortunes over the last few days, it was that there was little point in worrying about the future. One never knew what was just around the corner. Better to enjoy the moment.

"Is the plan the same?" Jaymes said quietly from her side.

"Yes, I think so," Caithlin said, her mind brought back to the present. "We'll head to the northeast of the Eleccian Isles, as we discussed. That seems to be fairly active at the moment. If we're going to find anything to flex our muscles against, there is as good a place as any."

The thought of looking for battle perhaps should have intimidated her more than it did. But, with a ship she knew better than any other under her command and eighty experienced sailors manning her guns, Caithlin felt ready for war. She looked along the deck ahead of her at the ship her father had entrusted to her. Images of the little model ships in her room at home suddenly flooded her mind as she remembered long evenings with her father patiently teaching her how to put the delicate models together. She remembered the frigate that had pride of place in the center.

"Something I've been meaning to ask you," she said as she glanced over at Jaymes.

"Yes?"

"I've heard others say that your Elohi-class frigates are special. Sacred, even. That in battle, the torch carried by the Elohi carved on the prow will glow with heavenly light."

The naval officer smiled for a moment before replying.

"I've never seen it myself, but I am still new to frigates. But yes, I have friends who have seen it. It is true. The stories would have you believe that the torch bursts with blue light with every battle we enter, but alas, it isn't so. I'm told that it is just in the big battles, when our going to war against the forces of evil is significant enough to warrant the attention of the heavens, and then the angelic Elohi descend and are with us. I would like to see it, one day."

Caithlin nodded slowly and then turned back to look ahead, the wheel of the brig seemingly lighter than ever in her hands. She thought upon his words and briefly on her own faith. She believed in the power of the Shining Ones and the forces of good above – she would be a fool not to – but she had never really relied on them. Perhaps, given the strange turn in events that had led to her now commanding a ship of war in a foreign navy, it was time to rethink that focus of faith.

"Let us hope the Elohi are with us when we need them," she said quietly, half to herself.

***

"They're here, sir."

Karnon slowly opened one eye and rolled over in his bunk.

"The orcs, sir," he now recognized the gruff voice of Sergeant Porphio Aeli. "They're here. They're in the bay."

His eyes shooting fully open as every last shred of weariness was flushed out by an instant surge of adrenaline, Karnon sat bolt upright and quickly hauled on his boots.

"How many?" he demanded. "Are the others awake?"

"One large ship at anchor in the bay," the round-faced sergeant replied as Karnon hauled on his mail hauberk. "They're sending small boats toward the beach, same way we got in. Captain Berso has been alerted and is organizing the remainder of the *Veneration* marines."

Karnon pulled his breastplate on and set about securing the buckles beneath his arms. Blinking sleep out of his eyes, he sighed in frustration as his fingers struggled with the intricacies of the new, naval-pattern 'quick release' buckles that had been designed specifically for the marines. The buckles allowed breastplates to be rapidly removed in the event of the wearer falling overboard. Karnon, like his soldiers, wondered over the wisdom of such an invention, given that the mail hauberk would happily make the wearer sink like a stone without the extra weight of the breastplate.

A few isolated rays of light blue shone through the window and into the little room at the end of the miner's hut as dawn approached. Fastening his sword belt around his waist and grabbing his helmet and shield, Karnon paused for a second as his eyes fell on the letter he had written to Sabine the night before. The simple, folded piece of paper lay on the crude, wooden stool next to his bunk. For not the first time, the severity of the immense pressure he put his wife under on a daily basis, simply by the unknown, forced itself to the front of his mind.

"Sir?" Porphio asked after a pause. "Captain Berso is waiting for us."

Karnon followed Porphio out of the mining hut and up the steep path to the north of the encampment, leading up to one of three shallow peaks that overlooked the bay. The narrow path snaked up between the dense, colorful foliage, only now transforming from a thousand shades of green and gray into an explosion of color as the rays of dawn sunlight peered over the horizon. The nocturnal rattle of night insects was replaced with the melodic, shrill calls of tropical birds from the surrounding trees and the jungle extending inland away from the sandy beach.

Karnon found Berso knelt by a copse of three palm trees on top of the stubby hill, a small map extended over his knee as he stared down across the bay. A hulking orc vessel sat in the dark, flat waters perhaps half a mile off the coast, lowering a second wave of small boats from both sides to catch up with the four boats that were already being rowed toward the beach. Two further orc vessels were just visible on the horizon, several miles off the coast.

"Time to earn our pay," Berso greeted as Karnon and Porphio jogged over to take a knee next to him. "Looks like there is a fair few of them."

Karnon accepted the older officer's telescope and used it to look down at the boats moving silently through the still waters. Each was crammed with orc warriors, clad in black armor and carrying vicious axes. There were perhaps fifty orcs packed into the boats – if the second wave was of a similar size, they would be facing a roughly equal number of warriors to what they had at the island.

"They've gone for the beach, as predicted," Karnon muttered, "and it looks like they're committing everything they have to a single attack."

"We've fought orcs before, sir," Porphio said. "Got to respect them as great fighters. But they ain't clever. I'm not surprised to see they haven't bothered with scouts or flanking units."

"I've sent a runner to wake up Vell and his men," Berso said, taking his telescope back from Karnon. "The orcs are expecting company mercenaries but not legion marines. Exactly as we discussed, Vell and his lot will let off a few shots on the beach and then fall back along the tracks we've prepared. Then we hammer them."

"*Pious* marines to take the westerly route, your lot to take east," Karnon said. "If it all goes to shit, we fall back to the rally point south of the settlement."

"Agreed," Berso glanced across at the taller marine, "let's give them a bloody nose. Send 'em out of here having learned what a Basilean marine is. I'll see you when this is done."

Karnon and Porphio rushed back down the path and off to the far side of the settlement, to the assembly point for the forty marines from *Pious's* ship's company. The drill had been practiced a dozen times already. Karnon found his men waiting in the small clearing on the far side of the ridgeline running along the top of the beach, each soldier already in armor and carrying their sword, shield, crossbow, and bolts. Sergeant Castus Erria rushed out to meet the two soldiers as they arrived, saluting Karnon as he drew alongside.

"*Pious* marines assembled as ordered, sir," Castus reported.

Karnon beckoned for his soldiers to move across to him, forming a rough semi-circle around him. He glanced across their faces – most of them were men he knew well enough from their time in the regular legion, or during their specialist training in their new role. None of them were new to warfare.

"You've no doubt already heard that the orcs are only moments away from that beach," Karnon said, his voice low as he gestured to the water's edge just out of sight on the far side of the low ridge behind them. "There's no way they're expecting us. You've all faced orcs before. You know that they hit hard, harder than we can. They're tough, tougher to drop than we are. But they're not clever. As long as we keep them confused, in the dark, and unsure what is going on, we have the initiative. The moment it opens up into a straight fight, we lose. Stick to the plan, but be ready to improvise. Split into your units. Let's go welcome them ashore."

Chapter Fourteen

Ghurak was the first to jump off the lead boat, his legs plunging into knee-deep water and his feet sinking slightly into soft sand. His first wave of warriors began to disembark from the rowing boats and wade toward the shore; his blooded, veteran greataxes doing so in disciplined silence while his younger, more eager axes grunted and nattered idly as they made their way to the beach ahead. He shook his head in disgust at their amateur approach to the landing; the gold mine would have a guard force of some sort, and while Ghurak relished a straight, bloody fight as much as the next orc, he also knew the value of not alerting an enemy to his presence until the last possible moment. However, shouting at his young, enthusiastic idiots to keep their voices down would be even worse.

The fifty orcs of the first wave made their way up onto the beach; a site not too dissimilar to the human colony he had successfully attacked only days before. That came as little surprise – a beach on a jungle-covered island was bound to be near enough the same as the next. But this one was denser, with steeper contours leading up the surrounding peaks of the bay, with the wooden huts of the miner's encampment far more hidden from view from the bay itself. Ghurak grunted. They would have a sentry posted, no doubt. And that sentry would have seen them come in – he certainly would have heard the tactically inept numbskulls of the axe units from near enough a mile off in the silence of dawn. He expected a response from the mine's guard force, and soon.

Ghurak paused as his orcs quickly formed up into their units on the beach. Caws, whistles, and shrill, annoying songs of tropical birds echoed from the dense jungle folding around the bay. The first thin line of yellow appeared over the horizon behind where the *Green Hammer* lay at anchor, silhouetting the second wave of his orc warriors in their small boats. Something did not feel right.

"Hrolk! Agash!" he called across to two of his leaders. "Get your warriors up on either side of the beach!"

Somehow it came as a comfort to Ghurak when a salvo of crossbow bolts suddenly whistled out of the tree line at the top of the beach, slicing through one of his axe units and felling an orc warrior.

"Up the beach!" Ghurak bellowed. "Go!"

Some twenty orcs rushed up either side of the beach toward the narrow paths leading along the edges of foliage – both groups of orcs made up of a mixture of axes and the veteran greataxes. Left with

174

a group of ten warriors in the center, Ghurak held his cutlass aloft and let out a long, guttural yell as he dragged his own heavy feet up and across the soft, slippery sand.

Emerging over the plant-covered ridgeline ahead, Ghurak saw a group of human warriors, at least twice the size of his own unit, form a shooting line with crossbows. Quickening his pace, he charged head-long toward them.

***

Crouched at the edge of the footpath leading down to the beach, Karnon watched as the opening stages of the battle unfolded before him. The orcs of the first wave were already off their boats with the second wave halfway across the bay. Two groups were moving up either side of the beach – one toward his own marines, and the other toward Berso's – while an enormous orc in a hat and red greatcoat led a charge up the center toward where Captain Vell's mercenaries were loading their crossbows for a second shot.

Karnon grimaced. The orc in the greatcoat and hat was truly gargantuan – he recognized a krudger when he saw one. Given the enormous orc's almost comedic wig of gray, gentleman's curls and his ornate cutlass, he would not be surprised if he was the captain of the large vessel at anchor in the bay. Even outnumbering the central group two-to-one, Karnon would not have been facing a krudger in open battle like that. He only hoped that Vell had the common sense to fall back. But there was no time for that now; a group of twenty orcs was heading rapidly toward the path leading to where his marines lay in wait.

Rushing back through the dense foliage, the rustling of leaves seeming to be deafening when stealth was key, Karnon returned to his soldiers. Sergeants Erria and Aeli were both in command of a unit of twenty marines, one hidden on either side of the path leading up to the mines, lurking in the cover of the dark greenery extending up the steep, surrounding slopes.

"Enemies, incoming!" Karnon called out. "Strength twenty! Wait for my order to shoot!"

He darted across to crouch down amid the thick, dew-covered leaves surrounding Castus Erria's marines to the left of the path. Finding his shield where he had left it, he quickly secured it to his arm and unsheathed his broad-bladed sword. Only moments later, the first few orcs appeared above the lip of the ridgeline, charging along the path toward the wooden huts at the edge of the mining settlement. Packed together in two lines, constrained by the narrow path, the orcs thundered up toward the gold mine. His heart thumping in anticipation of the oncoming fight, Karnon watched them in silence. He needed to time the order well; his two units were positioned properly and aiming slightly downhill from the slopes, but if he mistimed his order, there was a chance he would command his marines to shoot across the path perilously close to each other.

The first few orcs ran past him, close enough to touch, the stench of their sweat and the grime across their rugged armor overpowering even the strong smells of the jungle trees and plants. Karnon waited for just a few more moments until the last orc had passed him.

"Shoot!" he yelled.

The jungle to either side of the path came alive with the metallic clicking of triggers and the twanging of crossbow strings. Leaves flew up in the air as dozens of crossbow bolts sliced through branches and down into the closely packed group of orcs. Assailed on both sides by twenty deadly-accurate crossbowmen, the orcs were bloodily cut down where they stood. Bolts flew into their flanks, cutting through armor to plunge into their torso and limbs, or spattering blood on their comrades as metal bolt heads plunged through skulls.

The grunting cries issued by the dying orcs were more of shock and alarm rather than pain. Perhaps half of the group crumpled to the ground, but some ten remained standing, most with bolts emerging from wounds that would have killed a man, but it left the orcs merely looking around in confusion and awe for a clue as to the location of their assailants.

"Marines!" Karnon shouted as he leapt to his feet. "Attack! Attack!"

Charging through the foliage, Karnon emerged at the edge of the path at the head of his soldiers. With a fearless instinct for combat that nature did not grant to humans, the orcs turned in place and leapt out to meet their attackers. The first orc, a towering mass of green muscle armed with a heavy, double-handed axe, spat out an insult and swung his weapon toward Karnon's head. He ducked beneath, brought up his shield to deflect a rapid second attack, and then hacked down with his own blade into the side of the orc's neck to half-sever the creature's head. With dark blood gushing from the terrible wound, the ferocious creature somehow managed to attempt a third attack against Karnon before he plunged the tip of his sword through the orc's chest to kill him.

The fight ended that quickly. With forty marines descending on a quarter of their number, even the mighty orcs were cut down in mere moments. Karnon wiped sweat from his eyes, his breathing labored in his heavy armor in the hot, humid environment. His soldiers quickly and efficiently checked the fallen orcs, slitting the throats of any who showed even a glint of a sign of life. Karnon looked back along the path. The plan had called for Vell and his mercenaries to fall back to take cover at the settlement while Karnon's marines delayed the attack. There was no sign of Vell.

"Reload, quickly!" Karnon ordered his men. "We need to relocate to that ridge!"

***

The impact of the crossbow bolt slowed Ghurak down for a pace, throwing back his hip and sending a brief flare of pain along his leg. He looked down and saw the bolt protruding from a bloody hole in his thigh. Swearing, he attempted to quicken his pace to keep up with his stampeding warriors but found himself limping as his leg refused to respond correctly, despite the pain being not even close to unmanageable. The ragged line of human soldiers at the top of the beach had discarded their crossbows and were now unsheathing swords and axes, ready for the clash of Ghurak's approaching orcs.

Willing his leg into obedience, Ghurak charged up the shallow incline of the beach. He looked up and saw the human soldiers rushing down toward him, twice their number and led by a tall, broad man with a near shaven head and a double-handed sword. Forcing more haste out of his injured leg, Ghurak barged his way past the front line of axe warriors and held his cutlass up to attack.

The two forces met with a clash of blades and the dull thunk of weapons biting into flesh as the first casualties were inflicted on both sides. Ghurak met the leader of the enemy unit head on, swinging his curved cutlass around in an attempt to decapitate the man with his first strike. The human soldier held his own longer blade up to block the attack, but the sheer force of Ghurak's assault knocked it back, staggering the wielder. Regardless, the shaven-headed soldier stepped in and smashed a clenched fist into Ghurak's jaw. He almost laughed, a combination of admiration at the audacity of the assault and its ineffectiveness, and raised his sword again.

Out of the corner of his eye, Ghurak quickly saw one of his orcs being forced back by a skillful human soldier wielding a battle-axe; Ghurak swept his own blade across to lop off one of the human's arms before continuing down to clash against the veteran human's double-handed sword again. Shouting in anger and glee, Ghurak brought his arm tirelessly down again and again, part of him admiring his opponent's skill in blocking every attack and even managing the odd, rare counterattack of his own, but an equal part frustrated by the warrior's refusal to die.

A heavy blow from Ghurak forced the man back a pace, giving the orc pirate an opening and a brief second to assess the battle raging around him. He leaned over to effortlessly cut down another human warrior stood next in line in a shower of crimson blood. With a cry of rage, the veteran human swordsman leapt forward at Ghurak, swinging his heavy blade around. Ghurak batted the attack to one side with a clenched fist and thrust his cutlass straight through the center of the man's body, roughly where he figured a human's heart might be. The swordsman's life ended with the briefest look of utter surprise. He was dead before he even crumpled down into the bloody sand below. With an ecstatic battle cry, Ghurak limped forward to find another man to kill.

***

Karnon saw Berso and his marines arriving on the ridgeline only moments before him. The soldiers quickly spread out to crouch at the edge of the undergrowth cresting the ridge, each man rapidly preparing his own crossbow.

"*Pious* marines! Shooting line! On the left!" Karnon ordered, gesturing to the left of Berso's men with the outstretched fingers of one hand before rushing over to crouch next to his fellow captain.

"D'you get them?" he asked as he arrived.

"Yeah," Berso nodded wearily, blood dripping from an open wound across his upper arm, "they're dead."

Karnon looked down at the beach to see the final rounds of the battle between Captain Vell's mercenaries and the orcs led by the red-coated krudger. Only half a dozen of the mercenaries were left alive; a mere trio of orcs faced them in the center of the pile of dead bodies from both sides at the top of the sandy incline. One of those orcs was the krudger, his booming yells echoing up from the beach below as he swung a cutlass around to brutally hack down one of the human soldiers in a series of anger-fueled, ferocious blows. Karnon quickly considered giving the order to his men to shoot, but he realized they would only succeed in hitting their allies in the back. Charging down to help would also sacrifice the commanding position they held at the ridge; a situation they would soon need, given that the second wave of orc boats was already disgorging its brutish passengers.

There was nothing that could be done for the last of the mercenaries. Even faced with five armed men, the krudger fought on with a rage like a demon of the Abyss. He cut down a soldier before running through a second, leaving the last few to be torn apart by his surviving two orcs.

"Get ready to shoot!" Karnon called across to his marines as they rushed up to take position on the ridge. "On my command, you drop that big bastard in the center!"

The next wave of orc attackers formed up at the water's edge with surprising discipline. Karnon noticed anxiously that this wave was even larger than the first. The final mercenaries fell down dead, leaving the blood-soaked krudger and his final two veteran warriors atop a mound of corpses. Karnon and Berso shouted an order as one.

"Shoot!"

***

Hissed breaths escaping through gritted teeth, Ghurak looked down at the bodies of the fallen by his feet. The rising sun cast long shadows from the surviving trio of orcs over their fallen foes as, behind them, the boats carrying the next wave of orc attackers were rowed up to touch the beach. Ghurak heard the commanding shouts of Irukk and Shargol from behind as the two orcs took charge of the next wave. Then he heard the order shouted out from the undergrowth on the ridge above him.

A veritable rain of crossbow bolts shot down, thick enough in volume to seemingly combat the light provided by the morning sun. All along the ridgeline, dozens of projectiles were hurled at the three orcs as crossbows clicked and twanged from hidden positions in the foliage. Ghurak felt bolts strike him in both legs, his gut, chest, and neck. His legs buckled beneath him, the embarrassment of stumbling far outweighing any physical pain that manifested itself in his mind. The world lurched over and up to meet him as he crumpled to one side, falling face down into the bloody sand.

His breath escaping in wheezes, Ghurak dragged his head over to one side and saw Vurul, one of the two orcs that moments before was stood by his side, now lying face up and motionless with a crossbow bolt protruding from his forehead. His exhalations issuing in unhealthy crackles, Ghurak tried to move his legs. Neither responded. He tried his arms and felt a renewed vigor to return to the fight as he realized that his left hand was acting to his commands. He slowly brought his hand to his gut and, finding bolts protruding from his own body, grabbed them one by one and yanked them out.

He reached down to his legs and found more offending projectiles. His shaking hand continued to grasp onto each, pulling it free with a spurt of blood. With one of the projectiles removed from his knee, he found his left leg now bent at his will. He was nearly back in the fight. Bleeding from a dozen wounds, Ghurak pressed one hand against the ground and twisted around to plant his one responsive knee into the sand and slowly force himself up off the ground. Immediately, his vision blurred and a sickening nausea clutched at his head and throat. He tried to breathe in deeply, but he found only one side of his chest seemed to heave in and out. The other hurt, hurt like an ogre's headbutt, and succeeded only in bleeding from where a bolt had punctured straight through his ribcage. He could not breathe. All of the aggression and willpower in the world failed to stop him collapsing back down into the sand, amid the carpet of dead orcs and humans.

So this was death. It did not hurt, not physically. No more than any normal battlefield injury, at least. It was the mental anguish. The frustration. The humiliation of being defeated, and defeated by cowards at range, to make it even worse. Ghurak stared up at the clear sky above, blood trickling up through his dry, aching throat and out of both sides of his mouth. It should not have ended like this. He had more to achieve.

Then, from nowhere, a powerful hand grabbed him by his upper arm, and he was dragged slowly up to his feet. Another hand grabbed one of his shattered legs, and the world span again as he was hauled up onto the broad shoulders of an orc warrior. Crossbow bolts again spat down from the ridge above, at least one slamming into Ghurak's back, and another thudding into his orc savior's shoulder, but the warrior shrugged the impact off and sprinted back toward the water's edge and the waiting boats. Ghurak opened his mouth to yell at the idiotic orc, to scream from the bottom of his one working lung that Ghurak's warriors did not run from a fight, and that they needed to turn back around and get up to the top of the beach.

Then he realized that the two groups of orcs he had sent up toward the gold mine had not come back. But human soldiers had. His warriors were all dead. The entire first wave, gone, with Ghurak as the sole survivor. He had lost over sixty orcs. They had been massacred. Whether he alone was being saved, whether the second wave would carry on up the beach or would run away back to their boats, he did not know. He did not even know which course of action he would have ordered. The whole dim and ill-focused world around him darkened to nothing as consciousness slipped away.

***

The fresh winds of the past two days had given way to a void, a near absence of airflow that could barely be called a breeze. That being said, the horizon to the southwest was dominated with towering clouds of billowing white that reached up toward the heavens, a sure sign that far, far more active weather was on its way. But for now, there was a calm, and the midday heat was stifling as a result. Charn felt it most as he clambered up the narrow path that threaded between the palm trees, sweat soaking his entire body beneath his heavy coat and tricorn hat. The birds singing in the trees seemed to mock him with their chirpy optimism, as if their songs told the story of the Basilean frigate captain who continually failed to find the pirates he had been charged with eliminating.

Charn and Walt Ganto followed their two marine escorts up to the miner's accommodation huts, Charn bringing one hand up to touch his hat to return the salutes of the quartet of marines who stood waiting at the top of the path. A few rows of crude but sturdy wooden benches were arranged in uneven lines in a patch of open ground behind the long huts that served as accommodation for the miners. It was at the end of one of these benches that Charn saw Karnon Senne perched, a roll of paper spread out over his lap as he scratched away with a quill and ink. Swatting irritably at a large, fat insect that momentarily landed on the back of his neck, Charn quickened his pace and made a direct line toward his marine captain. As he rounded the corner of the last building, his uninterrupted view of the waters below showed just how obvious it was that three frigates sat an anchor in the bay. Charn expected more formality from his marine officer; there was no excuse for not realizing his captain had arrived.

Then Charn saw the rows of graves. Three neat rows, each of perhaps ten freshly covered mounds of earth, each headed with a temporary marker. The improvised graveyard was a few dozen yards away, by the front of a tiny stone chapel. Karnon looked up as Charn and Walt approached.

"You just missed them, sir," the marine said as he blew on the ink of the sheet of paper before carefully rolling it up. "They were here yesterday morning."

Charn looked down at the burly soldier. His eyes were dull and tired, his face unshaven.

"How many men did you lose?" Charn asked.

"Twenty-nine."

"I'm... sorry," Charn managed.

"Four from the ship's company of the *Veneration*. None of our own from *Pious*," Karnon added.

"And the other twenty-five?"

"Men hired by the mining company," Karnon said as he stood up, "their entire defensive force."

"So... only mercenaries, then," Charn shrugged nonchalantly.

Karnon's eyes darkened. For the briefest moment, Charn thought the young soldier might actually strike him.

"Ex-legion," he said, his tone aggressive, "and once legion, always legion. They're buried with our four marines. We made no distinction."

"I'm sorry we can't take them back with us for a proper burial," Charn offered.

Karnon paused for a moment before answering.

"This is still Basilean soil. They're buried by a chapel, on consecrated ground, in marked graves. That's better than the vast majority of legion soldiers could ever hope for."

Charn looked over pensively at the small graveyard. A handful of other graves circled the chapel, no doubt the tragic result of unfortunate mining accidents.

"And the orcs?" he then asked, finally cutting to the question he really cared about.

Karnon turned to look out across the bay.

"Sixty-three dead. There's a cliff not far from here. We dumped them there. They're shark food now. They deserve no better. We got them all on the beach and the paths, we never even needed to fall back to the defenses we had prepared. We saw their captain, too. Huge one. We shot him I don't know how many times. The tough old bastard survived it. He was still breathing when they carried him off. Whether he is still alive or not now, I don't know. I kept his sword for you."

Charn swore as he swatted away at another of the relentless, thumb-sized insects that insisted upon settling down on the back of his neck. A day late. He was that close. Yes, Karnon and the soldiers from the two ships had done a good job of defending the mine and inflicting significant casualties on the enemy; but now they needed to go back to Keretia to avoid the bad weather approaching from the southwest, and it was another chance lost. A wasted expedition save their brief success in intercepting the slaver ship several days before.

"Keep the sword," Charn said. "I've never been one for sentimentality. Tell your soldiers they did a good job. Then get them back onboard."

"We should leave somebody here, sir," Karnon said. "If those orcs come back, there is nobody left to defend this site."

Charn paused for a moment to contemplate the suggestion.

"A detachment of marines from the *Veneration* should do. Twenty men. We can't spare any more than that, not now. I'm going back onboard; the boats will be here for you and your men in half an hour. That should give you enough time to pack up."

Charn nodded to his second lieutenant to follow him. He had only taken a few steps back toward the beach, with Walt in tow, when he stopped again. Orcs were a remarkable breed of creature in a terrible sort of way, and he knew well just how frustratingly difficult they were to kill. Even with the Basilean legion representing the very best of all human foot soldiers, and with the marines in turn representing the best within that esteemed organization, humans did not routinely kill orcs at a rate of over two to one. It was all but unheard of. He turned back to face Karnon.

"Good job, Captain Senne," he said genuinely. "There'll be extra tots of rum for your men once they're back onboard."

"Aye, sir," Karnon replied wearily, managing to muster a slight smile, "I'll let them know."

***

The cabin lurched, pitching and rolling simultaneously to combine into a gut-churning, corkscrewing motion. His eyes opening to allow in a blur of light, Ghurak took in a slow, painful breath. He had been neither asleep nor properly awake for hours now, sitting uncomfortably in that useless limbo between the two. He opened his eyes a little more, but only a thin trickle of light illuminated the wooden planks above his head.

"He's waking up!" a high-pitched voice called. "Go and get the first mate!"

A groan escaping his dry lips, Ghurak slowly sat up. Even with his vision blurred, he recognized that he lay in his cot bed in the familiar cabin at the rear of the *Green Hammer*. The lamp suspended from the ceiling above him swung erratically, confirming his suspicions that it was not just his injuries that were making the world appear to churn around him; the ship was caught in a storm.

Four goblins stood at the end of the bed, staring at him in silence as they shifted and twisted to maintain their balance on the rocking deck. He recognized one of them as Ratchit. The second was Blaster; an encouragingly violent goblin who somehow managed to handle a full-sized cutlass in combat. The other two were generic, a pair of faces indistinctly lost within hundreds onboard, having never achieved anything noteworthy enough to warrant him learning their names.

Ghurak looked down at his body as his vision intermittently swam into focus. Puckered lips irregularly punctuated his skin, where wounds had been held shut and then crudely stitched back together.

"I sewed you up, Admrul," Ratchit reported eagerly, "just like a torn sail. Good as new."

Ghurak knew little about the intricacies of proper medical care, but he had been wounded so many times in his decades of war-mongering that he *did* know the orc body was quick to heal. Whereas humans, elves, and the like would need time for muscles to re-knit and fractured bones to strengthen, the process was far more simple for an orc. An orc ignored the pain and carried on, as long as they had stopped bleeding. And by the looks of his new set of scars, Ratchit had indeed stopped him bleeding.

"Get me some clothes," Ghurak ordered the goblin.

The simple act of pulling on a pair of black trousers took several minutes. As Ghurak was now discovering, stopping bleeding and ignoring the pain was one thing; but if breathing was still difficult and limbs did not work the way he expected them to, he perhaps needed to pause for a few moments' thought before committing himself back to battle. His thoughts were interrupted as Irukk appeared at the door to his cabin.

"You sent for me, Admrul," the burly young orc reported.

Ignoring another bout of dizziness and nausea, Ghurak looked up at the younger orc as he struggled to slowly feed his arms into his jerkin.

"The beach," Ghurak slurred slowly, "what happened?"

"We arrived and saw that our first wave was dead, Admrul," Irukk said solemnly. "All dead, except for you. So I came and got you, and we left."

"Why didn't you carry on with the attack?" Ghurak stared at Irukk as he slowly raised himself to his feet, stumbling as the deck continued to pitch and roll beneath him.

"The first wave was all dead," Irukk repeated, "and we saw how many shooters hit you and the others. There were dozens of them hidden on that ridge. If we charged, we would have been killed, too."

"All of you?"

"Maybe, Admrul. Dunno. But I made a decision."

The deck rolled suddenly as the *Green Hammer* continued to wrestle with the towering waves, and Ghurak collapsed back down to sit on his bed, one shaking arm reaching out to press a hand against the wooden bulkhead for balance. A goblin rushed over to his side to provide assistance – Ghurak reached out with his other hand in an attempt to grab the patronizing creature by the throat, but with the combination of the nausea and his blurred vision, he mistimed and the creature escaped his grasp.

"So it was you that dragged me away?" Ghurak asked Irukk.

"Yes, Admrul."

"Stupid thing to do, wasn't it?" Ghurak hissed. "You're the first mate. If I died, this ship would be yours. You'd be captin of a smasher."

Irukk paused. He looked down at his feet, his tongue picking idly at the root of one of his yellowed fangs.

"Drika said it's not our way," he finally replied. "He told us that orcs fight, and that we stand shoulder to shoulder in a fight. But… we're not just orcs, now. We're a crew. We fight against enemies, the sea, the wind, all of it. We don't stab each other in the back. We're a crew and we stand together. So I came and got you."

Ghurak let out a choked laugh and slowly shook his head. Drika had always thought too much. He could fight, sure, but there was something decidedly un-orcish in the way he made decisions. He placed value in concepts that should be alien to any proper orc. Yes, if Ghurak had seen Drika fall, he would have saved him. But Drika was a slave with Ghurak, one of the original crowd, they had history. Irukk was new. There was no loyalty. He had an opportunity to advance, and he threw it away for some soft concept that he would have expected from a foolish human or dwarf.

"You made a mess of it, Irukk," Ghurak scowled. "You should have left me. And you should have attacked. You could have sent a runner back to the ship and brought the guns around to blow the hell out of that ridge. You could have gone straight up that beach, lost half your warriors, but won with the other half. There were ways to take that mine, and you didn't try any of them. You're lucky I'm battered to hell, because if I wasn't, I'd be beating you to death with my bare hands right now. But I can't, so I'll let it go. But you're not fit to be first mate of this ship. Go find Shargol. Tell him he's first mate now."

Irukk looked down at Ghurak, his jaw set angrily and his eyes narrowed. He wordlessly turned to leave. Then he stopped, shut the door, and turned back to face Ghurak again.

"You want to see more bloody mindedness from me, Admrul," he said, "I get that. Thing is, you're here in pieces in front of me. So how's about I just beat you to death now, when you're all helpless, and then walk out of this room as a captin?"

Ratchit and his three goblin comrades exchanged nervous glances as they witnessed the threatening exchange between the two hulking orcs. Ghurak looked up at Irukk. He was not the most experienced fighter, but he was big, and a natural in battle. There was something about him, something that combined ferocity, fearlessness, and a natural instinct for war. Irukk might make it to krudger one day. And right at that moment, Ghurak knew his broken body would be powerless to stop Irukk if he decided to follow through on his threat.

Ghurak let out a low, choked laugh.

"Alright, Irukk," he nodded. "Alright. I like that. I like that instinct better. That's how an orc thinks. You're still first mate."

Irukk folded his arms. Ghurak watched him, stone-faced, realizing that he was currently closer to death than he had been when he was shot down on the beach by the line of crossbows. Irukk nodded.

"Thought so, Admrul," he sneered. "I'll get back to work."

Ghurak watched him leave, relieved that he was not going to die in bed, strangled to death without a weapon in his hand. But he was also aware that he had planted some seeds of thought in Irukk's head. He may have just made a dangerous enemy out of a tough, reliable subordinate. He would have to watch Irukk closely.

Chapter Fifteen

The admiral looked up from behind his gleaming wooden desk but did not invite Charn to take a seat. That spoke volumes. The office's east facing window allowed in the region's normal abundance of sunlight but conveniently did not allow a clear view to the south where the horizon continued to be dominated by the towering clouds that heralded the arrival of a hurricane. The path taken by the severe weather did, at least, keep it clear of Keretia, but Charn understood these waters well enough to know that hurricanes had a nasty habit of changing direction. Until it dissipated, nobody was safe.

"You appear," Jerris said as he finished scribbling his final comments on the document sat before him on the desk, "to have sent a ship ahead of you. A barque."

"That's right, sir," Charn said. "We intercepted the ship while it was making a run for Mos-Luxa, with a hold full of slaves taken from the Genezan Colony at Baudethra. We boarded her and took the ship."

The admiral smiled grimly. The reaction was quite the opposite to what Charn was expecting and certainly a good deal different to the jovial senior officer who had sent him on his way several days before. Charn swallowed uneasily.

"Yes," the admiral said, "your man... Lieutenant Innes. He came to report to me as soon as he brought that ship alongside here. Minus the freed slaves."

Charn's eyes widened.

"He did what?"

"Well," Jerris leaned back in his chair and interlaced his fingers across his belly, "rather than bringing the freed slaves back here to be correctly accounted for, given medical treatment, and then carefully reintegrated to their homes while informing the Genezan authorities, Kaeso Innes thought it better to just sail around to their island and drop them off home on his way past. You know, a sort of Basilean Naval door-to-door service."

Charn's head hung in despair as he closed his eyes. He let out a long breath. Rather than follow correct process, the Basilean Admiralty would be left having to explain to the Duma why they could not account for the names, numbers, and state of health of the Genezan citizens they had freed. An idiotic decision made by an overzealous junior officer would now cause embarrassment at a national level. Charn was beginning to see why he had not been invited to sit down.

"I've half a mind to confiscate the prize money from you and your crew for the sale of that barque you captured, and donate it to the colony at Baudethra," Jerris winced irritably, "but I can't do that, because if I take prize money from your crew, half of them will sod off and desert! But here's the thing. That's embarrassing for us, but ultimately rather inconsequential."

The admiral's annoyance escalated rapidly into a full-blown rage as he leaned forward to slam a hand against his desk.

"What is of consequence is that I entrusted one of my best captains with a squadron of three frigates to hunt down a pirate! That squadron is now back alongside, having not found said pirate, but instead completely missed the fact that the pirate's ships have sunken another Basilean warship and captured no fewer than three merchant vessels! Three! In the time you've been out there, those bastards have sunk one of our sloops and taken three ships from the lanes we are charged with defending!"

Charn's jaw dropped open in horror. The last time he had fallen so far short of the mark expected of him was when he crashed a frigate into a brig during a replenishment at sea exercise.

"So, tell me," the admiral continued, "while the orc pirates – who now reputedly have a second blood runner in their little fleet – were sinking one of our ships, capturing two in a single engagement, and a third on their way home, what exactly were you doing?"

Charn inhaled and took a moment to compose himself. While his exemplary record meant that he was not accustomed to reprimands from his seniors, he was not a complete stranger to it and so knew better than to blurt out the first answer that leapt to mind.

"Sir," Charn explained, "before our successful engagement and capture of the slaver barque, I landed a force of eighty marines at the gold mine at Kios, in accordance with my written orders. Our..."

"And was the gold mine attacked?" Jerris smiled sardonically.

"Yes, sir. It was."

The smile instantly faded from the admiral's wrinkled face.

"By whom?"

"The orcs, sir?"

"Was it successfully defended?"

"Yes, sir," Charn replied, "no damage to the installation. No casualties to the work force."

"How many marines did you lose?" the admiral asked.

"Four, sir, in addition to twenty-five soldiers contracted by the Capital Mining Company."

"Enemy loses?"

Charn managed to suppress a bitter smile as he reported Karnon Senne's outstanding victory.

"Just shy of seventy. Sir."

Jerris leaned forward over his desk, his elbows planted on the smooth wood and his fingertips pressed together in front of his thin face.

"I'm less angry now, Charn," he admitted. "I'm less angry. Good. That's gone rather well. Seventy dead orcs will hit them hard. You know as well as I do that their crews are enormous, but much of it is made up of the little runty ones rather than proper, fighting orcs. They'll be reeling from that."

"Yes, sir," Charn agreed coolly.

Jerris stood up, walked across to a cabinet in the corner of the room and produced one of his decanters of rum. Charn noted that Jerris only fetched a single crystal glass. Clearly he was not out of trouble yet.

"You've stopped a slave ship from reaching Mos-Luxa and saved a good number of innocent people," Jerris said as he poured out his glass of rum, "and you've protected one of our most profitable assets in the region, as well as inflicting significant casualties on our enemy for very little loss. That's all good. But measured up against that, we've lost four ships on your watch. Put those together, and neither side is clearly winning this battle."

Charn remained silent. The admiral emptied half of his glass down his throat, took a step away from the cabinet, thought better of it, and returned to top up his glass again.

"We're neck-a-neck," Jerris continued, "and that won't do. I don't send officers out to captain frigates based on their mediocrity. I employ winners, Charn. Victors. Men who come back having wiped the floor with the enemy, not exchanged a few blows and come out of it about even."

The words stung. Charn knew the admiral was right. There were plenty of officers who could captain a frigate to a decent standard and produce some minor successes. But being appointed to command a ship of war was based upon standing out from one's peers. From being exceptional. Charn had previously proven himself to be exceptional, but he was now falling short of the mark.

"When this storm passes, you get back out there. You get those three frigates out and you find that pirate fleet. You find them, and you send every last one of them to the bottom of the sea. No matter what. Understood?"

"Understood, sir."

Jerris looked out of the window at the masts of the three frigates, neatly lined up alongside the jetty on the far side of the sun-drenched naval yard, the three masts of the *Pious* standing out against the two masts of the older Batch One frigates.

"You've never let me down before," Jerris said, without looking over, "but you have to understand, Charn, that there is no quarter given for a captain who fails to achieve his duty. If you do not prove you are up to the job, there will be ramifications."

Charn swallowed again. He knew exactly what that meant. His rank was secure enough, but his command certainly was not. The *Pious* could be taken from him and given to another of the many captains waiting in the wings for an opportunity to command a frigate. That would leave Charn as a bitter, failed captain left to see out his days in some awful administrative position at the Admiralty; doomed to reminisce about the glory days of when he once commanded one of the Hegemon's frigates. The thought was unbearable.

"We'll get them, sir," Charn said quietly, careful to keep his tone serious and even. "As soon as this hurricane has passed through, the four of us will be back out."

Jerris glanced across at him.

"Four?"

"Yes, sir. *Pious*, *Vigil*, *Veneration* and the *Martolian Queen*."

Jerris raised his brow as he finished his glass of rum.

"Let's see if she survives this first," he said, nodding toward the horrific weather building to the south.

"Sir?" Charn asked.

"The *Martolian Queen*," Jerris replied. "Captain Viconti took her out days ago. They haven't come back yet."

***

The bows of the *Martolian Queen* fell down into the trough of the wave, impacting the dark blue water with a resounding thud as foam was fountained to either side and up over the fo'c'sle. The ship's bowsprit almost immediately charged up into the next wave, pointing toward the rain and dark clouds above, seeming to hang in space for a second before falling down the next wave with another thud that resonated across the entire ship.

Soaked to the very skin, her silk shirt plastered to her, Caithlin stood by the helmsman on the quarterdeck, her feet spread for balance as the brig continued to pitch up and down with every colossal wave she met. The eye of the storm was visible to the south, flickers of lightning sporadically illuminating the black clouds that corkscrewed up toward the heavens. She looked up at the top men clinging to the masts and yards above her, each sailor precariously balanced at their position dozens of feet above the deck and the churning seas, pitching forward and backward in space as the motions of the ship were exaggerated tenfold higher up.

Behind her, audible even over the howling wind and driving rain, the guns of the pursuing ship spoke for the first time. Caithlin looked over her shoulder and saw twin plumes of seawater shoot up in the brig's wake, not close enough yet to cause concern. The pursuing brigantine was drawing closer; a smaller, faster vessel than the *Martolian Queen*. Through her telescope, Caithlin could see the brigantine's colors now – a long, black flag depicting a red demon stabbing a heart. Captain 'Red' Gallo. A wanted man, one of the more notorious pirates known to sail with the infamous Cerri Denayo. It was not the orcs they were hunting, but it was good enough.

"If we turn to port, we have the weather gauge!" X'And shouted over the din of the wind. "We can give her a couple of broadsides before she can react!"

"No!" Caithlin yelled. "They still think we're a merchantman! I want them in closer! I want them to board!"

The salamander's serpentine eyes bulged in surprise.

"You want to do *what*?!" he exclaimed.

"I want them in closer!" Caithlin repeated. "Gun for gun, we're fairly matched! If we can board, I've got eighty armed sailors that he isn't expecting!"

"And he'll have over a hundred!" X'And shouted. "A hundred cutthroat bastards who aren't afraid to fight!"

"A hundred cowards and bullies who are expecting an easy target!" Caithlin corrected as she paced forward to the upper deck. Three sailors manned each of the eighteen guns – over half of Caithlin's crew, hunkered down in vain attempts to shield themselves from the weather. The rest were up top, clinging to the yards high above.

"Listen in!" Caithlin yelled above the whipping wind. "I'm bringing them in closer! I'm going to strike our colors and let them board us!"

A tirade of shouts and curses exploded from the enraged sailors, both the civilians and the naval ratings, until Caithlin held up both hands to silence them.

"Quiet!" she demanded. "Be quiet and listen! I want grapeshot loaded, port and starboard! Either side they approach us from, we'll be ready! I want five guns hidden on both sides! We need to look like a merchantman, not a privateer! Go down below; get sailcloth, anything you can find! As soon as those guns are loaded and ready, get half of them hidden from view!"

Anger was almost instantly replaced by eager anticipation as Caithlin's plan was revealed to her crew. Sailors quickly set about loading the cannons with deadly grapeshot while others disappeared below deck to find the necessary items to hide away half of the ship's guns. Caithlin turned to look across at X'And. The salamander nearly smiled as he flung out a clawed hand to grab hold of the mainmast for support as the deck heaved in the mountainous waves beneath them.

"We didn't make that orc pirate run aground by fighting fair," Caithlin beamed, peeling her soaked hair off the side of her face. "And I certainly do not intend to fight fair now."

"Aye, Captain," X'And grinned.

The pirate brigantine fired its bow chasers again, this time resulting in the unmistakable whine of round shot narrowly missing the *Martolian Queen* as a shot was flung by on either side. Caithlin looked up to the sailors clinging to the yards on the mainmast.

"Tear the sails!" she hollered up to them. "Cut them!"

"Captain?!" a naval petty officer shouted back down in bewilderment.

"Tear the sails!" Caithlin yelled. "Make it look like we've been damaged!"

Three of the sailors quickly drew their knives and set about cutting up the mainsail and the main topsail above it. Caithlin smiled grimly at the proficiency of their work; a long length of sail cloth fell down to the deck, splitting the mainsail neatly in two and leaving it flapping ineffectually in the wind. Almost immediately she felt the speed ebbing away from her brig. She turned and saw Jaymes waiting behind her.

"Strike the colors!" she called back to him.

The young lieutenant looked back at her with anguish in his eyes.

"I appreciate your plan, Captain," he replied, "but if it is all the same, even as a ruse, I would rather not lower the flag of Basilea in surrender."

Caithlin smiled sympathetically to him and nodded. Dashing back across the heaving quarterdeck, she reached the after end of the ship and quickly untied the flag's halyard from its pole and carefully lowered it, respectfully preventing the blue cloth from touching the deck by hauling it in under one arm and folding it as neatly as she could. She then handed it across to Jaymes.

"Put it somewhere safe down below," she instructed him, "then get back here, quick as you can."

"Aye, Captain."

Caithlin paced back over to the upper deck, looking down to admire the work of her crew. A sail was shredded convincingly above her; the guns were loaded and ready, ten of the eighteen cannon were hidden from view with their gunners lurking dangerously beneath the piled sailcloth.

"Be ready for my order to open fire!" Caithlin called as the pirate brigantine fought its way through the towering waves to close with them from astern. "Get pistols and boarding pikes up here, quickly! If they come alongside from port, then the port guns will fire grapeshot and the starboard gunners will be first to board! If they come from starboard, other way around; starboard gunners fire, port gunners to lead the boarding! Understood?"

The chorus of shouts from her crew was positive affirmation enough. She turned to face Jaymes as he arrived back on deck. The lieutenant passed Caithlin her sword belt. She took it and fastened it around her waist. Only then did she notice her hands were shaking. She looked up at Jaymes and forced an insincere smile. The gravity of her predicament hit her in an instant.

"I'm about to fight pirates, Jaymes!" she gasped. "One week of fencing lessons isn't enough! I can command a ship to line guns up, but I can't fight with a sword! I don't know how!"

Jaymes reached into his own belt and handed a pistol across to her.

"Keep your powder dry and make your shot count!" he smiled encouragingly, raising his voice above the roaring wind and blinking rain water out of his eyes. "Your job isn't to fight! Your job is to command! We've got this, Cathy! We've got this!"

Cathy accepted the pistol and tiny sack of shot and powder. The brigantine drew closer, close enough now for her to see the deck packed with armed pirates. Exactly as X'And had predicted, there were a good hundred sailors on the enemy ship. A lone figure jumped up to cling to the ratlines on the port side of the vessel, raising a speaking cone to his mouth.

"Haul your sails in and prepare to be boarded!" the pirate's gruff voice just about carried across the gap between the two ships and the howling wind.

Caithlin looked up at her sailors above her.

"Shorten sail!" she called up to them.

Again, the *Martolian Queen* slowed, a sickening list now being added to the rhythmic pitching of the bows as the ship floundered pathetically at slow speed in the heaving seas.

"Whatever happens, you stay on the quarterdeck, Cathy," X'And said seriously as the brigantine drifted alongside the *Martolian Queen*. "I'll lead the boarders across."

"I'll do it," Jaymes said. "They're mostly naval men. I'll lead the boarding party."

"I said I'll do it!" X'And snapped angrily.

Caithlin looked across at the two sailors, both well capable of leading her crew into battle. The Basilean lieutenant and the salamander corsair both looked at her eagerly for approval.

"Take them across, X'and," she said to her first mate. "Lieutenant, you stay on the quarterdeck."

The salamander grinned.

"You've got to time this right," he said to Caithlin, "we're dead in the water now, we can't maneuver. When you fire those guns, you've got to fire them late enough that those bastards are already committed to hitting us, but early enough that you'll hit them on their own deck."

"I know," Caithlin nodded, "that, I can do. Go to it, X'And."

The salamander rushed quickly down to take his place at the starboard waist, ready to lead the charge onto the pirate brigantine. The ship was all prepared; only a dozen sailors were visible on the upper deck, a convincing number for a merchant brig. Then, quite out of nowhere, a memory forced itself into Caithlin's mind.

"Shorten the sail, Cathy! That's it! Gentler on the tiller! Don't fight the elements, Cathy, and they'll become your friend."

Following her father's instructions, Caithlin set the sail on the small skiff as it wallowed across the choppy waves of the lake. She turned to look up at her father. Even as an eight-year-old girl, she could feel the warmth and love in his cracked face as he smiled proudly down at her.

"That's it! You've got it now!"

Her throat dry and her limbs suddenly cold and heavy, she turned to look at the more sympathetic face of Jaymes.

"I can't do this!" she repeated to him. "I'm not a soldier! I don't know how to fight!"

Jaymes smiled again, his face sorrowful.

"It'll be over in moments," he promised. "The men won't let you down."

"I'm not afraid to die!" she found herself suddenly babbling, her mind propelled to her father back home in Geneza, still completely unaware of the predicament providence had placed his beloved daughter in. "I'm not! But it'll kill my father! His heart won't take it! Don't let me die, Jaymes! For my father's sake! Don't let me die here!"

Her shaking hands clung to his as she stared up at him, the pirate brigantine now only seconds away from nudging into the starboard side of the *Martolian Queen*. Jaymes's sympathetic stare morphed into one of resolution and calm, assured determination. He rested a hand gently on hers and gave her an encouraging wink.

"Nothing's getting past me, Cathy," he beamed. "It's time. Give the order."

***

The sight of a fast brigantine plunging through the towering waves on the edge of a hurricane, its deck crammed with pirates, would concentrate the mind if viewed from the quarterdeck of a Basilean frigate. For Jaymes, with his vantage point being on the deck of a lightly armed brig, the sight was truly terrifying. His handful of actions had seen him largely confined to commanding banks of guns and occasionally leading a boarding party against the smallest of enemy units. Now, as the sea of grimacing, scarred faces on the brigantine drew closer, he knew that there was a very real chance he was facing his imminent death.

That was why, in something of a parasitic way, he appreciated the raw honesty of Caithlin's fear. It galvanized him into focus, forced him to muster his courage, and appear braver than he actually was. Similar to helping a friend being one of the best cures for sadness in oneself, holding Caithlin's hand and assuring her that all would be fine somehow took some of Jaymes's own fear away.

He looked across at the pirate brigantine, its bowsprit cutting in toward the *Martolian Queen's* starboard waist. Perhaps a hundred pirates were crammed on the deck, their terrifying grins and curved blades illuminated by flashes of lightning on the southern horizon. Whistles and catcalls shrieked across the gap between the two ships, no doubt initiated by the view of the brig's beautiful captain. This was win or die. Caithlin's fate would be worse than death if the pirates captured the *Martolian Queen*.

Half a dozen pirates stepped up to line the port side of their vessel, ropes and grappling hooks held ready to secure the two ships together for boarding. Only a handful of yards separated them now. Jaymes rested a hand on the rough, white sharkskin handle of his saber, threading his wrist through the blue and gold sword knot attached to the hilt. He noticed with some relish that the brigantine's guns were not manned. They were not expecting any resistance. They were careless. Sloppy. It would cost them.

The brigantine's bows came about a little to starboard to avoid ploughing straight into the side of the brig. They were committed now; there was no chance of opening up the gap again in time. Realizing that Caithlin's terror had made her ineffective, and that a moment's hesitation could be disastrous, Jaymes opened his mouth to issue the order.

"Gunners! Starboard side! Run 'em out!" Caithlin yelled above the roaring wind. "Fire!"

The next three or four seconds passed by in a whirl of bloody violence. Sail clothes were torn off the hidden guns on the starboard side of the *Martolian Queen* as gunners rapidly opened up the brig's gun ports. The order to fire was echoed by each of the nine gun captains on the port side, and with a deafening ripple, the cannons fired. The nine guns spewed out their deadly canisters of grapeshot, the cones of fist-sized metal balls cutting across the upper deck of the pirate brigantine in a bloody swath of carnage. Scarlet fountained up from the packed bodies on the enemy ship, the front waves of men flying back in the deadly storm of metal as bodies and faces were torn open and limbs were ripped off.

Simultaneously, the *Martolian Queen's* port side gunners leapt up from their hiding places beneath the sail cloth and charged forward with their own ropes and grapple hooks. Jaymes noticed that some of the Basilean sailors had found the time to quickly grab their blue jackets and red bandannas, eager to show their true colors as naval men, now that the fighting had started. His hearing replaced by the familiar, high-pitched whine of his muted eardrums after the banging of the guns, Jaymes watched as their sailors crossed the heaving deck to throw their lines and hooks onto the brigantine, securing her alongside as they tied their ropes to the cleats on the *Martolian Queen's* deck.

Then, with a thud and a squeal of protesting timbers, the pirate brigantine hit the side of the privateer brig. Above them, the yards and rigging of the masts clattered and tangled, leaving the two ships locked side-by-side in a deadly embrace as they rose and fell together in the furious waves of the Infant Sea. X'And was the first across, a curved blade held high in one hand as he leapt over to the brigantine and across her bloody, corpse-filled deck. The salamander first mate threw himself into the fight, leaping forward to clamp his fanged jaws around the face of the first pirate he encountered. The other four salamander corsairs were close at his heels, pistols barking and swords hacking down into the center of the bloodied and confused crowd of pirates they faced.

With a combined roar, the boarding parties of the *Martolian Queen* followed the salamanders into the fight, cutlasses and boarding pikes slashing out into vicious attacks as soon as they bridged the small gap between the two vessels and engaged their piratical foes. Jaymes unsheathed his own saber, and he looked across at Caithlin. Having acquired a second pistol, she held both weapons at the ready and cocked their hammers with her thumbs. Any sign of the fear she had displayed only moments before had now evaporated completely.

The roaring mass of perhaps fifty privateers and Basilean sailors cut through the ranks of pirates amassed on the deck of the brigantine, driving into their midst and separating them into two. With the waists of the two ships now locked together, they continued to ride the turbulent waves as one, the natural lines of their hulls sweeping away from each other at the bows. This left a gap too large to be traversed at the front of the ships but kept their quarterdecks at the rear pressed against each other. Seeing an opportunity to counterattack, a group of five pirates leapt from the brigantine onto the *Martolian Queen*, right next to where Jaymes and Caithlin stood.

***

The cataclysmic effect of the broadside of grapeshot had stirred two emotions within Caithlin; hope that they could actually win this encounter and shock at the sheer levels of bloody carnage her order to fire had inflicted. There was no way to begin to estimate how many of the pirate crew had been killed by the salvo. The deck of the pirate brigantine was slippery with blood from the dead and dying, now only intensified as the vicious melee between the two crews raged on.

Caithlin had the briefest of moments to contemplate her orders, the ramifications of her decisions, and the hellish image before her of the men her plan and order had killed. She found in that brief moment that she did not need to think very hard to justify her actions to herself. These men were pirates; violent killers and self-serving thieves without a shred of honor or decency. The act of killing them was more akin to exterminating vermin rather than taking away an honest life in battle. Her eyes narrowed and her jaw clenched shut, she watched with growing satisfaction as her sailors tore through the ranks of pirates.

Then, as the clash of blades rang out over the wind and rain, and the screams of the wounded and dying cut through the shouting of orders, Caithlin looked up to see five pirates leap across from the enemy ship to board her own quarterdeck. For the second time in less than a minute, a thousand thoughts raced through her mind as the intensity of the situation in which she suddenly found herself sank in.

As they dashed across toward her, soaked by the crashing waves and driving rain, the five pirates were all but impossible to tell apart from her own crew. Men in their twenties and thirties, dressed in the simple garb of sailors, armed with cutlasses. The first man across was perhaps the youngest, barely out of his teens with a neat, dark beard. Barely before she even realized what she was doing, Caithlin raised her right hand, aimed her pistol, and pulled back on the trigger.

The gun clicked, and the moment between the snap of the hammer and the ignition of the charge seemed to last a lifetime. The gun jumped in Caithlin's hand, a plume of pungent smoke sprouted from the barrel, and a thin stream of blood sprayed out of a dark hole in the pirate's chest as he was flung down to the deck. The whole action was so easy that it surprised her. Not only the act of extinguishing a life, but also the complete lack of guilt or remorse she felt in the instant after it.

Emboldened by the success of her last shot, Caithlin took two paces forward to meet her attackers, raising her left hand and her second pistol. Lining up her shot with her next assailant, a tall, wiry sailor with gray stubble, she pulled on the trigger again. Again the pistol jumped, the air around her stank to the high heavens of burnt powder, and again a man fell down dead with utter ease. Jaymes dashed out to meet the remaining three pirates, cutting down the first before raising his saber to defend himself from the next in line.

Caithlin glanced down at the smoking pistols in her hands. She looked back up as Jaymes struggled in his fight, holding back two furious buccaneers who forced him back toward the mainmast. She looked down at the sword by her side, the weapon she barely knew how to use, and then at the empty pistols that proved so useful but now lay harmless. It was at that moment, faced with the seemingly simple decision of whether to draw her sword or reload a pistol, that she froze in panic.

***

Jaymes watched in surprise as Caithlin paced forward fearlessly, her chin held high as she calmly raised her second pistol and gunned down another pirate. With three remaining, the odds had changed from certain death but were still not in their favor. Jaymes dashed across the heaving quarterdeck and lunged forward to meet the first pirate, the tip of his saber lancing straight through the charging buccaneer's gut to emerge out of his back. Jaymes quickly withdrew his bloodied blade as the pirate crumpled to the deck, raising his sword to defend himself as a lumbering, bearded corsair hacked down at his head with a heavily notched cutlass.

Their blackened teeth bared, the two remaining pirates attacked Jaymes with a flurry of blows, forcing him to step back and bring his saber up in a series of parries as he frantically defended himself against his two opponents. Both men were about his own age, both let out a series of violent threats and insults as they bore down on him, both of them doing so in an accent that placed them as Basilean-raised. They were from his own nation.

Jaymes quickly side-stepped around the back of the mainmast, moving in an attempt to line both pirates up so that he would only need to fight against one at a time. The larger of the two swung a heavy blow down toward Jaymes's neck; he managed to parry, but his counterattack was immediately batted aside by the second pirate; a lithe man with a thin, blond moustache. The blond pirate thrust his own blade forward; Jaymes side-stepped again to avoid the blow and saw the cutlass dig into the mainmast, locking in place in the thick wood of the beam. Before he could take advantage of his opponent's error, the tall pirate attacked him again.

Jaymes parried three attacks, unsuccessfully attempting to land a few blows of his own, before he found himself once again facing two armed men as the blond pirate returned to the fight. He heard a roar and saw another half-dozen pirates leap over from the brigantine onto the quarterdeck of the *Martolian Queen,* and his situation transformed back from one of desperation to one of certain death. Seeing the briefest of opportunities as the two pirates looked over to see their comrades rushing to their aid, Jaymes stepped forward to attack and thrust his blade through the shoulder of the lithe, blond pirate. As the taller pirate hacked down with his cutlass to save his wounded shipmate, Jaymes parried the clumsy blow and drew his own blade across his opponent's throat, neatly slicing it open to the bone and sending him toppling down in a fountain of crimson.

Their cries joining those of their enemies, three Basilean sailors charged across from the starboard cannons to join the fight on the quarterdeck, the first managing to run through one of the buccaneers with his boarding pike. Jaymes jumped in surprise as a pistol boomed from right next to his ear; Caithlin's shot winged one of the pirates as he jumped onto her ship, but the rotund sailor remained on his feet. She brought up her second pistol and fired again, this time shooting him square in the center of the forehead and sending him down amid the growing pile of corpses on the deck.

Steeling his courage, Jaymes raised his blood-streaked sword and hurled himself back into the attack against the pirates. Standing front and center with the sailors from the guns, he held his ground as the veteran Basileans fought against the seemingly fearless pirates. Jaymes traded blows with a gray-bearded man whose gold-handled cutlass spoke of wealth from years of plundering, coupled with a skill forged from a life of seaborne warfare. More sailors from both crews joined the swirling fight on the quarterdeck that raged to either side of the swordsmen as Jaymes held his ground, aiming cuts and thrusts at his adversary while desperately defending himself from rapid ripostes and lunges.

With another roar, the attention of every fighter on the quarterdeck was brought to the crowd of twenty sailors that swept across from the pirate brigantine. Jaymes let out a gasp of relief when he saw X'And leading the charge. The brigantine had been cleared of enemy sailors, and now the *Martolian Queen's* crew were doubling back to finish off the last remaining pirates. At the sight, the gray-bearded pirate threw down his blade and held his empty hands aloft in surrender. Within seconds, the act of submission spread across the other pirates, and the fight ended as quickly as it had begun.

The palm of his hand nearly red-raw from where it clutched the rough, sharkskin handle of his saber in desperation, Jaymes struggled to control his breathing as adrenaline continued to surge through his limbs. He looked across the quarterdeck and saw Caithlin staring at the pirates who had surrendered, a smoking pistol in one hand and a saber in the other. Nauseous with the relief of having somehow survived, he offered her a friendly smile. She did not return it.

"X'And," she called across to her first mate, "secure the prisoners. Throw their dead overboard. Get both of these ships ready to sail."

"Aye, Captain," the salamander replied, lowering his sword calmly.

The towering reptilian seemed completely unruffled, as if victory and his own survival had been assured before the battle had even commenced.

"Captain!" he called back to Caithlin. "I'd suggest a prize crew of twenty would manage her back to Keretia. Perhaps thirty if we are placing men in irons down below. I can take her back, if you wish."

Caithlin looked across at X'And, and then the growing number of Basilean sailors who made their way back over from the bloody fighting aboard the brigantine. She looked at Jaymes, her eyes cold and distant.

"No," she said, "he can take it. The lieutenant can take this ship back to port."

His hand shaking, Jaymes sheathed his sword and released his aching wrist from the confines of his sword knot. He paced over to Caithlin.

"You don't want me to stay aboard the *Martolian Queen*, Cathy?" he asked quietly.

The blonde privateer captain looked up at him with pitiless eyes.

"Lieutenant Ellias," she said coolly, "take a prize crew to that brigantine and take her to Thatraskos. Obey my orders. And get off my ship."

His throat dry, his eyes narrowing in confusion, Jaymes took a step back as Caithlin looked away from him.

"Aye, ma'am," he managed, "at once."

"And this one?" X'And asked, pointing his blade at the gray-bearded pirate who Jaymes had faced. "This is Gallo, I think? He's wanted."

Jaymes's eyes opened again in disbelief. 'Red' Gallo, a man who had terrorized various parts of the Infant Sea for a decade. They had just defeated him. Jaymes had personally fought Red Gallo to a standstill in one-on-one combat. He let out a choked laugh of surprise. Caithlin walked across to the indignant, silent pirate, her saber resting over one shoulder and her smoking pistol held by her thigh. She looked at the notorious buccaneer, her cold eyes narrowing. Jaymes watched in concern, wondering if he would need to intervene. There was a legal process to adhere to. X'And, perhaps anxious of the same issue, stepped across to stand next to the angry looking privateer captain.

"Captain Viconti? I assume you wish this man to be placed in irons along with his crew?"

Caithlin took a slow step back and nodded.

"Yes," she finally said, "he's for the hangman, not us. Get him locked up and out of my sight."

Any response was cut off as an excited scream echoed up from the hatch leading down below from the center of the brigantine's upper deck. Footsteps thudded up until one of the *Martolian Queen's* sailors appeared at the hatch, a jubilant grin plastered across his face.

"Captain!" he yelled across from the defeated pirate vessel. "You have to see what's down here!"

Chapter Sixteen

The bell on the mainmast sounded eleven times, reminding Caithlin just how long she had been awake for. Suppressing a yawn, she dipped the nib of her quill back into the small pot of ink and resumed her calculations on the parchment spread out over her desk. The division of prize money was something she had never needed to deal with before; a merchant captain's terms gave no leeway and were set in stone, and she would normally have a representative of the company onboard to ensure pay was evenly distributed. Likewise, a proper warship would employ a purser as one of its warrant officers – as *Pious*, and the other frigates did. But Caithlin was left with the mathematics to carry out herself as, being a privateer, the constitution of her crew was entirely under her rule and she had not thought to hire a purser.

As a commissioned privateer, the rules for the distribution of prize money were the same for her as they would be for any proper warship in the Basilean Fleet. She stared down at the calculations again in disbelief, the numbers jumping off the page. As captain of a privateer, she was entitled to a staggering three-eighths share of the prize money. Three-eighths of the money made from selling a brigantine was significant. Three-eighths of the reward money of a relatively notorious pirate captain made it even more so. Then there was the cargo hold packed to the brim with valuable spices. Three-eighths of all of it was hers and hers alone.

Caithlin worked through the calculations again. One-eighth would go to the ships officers, one-eighth to the ships junior officers, and one-eighth to the midshipmen and warrant officers. The simple fact of the matter was that she had next to none of these; she was not training any midshipmen; she had no surgeon, master, purser, or any of their mates. All she had was a first mate and a lieutenant borrowed from the Basilean Navy. Very technically, that should give three eighths to be equally divided between X'And and Jaymes Ellias, while the final two eighths, or one quarter to satisfy her need to round the numbers properly, would be evenly distributed between the entire crew, including the families of the twelve sailors who had lost their lives in the fight.

That simply would not do. She would take a quarter share for herself, a quarter to be split between X'And and Jaymes, and half to be split between the rest of the crew. Of course, some cultures would look at that divide and snort in disgust at the apparent contempt with which the common sailor was treated, but from Caithlin's point of view, she was breaking regulations by giving each of her sailors quadruple what they were legally entitled to and penalizing herself and her two officers to achieve it.

She remembered her father telling her that the Genezan Navy insisted upon a share of prize money being sent to their own Admiralty toward the upkeep of the fleet. This practice was not routinely carried out in the Basilean Fleet, most likely because the Basileans were so abundantly wealthy, Caithlin figured. She let out a brief, bitter laugh. The Basileans would rather give more prize money to their sailors in an attempt to combat the rising problem with desertion and even mutiny. Perhaps addressing living conditions and basic pay might be a better place to start.

She ran the numbers through on the parchment for a third time. There were still variables based on what the market was currently paying for spices and what the brigantine and its guns would fetch, but she reckoned that the money she would be left with would knock a staggering two years off her ten year debt in one fell swoop. She paused in contemplation as she stared down at the page. If only it would always be this easy. But she knew full well that this first haul was luckier than most privateers would see in their entire career. It was a one off. But what a start.

A polite knock at the door of her cabin brought her attention away from the numbers on the table in front of her.

"Yes?" she called out.

The door opened to admit X'And. The tall salamander lowered himself to squeeze through the archway and into the cabin. He closed the door behind him, the moonlight shining through the windows on the stern of the brig illuminating his harsh, reptilian features.

"You planning on getting sleep any time soon?" the salamander sailor asked, a hint of admonishment in his tone.

"I'm working through the figures," Caithlin replied. "I think it best if we both accept a slightly smaller share than we are entitled to. It would be more appropriate to reward the men."

"Well," X'And exhaled, "I agree with the principle, certainly. But don't be so eager to reduce your own share. You'll only end up paying off the interest of your debt at that rate. But anyway, why are you up at close to midnight doing calculations that could be done in a few minutes by a purser once we are ashore?"

"Because I'm perfectly capable of doing them right now," Caithlin replied with some venom, her dark eyes fixed on his.

The salamander did not flinch for a moment beneath what was supposed to be a withering stare.

"You're doing them because you are trying to take your mind off all of the things that bothered you about that fight today." He folded his arms. "You're working yourself into a frenzy to avoid facing the thoughts that you need to face. I've known you long enough, Cathy. Don't pull my tail."

"Go on, then," Caithlin retorted, tossing her pen across her desk and leaning back to fold her arms. "You're the self-appointed expert on all matters of humanity. What contemplations am I eschewing?"

"Well," the salamander replied calmly, walking across the cabin to pull up a chair and seat himself opposite Caithlin, much to her annoyance, "you've just killed three men. Not ordered a killing, but actually committed the act yourself. Gunned three men down, dead by your own hand. First time you've ever done that. Are you telling me that this is not weighing on your mind?"

"That's precisely what I'm telling you!" Caithlin snapped. "They were scum! Murderers! Vermin! I won't lose a moment of sleep over them! So perhaps you don't know me as well as you think you do, if you've come to the conclusion that wiping killers off the face of the world is what is upsetting me!"

"So, you do admit that you're upset," X'And leaned back and interlocked his clawed hands behind his long head, his scaly face smug from his little victory. "Perhaps we had better talk about that instead."

Caithlin opened her mouth to snap out another angry response but stopped almost immediately. He was right. He nearly always was, when it came to matters of the heart. From what little contact she had made with other members of his race, she had determined that salamanders were very much unique in that regards. A strict moral compass that always prioritized goodness of the heart and soul over common sense and logic.

"I made a fool out of myself today," Caithlin finally admitted, leaning forward and resting her head in her hands. "Before we went into the fight, I found myself babbling like a coward. I came apart. When the swords were clashing all around me, I froze. At one point, I even dropped a shot when I was trying to reload a pistol. I let fear get the better of me. I acted like a coward."

X'And's features contorted as he cocked his head to one side. He remained silent, his facial expression unerringly human for a few moments. Then, he spoke.

"Oh, that's it? I thought there would be more. I was rather expecting more."

"Are you mocking me?" Caithlin growled.

"Well... yes, I suppose I am," the burly salamander shrugged, "because you are making something out of nothing. I fully appreciate that you've never been in a battle before, so you don't actually know what is normal, but let me assure you that what you are describing is absolutely normal."

Caithlin opened her mouth to object, but X'And carried on regardless.

"Hake Rawen was on number four cannon. He froze at his gun when you gave the order to fire. He needed a kick up the arse from Trill. He fired a second late, but the world kept turning, and we still won. I can guarantee you, absolutely guarantee you, that every one of us was scared going into that, and every one of us made mistakes. I've done a lot worse than drop a shot while trying to load a pistol."

"But I made a fool out of myself!" Caithlin protested. "When they were coming alongside us, I grabbed Jaymes Ellias's hand and started telling him not to let me die!"

X'And leaned back again and narrowed his eyes.

"Aha," he said simply.

"What in heavens is that supposed to mean?" Caithlin spluttered.

"That explains why you lashed out at him and sent him off to that brigantine. You're embarrassed."

"Of course I'm embarrassed!" Caithlin hissed. "That's precisely what I've been trying to tell you!"

"But if it was my hand you grabbed, you would not be embarrassed."

"And what exactly do you mean by that?"

"I mean that you're rather taken by him," X'And replied, "and not the wisest of choices, if I may say so."

"Right, first off, I'm not taken by him," Caithlin snapped. "Second, even if I was, why would he be a poor choice? Finally, and most importantly, you're completely off the mark. That's not why I'm embarrassed. I'm embarrassed because I'm the captain! I'm supposed to set the example! I'm supposed to be the one flinging myself headlong, outnumbered, into a crowd of pirates and dropping them with a saber, not Jaymes! I made myself look like a fool, and then he made me look even worse! I was left simpering at the back, like some awful storybook princess who needed rescuing! I'm not being that woman! I'm stronger than that!"

"What, stronger than feeling any fear whatsoever in your first ever battle, is that what being a strong woman means? Don't be ridiculous! Well, I'm certainly glad I came in to check on you, because we are unpacking all sorts of problems here, aren't we? You've never mentioned any of this insecurity to me before!"

"That's because I've never nearly had my head removed from my shoulders by sodding pirates!" Caithlin yelled. "And wipe that smirk off your stupid snout, that wasn't supposed to be funny!"

X'And's grin slowly faded away. He tapped his thumbs together with a clinking of claws as he looked past Caithlin and out of the stern windows to the moonlit night sky. The ominous flash of lightning still occasionally crackled across the dark, southern horizon, lighting up the silhouette of the captured brigantine following in the *Martolian Queen's* wake.

"I'm sorry," the salamander admitted, "but you've got a lot of things circling around in your mind, and I think you need a friend to help you unravel them. That's not weakness. That's just life. Human… salamander… no difference. It's life."

"So what do I do?" Caithlin said in despair, her head sinking into her hands again. "What now?"

"I'm here to listen," X'And cast a friendly smile.

"No, don't hit me with that nonsense," Caithlin sneered, "I don't want any of that sentimental clap-trap. Just tell me what you think I need to do. Bluntly and clearly."

X'And cocked his head to one side again.

"Alright. First off, stop worrying about what others think about you. Yes, you are being judged, but only to the same extent you are judging others. We all do it. Second, stop setting your standards so impossibly high. We all get scared. You need to get used to that. It doesn't go away. Third, when we get back to Thatraskos, you go find Lieutenant Ellias, you apologize for acting like an idiot, and then you shake hands and you say goodbye to him."

Caithlin nodded, a brief and slightly playful hum escaping her lips as her brow raised in amusement.

"You really don't like him."

"No!" the salamander snapped. "No! I don't! I know his type; I've seen them before! Pretty face, silver tongue, and a trail of broken hearted girls left in every port he visits!"

"He's not like that," Caithlin said, quite forcefully.

"He is exactly like that!" X'And scowled. "You just don't want him to be! Naval officers are not gentlemen, even their own Hegemon said that after they put down the Ekhos Mutiny! Look, you made a good decision by sending him off to that other ship, now put your conscience to rest by apologizing to him when you see him, give him his share of the prize money, and wish him luck. You don't need his sort in your life. By the memory of the Deliverer, Cathy, you've just gunned down three men without flinching, but you're worried about what some pretty fop thinks of you?"

Caithlin looked over her shoulder at the brigantine, pitching gently in the easing waves as they made their way north, away from the hurricane and toward Keretia, a strong wind at their backs.

"You're right," Caithlin sighed. "You're right. Look, I should get some sleep. It's been a long day, and I'm utterly exhausted."

After letting out a long sigh, X'And slowly stood up and took a pace back toward the cabin door.

"Yes, get some sleep. You'll feel better in the morning. When we're up there, on deck, you're my captain and I respect you whole-heartedly. But outside of that, know that you're more like a little sister to me. Family. I care about my family. I just want what's best for you, as I know you do for me."

Caithlin returned her friend's smile with genuine gratitude. The feeling was reciprocated. After two years of sailing together, he was like a big brother to her.

"Thank you, X'And. Honestly. Thank you."

"Get some sleep!" the salamander warned her with a glare as he opened the door. "Good night, Cathy."

Caithlin locked the door behind him before kicking off her boots and unbuttoning her shirt. She walked over to the lamps hung from the wooden bulkheads, blowing them out in turn until her cabin was lit only by the moonlight pouring through the stern windows. Above them, the twinkling points of light of the Constellation of Elinathora guided them back to the north. She walked over to lean against the window, spending a few peaceful moments watching the deep, blue waves beneath the starlit sky and the brigantine that drifted serenely behind the brig, leaving the tumultuous hurricane far behind.

***

The sun rose steadily over a blurred horizon, casting light down on the armada of little fishing vessels that were already clear of Tha-traskos harbor and heading south. Karnon leaned on the taff rail running along the stern of the *Pious*, the morning breeze already warming as he watched the naval dock slowly come alive. Crews brought supplies out to the small sloops moored up alongside the shallow-water jetties, a messenger on horseback arrived at the admiral's offices, and dockyard workers set about affecting repairs on a storm-damaged frigate that had returned to port the previous evening.

"You have to take advantage of moments like these."

Karnon looked over his shoulder and saw Charn standing a few paces behind him.

He went to stand up straight, feeling like a wayward child for being caught committing the cardinal sin of leaning on a rail on Charn's quarterdeck, but the grizzled captain held up a hand to stop him.

"Don't let me disturb you, I was just up for some morning air and thought I would say hello. Do you take tea? I can have my steward rustle something up."

"Yes. Sir," Karnon answered hesitantly. "Tea would be much appreciated."

Charn made his way over to the forward end of the quarterdeck and shouted a brief instruction down before he returned to stand next to Karnon again.

"I don't stop and enjoy these moments enough anymore," Charn said, almost to himself, as he looked out across the calm bay. "It doesn't come as naturally as one is rapidly approaching middle age."

Karnon watched the normally harsh man with some curiosity, finding himself caught off guard by the flow of the conversation.

"I'm obviously no sailor, sir," Karnon said after searching his mind briefly for a subject to divert that flow back to matters professional, "but the horizon to the south looks a little clearer. Do you think we might be putting out to sea again today?"

Charn narrowed his eyes and sucked in a long breath through his teeth.

"Not today," he finally replied. "First off, we're having the hull blessed by the priests from the naval chapel. That's quite an event. Shame we can't do it in dry dock, as there is a lot more ceremony then, and it becomes a lot more meaningful. But I'll still happily take the interim procedure from them. As for the weather, these hurricanes are as unpredictable as they are violent. I'm very eager to get back out there, but I think we're better off giving it one more day at least. Let's let it spin itself out first."

Karnon stopped to think over Charn's words regarding the religious ceremony. He had always prided himself as a rational man, never given to emotional outbursts and always prioritizing a pragmatic and reasonable approach to problems. He had, at one point in his adolescence, even inwardly questioned his faith, led on by a small crowd of rather pretentious friends who claimed that their college studies had indicated that some aspects of religion could even be called into question, and that the advancing fields of science could prove some of what religion credited to the Shining Ones above.

And then he had seen Elohi on the battlefield. On the outskirts of Tragar, as a newly qualified man-at-arms on his first campaign, he had seen the red skies suddenly light up as angelic hosts flew down from the heavens above, one moment a line of perfectly elegant celestial beings in shining gold and silver; the next moment a fighting force of towering giants, tearing the Abyssal demons apart with their flaming swords. Karnon believed. He had seen, and he believed.

"Will blessing the hull give us the favor of the Elohi, sir?" he asked, nodding at the wooden effigy of an angelic Elohi at the *Pious's* bow. "Do you think the ship's light will shine?"

Charn looked across at the younger officer and issued a slight, grim smile. After a brief silence, he nodded.

"The stories will tell you that the beacons of the Elohi frigates shine in every battle we enter," Charn said, "but you've already seen that that is not true. I've been captain of Elohi frigates for four years now. A Batch One before *Pious*; the *Devout*. I've seen the beacon shine five times. What a lot of people don't know is that the Elohi-class frigate was named so because it was the first ever warship to be built with an area to secure holy relics actually incorporated into its design. All the larger, older Basilean warships are also fitted with holy relics, but that was an afterthought once the Hegemon decreed that warships should be blessed with their own relics."

Karnon watched as the older officer displayed an uncharacteristic enthusiasm, an animated energy and interest in the conversation as he briefly explained the history of his own, beloved frigate. Karnon wondered at this new revelation that somewhere on this very ship, holy relics had been built into the actual hull. He began to question what relics the *Pious* was blessed enough to carry but was cut off as the captain began to speak again.

"But I digress, the lighting of the torch doesn't happen often. But when they come... it is beyond magical, Karnon. It is... beyond words. Ah! Here's tea."

The majesty of the moment was destroyed by the arrival of Samus, the captain's steward, with a tray of tea. As if sensing the arrival of more officers on the quarterdeck, he had brought four cups. In turn, as if sensing the opportunity for a freshly poured drink, Walt Ganto followed the steward up to the quarterdeck.

"Good morning, sir," he nodded to Charn before offering a smile to Karnon. "Good morning, Mister Senne."

"*Captain* Senne," Charn corrected, "you're addressing a legion officer, not a naval officer. Be good enough to observe their customs and protocols while you are on my ship, Mister Ganto."

"My apologies," Walt grimaced, "Captain Senne."

The stern naval captain's inevitable follow up was curtailed as his eyes drifted to the south, out past the breakwater at the slow flow of traffic to and from the harbor.

"Hullo," he said pensively, "she survived the storm, then. And it appears she's been busy, too."

Karnon and Walt both looked over to the far side of the breakwater and saw two ships, both twin-masted and smaller than a frigate, sailing steadily into Thatraskos harbor. Karnon watched the ships – which to him could have been brigs, barques, skiffs or cutters, they were all something generally smaller than a frigate – gracefully round the corner of the harbor entrance and alter course to head for the naval dock. He could just about make out that both ships were flying Basilean flags, but not the Basilean Naval ensign.

"I'm sorry," he confessed to the two naval officers, "I'm afraid I have no idea what the significance of those two particular ships is."

"That's the *Martolian Queen*," Charn nodded at the lead ship, "the privateer brig that will be joining us when we put out to sea again. And the brigantine following her? She's a twenty gunner. Count 'em, Captain. And you don't put twenty guns into a brigantine if you intend to move cargo. You put that many guns in a ship if you intend to fight. So, given that Captain Viconti's letter of reprisal from the governor has only authorized her to engage pirates, that means she has had some success."

"And," Walt continued as the two ships brought in their sails and prepared to come alongside their jetties, "correct me if I'm wrong, sir..."

"You need not fear me not doing that, Mister Ganto. Ever."

"...but if that's a twenty gun brigantine sailing in, it's likely to be a criminal of some notoriety. Most of the pirates will rely on small, fast ships like sloops and schooners to get alongside a merchantman and board them. Running a brigantine with twenty guns is quite a statement."

"For once," Charn growled, "as much as it pains me to admit it, Mister Ganto, you are not talking complete drivel."

The sun continued its pathway up into the morning sky as the docks grew busier and the two ships carried out their laborious process of approaching the jetties, coming alongside and securing. Kaeso Innes and Iain Kennus, the ship's surgeon, joined them on the quarterdeck for a second tray of tea as they watched the events unfold. But, as much as Karnon found himself only marginally interested in the decidedly nautical conversation – perhaps less so given that he could only decipher half of it – he did find himself relaxing a little in this decidedly new environment.

When he had first been shown around the vessel and the idiosyncrasies of naval life had been explained to him, Karnon found them pointless at best and pretentious at worst. But now, perhaps realizing that something as simple as the freedom to walk upon the hallowed quarterdeck at his leisure, a privilege of his rank, was actually something to be grateful for, he found his new and bizarre environment and company a little more comforting. He accepted a fresh cup of steaming, spiced tea and watched the morning unfold from his lofty perch on the quarterdeck, occasionally suppressing a smirk as the frigate's captain continued to berate and rebuke his two young lieutenants at every opportunity.

***

Struggling through the late morning heat in a heavy greatcoat and hat was already becoming somehow familiar. Caithlin made her way across the naval dockyard, heading around the edge of the bay toward the merchant docks. She found herself walking, almost strutting, with a brash spring in her step, her saber and scabbard held in one hand as it dangled from two leather straps at her waist, carried rather than worn as was the current fashion with naval officers. She ignored the same repetition of stunned looks she received from sailors and dock workers as she passed, telling herself that her rapidly repairing ego was not further flattered by their attention.

It was good to be back in the idyllic setting of Thatraskos, the gentle slopes around the bay covered by the neat, pretty white buildings with their terracotta roofs, the gentle waters of the bay acting as a carpet for the fleet of tiny yet charming fishing vessels and the impressive array of larger merchantmen and warships. A few good nights of sleep on the return voyage had done her a world of good, and the reality of just how much she had knocked off her debt in her first sea engagement had given her a real confidence for her future in her new career.

Rounding a corner in the administrative center of the merchant dockyards, Caithlin approached the now familiar building of the harbormaster's offices. Before she even reached the front door, she was greeted by a whistle and looked up to see Kassia Rhil stood by the open second floor window of her office.

"Hello, sailor!" she called down. "Somebody's been making a name for herself!"

Caithlin grinned and removed her hat, bowing with an exaggerated flourish.

"Come on up," Kassia called, "I'll pour you a drink."

A few minutes later saw Caithlin sat on the windowsill of the harbormaster's office, her heavy coat, hat, and sword discarded in favor of a glass of local fruit juices.

"You were seen by quite a few fast ships on your way back in," Kassia said. "That brigantine you've brought in is known to quite a few. Captain Gallo, no less. You've set your bar quite high for your first venture out as a privateer. How are you going to top that one?"

"I'm going to bag myself an orc blood runner," Caithlin winked, "that bunch that rather rudely put me in this predicament in the first place."

"Well, don't get ahead of yourself too quickly," the harbormaster smiled. "Don't let the success get to your head, or you'll end up biting off more than you can deal with. You keep yourself and your crew safe, first and foremost."

"I know, I know," Caithlin waved a hand dismissively, "don't worry about me. I know what I'm doing. I might be new to cannons and sabers, but I know sailing very well, and that's most of my job."

Kassia exhaled quietly and shook her head.

"Well, your reputation is on the up already. We knew you were coming back in, but next time do yourself a favor and come alongside at midday, not dawn. You'll get more of an audience then. That aside, I've already had five sailors in here asking after you this morning, looking for work on your crew. There'll be more as soon as people see that brigantine and word gets around."

"If they know a tiller from a touchhole, I'll take 'em," Caithlin yawned. "I'll have to give the navy their sailors back, so I need every man I can get. As for this brigantine, can you arrange a sale?"

Kassia frowned.

"Are you not keeping her? She's got more guns than you'll fit on your brig, and having a fore-and-aft rig at the tail end will give you more flexibility in quite a lot of scenarios. Don't you want to put your brig up for sale instead?"

"Absolutely not," Caithlin sat upright, "that's my father's ship. Once I've sorted this whole mess out, I fully intend to sail it right back to him. I'm not selling the *Queen*. Not now or ever."

Kassia shrugged nonchalantly and smiled.

"Right you are, Cathy, I can understand that. Leave it with me. I'll get a good price for you."

Caithlin glanced across at the middle-aged woman. A surge of gratitude washed over her as she recalled their first meeting and the sorry state in which she had arrived at this very office. Caithlin had never been good at talking about her feelings, that much she knew well. She took some pride in her self-awareness in that regard, but it was of little help when it came to matters of the heart. She ran through a few different approaches in her mind, ways of phrasing just how much she appreciated Kassia's care and charity, but nothing seemed to sound quite right.

"Your share when you sell that brigantine..." Caithlin started.

"One-twentieth is standard, but I can take a little less for a friend."

"Half."

"What?!"

"Half. Take half of the sale."

Kassia shot to her feet, both hands held up in protest.

"Don't be ridiculous! Cathy, I appreciate the gesture, but you are talking about a lot of money! You know how much you owe! Don't throw this opportunity away!"

Caithlin looked out of the window, a smile tugging at her lips as she saw the sun drenching the picturesque port with warmth and light. She thought of some of the horrific ports she had visited along the coastlines of the High Sea of Bari to the Bitter Lands. This place was heaven in comparison. It was a good place to be stranded.

"You saved me," Caithlin said evenly, "you saved me from prison or worse. You saved my father's company, and that means even more to me. Look, I owe ten years of debt. I've knocked that down already in my first voyage out. You might call it luck. I don't. I call it skill. I don't think I'll be here for ten years, I reckon on about two. So that's two years of us working together. Take the half share. I owe you that much for your kindness. I'll only go out and bring another two ships back next time. I want to give you the money. I want to thank you properly."

Kassia sat back down slowly behind her desk. She leaned forward, her eyes regarding Caithlin pensively as she rested one lightly clenched fist inside her other hand.

"Let me be blunt," she said, "because I care. You struck gold first time out, and I think it is largely because nobody was expecting you. Everybody will know who you are, soon enough. Everybody will know your ship. It will only get harder from here. You'll need to get smarter. Don't get cocky, Cathy, they'll kill you. As the Shining Ones above are my witness, the people you are facing will kill you."

Caithlin found herself tempted to give a nonchalant reply but stopped. Kassia had not always worked in a harbor office. She knew ships and she knew the sea. Caithlin, in turn, knew she needed to listen. She nodded slowly.

"Alright. I'll be more careful."

"Good. Now regarding this debt you owe me, if you are so grateful, would you consider allowing me to name my terms? If you are that indebted to my kindness, would you do anything for me?"

"Yes," Caithlin responded, "I think so. Within reason, yes. Name your price."

"Alright. First off, I'll take the standard one-twentieth share for the sale of the brigantine. You use the rest to pay your crew and chip away at those debts. Second, you pass on the favor. I've already told you that somebody once took care of me when I was also in trouble, back when I was your age. This is the Basilean way, this is what separates us from other nations. So, you give me my standard share, and you assure me, you *promise* me, that when the day comes, that you encounter somebody who needs your help as much as you needed mine, you'll do the right thing. You'll pass on the kindness of charity, just as I did to you. Those are my terms."

Frowning in confusion at how that was even close to repaying her debt to Kassia, Caithlin slowly stood and offered her hand. Kassia shook it firmly.

"Done. When that day comes, I'll do the right thing. I assure you."

***

It was now decidedly late for lunch. Charn did not care. Thaddeus Just had joined them on the quarterdeck, and now with the captain, the marine officer, two lieutenants, the master, and the surgeon, they had a true social gathering. Charn leaned back against the taffrail, his fingers interlocked across his belly as he listened to Walt Ganto prattle on about his wild theories of fitting a first-rate battleship out with fore-and-aft rigged sails, much to the disgust of Thaddeus. Kaeso Innes listened in attentively to the uneven trade of professional opinions, while Iain Kennus engaged in a much less heated conversation with Karnon Senne about good taverns in the City of the Golden Horn.

Charn watched and listened with interest; something that deep down he knew he did not do enough. Yet he found himself in an uncharacteristically contemplative mood, and it had taken him a good few moments of soul searching to discover why. The admiral's words at their last exchange had bothered him. Yes, Charn took great pride in being a moody, unapproachable sort of bastard, but that pride also extended to his own professional competence and reputation. In many ways, that was all he had. Long years at sea – many of which were arranged at his own behest to ensure his professional advancement – had left a neglected wife who, after just as many years of isolation, had finally told him that she was done. He could not blame her for that.

But the admiral had threatened to take the *Pious* away. *That* weighed heavily on his mind. That was perhaps why, rather than attending his own duties and allowing his subordinates to see to their own, Charn had encouraged them to sprawl around the quarterdeck, for over four hours now, simply engaged in idle chit-chat. It was the sort of thing he would have scoffed at, if he heard of it on another ship of war. But this was his ship of war, and if he did not find that orc fleet and send it to the bottom of the Infant Sea, it would be taken away from him. His entire life had been geared around command at sea. He had neglected his family, friends, everything else for command. If he lost it now, he was nothing.

"Samus!" Charn yelled down to the hatchway leading below. "Samus! Get up here! I've decided that we will take lunch on the quarterdeck. Bring some chairs up!"

The two separate conversations to either side of him died away abruptly.

"That's a little unconventional, sir?" Thaddeus risked.

"It's my bloody ship!" Charn boomed with a grin. "I shall do as I damn well like!"

He was greeted with overly sincere, exaggerated laughter from his two lieutenants. Career laughs. He let it go. Yes, it was his ship. For now.

As three of his sailors struggled to drag chairs up the narrow stairway leading to the quarterdeck, Charn heard the bosun's call announce that an officer had just arrived on deck. Wondering if that infernal captain from the *Vigil* had made another unannounced visit, Charn stormed across to the stairs to look down at the gangway leading from the quayside to the ship's starboard waist.

Jaymes Ellias stood to attention as he arrived onboard, bringing a hand up wearily in salute, as was protocol for an officer arriving onboard a warship. Beneath his blue jacket, his white shirt was spattered with rust-colored stains. His eyes were dull and tired. Wordlessly, he headed for the hatchway leading down to the gun deck.

"You're back," Charn declared simply from his elevated vantage point on the quarterdeck.

Jaymes stopped in his tracks. He looked up at his captain. Charn's bitter smile faded away. Even though he had seen that look on many an officer for the last year he had been in command of the *Pious*, the implications of Jaymes's expression suddenly hit home. He was propelled back some fifteen years, to a time when he was a bitterly unhappy lieutenant aboard the HW *Faithful*, and when the reign of terror inflicted by the ship's captain resulted in a disastrous turn of morale.

He remembered that awful sensation of stepping back onboard after a miserable night ashore with his fellow junior officers, wiled away with morose conversation about how miserable life onboard was. That awful memory of the smell of the warship, in stark contrast to the smell of normal life ashore, when one was back onboard. The sounds of sailors at work, the clinking of halyards against wood, the creaking of the wooden boards. Everything that reminded an individual about how bad life on a warship was compared to life ashore for ordinary folk. And right now, the look in Jaymes's eyes told Charn that he, as captain, had created that exact same environment. His officers hated life onboard the *Pious*, just as he had as a younger man. And he was responsible for it.

"Welcome back aboard, Mister Ellias," Charn said sincerely. "I gather you've had an eventful few days?"

"Aye, sir," Jaymes replied quietly, his tone monosyllabic and lacking any real emotion.

"You took a pirate brigantine?" Charn leaned forward to fold his arms on the wooden rail skirting around the forward end of the quarterdeck.

"The ship's company did, sir," Jaymes replied. "I was more of a witness rather than a participant."

Charn stared down at his first lieutenant. The man was broken. Whatever had happened or, more likely, whatever state Charn had sent him off the *Pious* in, the man was utterly disillusioned. Charn made his way down the stairs to stand by Jaymes, out of earshot of the comings and goings of sailors on the upper deck.

"I'm glad to have you back onboard, Jaymes," Charn said. "Your absence has very much highlighted your competency. Look, we're having a spot of lunch on the quarterdeck. I'd be delighted if you would join us, but there is honestly no pressure to do so. Go down below and either get yourself washed and into a clean uniform so that you can join us, or if you'd rather, then feel free to step ashore and take some time to yourself."

The sound of laughter drifted across from the after end of the quarterdeck as Samus brought across the first tray of food. Jaymes stared down at his feet.

"I shall be up presently, sir," he mumbled.

"Take your time," Charn said.

He risked clapping a hand against one of Jaymes's shoulders.

"This is your home," he told the younger officer, "I'm sorry you don't feel as welcome as you should."

Deciding that any further attempt to bridge the gap between them would be even more uncomfortable for them both, Charn headed back up to the quarterdeck and left Jaymes to make his way to his cabin.

"Samus!" Charn yelled as he claimed a seat on the quarterdeck, "be a good fellow and crack open a couple of bottles of wine, would you?"

Again, Charn recognized the looks of confusion on his subordinates as he took his seat. Baking in the midday sun, it felt almost as if this was his leaving party, his final hurrah onboard before moving on to other things. It was as if he was accepting defeat after the admiral's reprimand. Deep down, he knew he was overreacting, but somehow could not muster up the strength to carry on as normal. Perhaps he, too, was as tired as the young officers he commanded.

Food and drink was brought up, and the gathering on the quarterdeck grew as Prost, the ship's gunner, and Miko, the carpenter, joined the assembly. Realizing that time was marching on and that it was only a little under two hours until the chaplains were due to turn up to conduct the ceremony for the blessing of *Pious's* hull, Charn was about to begin bringing proceedings to a halt when he heard the shrill bosun's call announce the arrival of another officer from the gangway. Charn leapt to his feet and made his way over, when the new arrival appeared on the quarterdeck.

Caithlin Viconti made her way up from the upper deck, flashing a brief smile to Charn as she arrived. The assembly of ship's officers at the impromptu quarterdeck lunch raised themselves to their feet as she arrived, either out of respect for a visiting captain, a lady, or both. Charn noticed a certain self-assurance in the privateer's manner; a swagger to her step that accompanied the darker, more piratical make-up around her eyes and the daring neckline of her half unbuttoned shirt.

"Don't worry about that," Caithlin said, holding up a hand to stop them. "I was just passing by and wanted to pay my compliments and pass on my gratitude for the loan of your sailors."

The buzz of conversation returned to normal behind Charn as he gestured for Samus to climb back up to the quarterdeck.

"Samus, bring a glass of wine over for our visitor," he ordered the steward.

"Not for me," Caithlin said, removing her black tricorn hat, "I don't really drink. Besides, as much as I appreciate the invitation, I'm not stopping. It was really just a quick visit to thank you face-to-face. And apologize for bringing back a few less sailors than I took away with me. Their bodies were given the proper marks of respect after the engagement."

Charn nodded slowly. Nothing could be done about that, no point in losing his temper over some of his men being killed in battle. Technically, they were Alain Stryfus's men, but that mattered little.

"Thank you for that," Charn said, "and I am glad that you had some success. Mister Ellias has just returned onboard and should be up here shortly. He described his role in it all as something of a bystander."

"Did he indeed," Caithlin said quietly, absent-mindedly biting the corner of her bottom lip. She looked across at the stormy southern horizon for a moment and then back at Charn. She stepped in closer, her tone low and conspiratory.

"Your lieutenant is too modest," she half-whispered. "He took charge of the training of my crew and personally instructed me in fencing and pistol marksmanship. When we went up against that brigantine, he followed my orders and remained on my quarterdeck. The captain of the opposing vessel, a rather unsavory character by the name of Gallo, led a counterattack against my ship. Lieutenant Ellias stood alone, outnumbered, and stopped the counterattack dead. He fought Captain Gallo to a standstill until he surrendered."

Charn listened intently as Caithlin continued. While he had assumed the brigantine had belonged to a pirate of some notoriety, he had not realized it was the infamous Red Gallo. And Caithlin had taken him down on her first voyage as a privateer.

"Then, after I ordered Lieutenant Ellias to captain the brigantine back here, there was a brief attempt at an uprising from the pirates, who attempted to re-take their ship. Lieutenant Ellias successfully put them back down, without any loss of life. So, in summary, I could not disagree more with his report of being nothing more than a bystander. I would go as far as to say that he was the most valuable individual in my entire crew. What a shame that he intends to leave the naval service."

Charn was about to reply when he noticed the very subject of the conversation stood at the foot of the stairs leading up to the quarterdeck. Jaymes, looking a little fresher in a shirt devoid of bloodstains, looked up uneasily at the two captains, clearly having heard every word exchanged about him.

"I was just leaving," Caithlin cleared her throat uncomfortably. "Captain Ferrus, thank you for your hospitality and for all of your assistance in preparing my ship for service. I always admired your navy's frigates, but having now lived through a battle and seen firsthand how a warship is to be used, I only appreciate more the absolute magnificence of your vessel."

A few days ago, Charn would have taken that as a compliment. Now, having convinced himself that the magnificent vessel in question would soon be wrenched from him, he could only smile uncomfortably. Caithlin nodded a farewell and then made her way down the stairs to stand in front of Jaymes.

"I owe you an apology," she said clearly enough for Charn to hear. "I was discourteous to you when you did not deserve it. The simple fact of the matter is that your competency and professionalism made me look rather stupid. That was my fault, not yours. I apologize for my words."

"Not a problem, ma'am," Jaymes replied formally.

Caithlin extended her hand. After a brief pause, Jaymes shook it.

"Goodbye, Jaymes," she smiled warmly, "and thank you. I hope life outside the naval service is everything you want it to be."

The two Basilean officers watched the privateer make her way back down the gangway to the quayside and stride confidently away from the trio of frigates.

"You don't have to leave this, you know," Charn offered as Jaymes clambered up to the quarterdeck. "One has to wonder whether life on the other side of this is indeed all it is cracked up to be."

"I have to try, sir," Jaymes replied. "Better for me and better for the service."

Charn watched as his first lieutenant walked over to take a seat next to Karnon Senne. A sailor from the duty watch rang the ship's bell to signify the passing of the hour, reminding Charn how little time he had until the blessing ceremony. Content that he was, for once, leaving his officers to enjoy what little spare time they were allowed, he quietly left the quarterdeck and made his way to his cabin.

Chapter Seventeen

"I'm not for a second suggesting anything close to sacrilege!" Captain Alain Stryfus countered as he emptied the last of the decanter into his glass. "I'm merely saying that – while I acknowledge the power of our deities above – I do not place ultimate faith in our clergy! I do not for a moment think that our mortal priests below are the chosen of the Shining Ones or wield their power and authority!"

Charn narrowed his eyes in disapproval as he leaned back in his chair. The sun had only an hour or two left before dipping beneath the horizon, but the early evening light showed a clearing horizon to the south through the tall windows of the Thatraskos wardroom. They would be sailing the next morning, of that Charn had no doubt.

The three frigate captains sat alone at a long dining table in the naval base's plush wardroom; the accommodation and living area for the naval port's officers. A dozen officers of varying ranks were scattered around the room, all seated perhaps a little unsociably in their various groups rather than together at one table. The large room was wood-paneled to give it the feel of a ship at sea, although the realities of life onboard a dark, cramped warship were not replicated in the room's open nature, large windows, and tall ceiling. Perhaps fifty meticulously constructed model sailing ships hung from wires above them, carefully arranged in place to replicate the climax of the legendary Battle of Star Point.

"You're missing the point entirely," countered Captain Marcellus Dio, with not a little irritation evident in his tone. "Our chaplains claim no such thing! You can't honestly believe that a man or woman who feels a stronger pull toward a life of servitude, driven by their faith, is some sort of magic-wielding fraud who wishes to hide behind the vestments of the clergy for their own betterment! That's utterly ridiculous! The ceremony to bless each hull takes a long time because it has real purpose and sincerity! Not because it is some charlatan making something out of nothing and wafting their hands around pointlessly!"

"Gentlemen," Charn interjected, "I think we have strayed from the point. What I was saying was that this afternoon's ceremony to bless the hulls of our frigates was, in my opinion, a welcome gesture; and while I certainly do not for a moment believe that it will be the deciding factor that differentiates victory from defeat, I do believe it to be fully worthwhile. Even for those who doubt the extent of the powers of the clergy, there can be no denying the powers of the Shining Ones and our gesture does, at least, shine a beacon on our good intentions."

"Agreed," Marcellus said simply.

Alain removed his napkin from his shirt collar and placed it on the empty plate in front of him but remained silent. The silence was infectious; making the next few moments pass by in some discomfort before laughter from another table galvanized conversation to begin again.

"So tomorrow is the day, then," Marcellus stated, nodding out of the windows toward the southern horizon.

"Yes," Charn said, "I expect so."

"We thought that last time," Alain commented dryly.

Marcellus took in a long, slow breath in response to the younger captain's complaint. Charn, too, found himself somewhat annoyed by Alain's incessant negativity, but his mind wandered elsewhere. He had received another letter from his wife, explaining why she had made the decision to terminate their relationship. It was almost apologetic, despite her years of faithfulness and strength in the face of loneliness while Charn was at sea.

Her points were all valid and perfectly reasonable. They both knew that Charn had engineered his own destiny, and that he had consistently pushed hard for more sea time to increase his prospects for advancement. He had left her alone and ended the marriage; not the navy. But that left him with the navy and the navy alone, and the admiral's thinly veiled threat still burned within him. This was all he had left.

"We'll get them this time," Charn grumbled as he re-filled his glass of rum. "We'll get them. I'm not coming back into port until we do."

***

A string of expletives echoed out of the cabin on the far side of the passageway as Jaymes splashed a drop of scented lotion onto his neck to complete his rather half-hearted preparations for an evening in town. Karnon, the source of the disturbance, shot out of his cabin and slammed the door behind him. Jaymes flinched as he noted the vivid, maroon breeches that Karnon had elected to wear; more offensive to the eye even than the mustard-colored affair he had sported on their last outing into town.

"Sodding little bastards!" Karnon growled. "That bloody island was covered in them! As if it isn't bad enough having to defend a gold mine from a horde of orcs, the island's original natives have bitten me to buggery!"

"I have no idea what you're talking about," Jaymes admitted as he closed the door to his own cabin behind him.

"Insects!" Karnon grimaced. "Every morning was the same routine! Wake up and find out how many *dozen* times you've been bitten overnight! I mean, what sort of little shit of a creature bites a man in between his toes?! And on the anklebone! And it hasn't stopped! I think I've brought back an entire colony of them in my socks, because the new bites are still arriving!"

"Have you spoken to the surgeon?" Jaymes offered.

The burly marine shook his head.

"That man is about as useful as a halfling in a spear rank," Karnon grumbled. "Come on, I assume it's just us two again."

"Yes. Walt is off at the Bay View again..."

"In uniform?"

"In uniform. And Kaeso is staying here to revise."

"Hasn't he just passed his lieutenancy exams?" Karnon asked.

"Yes, but he'll have another board to sit in about ten years, and I think he's the sort of fellow who likes to prepare a little bit early."

The two men clambered up to the upper deck where the western horizon was just beginning to grow darker as the sun set. With the afternoon's gentle breeze dying away to nothing, the evening sky was still ferociously hot. Jaymes walked over to the gangway, standing to attention at *Pious's* waist, out of reverence to the ship's ensign, but not saluting as he was now in civilian attire. Karnon followed his example and then followed him down the gangway to the quayside.

"About time you showed up," a voice called from where a figure leaned against a wall of empty supply crates. "I've been waiting for over an hour."

Jaymes looked across and saw Caithlin standing by the crates, arms folded, wearing a short dress of elven styling in white that emphasized her tanned limbs and blonde hair. He stopped in his tracks, completely caught off guard by her appearance. The privateer captain, now devoid of nautical attire and looking far more like a regular citizen of the island, made her way over.

"Shall we go and get something to drink?" she greeted the two. "I'd rather like to leave the docks. I've been propositioned four times while I've been waiting here, which tells me as much about this dress as it does about waiting on corners in docks at sunset."

"How come you're still here?" Karnon grumbled. "Didn't any of them offer you enough?"

"My prices have gone up since I made a ton of money bringing in a famous pirate that the Basilean navy couldn't deal with," Caithlin smirked in response.

"Probably should have relied on marines instead of sailors, then," Karnon countered.

"Oh, is that what you are?" Caithlin queried. "I hadn't even heard that the Basilean fleet had officially adopted a marine force. Perhaps they're waiting for a special occasion before they make the announcement. Come on, I'll buy."

Jaymes exchanged a wary glance with Karnon as the young woman led the two off toward the southwest quadrant of town.

"Palm Spring alright for you two?" she asked, sliding her arm across to link it through Jaymes's as she walked alongside him.

"Fine by me," Karnon said. "I think that's my favorite place here so far."

The trio made their way out of the naval dock, idly passing the time on the journey by talking about the weather, options for taverns and inns, and other low-key subjects. Caithlin's sudden, more talkative nature did, however, elicit a few exchanged glances between Jaymes and Karnon as they crossed the town.

The evening had grown a little cooler and more comfortable by the time they reached the Palm Springs Inn and made their way up to the seating area on the roof, overlooking the bay. In the corner of the roof terrace a middle-aged man, whose olive skin marked him out as a native islander, plucked away tunefully on a miniature Keretian lute. Jaymes picked out a small table and moved across to pull a chair out for Caithlin.

"Hey!" Karnon suddenly shouted across the roof, drawing attention from the two dozen or so well-to-do patrons gathered at their tables. "Hey! Morgan! Is that you?"

A small, wiry man with a shaven head and ratty features turned around from another table at the far side of the roof and looked back at Karnon, his features startled. He held a hand up in recognition.

"Old legion mate of mine," Karnon explained, slapping a hand on Jaymes's shoulder. "Sorry if I'm rude, but I really should go and say hello. I might be a while catching up, it's been years. Start without me, I might see you later on."

The marine captain quickly made his way over to see his old comrade, leaving Jaymes alone at the small table at the edge of the roof, opposite Caithlin.

"What shall we have?" she asked.

"Are you not drinking water?"

"Oh no," Caithlin said, "I've come across here from visiting a friend of mine. We've already had a glass or two of wine, so I might as well carry on."

That explained her uncharacteristic behavior, Jaymes mused, knowing from previous conversations with her that as a non-drinker, a glass or two would be more than enough to loosen her up significantly. He gestured for one of the inn's staff and ordered a bottle of wine that he knew to be very light on alcohol. The music from the lute seemed to blend in with the evening songs of the colorful birds in the surrounding trees to create that optimistic feeling that Jaymes felt to be unique to the islands of the Infant Sea.

"I'm buying," Caithlin said, reaching into her pocket. "I still haven't sorted out your share of the prize money from our escapades."

"Quite alright," Jaymes said, producing three coins. "I've still got the last remnants of what the admiral sent me across to you with."

"Weren't you supposed to give that back?" Caithlin asked.

"Yeah," Jaymes admitted, "but I lied and said I spent it all. Anyway, how's about one of these coins pays for the overpriced wine, and we both pocket one each out of these last two?"

He looked down at the coins, the noble dragon showing on one of them and the Hegemon's crown emblem on the other two. There was an old saying about accepting the Hegemon's coin for a life in the navy. Aside from his final payout, these three coins would be his last payment for the years he had given. That made them symbolic. But giving one to Caithlin felt right, even though he knew the cool, detached privateer would never return his accursed sappiness and sentimentality.

"That sounds fair," Caithlin smiled, sliding one of the heavy, gold coins across the wooden table.

She looked up at him, her expression slipping from joviality to discomfort, and even a little nervousness. The show of emotion looked out of place across her flawless features. The gentle plucking of the lute continued to stir at Jaymes's emotions.

"I had to come and find you," she said quietly. "I know I apologized before, but it was rushed. I wanted to properly say sorry for the way I spoke to you."

Jaymes looked away to the south at the now clear horizon. Two or three staggered lines of little fishing boats funneled into the bay at the end of their long day at sea. He looked back at Caithlin.

"It's alright," he shrugged, feining indifference, "I think I was annoying you. I probably deserved it."

"No. No you didn't," Caithlin said seriously. "I was coming apart at the seams and you were trying to help."

"For what it's worth," Jaymes said as a server brought over their wine and poured out two glasses, "I was terrified myself. I'm not saying that to appear... I don't know. It's the truth. Anyway, it really doesn't matter, so let's not worry about it."

Jaymes sampled the wine; the exquisite nature of the liquid was rather lost on him and his simple palette. He watched Caithlin take a silent sip from her own glass, deciding that the gentlemanly thing would be to stop her from drinking anymore, even though he risked being rather patronizing by doing so.

"So what happens now?" Caithlin asked. "One last patrol and then you're done? You're leaving?"

"That's the plan," Jaymes said, smiling at the thought of returning to the mainland. "I have a friend who was a midshipman with me when all this first started. He had the good sense to leave the navy about two or three years ago. We spoke about starting up a small business in the capital, buying a few small boats to ferry people around. Little coastal trips, taking wealthy people from place to place, that sort of thing. A couple of old friends are now actually invested in it and wrote to me to see if I was still interested in joining them."

"And that's what you want?" Caithlin asked, resting her chin on the tops of her hands as she leaned across the table.

"Yes," Jaymes answered hesitantly, "I think so. My parents and my sister all live in the capital, and it would be nice to see more of them. I... don't think there really is a perfect solution to any problem. But being in the navy is definitely a problem for me, and while this isn't a perfect solution, it is still a solution. Yes, I think I'd like to give this a go."

Caithlin glanced across at him, then looked away and nodded to herself as if briefly running a conversation through in her head before looking up again.

"I hope it works out for you," she smiled warmly. "You deserve every success with it. I think you'll do well. You have a way with people."

"I don't know about that," Jaymes winced.

"Oh? I think you do."

"Your first mate doesn't," Jaymes replied.

"What makes you think that?" Caithlin asked.

"Well," Jaymes said pensively, "I picked up a hint of sorts just before I left your ship, when he took me to one side and said, 'Ellias, let me make one thing perfectly clear. I don't like you.'"

Caithlin unsuccessfully attempted to suppress a smirk and narrowed her eyes as if deep in thought.

"I wouldn't look too far into that," she offered, "I think that's a fairly ambiguous statement. Could mean nearly anything."

Jaymes laughed quietly as he reached for his wine glass.

***

Thaddeus Just yelled up a command to the top men on the yards, and the sails on all three masts were let out. The *Pious* pulled ahead a little, leading the line of three frigates across the bay and toward the opening to the Infant Sea. The mid-morning sun blazed away incessantly, its rays of heat combated only by a stiff, unseasonal northwesterly breeze that flowed over the peaks of the island to push out the sails of the frigates. Charn wondered if such a rare wind in the bay was a good omen, it being positioned nicely to help the ships sail for the breakwater and then south for the open sea.

Aside from the top men who were busily engaged in trimming the frigate's sails, the remainder of the ship's company stood to attention in a continuous line leading around the edge of the fo'c'sle, upper deck, and quarterdeck. Charn stood centrally with his officers, each of them resplendent in their blue jackets and black hats. The *Veneration* followed the *Pious* out, then the *Vigil*, and finally the *Martolian Queen*. A squadron of three sloops – a last minute but very welcome addition to Charn's hunter force – waited for the frigates outside the breakwater.

The *Pious* headed past the tall tower of the naval administration building, and the office of Admiral Sir Jerias Pattia. The line of warships was close enough to the shore that Charn could see a lone figure at the office window as the admiral watched his frigates heading out to the open sea to resume the hunt. Again, the last words he had received from the admiral weighed heavily on Charn's mind, and again he cursed himself for his lack of mental fortitude in failing to adequately deal with them. It mattered not. One way or the other, he would not be returning to this bay, this picturesque coastal town, and this island without victory assured.

***

His fists clenched and his arms locked in at his sides as he stood rigidly to attention on the quarterdeck, Jaymes watched enviously as the normal world slipped by at the edge of the bay. Ordinary folk carrying on with their business and day-to-day chores, completely disinterested by the three towering warships that drifted silently past the carpet of little fishing boats in the bay. Perhaps, just perhaps, it would be him soon. *If* they finally found this orc pirate fleet. And if he survived.

Slowly, carefully to avoid detection, Jaymes eased one hand into his pocket and found the last remaining coin he had been given to pay for his first meeting with Caithlin. He curled his fingers around the metal and held on tight to it, thinking of the perfect evening he had spent with her before he walked her back to her ship just before midnight. It certainly was a better way to say goodbye. *If* they found the orc pirates, and if he survived the subsequent encounter, he would miss her when he resigned his commission, left the navy, and returned home. He would always keep the coin to remember that last, perfect evening ashore before his final voyage as a naval lieutenant, and his final battle.

The four ships curved gently around and past the breakwater. As planned, the *Vigil* and *Veneration* altered course to port and starboard respectively, the two smaller, Batch One frigates easing out to take station off the *Pious's* quarters and form an arrowhead of warships. The *Martolian Queen*, not as fast as a frigate but clearly quicker to accelerate, swept in between the *Vigil* and the *Pious* as her sails were set to full. Her crew, now made up of a vast influx of new sailors as the loaned men were returned to their frigate, ambled about the upper deck as they carried on their business in stark contrast to the rigid formality of the three Basilean warships.

Jaymes looked down from the edge of the frigate's quarterdeck to the smaller ship below. He saw Caithlin removing her heavy jacket and tossing it to one side. Cursing himself for his incessant sappiness and sentimentality, Jaymes felt himself pining like an adolescent as he watched her. It was like the women he had thought he had fallen for before her, only a hundred fold. One hand wrapped tightly around the coin, he stepped forward out of the formal line of officers and held a hand up high to wave down to her. Caithlin looked up at him, too far away for him to make out any facial response, but close enough for him to see her return the wave.

Jaymes looked across at the harsh, terrifying face of Charn Ferrus as the weathered captain stared icily at him.

"Back in line, Mister Ellias, stand to attention," the captain ordered sternly.

Jaymes took a pace back and resumed his place next to the captain as the brig opened out to port ahead of the *Vigil*.

"She'll be alright, Jaymes," Charn muttered under his breath to him, "she's one of the good ones. Don't worry about her."

Surprised at the exceptionally rare show of compassion from his captain, Jaymes stared ahead as the four ships met up with the trio of sloops and headed out to the open sea. For the first time in the months he had been a part of the *Pious's* ship's company, he genuinely appreciated the words of his captain.

"Mister Ellias!" Charn called, his tone formal again. "Fall out the ship's company!"

"Bosun!" Jaymes shouted. "Pipe the carry on!"

The bosun raised his metal whistle to his lips and let out a long, two-tone blast. In response, every sailor on the deck turned to their right and, with the formalities of leaving harbor completed, quickly set about their routine tasks. Jaymes remained at the quarterdeck, watching the three small sloops swing by to take station by the four larger ships as they headed south to the open sea.

"You were back before me last night," Karnon said as he wandered over to the corner of the quarterdeck. "Didn't it go well?"

"All went fine," Jaymes said, his hand still gripping the coin. "What about you? Did you have a good evening catching up with your friend?"

"Friend?" Karnon scoffed. "The man's a complete arsehole. I can't stand him. Never could. But even a heartless bastard like me knows when to make himself scarce."

Jaymes smiled in gratitude as Karnon headed back down to the upper deck. He glanced across at the brig and, deciding that the time for sentimentality was over and the time to concentrate on the business of waging war had again begun, set about seeing to his duties.

***

Ghurak looked up at the door as a fist hammered into the thick wood. The shutters to his quarters were tilted to allow a few lines of sunlight into the cabin, illuminating his throne, planning table, and personal collection of weapons that hung from the walls and racks around him. There was still an empty space where his prized cutlass had been kept, before he had lost it at the failed attack on the Basilean gold mine. The recollection made him clench his powerful fists in anger. Struggling to his feet – the struggles driven by his physical injuries but certainly not any reluctance to face the pain, Ghurak reminded himself – he limped over toward the door.

The hammering came again.

"Wait!" Ghurak bellowed.

After bringing the smasher back to Axe Island, Ghurak's crew had tracked down a goblin from the *Devourer* – Admrul Urugag's smasher – who boasted a reputation for being able to stitch up any wounded green-skin who still breathed. Despite being a rival island chief, Urugag had allowed it and sent his goblin scab-lifter over to where the *Green Hammer* lay at anchor just off the coast of Axe Island. The goblin only confirmed what Ghurak already knew – the injuries to his left leg were permanent, and he would in all likelihood never be able to bend his knee to its full extent again. Given the sheer number of crossbow bolts that had penetrated his thick hide, he had escaped lightly.

Ghurak reached the door to his cabin and paused. He knew the warriors were beginning to talk. He had hidden the extent of his injuries for some time by remaining seated at the throne in his cabin and ordering his subordinates to report to him, rather than stomping around his own ship. But his loyal goblins were nosey little bastards and eager to earn his favor by reporting anything they overheard to him. Ghurak knew that some elements of the crew were beginning to doubt him. A crippled orc admrul could just as easily be replaced by a younger, more fit leader.

Ghurak flung open the door to reveal Irukk and, more to his surprise, the human pirate captain, Cerri Denayo. Irukk looked at the wounded krudger with barely hidden surprise.

"You're… up and moving again, Admrul."

"I've been up and moving for days, Irukk!" Ghurak snapped. "What of it? A few sticks and stones are not going to stop me!"

"Captin Cerri wanted to talk to you, Admrul," Irukk said, his respectful tone still in place despite the reports from Ghurak's goblins. "It's important."

Grunting, Ghurak turned and concentrated with every fiber of his being in walking normally and evenly back across his cabin to his throne. He stumbled, blatantly, halfway across the cabin. It was in full view of his first mate. Suppressing a curse, Ghurak continued and turned to sit down on his throne.

"Well?" he demanded.

"I've had a message from a contact at Thatraskos," Cerri said, his lithe arms folded across his thin chest. "The Basileans have sent a force out to sea. They're hunting for you."

"How long ago?" Ghurak narrowed his eyes and leaned forward, planting his grizzled chin on one fist.

"Two days."

"How many?"

"Seven ships," Cerri said seriously, "three of them are frigates; the others are smaller."

Ghurak nodded. A smasher could better a Basilean frigate, but not three of them. His two blood runners would begin to even the odds, but he still needed more.

"Then we'll go out and stop them," Ghurak grunted. "You and me, Cerri. Finally. We'll go out alongside each other."

"We?" the human pirate laughed. "What's this 'we'? I told you when this all started that it would end in disaster. I told you to leave the Basileans well alone. It's the unwritten rule around here! I'm not going out there with you, Ghurak, this is on you to fix. Even the other orc captains at Axe know that! No, I'm being neighborly by bringing this information to you. I'm already helping you enough as it is. But this is where my help ends."

Ghurak glowered up at the human pirate chief. He briefly considered killing him there and then, but he had naval warships scouring the seas to the north for him already and could not afford to have the entire human pirate population doing the same.

"Then I'll do it without you," Ghurak said simply.

"And then what?" Cerri snapped. "Let's say that somehow you send seven Basilean warships to the bottom, then what? Do you think their Admiralty will sit back and think, 'well, fair enough, we clearly can't stop him!' No! The more you insult them, the more they'll send down! If you go out and sink them, then they'll send more! When will you be satisfied? When they send down a Dictator-class battleship from the capital? What is it you want, Ghurak? The rest of us, we want to make as much money as we can for ourselves and our crew. What do you want?"

Ghurak smirked at the thought of a Dictator-class battleship being sent down from the capital to look for him. Now *there* was a fight that would be worth his time. As for what he wanted? That was a stupid, narrow-minded, childish question that he would expect from a human. He wanted what all orcs wanted. Power and respect. Concepts that seemed secondary at best in the priorities of even the mightiest human warlords.

"Go on, Cerri," he said dismissively, "you've delivered your message. Go back to your whores and your rum, I've got some proper fighting to do."

Scowling, Cerri turned on his heel and stormed out of the cabin. Irukk watched him go and then turned back to face his leader.

"What orders, Admrul?"

Ghurak leaned back in his throne for a brief moment's contemplation.

"Get the ship ready to sail. Send a message to Kroock and Drika and tell them to be ready, too."

Irukk turned to leave.

"Wait."

The orc first mate stopped again.

"Send a message out to every captin of these little rabble ships around the island. Tell them I'm going to war and I'll allow them to join me. Tell them... the captin who impresses me the most will be given command of the next blood runner I have built."

"You're going to let a goblin be captin of a blood runner?"

"No! No, I'm not! But you tell them what I've told you to tell them!"

"Aye, Admrul," Irukk replied.

Chapter Eighteen

The winds veering around to give a northerly flow had pushed away the last remnants of the hurricane and presented an entirely different view of the Infant Sea to the one Jaymes had experienced when bringing the captured brigantine back to port a few days before. With spring having now well and truly surrendered to summer, the skies were blue and the turquoise waters calm, with just a hint of cool refreshment in the breeze from the northerly, polar flow.

The three frigates continued to surge on southward, *Pious* front and center, while the *Martolian Queen* kept station to the east, leaving the squadron of small sloops out to the west. The extended line of seven warships must have been quite a sight as they crossed the Sand Lane, a show of force reminding the traders and merchant captains that Basilea still controlled these waters, despite the outlier, rogue successes of one orc captain with providence temporarily on his side.

Jaymes made his way up to the quarterdeck and saw that Francis currently held the duty of officer of the watch. He doubted that any civilian shipping company, or any human or dwarf sailor for that matter, would agree with the policy of entrusting a warship and its conduct to the leadership and authority of an adolescent. But, in the captain's absence, there were not enough experienced officers to take charge of the quarterdeck around the clock as officer of the watch, and in more sedate periods of sailing such as this, it was a fantastic way to build experience in the navy's future commanders.

"All quiet, Francis?" Jaymes greeted as he paced over.

"Aye, sir," the young midshipman nodded. "Wind's coming around a few points toward the nor'west, but nothing else of note."

"Right," Jaymes suppressed a yawn, "fingers crossed we find something this time out, then."

A minute or two passed in silence as Jaymes walked across to the port taff rail, staring out across the warm waves at the *Vigil* and the *Martolian Queen*. He fished a hand into his pocket and found the solitary gold coin he now kept with him at all times.

"Sir?" Francis interjected uncomfortably as he appeared at his side. "If you don't mind, what was it like fighting against Red Gallo?"

Jaymes paused in contemplation. Only a moment after he had begun to process his memories of the event, he was interrupted by a shout from the top of the mainmast.

"Sail ho! Mister Ellias, sir! Sail ho to the south!"

Jaymes rushed over to the forward end of the quarterdeck.

"What is she?" he shouted up at the lookout atop the mainmast, his hands cupped around his mouth.

"Can't tell, sir," the reply was hollered back over the rush of the wind, "but she's got red sails!"

Jaymes eyes widened in alarm. Remembering procedure – he was merely an off-watch lieutenant, despite being the ship's second-in-command – he looked across expectantly at Francis Turnio.

"Just one sail, sir," the young officer stammered. "It could be nothing. I... we're heading south anyway, I think we should monitor it before we..."

"Francis," Jaymes interjected, "have you ever even heard of anybody except the orcs dying their sails red?"

Francis swallowed and then nodded.

"Understood, sir," he said, before turning to bellow out an order down to the upper deck. "Beat to quarters!"

***

"What is it?" Karnon demanded as he ducked beneath the narrow hatchway entrance into the dimly lit, cramped armory. "What's going on upstairs?"

Six of his marines had already arrived in the frigate's armory, including his deputy, Sergeant Castus Erria, and they were busily setting about unlocking the supply of personal arms.

"Not sure, sir," Erria said as he passed across two heavy crossbows to one of his marines to take to the upper deck, "came straight here as soon as they beat to quarters. Must be the orcs, though. I can't see what else would cause the alarm to go."

"Right," Karnon nodded, "get everybody armored up. I know some of the lads are still cagey about wearing full armor at sea, but if it is the orcs, I'm willing to bet that they'll be more of a threat to us than drowning will. Everybody in full armor."

"Got it," Erria replied as he shoved a clunky, pitted key into the lock of one of the armaments crates and opened the lid to reveal rows of deadly boarding pikes. "And the firearms, sir?"

Karnon paused for a second. He found it incredulous that, not yet out of his twenties, he was already suspicious of new weapon technology. As a man-at-arms in his adolescent years, muskets and pistols were something almost exclusively used by dwarfs. Now, with trade relations between the dwarfs and Basilea on the rise again, more of these brutal but expertly crafted weapons were finding their way into the Basilean fleet, who seemed to embrace them far more readily than the legion.

"Give the pistols to the sailors," Karnon replied, "we'll be fine without them. Give them to the officers first, then any left over go to the petty officers of the boarding parties. As for the muskets… get three marines at the top of each mast. Tell them to stay there no matter what and shoot down with the muskets."

"And the shields?"

Karnon exhaled.

"Get them on the upper deck. If we end up facing that big orc ship, there might just be enough room to use them."

Content that there was an embryonic plan beginning to formulate, Karnon grabbed one of the boarding pikes for himself and turned to head to the upper deck.

***

Initially, little more than a scarlet smear on the horizon as viewed through his telescope, Charn had nothing to compare the ship to and so could make no accurate assessment regarding its size. Then a second, smaller sail appeared not far from the first, identifiable after a few minutes as triangular; fore-and-aft rigged. That contrast gave Charn exactly what he needed to visualize what he was facing. It was two ships he had met before. From his vantage point on the fo'c'sle, Charn grimaced and lowered his telescope.

"That's them," he grunted, "that's the bastards. Smasher and a blood runner."

He allowed himself a slight, vicious smile at the thought of moving to engage the two orc ships with the power of the seven ship fleet at his disposal. The three frigates alone could take down the smasher, of that he was confident. The presence of the blood runner would only slow down the inevitable, and not by much.

"There's another one, sir," Jaymes said, one elbow placed against the base of the bowsprit as he leaned over with his own telescope. "Third ship, just off to the west. Looks like the smasher is flanked by two blood runners."

"Two?" Charn spat, raising his telescope again to confirm the report presented by his first lieutenant.

Sure enough, a third sail polluted the otherwise clear horizon. Not to worry. They had the weather gauge with the wind now off to the northwest and had seven ships facing only three, with only the smasher being able to stand up to the might of a Basilean frigate. But not three of them. Charn would just have to think that little bit harder to minimize his casualties before claiming the inevitable victory.

He brought his telescope back to line up on the large, central ship. The smasher and its crude, metal bow grew ever so slowly larger as the two opposing forces sailed directly toward each other. Then, just becoming visible behind the smasher, Charn saw something. He let out a gasp as a sudden sense of nausea clutched at his throat.

"Sir?" Jaymes muttered.

Charn brought his telescope down and snapped it shut.

"I know. I've seen them."

***

Ghurak allowed himself a low chuckle as the line of Basilean warships on the horizon began to open out in preparation for battle. They were close enough now for him to even make out the small ships. Three frigates in the center, a familiar looking ship with the lines of a fast merchantman off on the right, and three of the tiny, fragile sloops on the left. That was what made Ghurak laugh. They had come out to fight, expecting to outgun him. But those last few hours and the promises of reward he had put out across the coast of Axe Island had combined together with his growing reputation for success after bringing in three captured ships from his last voyage. He looked out with pride at his own assembled fleet; an armada fit for any admrul.

The *Green Hammer* surged forward in the center of the fleet, flanked by the *Driller* and the *Blood Skull*, commanded by his captins – Kroock and Drika. No fewer than six single mast rabbles – tiny warships of a similar size and role to the sloops – had responded to his call. But that was not all. Captin Drethug, one of Admrul Urugag's most trusted subordinates, had clearly exchanged harsh words with his krudger; Drethug's own blood runner, the *Wave Rammer*, had unexpectedly appeared to join Ghurak's fleet as he departed Axe Island. That allowed him to arrive to face the Basileans with ten warships to their seven, five of which packed a worthwhile punch.

Ghurak snapped his telescope shut and limped across the back of the ship to stand by his wheel goblins. He saw Irukk watching him out of the corner of his eye. Yes, they all knew now that one of his legs was crippled, most likely permanently. And yes, that meant he could not run as fast, but he only needed his hands and his head to fight, and those still worked just fine. But Irukk and his gang of warriors were growing increasingly suspicious in their behavior; the conversations that hushed as soon as Ghurak hobbled near, the disapproving looks from the angry, ambitious, younger orcs. Even the way they watched him now, his first mate and the orc gun captins of the cannons that bristled from the deck to either side of the wheel. They watched him like little sharks, eagerly waiting to devour a wounded kraken. But this kraken had plenty of fight left in him. If anything, more than ever.

"Irukk!" Ghurak boomed to his first mate.

"Admrul," the burly orc replied.

"Get the signal flags up!" Ghurak growled, well aware that this was not a job for the first mate but eager to take any opportunity to remind Irukk who was in command. "Tell the rabble captins to take out those sloops. Order the blood runners to follow me in on the frigates."

***

Her eyes narrowed as she contemplated the enemy fleet on the southern horizon. Caithlin flipped her gold coin up into the air, where it hovered for the briefest of moments at shoulder height before she snatched it out of space with the same hand. She repeated the flip and catch again and again as she glanced at each of the orc ships in turn, assessing the trim of their sails relative to the course they had selected against the wind, in an attempt to ascertain the experience of their captains.

The two fleets were closing fast, almost close enough now for the first bow chasers to open fire and truly initiate the battle. She was nervous – she admitted that much to herself as she flipped the coin Jaymes had given to her – but certainly far less so than prior to her last battle. Even though they were outnumbered, they had a far more advantageous position with the wind off their starboard quarter; and being but one ship in a force of seven made her feel far more absolved of responsibility of the outcome. She could only do her best. No more.

"Flagship is signaling, Captain!" X'And called from the starboard waist.

Caithlin pocketed the gold coin and raised her telescope to her eye. The signal was clear enough.

M-Q-Attack-West

"They want us to cross the line of battle and attack the rabbles," X'And muttered.

"Yes, I can see that," Caithlin replied irritably.

The six rabble ships were plunging through the waves toward the three sloops on the western end of the line of Basilean ships. Caithlin knew the handling characteristics of a sloop well enough and could guess at the deficiencies of a rabble just by regarding one through a telescope, but even as a newcomer to naval warfare it was obvious to her that six rabbles would defeat three sloops. Charn Ferrus was clearly ordering her over to the west to protect the sloops. Then again, why bother even bringing the sloops if they needed a larger, more capable ship to defend them? They were the fastest ships in the Basilean fleet. They would do better by exploiting their advantages and keeping their distance, perhaps even leading the rabble away.

"What do you think?" Caithlin asked X'And after making her way over to his side.

"Orders are orders," X'And shrugged.

"It's a request, not an order," Caithlin countered. "I'm a privateer, not a naval officer."

"Regardless, it makes perfect sense. That frigate captain knows his business, better than you or I. He is trying to quickly flip the balance of numbers. He wants us over there, sinking the little ones so that his three frigates are not surrounded. A Basilean frigate can take on a blood runner without much trouble."

"But not that big orc flagship," Caithlin shook her head. "No. This won't do at all. A red shark doesn't turn around and bite at a shoal of mackerel following it. Those rabble can barely harm us, let alone a frigate."

"A red shark certainly doesn't go attacking a dragon shark, either!" X'And exclaimed, gesturing at the orc smasher. "You can't seriously be thinking about engaging that monstrosity! You've asked for my opinion, now listen to it!"

Caithlin resumed flicking and catching the gold coin, a metallic ping ringing out with every tap from her thumbnail.

"I've asked for your opinion, and I've considered it, but I'm not the sort of captain who merely defaults to the advice they are presented with. No, I've made up my mind. We're not going to do much to that flagship of theirs, but that blood runner that has strayed from its station ahead of us? If we keep them busy, that'll leave the frigates facing an equal number of ships. That's a worthwhile contribution. That's what we're going to do."

Before X'And could respond, a loud, staccato crack echoed across from the *Pious*. Not the blast of cannon fire but nearly as loud. The same crack sounded from the *Vigil*, and then finally the *Veneration*. Caithlin stared over the waist of her brig at the three frigates in amazement as she saw a ball of blue fire erupt into life on the bow of each of the mighty warships.

***

"Why are they hesitating?" Charn snapped, staring across at the privateer brig that obtusely held station to port, despite the clarity of the orders hoisted up on the signaling flags. "I need the rabble cleared away! Why is she not turning?"

Jaymes watched the brig continue on southward momentarily before diverting his eyes back to the orc fleet ahead. He found himself feeling surprisingly exposed and vulnerable in his new duty position on the fo'c'sle; previous encounters had seen him taking charge of cannons on the upper deck, but now as the new first lieutenant, his job was to take charge of the battery at the very front of the ship, including the bow chaser guns that would undoubtedly be the first to fire. It struck him as incredible, he realized as he stared out at the rapidly approaching orc smasher and its accompanying blood runners, that he had gone from a role that was so practically useless to something of value in a very short space of time.

Only weeks ago, he had arrived on the *Pious* as a sloop officer with no recency in post, having just completed the better part of two years attempting to provide advice in a civilian design office from behind a desk. Now, with Gregori Corbes dead and gone and no experienced officers provided in his stead, it fell to Jaymes to set that example. Only now, mere moments from the commencement of the largest battle of his entire life, did Jaymes realize the importance of his role and, more importantly, how infinitely more difficult it was for Charn to run a ship with no experienced mid-tier leaders to rely on.

"We've got it up here, sir," Jaymes said to Charn with a counterfeit confidence he certainly did not feel internally. "We'll be ready to engage on your order."

The graying captain looked around the guns of the fo'c'sle and the blue-uniformed sailors standing by to operate them.

"I'm going back to the quarterdeck, Mister Ellias," he said. "I'll let you know who I want you to fire upon as soon as we are within range. At that point, I'm fully entrusting you to give them hell."

Jaymes's reply was cut off when a sudden tremor swept through the wooden boards beneath his feet. It was only a small shimmy, but it was unlike anything he had ever felt from a ship, unlike anything he could imagine being inflicted upon a vessel by the elements. He heard a mild rush of wind yet felt nothing. Then, even more inexplicably, he felt hope. A calm serenity washed over him, inspiring him and strengthening his resolve from the very core. From the looks of the sailors around him, he was not alone in this sudden, joyous feeling.

With an ear-splitting crack, the carved wooden flames atop the ship's Elohi-effigy suddenly exploded into a shower of splinters, immediately replaced by the warm glow of blue fire sprouting up from the torch. His eyes wide with wonder, Jaymes let out an excited breath. One of the sailors by the bow chasers dropped to one knee in reverence and bowed his head. Others followed his example, including Jaymes and Charn. The Elohi were with them. They could not fail now.

***

The cannons blasted away from the front end of the smasher, the now familiar acrid smoke rolling back across the deck to cloud Ghurak's vision and overwhelm his barely functional sense of smell. Grinning viciously, he hobbled forward to the side of the deck, pushing a duo of absent-minded goblins out of his way as he did so. The smasher was the first ship to open fire in the engagement, as well it should have been. His ship headed straight for the center of the three frigates which, he noted with mild curiosity, had set about changing their formation from sailing side by side to now adopting a long line where two of the frigates turned in to follow their leader, cowering behind.

No matter. Ghurak would destroy the lead frigate and then turn his attentions on to the two following behind. Off to his left, the six rabble ships had swept ahead of the orc fleet and were now firing, their lighter guns banging away as each of the small ships rode the rise and fall of the warm waves with decidedly more effort than the *Green Hammer* and the accompanying blood runners. The three Basilean sloops swept out to meet them, puffs of black smoke appearing above their bows as they returned fire. A lucky shot from one of the sloops hit the lead rabble ship, crumpling its bow a little on impact. The tiny warship continued on regardless, its own guns soon thumping into action again as the small ships of the western flank continued to rapidly close with each other.

Up forward on his own ship, his front gunners fired again. Seconds later, they were joined by the lighter forward facing cannons of the *Driller* as Kroock's gunners targeted the lead Basilean frigate.

"Ratchit!" Ghurak yelled. "Get the order flags up! Tell everyone to fire at that lead frigate!"

***

"Fire!"

The cannons thundered to either side of Jaymes, jumping back on their restraining ropes. His ears rang out with a high-pitched, shrill whine as he saw columns of water shoot up to either side of the blood runner. A small puff of brown briefly appeared on the grotesque ship's fo'c'sle, from this range a mere patch of color; but from what Jaymes had experienced firsthand, evidence that on the deck of the orc ship there were deadly splinters of wood cutting down the crew from the one shot that was on target.

The three frigates had formed up in line astern now, evidence that Charn's plan was clearly to surround and engage one unfortunate orc ship that would soon suffer the withering effect of the combined broadsides of the three ships. To the west, the three sloops were bravely engaging twice their number in rabble ships, the agile vessels already changing course to weave between each other in a bitter fight. Off to the east, the *Martolian Queen* continued to plough on toward the orcs, on the periphery of the fight and all but completely left out of the opening rounds of the action. That left *Pious* front and center. And that, in turn, left Jaymes stood at the front of the fo'c'sle, on the very spot that would be targeted by every forward facing cannon on the orc smasher and three blood runners.

As if hearing his thoughts, the smasher's bow chasers fired again. Jaymes hunkered down involuntarily, turning away and leaning over as his fists clenched in fear. An intermingled symphony of dull zooms whooshed through the air, and the deck jumped from beneath his feet, a deafening clang sounding as a cannonball smashed into the scant armor plating on the bows of the frigate. Jaymes looked up and practically saw the next cannonball hurtling toward him in a dull blur of black, its constant bearing showing that it was heading right for the *Pious*. Right for him.

Frozen in terror, Jaymes watched in amazement as the cannonball split in two in the air before his very eyes, a flare of vivid, unnatural blue light shining momentarily in the air before him. The broken halves of the projectile fell harmlessly to either side of the frigate, splashing down into the green sea. Above the heads of Jaymes and the fo'c'sle gunners, the wooden Elohi's torch continued to blaze away proudly.

"Shining Ones above!" a young gunner exclaimed joyously. "They saved us! They saved us!"

Jaymes paused, astounded that he stood unhurt. For the briefest of instances, the most ridiculous and selfish thought forced itself into his head. He wondered why he was stood on the front end of a warship, being shot at by an armada of orc pirates, when the children he grew up with all had normal, safe lives in normal, safe jobs in the City of the Golden Horn. He just needed to survive one more battle. One more. But it was the biggest fight of his life. Mentally chastising himself for losing concentration, he turned back to face the fo'c'sle gun crews.

"Stop vents!" Jaymes yelled, looking up to the blue flame to quickly issue a very sincere nod of gratitude to the powers watching over him before returning his attention to his duty. "Sponge the guns!"

***

"Mister Just!" Charn shouted across the quarterdeck to the ship's master. "That blood runner to the west of the smasher! The one two points to starboard – he's the one getting it in the neck! Position us between him and the rabbles, port broadside to fire on the way past before we alter to port for a quarter wind again! Starboard gunners can hit any of those little bastards fighting against our sloops!"

"Aye, Captain!" Thaddeus shouted his response. "Position to engage blood runner and then turn to port for an easterly course!"

The guns of the orc fleet banged out again, and the hideous whooshing of round shot tore through the clear skies. The *Pious* jumped with enough ferocity to knock Charn off his feet as cannonballs smashed into her bows. Charn reached out to the base of the mizzenmast, dragging himself back up to his feet. He looked forward and saw the fo'c'sle guns still firing, a jagged hole blown in the wood of the upper deck just on the forward curve of the port waist. Four marines were hurriedly taking two of his wounded sailors toward the hatchway down below where only Iain Kennus, the surgeon, would be able to save them now.

Charn swore under his breath. They would be the first of many.

"Mister Turnio!" Charn shouted. "Hoist signals to the squadron! Frigates are to engage westerly blood runner, port guns! Starboard guns into the rabble! Follow us in!"

"Aye, Captain!" Francis shouted in response, hurriedly opening the wooden locker of signals flags to set about the complicated task of arranging the colored, coded pennants in the correct order to accurately and succinctly relay his captain's orders to the other frigates.

Charn raised his telescope to regard the line of orc warships. Only moments to go now until they were all among each other. So far he had only needed to weather the bow chasers, but it would soon be all out war as the powerful, thunderous broadsides of both fleets would be lined up. And if he could cripple one of those blood runners in the opening rounds, he would skew the odds in his favor.

The dull crump of cannonballs impacting against wood followed by shouts of anguish from his crew brought Charn's attention away from his telescope. He looked out to starboard and saw one of the little sloops list to port and then suddenly turn over fully to present its hull to the skies, its single mast disappearing beneath the waves as it rolled over to its doom.

***

A salvo of fire from the *Blood Skull* smashed into the lead frigate, tearing shreds through its front sails as the line of Basilean warships approached. Irukk swore in frustration. The deck, crowded with diminutive goblins in their striped shirts and black-armored orc warriors, eagerly watched over either side of the *Green Hammer* as the battle unfolded around them.

"He's firing chainshot!" the young first mate yelled. "He'll never sink them with that!"

"Shut up!" Ghurak yelled, even though he agreed with Irukk. "That's Captin Drika! He knows what he is doing!"

But Ghurak disagreed with the choice. The frigates were tearing through the seas toward him with the wind off their quarter, and Ghurak knew enough to realize that they had the advantage of speed. But once they turned in, that advantage would be lost and it would be down to raw firepower. There, Ghurak would win.

"What are they doing?" Irukk grunted.

Ghurak looked up again. The lead frigate had swung its battered bows off to starboard, suddenly heading a few points away from Ghurak's flagship and toward a gap between the *Driller* and the furious fight between the small rabbles and sloops. The second frigate turned to follow, and then the third. Ghurak's jaw dropped.

"Where are they going?" he demanded, utterly perplexed as to why the Basileans would want to turn away from a fight with his smasher.

He was the admrul, and this was his flagship. He was the priority target. They should be engaging him. Up forward, his orc gun crew captins screamed orders to their goblin gunners as his forward guns were again readied. The cannons belched out their symphony of noise and smoke, and projectiles were spewed out at the Basilean frigate at the head of the column.

The orc and goblin gunners alike cheered as the salvo ploughed into the front of the frigate, crumpling the bows and tearing apart the wooden carving of the Elohi figure. The blazing torch above flickered momentarily, but the blue flame refused to die. Still, Ghurak thought as he chuckled to himself, regarding the utter carnage at the front of the lead frigate, he would not want to have been stood anywhere near the point of impact. He doubted even an orc would have survived that.

His joy was short lived. The Basilean frigate continued on, barely slowed by the tears in its sails and the broken, splintered wood atop its bows. The three frigates swept serenely past to curve around gracefully to the west, gliding along to sail past Kroock's blood runner. Ghurak let out a yell of anger as he realized the Basilean plan; positioning themselves well off to the left of his fleet's heavy hitters, they needed only brave a single broadside from Kroock's *Driller*, while the position of the blood runner prevented any of the other orc ships from firing on them.

The lead frigate opened fire from both sides simultaneously as it approached the *Driller*. The starboard salvo tore into one of the little rabble ships that had foolishly neglected to distance itself from the battle of its larger cousins. It somehow managed to survive the first few impacts, but then was blown apart spectacularly as its powder magazine was hit, instantly transformed from a vessel into nothing more than a smoking hulk, surrounded by twirling planks of broken wood. The frigate, looming over the blood runner, then fired with its port guns.

Cannonballs smashed into Kroock's ship, clanging off its metal bows, tearing through the rigging, obliterating crew on the upper deck, and punching holes through its timber flanks. The orc gunners returned fire as the frigate sailed past, repaying the bitter compliment with their own guns. The frigate lurched as the *Driller*'s broadside smashed into it, the thumping of metal projectiles against solid wood was clear even from where Ghurak watched from his own ship. Kroock's gunners did well, planting nearly every shot on target, but measuring the blood runner up against a frigate was no even fight. The frigate, wounded as she was, sped on while the blood runner reeled from the impact of the human guns.

And then the second frigate sailed by and fired. Again shots ripped into the blood runner, smashing through its sides and ripping down green-skinned sailors on its deck. Sails were torn, rigging lines snaked down to the sea, and wooden splinters twirled up in the air around it. The starboard guns then fired, bracketing another rabble with shot before the aim was corrected and the little orc ship was crippled, its mast falling down forward over its bows to leave it dead in the water. From somewhere in the center of Kroock's vessel, fire broke out and flames began licking their way up the mainmast.

Ghurak could only watch helplessly as the third frigate swam into view. The lead frigate, damaged as it was, turned to the left to sweep around the back of the *Driller*. The line of three frigates formed a half circle around the smaller orc warship and then, with a display of gunnery that Ghurak thought never possible from mere humans, the frigates fired as one. The explosion of violence was deafening, with gunfire rippling along the sides of each of the frigates. The *Driller* was blasted apart, more holes opening up in its sides, its front mast collapsing as it was snapped near the base, and its rigging was shot away. The top of the rudder was blasted off, the bows dug in to the waves but failed to lift again as sea water flooded through holes in the hull, and raging fires jumped from sail to sail.

Shaking his head in disbelief, Ghurak watched as orcs and goblins began jumping off the deck of the decimated blood runner, more of their shipmates forcing themselves out of gun ports on the lower deck. Flames tearing across the upper deck, the hull sinking lower and lower as floods claimed the bowels of the ships, Ghurak could only watch as his old comrade Kroock's vessel was lost to fire and flood. He turned to face Irukk.

"That lead frigate," he growled his pure hatred, "no matter what it takes, no matter what the wind is doing. Get me next to that ship. Now."

Chapter Nineteen

Jaymes's entire world consisted of nothing more than pale beige and a shrill whining. Then, as his impaired senses slowly began to function again, the pain hit in. A dull pounding at his temples seemed to almost fit in naturally with the buzzing in his ears as the sea of beige slowly began to focus into wooden planks, their lines of grain sharpening and then blurring. He felt hands grab him by the armpits, and then he was spun over to face up at the sky before being dragged off. He could just about hear shouts and screams over the incessant buzzing and whining, and he made out the tattered foremasts above him. He tilted his head weakly to one side and saw bodies of sailors, their lifeless eyes staring ahead, some with faces set from their final moments of pain, others in terror, others still in quiet and calm acceptance of their final fate.

"Wake up!" he heard a muffled, but familiar voice from close by. "Wake up, you stupid bastard! Come on, Jaymes!"

"Karnon...?" Jaymes muttered weakly.

He felt himself propped up against a solid surface and recognized his location as somewhere near the base of the mainmast and the front of the quarterdeck. The upper deck of the *Pious* was shattered along the port side, wood splintered and rigging torn, the deck piled with corpses. The air tasted of burnt powder and smoke, causing Jaymes to cough and splutter. Karnon crouched down in front of him and leaned in to shout over the shrill whine of his damaged hearing and the thunderous roar of guns as the cannons around him continued to fire.

"Head wound!" he yelled. "Looks worse than it is! You're bleeding all over the place, but I've stopped it! Just sit tight and stay here!"

Jaymes nodded groggily, only now remembering his final moments in command of the fo'c'sle guns as they approached the blood runner before suddenly all hell broke loose. Karnon stood and rushed back off to the forward end of the ship, no doubt to continue recovering casualties from the shattered fo'c'sle. Jaymes closed his eyes for a moment and took in a deep lungful of air. It did not hurt. So his lungs worked. That was something. He reached up to his throbbing temples and found a bandage wrapped around his head. Slowly but surely, his eyesight was focusing better and his hearing was able to discern more around him. Content that he could still fight, Jaymes clambered back up to his feet.

Pious

***

His face twisted in a malicious grimace, Charn let out a hissing growl of victory through his clenched teeth as he watched the blood runner sink and burn off *Pious's* port side. The damaged frigate swung around onto an easterly course, ready to either open out and reposition or move in to fire again as the battle dictated. Behind him, the *Veneration* followed with the *Vigil* taking the tail end of the line, guns still bellowing out magnificently from both warships.

Charn's grin immediately turned to a gasp of despair as he turned to look across the crumpled upper deck beneath him. From somewhere within his soul, the urge for emotion to override common sense and duty told him to leave the quarterdeck and rush down to the base of the mainmast, where Thaddeus Just lay dead. He overrode the useless sentimentality of seeing the corpse of his admired colleague and muttered the briefest of prayers before turning back to reassess the flow of battle.

The *Pious* continued to lead the line of frigates around the sterns of the orc warships, now heading east with the wind off the port quarter, while the orcs attempted to turn through the wind to face them. One blood runner burned fiercely, the second followed close at the heels of the looming orc smasher. The final blood runner, much to Charn's delight, had been forced to turn eastward and was now side-by-side with the *Martolian Queen*, exchanging fierce broadsides with the privateer brig. *Pious* herself had taken a beating; a good few shots from leading the column south into the bow chasers of the orc fleet, but then even more from the first and only broadside of the blazing blood runner. But it looked worse than it was. The damage reports told of no floods; his masts were all intact, his steerage gear responded, and with the exception of his fo'c'sle, all of his guns were still firing.

"Helmsman!" he yelled over the constant blasting of cannons. "Starboard your helm! Bring us to port, three points!"

A more cautious man would have opened out to take advantage of the speed and agility a frigate had over a smasher before repositioning to repeat the broadside encirclement that had just worked so well on the blazing blood runner. But with the orc flagship aggressively and recklessly turning through the wind in an attempt to close with the frigates, Charn would be wiser to leap on the display of tactical ineptitude and move in to engage.

"Mister Turnio! Order the others to remain line astern and engage their flagship!"

The deck tremored beneath Caithlin's feet as the starboard side cannons rippled fire from stem to stern, their crews firing on the blood runner as they turned together through the green waves. Most of her crewmembers were complete strangers; men, a handful of salamanders, and even fewer women who had flocked to her ship after her success on her first voyage. She watched them with a strange mixture of pride in their professionalism and relief at her risk in hiring them paying off. The crews responded smoothly and rapidly to the commands of their gun captains, quickly sponging out the barrels of the cannons and reloading the guns with chain shot as she had commanded.

"Do you want round shot, Captain?" X'And asked from his position next to her on the quarterdeck.

"No," Caithlin replied, "I want them crippled and dead in the water. Smash up their sails and masts with everything we've got. Then we can stand back and run rings around them."

As if arguing the statement, the port guns of the blood runner blasted out in a stuttered, uneven volley. Round shot pounded against the hull of the *Martolian Queen*, splintering boards along her curved flank and blasting holes through her stern. Caithlin was knocked down to one knee by the force of the impact but, hearing the screams of the wounded around her, considered herself lucky as she clambered back to her feet.

"Captain!" X'And yelled as another wave of bitter, black smoke drifted back across the quarterdeck from the guns. "We need to back off! We're standing alongside an orc ship of war with an armed trading brig! We can't exchange punches like this!"

Caithlin looked over her shoulder at the fierce center of the maritime battlefield behind her. The *Pious* led the three frigates around to charge down the smasher and the second blood runner, while way off behind them, the equally brutal fight between the remaining two sloops and three rabbles continued almost independently.

"I need to keep this last blood runner away from the main fight!" Caithlin insisted. "We can take a few more hits! The *Queen* is good for it!"

"Cathy," X'And shouted, grabbing her by both shoulders, "listen to me! You cannot go toe-to-toe with them! Not like this! I've seen more sea battles than you ever have, and even I've never been in something like this! You need to back off, before more of our sailors die needlessly! You need to listen to me!"

Caithlin stared into the desperate eyes of her friend and comrade. A life of sailing had not prepared her in any way for a full battle. She was in over her head. She needed to listen to advice.

"Helmsman!" she called out as she turned away from X'And. "Hard a port! Alter course to the north and open us out!"

***

Charn lowered his telescope, shaking his head as he saw the *Martolian Queen* finally lose her resolve and break off the engagement with the blood runner. The *Pious* continued in her arc back around to face the smasher and second blood runner, guns loaded and ready with round shot. The *Veneration* and *Vigil* followed behind, barely damaged by the action so far. The two orc ships had been slowed tremendously by their aggressive attempt to turn through the wind to engage, leaving the initiative still with Charn and his frigates. He needed to hit the smasher.

"Sir," a weary voice muttered from next to Charn, "my station has been rendered inoperative, so I thought best to report for duties here on the quarterdeck."

Charn turned to see Jaymes Ellias, his white shirt drenched down one side with blood from a head wound, his dark hair falling limply over his bloodstained bandage. Charn withheld a smile of pride at the young man's bravery and dedication to his duty. He had seen the impact on the fo'c'sle earlier and written Jaymes off for dead. He clasped a hand on the young lieutenant's shoulder.

"Good man, Jaymes, good man. I'm afraid we've lost Thaddeus. Get back down on the upper deck and assume the duties of master."

"Aye, sir," Jaymes said, turning to stagger back down from the quarterdeck.

Charn looked back up at the two enemy ships still attempting to turn around eastward in a merry but fruitless chase after the frigates. Glancing up at his squadron commander's pennant above, Charn smiled at his fate as an unspoken prayer was answered. The wind had veered north. The Elohi above were watching over him.

"Mister Ellias!" he shouted down to the upper deck. "Put us north of their flagship, port side to! Let's give the bastards a few punches on our way past!"

Charn looked back at the *Veneration* and the *Vigil* behind him. He narrowed his eyes, confused, as he saw the *Vigil* alter to port, breaking away from the line astern formation he had ordered. He let out a gasp as he saw a new line of signal flags hoisted up on the outer halyards. He did not need to translate the line of symbols and colors; any naval officer knew them by heart.

"No…" Charn breathed.

'Tell the Hegemon we died willingly.'

The last signal given by the legendary Captain Norre Vistus at the Battle of Chy Bay. The signal he gave before placing his ship right between two enemy battleships and firing until he was overcome.

"No!" Charn yelled in frustration. "Don't do it, you stupid bastard!"

Charn watched in anguish as Captain Alain Stryfus steered his frigate directly toward the narrow gap between the smasher and the blood runner to the south.

***

The three Basilean frigates approached rapidly from astern, their sails billowing out in a wind that seemed to knowingly change in their favor, their blue torches still blazing. Ghurak watched as the lead frigate approached from his starboard as he continued to turn to port in an attempt to line up his broadside. The second frigate followed close behind, but the third broke away and altered to the southeast.

"What's he doing?" Ghurak growled.

The sleek frigates, handled with an expertise Ghurak could only dream of, bore down from the west and back toward him. He was in a position to fire now but knew his crews could never reload in time to get a second salvo off as the frigates drew closer to fire their own broadsides.

"Guns! Right-hand side!" he shouted down to the massed deck below him. "Wait for my order to fire! Wait!"

The third frigate concerned him more. It, too, sped on westward but now far enough away from the others that it clearly had a different plan. That plan dawned slowly on Ghurak. Judging by his explosion of expletives, Irukk had understood it, too.

"He's coming around the other side of us!" the first mate yelled. "They'll fire at us from both sides! That third one can hit the *Wave Rammer*, too!"

"Let him!" Ghurak grunted. "Let the stupid bastard put himself between a smasher and a blood runner! See how long he lasts!"

"He's coming in right next to us!" Irukk yelled. "We need to load grapeshot on the left side! He'll rip us to shreds!"

Ghurak glared over at his increasingly insubordinate first mate.

"Get a hold of yourself, you soft bastard!" Ghurak thundered. "I'm in command here! Those sods can't reload in time! We'll hit him with what we've already got loaded! Gunners, left and right, wait for my order!"

***

His hearing returning was one sign that his senses were back to normal. The other was the hammering pain from the wound above his right ear. Jaymes looked up at the three masts above, the few top men still on station on the yards still bravely setting the sails under his commands while the majority of the crew manned the guns. It would be the port side guns again that would be in action, this time against the orc flagship. Jaymes looked forward and saw both Walt Ganto and Kaeso Innes ready to give the orders to fire.

The *Veneration* followed them close behind, but for some reason, the *Vigil* had broken away to the south and looked intent on suicidally positioning itself between the smasher and the blood runner ahead. Then Jaymes saw the signal flags flying from the *Vigil* and shook his head in amazement.

"Alain, you stupid bastard," he breathed. "You'll kill them all..."

Then, quite unexpectedly, the smasher altered course. Its brutal, dull metal bows dug into the waves as it came about to starboard, suddenly turning as if attempting to cut off the advancing frigates. Then, lined up neatly at a range of only a couple of hundred yards, the smasher's colossal broadside fired. In the normal manner of the undisciplined orc gunners, each gun fired sporadically in turn. The first half-dozen either fell short or plunged into the foamy wake left behind by the the *Pious*, but then the round shot started to strike home.

The world exploded around Jaymes. The already devastated port side of the frigate seemed to be torn open as two cannons, still clinging to their wooden trolleys, were flung up into the air. Men were hurtled back in a brutal mist of scarlet as they were torn apart by the deadly wooden shards that had once formed a part of their own vessel. Jaymes saw Walt Ganto simply disappear – standing by his crews one moment and then gone the next, the only evidence to his existence being a pool of blood and entrails, and a fist protruding from a severed sleeve.

The noble frigate, somehow still afloat and surging forward, lurched drunkardly from the impact with a squeal of broken timbers that sounded like a howl of pain. Up forward, still stood dutifully by his guns, Kaeso Innes yelled out an order.

"Port guns! Fire as she bears!"

The order was taken up by the gun captains, and the disciplined ripple of return fire from the *Pious* boomed out from bow to stern, each cannon blasting in quick succession and leaping back on its wooden wheels. The firing stopped at the after end of the upper deck. There was nothing from the quarterdeck. Jaymes turned and looked up to see the taff rail of the quarterdeck torn into shreds. He let out a breath of panic.

Ignoring the ceaseless buzzing in his ears and the pain hammering in his head, Jaymes sprinted across the blood-soaked deck to the steps leading up to the quarterdeck. The after end of the frigate was a scene of utter devastation. The guns lay broken where they had been hit, their crews reduced to piles of bloodied waste, torn apart by the deadly splints of wood around them. A solitary sailor clung tenaciously to the ship's wheel, bleeding from wounds in his legs but still valiantly keeping the frigate on course. Francis Turnio, not yet old enough to be called a man, lay crumpled and gasping for breath by one of the broken guns, a splint of wood the size of a limb protruding from his shoulder.

A few paces away from him, Captain Charn Ferrus lay motionless in a pool of scarlet, his eyes staring up to the sky above. Jaymes ran over to drop to one knee next to him, helplessly checking over his captain for any injuries he could stem. Charn's body was broken, bleeding from a dozen wounds as his final few breaths escaped in weak, wheezy gasps. His bleary eyes looked up at Jaymes. Helpless, utterly at a loss, Jaymes could only grab one blood-soaked hand and stare down at his captain.

Charn gazed back, an expression that Jaymes had never seen on the captain's face now twisting his features. It was one of confusion, of utter bewilderment. He was not expecting to die. His labored breathing growing weaker, more silent, he squeezed gently on Jaymes hand and opened his mouth. Blood trickled out of both corners. He whispered a final word.

"...Sorry..."

Jaymes froze in place. Charn was dying. The invincible captain was done. After decades of fearless servitude, Charn would now leave the world with his last mortal view being his useless first lieutenant. Jaymes frantically struggled to find the words to see the intrepid captain off, to say something meaningful in that final second. Should he say something about duty? Promise him that this battle would be won? No. Sincerety was more important, and even in death, Charn knew the man Jaymes was.

"Thank you, sir," Jaymes gasped, "thank you for everything you have taught me. I'll never forget you, Captain."

A chill washed over Jaymes. Around him, the world changed. It was only for the briefest of moments, but in those few seconds, Jaymes saw a sight that he would never be able to ascertain was reality or his imagination. The blue light of the Elohi's torch flared up.

Above him, majestically clothed in robes of purest white over armor of gold and silver, a trio of Elohi clung to the frigate's masts, their noble faces contorted with exertion as they pushed with all of their unnatural might to propel the ship forward. All around him, across the shattered quarterdeck, pale and translucent facsimiles of the dead clambered to their feet, the spirits calmly and peacefully leaving their bloodied corpses behind on the hellish deck of the warship. Hooded figures flew down from the heavens, taking each sailor by the hand to guide them a few steps forward until they faded from view.

Jaymes watched in amazement as Charn Ferrus stood, his uniform immaculate again, his face pristine, ten years younger without the lines of worry and the burden of duty. A towering, hooded figure took him by the hand. Charn turned one final time to look down at where Jaymes knelt, still clinging to the bloody hand of his dead body. The captain smiled at him. A slight, barely perceptible smile. But a warm, sincere one. In that moment, Jaymes knew that Charn had heard his final words of gratitude.

"Jaymes!" Karnon yelled, clamping a hand on his shoulder. "He's gone! You have command now! Jaymes! Get up!"

The serene view of blue spirits and angels was gone. The noxious stench of fumes, sweat, and blood returned, along with the screams of the dying and the blasting of cannons. Jaymes jumped up to his feet and looked around him, quickly assessing the wind, the *Pious's* speed, and the positions of friend and foe alike.

"Kaeso!" he yelled down to the upper deck. "Get the port guns loaded with grapeshot! We'll come around the front of that bastard and blow them to hell! Bosun! Bring down the command pennant! The captain is dead! We're no longer in command of this squadron! Helmsman, starboard your helm! Get us in closer!"

***

Another barrage of fire spat out of the port side of the *Martolian Queen*, propelling a salvo of deadly round shot off toward the blood runner. The two ships had been trading shots for over an hour now, the privateer brig landing more hits, but the heavier guns of the orc blood runner caused more damage when they did impact. X'And appeared from the hatchway leading down below and clambered onto the upper deck.

"How bad is it?" Caithlin asked, irritably wiping tears from her eyes from the near constant plumes of acrid gun smoke.

"Two feet, slowly rising," X'And reported the level of flooding from the wells below. "We've got some sailcloth over the hole, but we'll need to do something properly about this soon."

"She'll take a lot more than two feet," Caithlin said, "and while we're barely scratching that blood runner, we've kept them out of the fight for a good while now. Every minute they waste on us is another minute those frigates are outnumbering the other orcs."

When she had initially been approached by the Basilean Navy with a view to coercing her into a career as a privateer, she had wondered why the desperation over something so mediocre and comparatively insignificant as a brig. Now she knew. A brig could keep something a bit larger at bay, and in turn, that could lead to something larger still being engaged and destroyed. Caithlin looked through her telescope at the raging battle to the west, watching in confusion as two frigates sat to either side of the smasher, one of them caught in a deadly crossfire between two orc ships while another limped in closer, its sails in tatters and the clean lines of its deck ruined from battle damage.

She could not tell which one was the *Pious*, not from this range and with all ships being enveloped in dense smoke from their guns. The whole ordeal felt hollow, utterly detached when compared to the fast, frenzied fight against Gallo's brigantine. She reached into her pocket and pulled out the gold coin, looking down at it for a few moments.

"Let's get back into this fight," she declared.

"What?!" X'And exclaimed.

"We can't just languish over here while those frigates are getting blasted apart. We need to head west."

"We're leaking!" X'And snapped. "We've got less guns than everybody else, and we're leaking!"

"Then we need to win!" Caithlin growled. "Because the state we're in doesn't give us any other options! If those frigates lose, nothing will come to our rescue! We're taking on water, and without a proper break from action to repair, we're only going to get slower! And I'm quite happy to state openly that being boarded by orcs is not part of my battle plan!"

X'And watched in distress as Caithlin paced over to the brig's helm.

"West!" she called to her helmsman. "Point her west! Get us over to that fight!"

***

Jaymes watched in anguish as the *Vigil* sat between the smasher and the blood runner, her sails taken in to match the speed of the slower orc ships and hold position next to them. The frigate's guns bellowed out again, broadsides firing from port and starboard simultaneously, fire raking the decks of the two enemy ships bracketing her in place. In response, the two brutish orc vessels returned fire, their own guns tearing into the *Vigil* and blasting away at her hull and upper deck. The *Vigil's* mainsail collapsed forward, tangled up in the maze of rigging from the foremast, eliminating any chance of escape if her captain changed his mind on the aggressive plan of action.

"Closer!" Jaymes called across to the helmsman. "Get us right next to the bastards!"

The wounded *Pious* limped around to port, her tattered sails catching the northerly wind again as she swung about to drive back toward the smasher. The *Veneration* still followed, despite acknowledging the signal that the *Pious* no longer held the role of squadron command. She had hoisted her own signal flags, her sympathies clear in a message which indicated that her captain knew precisely what had happened to Charn.

Shining-Ones-Bless-Pious

The *Veneration's* port guns fired, sending an accurate salvo tearing into the bows of the blood runner to the south of the *Vigil*, blasting away at the orc vessel's crude drill and dark wooden fo'c'sle.

Through his telescope, Jaymes could see the havoc that Alain Stryfus had wreaked upon the two orc ships. The blood runner's quarterdeck was shot to pieces and her helm shattered, while tell-tale heat haze wafted up from a hatchway up forward, indicating a fire below deck. The smasher was sitting just a little lower in the water, the top half of her mizzenmast blown off and her flank creased and crumpled from the ceaseless Basilean cannon barrage. In turn, the *Vigil* was a sorry sight; her waist was splintered and torn, and her sails shredded.

The *Vigil* fired again, her crews loading their guns faster than any orc, but each salvo firing fewer cannons than the last as damage consumed her. The devastation inflicted on both orc ships was again obvious, even from a few hundred yards away, but moments later they returned fire again. The valiant frigate shook and shuddered from the impact, but initially seemed to weather another storm of metal. Then, with a sickening lurch, the *Vigil* listed off to port, her stern sinking into the waves.

Through his telescope, Jaymes saw sailors leaping off the deck of the dying frigate as a handful of her guns bravely continued to fire. Jaymes tightened his grip around the abrasive handle of his saber as the *Pious* drew closer, guns loaded and ready for vengeance.

***

"Left side guns, load!" Ghurak snarled as he paced along the center of the upper deck, barging his way past orc warriors and back-handing goblins aside.

The *Green Hammer* was battered, more so than he had ever seen, but still very much in the fight. Damage reports from down below told him that they were taking on water, but he had dispatched enough of his crew to put pay to that. With the relentless fire from the three frigates, Ghurak was slowly beginning to worry about one resource that was now noticeably dwindling. His crew. With enemies on all sides and a need to man every gun, he was down in some places to only a pair of goblins on each cannon.

Between him and Captin Drethug of the *Wave Rammer*, they had finally put pay to the audacious frigate that had dared plant itself between the two orc warships. He briefly toyed with the idea of calling for grapeshot, but as satisfying as it would be to see his guns tearing the human sailors limb from limb – especially at such close range – he knew that a cooler head was what would win the fight, and that continuing to blast the frigate into oblivion was the way to victory.

The second frigate – the one that had skulked at the back and avoided any real damage – now turned in toward the *Wave Rammer*, raking the crippled blood runner with another broadside. The leader of the frigates, its deck smashed apart and its guns only sporadically firing, limped across toward the smasher to attack again. At least that crew had a spine, Ghurak mused.

"Those cowards!" Irukk thundered as he leaned over the port side of the *Green Hammer*. "Those cowardly bastards! They're leaving us!"

Ghurak looked across and saw the remaining three rabble ships speeding off to the south, fleeing toward Axe Island with the wind caught firmly in their sails. One part of him was furious for their betrayal; the other could not give a damn due to their near totally ineffectiveness. Two Basilean sloops were now freed up from the west and sailed over to join the fray in the center of the battle. Looking across to the east, Ghurak saw the brig that had picked a fight with Drika's blood runner also charging down toward him, Drika giving chase with his forward facing cannons blazing away.

"Let them go!" Ghurak hissed, his face twisted in fury. "I'll deal with them when we get back to Axe!"

"Deal with them?!" Irukk roared as he turned to face the admrul. "Deal with them?! You haven't dealt with anything since you started this whole mess!"

Ghurak glowered down at Irukk, his red eyes ablaze with fury at the younger orc's insolence. Goblins scuttled to either side in a panic, clearing the deck between the two lumbering orcs.

"You don't dare talk to me like that, you cowardly little shit!" Ghurak boomed, snatching his axe from his side. "Who the hell do you think you are?!"

"Who do I think I am?" Irukk snarled, bringing his own axe around to hold across his muscular chest. "I'm the captin of the *Green Hammer*, once I've had your head! You're nothing more than a weak old fool, Ghurak! Weak! You've led us to failure, and now it's time for new blood!"

To the south, the crippled Basilean frigate slipped down into the waves as the gunners continued to fire, the doomed ship raked from cannons from both the *Green Hammer* and the *Wave Rammer*. With two frigates, a brig, and two sloops hurtling toward him and two blood runners still barring their way, Ghurak knew he could still win. He just needed to put Irukk down first. With a ferocious yell, he limped toward his first mate with his axe held high.

Chapter Twenty

The *Vigil* sank down beneath the waves, her Elohi figurehead on her bows being the last part of the valiant vessel to slip away. The carved wooden figure seemed to stay afloat for just a few moments more than she should have, as if gasping for last breaths before slipping into darkness. The noble figurehead slowly sank down, her torch still blazing blue, the holy fire lighting up the sea around her as it disappeared.

From the smashed quarterdeck of the *Pious*, Jaymes watched in horror as the gunners of both orc ships tiled their cannons down to fire grapeshot into the Basilean survivors below. Roars of anger, threats, and curses were shouted out from the watching crew of the *Pious*. Shaking with anger, Jaymes set his sights on the orc flagship ahead.

"Message from the *Veneration*, sir!" Francis Turnio called weakly from where he clung to the taff rail. "She's ordering an attack on the westerly blood runner!"

"Let them take her down themselves!" Jaymes grimaced. "We're going for the flagship!"

The carnage inflicted on the smasher grew more apparent as they drew alongside. Alain Stryfus may not have been Jaymes's friend, and Jaymes might have vehemently disagreed with his choice to sacrifice his ship and crew to deal the blows he did to the two orc ships, but there was no denying the effectiveness of his final actions. The *Pious* sailed down from the smasher's starboard quarter, only seconds away now from lining up for another withering broadside at only a hundred yards. The battered frigate drifted in alongside the larger orc vessel. Jaymes looked up at the hideous display of green-skinned engineering looming above him. He felt nothing but hatred as he gave the order.

"Port guns! Fire!"

Tirelessly, the *Pious*'s cannons fired once more. Canisters of grapeshot spewed over the deck of the smasher, the lethal balls cutting down orc and goblin alike. As if a holy wind of carnage were sweeping across the deck of foul creatures, orcs and goblins were cast down in showers of blood. Jaymes noted that some of the guns on the upper deck were now left unmanned, surrounded by dead green-skins and wrecked planks of wood.

"Port side, load grapeshot!" he shouted. "Be ready to hit them again! Top men; shorten sail! Match their speed, keep us in position!"

Karnon Senne appeared at the top of what was left of the stairs leading up to the quarterdeck, his steel breastplate covered in the blood of the sailors he had been lending aid to.

"Jaymes!" he shouted across. "The sailors down below are say-ing we're ignoring orders from the *Veneration*! What's the plan?"

"We're taking the flagship!" Jaymes shouted back. "They're low on gunners, and they can't match our rate of fire! We're going to sit off her starboard bow and blast her to the Abyss until we're ready to board! Get your marines ready!"

"Nothing to prepare! We're all ready now! Just give the order!"

Jaymes nodded an acknowledgment to the marine captain and then turned his attention back to the fight. He felt a slight smile grow as the guns of Captain Marcellus Dio's frigate blasted into the stern of the blood runner on the far side of the orc flagship, tearing a series of rag-ged holes below her quarterdeck. Orders were shouted from the bat-tered and bleeding gun crews on *Pious's* upper deck as more canisters of grapeshot were loaded into the smoking cannons. Shot was rammed home and arms elevated to signal guns were made ready. His throat hoarse from the bitter smoke and shouting of orders, Jaymes yelled out another simple command.

"Port guns! Fire!"

***

With a vicious roar, Ghurak flung himself forward against his opponent, swiping out with his axe at Irukk's throat. The younger orc brought his own axe up to deflect the blow before slamming a fist into Ghurak's face, crunching the bones of his nose audibly and snapping his head back. Ghurak piled forward again and drove his shoulder into the shorter orc's chest, propelling him back across the upper deck as orc warriors and goblin sailors struggled to throw themselves clear of the violent confrontation. Irukk's back slammed against the mainmast and Ghurak brought a knee up into his gut, bending him over dou-ble before slamming his elbow down into the back of his former first mate's neck.

Irukk crumpled down to the deck but quickly rolled clear of Ghurak's axe, which flew down and embedded itself firmly in the wooden planks where Irukk lay only a second before. Before Ghurak could recover his own weapon, Irukk was on his feet and back on the offensive. The powerful orc warrior sliced down with his heavy axe, again forcing Ghurak to take a step back. The younger orc followed his own blade, overbalanced and overextended, giving Ghurak the brief-est moment of opportunity.

Before he could take advantage, a shrill scream announced the arrival of one of the goblin sailors. Somehow finding the courage to intervene in a fight that would decide who would be the krudger of the fleet, Ratchit the goblin dived down from the mainstaysail above. The loyal goblin landed on Irukk's back and drove a vicious dagger into the orc's shoulder, leaning down to press the blade into the base of the orc's neck. Irukk let out a snarl of rage and picked up the savagely squirming goblin by his face, holding him at arm's length before snapping the valiant creature's neck and tossing him aside.

With a rage-filled growl, Ghurak brought his head back and then flung himself forward, planting his thick skull against Irukk's with a resounding crack. The orc staggered backward from the tremendous force of the blow, his arms hanging to either side uselessly as his red eyes blinked rapidly, stunned and confused. Rage tearing at his mind, all semblance of control and rational thought long gone, Ghurak bellowed out a yell from the bottom of his lungs and charged forward. He advanced only a single step.

The relentless broadside from the lead Basilean frigate, now practically jumping distance from the side of the *Green Hammer*, blasted out its repetitive chorus in unison. The combined might of the cannons, firing as one, was even more deafening than anything Ghurak had heard from his own, mighty flagship. The air was enveloped with black smoke, hiding the thousands of small metal balls that tore across the deck of the *Green Hammer*. Waves of goblin gunners were slain spectacularly, the taller orcs driven down by the hail of cannon fire and torn asunder. Ghurak felt the impact of numerous grapeshot rounds, digging deep into the flesh of his arm and tearing through his guts. Much to his shame, he dropped to one knee.

"They're boarding!" Ghurak heard Irukk splutter from within the smoke. "They're coming alongside! We need to fight them back!"

Ghurak staggered back up to his feet. He heard the familiar bellows of orc warriors preparing for battle, the panicked cries and screeches of goblin sailors, and the snap-crack of muskets from somewhere above. The smoke began to clear. The frigate was moving alongside the *Green Hammer*, sailors waiting along the ship's side with ropes and hooks to secure them together for boarding. Ghurak's eyes opened wider in amazement. *They* wanted to board *him*?

Lines of orc warriors were already forming up, ready to receive the visitors. Another salvo of muskets fired down from the tops of the frigate masts, and two of the orcs dropped down dead. Ghurak looked across at Irukk. His first mate staggered in place, blood dripping from vicious wounds across his chest and arms from the broadside of grapeshot.

"We need to fight them back!" Irukk repeated.

The humans boarding his flagship was a bitter insult, but at that point, it paled into insignificance next to the betrayal and attempted usurping by his first mate. At least the Basileans were supposed to be at war with him. He had some grudging respect for that. But, looking at Irukk, Ghurak had no respect whatsoever. Only a deep-seeded, burning hatred. His jaws open to emit a booming scream of rage, Ghurak charged at Irukk again. He slammed himself into the shorter orc, wrapping the thick fingers of one hand around his squat, muscular neck. Irukk slammed a fist into the side of Ghurak's jaw but to no avail. Fueled by such fury and hatred, Ghurak felt nothing.

Grabbing Irukk's head with both hands, Ghurak slammed the orc's face against the mainmast. Still Irukk resisted. Letting out a long, continuous yell, Ghurak smashed his face into the sturdy, immovable wooden post again, and again. The mast was now spattered with blood, each smash of Irukk's face adding to the macabre scene and now even denting the dense wood. His biceps bulging, his body drenched with sweat, Ghurak continued to pulverize his would-be usurper's skull into the mast. Irukk stopped moving. Ghurak continued, regardless.

By the time he finally stopped, the frigate was alongside and boarding lines were secured to the *Green Hammer*'s deck. Ghurak looked down at Irukk. The entire front half of the orc's head was completely missing. Letting out a grunting laugh, Ghurak threw the corpse aside. He looked down and saw a fist-sized chunk of meat protruding from a tear in his own side, no doubt caused by the grapeshot. With a hiss and a grimace, he poked the protrusion back inside his abdomen. It might have been something important he needed. Retrieving his own axe in one hand, and Irukk's in the other, Ghurak turned to stomp over to meet the humans who dared to board his ship.

***

Karnon looked up at the towering smasher as the *Pious* drew alongside. Smoke still wafted back from the glowing cannons, another broadside of grapeshot having just torn into the orc vessel. The bitter smoke was everywhere; it never truly cleared. It was like nothing Karnon had ever seen on the battlefields he knew on land. The dark wood of the orc ship was cobbled and nailed together in a seemingly random order, its lines brutish and threatening in stark contrast to the elegance and beauty of the Elohi-class frigate, even when crumpled and damaged.

Six sailors stood ready at the waist, their ropes and hooks in hand to secure the two ships together. Behind them waited another line of sailors with planks of wood, ready to rush forward and position a makeshift ramp to clamber up to the taller orc deck. Karnon turned around to regard his marines. Eight had already been killed by orc gunfire, but that left him with three lines of soldiers, armed and ready to board.

"First wave, stand ready!" Karnon commanded.

The first wave was armed with swords and shields. They would rush onto the enemy deck and form a shield wall to hold position while the second wave moved up to shoot with crossbows. Off to the south, the *Veneration* fired another broadside into the nearest blood runner, pounding the dying ship as flames rose up from the orc vessel's fo'c'sle.

With a clash, the *Pious* thumped into the side of the smasher. Wooden beams from both ships squealed in protest, and up above, rigging lines snapped as the two vessels entangled with each other.

"Boarders," Jaymes shouted from the quarterdeck, "secure!"

The six Basilean sailors rushed forward and launched their hooks up onto the deck of the orc ship. Before they had even secured their ropes to the cleats on *Pious's* deck, their comrades with the boarding planks were already at work. Muskets fired from the masts above as Karnon's sharpshooters blasted away at targets on the upper deck of the orc vessel.

Then, quite against the plan, the first reaction came from the orc ship. Long wooden beams, hastily constructed from numerous wooden planks, their ends bristling with metal spikes, suddenly folded down from the orc ship to dig into the *Pious's* deck. Then, with a combined, deafening scream, the green-skins attacked.

Waves of goblins poured over the very planks that the Basilean sailors had put in place, charging down toward Karnon's lines of marines. More goblins still scuttled rapidly over their own, spiked boarding ramps, jumping down onto the deck of the *Pious* and rushing in to attack the Basilean sailors. Towering orcs, their war cries booming and guttural, ran amid the goblins; others swung across using the broken rigging lines from their own ship to tumble down onto the deck of the *Pious*. Up above, goblins scurried from their own yards and rigging onto the *Pious's* masts, screeching as they attacked the Basilean top men.

"Front rank – form shield wall! Second rank – shoot!" Karnon yelled.

Abandoning the plan of attacking the enemy vessel, the front rank of marines clamped their shields together to form a defensive wall at the base of the boarding planks. The second row immediately leaned over the first, raising their crossbows. Each marine shot independently, targeting the more dangerous orc warriors and ignoring the hordes of charging goblins. Crossbow strings twanged, and deadly bolts flew out to thud into their targets; orcs fell down dead on the ramp between the two ships or tumbled screaming off the edges to fall into the sea below.

Goblins armed with cutlasses and axes hurled themselves against the shield wall, but the marines stood firm. The veteran soldiers furiously hacked down with their own swords, carving a bloody arc into the advancing green-skins as they continued to trample down the boarding ramp. Karnon looked up at the edge of the smasher. The orcs and goblins were still coming. There was no end to them.

"Second rank, load!" Karnon yelled, content that it was not yet time for them to abandon their crossbows and draw swords. "Third rank, advance!"

The marines armed with boarding pikes rushed past their cross-bow-armed comrades, taking their place behind the shield wall to stab through the gaps at the charging orcs and goblins. The wall was holding, but the orcs and goblins pouring onto the deck of the *Pious* from their own ramps were faring much better against the Basilean sailors. Karnon looked up and saw a pair of goblins leap dramatically across from the deck of the smasher, landing with a thud on the *Pious* only a few paces from him.

Karnon immediately stepped across and lanced his boarding pike through the belly of the first goblin before flicking it across the deck, trailing blood. The second goblin, letting out a vile and rage-filled chatter of staccato screams, sprinted headlong at him with an axe held high. Karnon smashed his shield into the goblin's face to stun the hideous, little creature before grabbing it by one ankle and flinging it screaming overboard to its doom. He turned his attentions back to his ranks of marines.

"Crossbows – shoot at will!" he commanded, seeing them finishing off their loading procedure.

The crossbowmen let loose a salvo of bolts, again targeting the main push of orcs that continued to sweep down the ramp. At that range, against the wall of green-skins, they could not miss. More orcs fell off the sides of the ramp, others dropped dead at the feet of the first rank shield wall. But the marines were giving. Karnon saw that three of his men were dead and the shield wall was being forced back. He looked up at the top of the ramp, desperately hoping to see the numbers of orcs thinning out.

Instead, he saw a single orc that he somehow recognized. A gargantuan green-skin, distinct in his red greatcoat, stood at the top of the ramp with an axe in each massive fist. The orc was drenched in blood, his red eyes open wide with fury as saliva dripped from both sides of his huge lower jaw. It was the orc krudger that Karnon had seen cut down by crossbows on the beach by the gold mine. Somehow, that thing was still alive. With a roar that echoed over the chaos and gunfire, the orc krudger rushed down the ramp to attack.

***

From his elevated position on the quarterdeck, Jaymes could see the waves of green-skins pouring down onto the *Pious*. Hatchways on the deck of the smasher opened up to allow hordes of the creatures to scuttle out from the lower decks, like deadly, axe-wielding ants. Nearly two hundred sailors and marines were crowded onto the deck of the *Pious*, shoulder to shoulder to face the screaming army of orcs and goblins. Looking up onto their ship, Jaymes reckoned they faced double that many.

The ubiquitous goblins continued to practically pour down from the smasher, hurtling over the ramps to pollute the *Pious* with their presence. Most were dispatched quickly; Karnon's marines on the center ramp held their ground and cut down the goblins with ease, while the sailors on the quarterdeck and fo'c'sle were more than able to hold their ground. If the Basileans were outnumbered two-to-one by goblins alone, Jaymes would not have worried. But it was not the goblins that were the problem; it was the hulking, black armored, axe-wielding orc warriors.

"Sir!" Francis shouted from next to Jaymes, bringing his attention back from the fighting below to his more immediate predicament on the quarterdeck. "There's more of them coming!"

Jaymes looked up to see a fresh wave of goblins scurrying down the two ramps connecting the quarterdeck to the smasher. The twenty sailors he had stationed on the quarterdeck wearily raised their boarding pikes and pistols and turned to face them. Jaymes unsheathed his saber. The lines of green flowing down onto the *Pious* were more than he had expected; much more. He had badly misjudged how many of the orc crewmembers were still left alive. He thought of Charn, Walt, Thaddeus, and the scores of other dead sailors from the battle and realized that he had no more right to live than any of them.

Putting aside his silly thoughts of surviving this last battle to live happily ever after with his friends and family in the capital, Jaymes looked up at the charging masses of goblins and orcs, and he accepted that this was his fate. This was how it ended. There were worse ways to go.

"*Pious* ship's company!" he cried, his sword held aloft. "On me!"

Renewing their vigor, Jaymes's sailors let out a yell as they charged into the fray alongside him. Jaymes met the leader of the wave of goblins head on, a larger creature who felt entitled to wear an over-sized bicorn hat. The goblin fired a pistol at Jaymes, missed, and then swung up with a straight-bladed dirk. Jaymes parried the attack and hacked down, slicing open the goblin's chest before punting the dying creature to one side and lunging forward to pierce the guts of a second opponent.

To Jaymes's left, a screeching goblin savagely cut a blade across the thighs of a gray-haired Basilean sailor. The man let out a cry and tried to hack down at the evil creature with his cutlass, but a second goblin leapt on him with a yelp, pushing him back until the sailor and both goblins plummeted overboard. To his right, an orc warrior cut down two sailors before turning to fix his blood red eyes on Jaymes. Deciding that several years of fencing lessons definitely had their lim-its, Jaymes snatched his pistol from his belt, cocked the hammer with his thumb, and shot the orc in the face.

"Reload, sir?" Francis asked from behind Jaymes, one hand pressing a bandage against his wounded shoulder.

"Much obliged, Mister Turnio!" Jaymes grinned, holding the smoking pistol out to the young midshipman before charging back into the fight.

***

The smasher and the *Pious* were locked together, the decks of both ships awash with sailors. Caithlin looked off to the south and saw the penultimate blood runner burning, while the *Veneration* swept around toward the final blood runner that doggedly chased the *Mar-tolian Queen* down. The only other ships left were two of the Basilean sloops who, clearly having decided that their miniscule firepower would be of limited use, were now recovering survivors from the water where the *Vigil* had disappeared beneath the waves.

Caithlin looked over at X'And.

"What now?" she asked. "I can't shoot at their flagship with Basilean sailors so close."

"You *could*," the salamander countered as the two towering ships loomed closer, "but you won't do much. I think it better if we board her."

Caithlin looked across, wide-eyed, at her first mate.

"*Board* an orc warship? That size? And you've been accusing me of being reckless?"

The salamander corsair flashed a sharp-toothed grin.

"Every last one of those green-skins is up on deck, fighting. It'll be all but deserted down below. We could do some real damage down there."

Caithlin looked across the bows of her brig, wincing involuntarily as the bow chasers of the pursuing blood runner behind them fired again. The gun ports of the smasher were open on both sides, and she lay dead in the water, tangled up alongside the *Pious*. Caithlin shuddered as she saw the devastated state of the Basilean frigate.

"What damage can we do down there?" she asked X'And.

"We can set fire to the powder magazines," the salamander replied simply.

Caithlin looked forward across the deck of her brig at the hulking orc warship. With the frigate to the south turning in to attack the blood runner behind her, only the flagship remained as any viable threat. If the smasher could be destroyed, the battle was won. She looked over her shoulder at her helmsman.

"Put us next to their flagship," she commanded, before turning to shout down to the sailors manning her guns. "Prepare for boarding!"

***

With a feral roar, Ghurak swung one of his axes down into the shield wall on the far side of the ramp. The sheer force of his strike buckled the metal of the shield, flinging the human soldier off balance. With his axe wedged in the metal, Ghurak hauled back and physically dragged the soldier out of his line and then lopped off his head with his second axe. A fresh wave of orc warriors charged down the ramp, hurtling past either side of Ghurak to smash their way into the slowly dissolving shield wall.

Up forward, the orcs and goblins had all but claimed the front of the Basilean frigate, having fought their way across the smashed deck and forced the human sailors down to stand their ground amid their cannons. Back aft, it was a different story entirely. A ferocious counterattack by the humans had beaten the orcs and goblins back, and Ghurak could only let out an agonized howl of rage as he saw a blood-drenched human officer lead the charge up the orc's own boarding ramps and onto the deck of the *Green Hammer*.

Batting aside a sword strike from one of the armored human soldiers, Ghurak rained blows down with his axes until he beat an opening into the shield wall. Forcing his way inside, he headbutted a human warrior down to the deck and then flung an axe down to embed itself in the screaming soldier's guts. The shield wall dissolved and the fighting broke down from ordered attacks into a furious, frenzied melee as orc fought human in a vicious bloodbath.

A tall, powerful looking human soldier with a plume of blue feathers atop his helmet stepped out in front of Ghurak. The man's bearing, as well as his helmet, marked him out as a leader. The human warrior charged at Ghurak with a boarding pike in one hand and shield ready in the other. Spitting out a mouthful of blood as he recovered his second axe, Ghurak lunged forward to meet the challenge. He swung an axe down at the human's head, but the warrior nimbly ducked beneath it and smashed the butt of his pike across Ghurak's face. Ghurak lashed out with his offhand axe, scything it through the air at chest height toward the soldier. The warrior took the blow on his shield and stabbed out quickly with his pike, tearing a wound through Ghurak's bicep.

Undeterred, the orc admrul swung both axes down toward his adversary, linking a furious flurry of blows at the skillful warrior. The human was forced back, ducking and dodging some blows while deflecting the others aside with his battered shield. Tirelessly, roaring savagely, Ghurak continued the assault until he finally saw an opening and planted a foot against the human's gut, kicking him down to the deck forcefully. The warrior clattered down, his pike rolling away from his outstretched hand. Ghurak grinned as he limped over to finish off the warrior.

Another soldier, also clad in the same platemail armor, dived out from one side and swiped down at Ghurak with a broad-bladed sword. Ghurak took the blow against the haft of one of his axes and then felt his head snap back as his new opponent slammed his shield into the orc pirate's face. With a roar, Ghurak smashed a fist into the shield and flung the warrior's arm aside. Powerless to stop the raw, physical strength of the orc krudger, the soldier's shield was forced to one side. Ghurak grinned in victory as he swung an axe down to embed in the man's chest, killing him instantly.

***

Karnon let out a cry of anguish as he saw the gargantuan orc cut down Sergeant Castus Erria. Snatching up his pike again, Karnon yelled furiously as he charged the orc, stabbing out with the tip of the weapon. He caught the orc pirate off guard, lancing the blade of the pike though his thigh and forcing him back a step. One wounded leg quivering, the enormous orc staggered back into a small opening in the brutal fight on *Pious's* upper deck. Then, from above in the rigging, Karnon heard the snap of a musket shot.

The orc leader's head was flung back from the impact, a great stream of blood and gore fountaining out of his now empty eye socket. Dropping one axe and clutching desperately at his mutilated face, the orc thrashed around blindly with his remaining axe, howling in pain and rage. Still screaming in anger, Karnon charged forward and planted his shoulder against the orc, pushing him back a step toward the ramp leading back to his own ship. He was quickly joined by two of his marines, ploughing their metal shields into the savage pirate and forcing him off the deck of the *Pious*.

With Jaymes leading the counterattack across the smasher's quarterdeck, and Kaeso Innes frantically trying to hold back the advancing orcs and goblins on the fo'c'sle, Karnon drove back the orc warlord in a desperate attempt to win back *Pious's* upper deck from the attackers. The fight hung in the balance.

Chapter Twenty-One

The *Martolian Queen* crashed into the battered, broken orc flag-ship at speed. Caithlin was knocked from her feet by the impact, her world lurching around her as the brig pitched up to port, the prow bursting through a ragged hole in the orc ship's side. The violent motion ceased as suddenly as it had begun, and Caithlin jumped back up to her feet. Retrieving both of her pistols from her belt, she cocked the hammers on both weapons. Her crew stood ready around her on the brig's fo'c'sle. Repressing the urge to attempt to prove her mastery over her own fear by unwisely leading the boarding, she shouted an order out to X'And.

"Boarding party, away!"

The salamanders were the first up across the prow of the *Martolian Queen* and in through the ragged hole in the orc ship's hull. Caithlin followed close behind, the sound of screams and the clashing of blades echoing from the darkness within. No sooner had she set foot inside the dark, dank, and stench-ridden orc vessel than a goblin charged at her with a wood axe. She brought a pistol up and shot the creature in the chest. A second diminutive monster ran at her, suffering the same fate as she raised her second pistol.

Scores of her sailors charged past her and into the smasher, rushing to engage the dozens of green-skins that were still inside the hulking wreck. Eager to finally overcome her fear of engaging in face-to-face combat, Caithlin rushed over to aid one of her sailors who was desperately fighting off two goblins alone; she smashed the butt of one of her pistols down onto the enemy's skull with a resounding crack, and then swept a foot up into the creature to punt it overboard.

"X'And," she shouted across to her first mate, "take your lot and get below to the powder stores! I'll lead the rest up top and take the upper deck!"

Retrieving his fiery blade from a butchered orc, X'And looked over at his captain.

"Ten minutes!" he shouted across. "Ten minutes and then we need to be clear!"

***

Fighting his way across the crude, grapeshot riddled quarter-deck of the smasher, Jaymes looked back down at the deck of his own frigate. A surge from Karnon and the marines had driven the orcs back off the upper deck, up along the boarding ramps toward their own vessel. However, orcs and goblins still fought against Basilean sailors on the fo'c'sle of the *Pious*, the green tide showing no signs of giving in.

Three orcs warriors surrounded by at least triple their number in goblins charged over from the forward end of the quarterdeck toward Jaymes and his surviving ten sailors. He quickly brought his pistol up, took aim, and shot one of the orcs square in the chest before handling the weapon across to Francis to reload.

"Make it quick!" he urged the midshipman before bringing up his saber and rushing out to meet the charging orcs.

Emboldened by a string of successes in cutting down goblins, Jaymes thrust the tip of his saber forward as he leaned in to the attack the first orc. Far quicker than he thought possible for such a hulking creature, the orc warrior dropped his shoulder and swung out at Jaymes's head with a heavy hammer. Jaymes quickly ducked beneath the blow and drove a fist into the orc's armored belly, succeeding only in cracking his own knuckles and letting out a gasp of pain.

Ducking beneath a follow up attack from the brutal hammer, Jaymes felt the air parting above his head as he avoided a killing blow by a hair's breadth. Standing up straight again, he darted in to attack and aimed a cut at the orc's wrist. Not quick enough to react this time, the orc dropped his hammer as Jaymes's blade half-severed the top of his hand. Bringing the saber arcing around, he sliced open the green-skin's throat and then leaned in to thrust the blade through the orc's gut.

As he pulled his blade clear, Jaymes glanced up just in time to see the second lumbering green-skin standing over him, a heavy axe held above his head in two mighty hands. Jaymes looked up and saw the blade glinting in the sun, below a clear blue sky, the weapon somehow at odds with the idyllic seascape and heavens above. He smiled. He would have given nearly anything to survive the day, but at least he finished it fighting, with his head held high.

Two pistol shots cracked out in quick succession, and the orc was flung forward. Blood flowing from his mouth, the green-skin collapsed to the deck as Jaymes's sailors surged past him to tear through the goblins. Astounded, Jaymes looked up. At the far side of the quarterdeck, he saw some forty human sailors, their non-uniform clothing and assortment of blades and swords marking them out as privateers. Stood in their midst, a smoking pistol in each hand, stood Caithlin. She rushed over to stand by Jaymes.

"Are you alright?" she asked, looking up at his blood-soaked head. "Do you need help?"

"It's worse than it looks," Jaymes said. "Thank you for shooting that bastard. I was in a spot of trouble."

"We all are, unless we move quickly!" Caithlin urged as her mob of privateers charged down screaming into the smasher's upper deck to attack the orcs from behind. "My sailors are going to light the powder magazine! We need to get clear!"

Jaymes's eyes opened wide in alarm.

"Then we need to cut ourselves loose! The *Pious* is locked in with this thing!"

Caithlin looked desperately to either side of the orc ship.

"You cut down the ramps back aft, I'll take forward!" she breathed.

"How long have we got?"

"About five minutes!"

"Let's get to it!" Jaymes urged.

Caithlin grabbed him roughly by his shirt collar and quickly pressed her lips against his.

"Don't do anything stupid!" she ordered before turning to rush off toward the fo'c'sle with her men.

Jaymes wasted a good ten seconds of his already severely limited time, standing in a shocked silence before the threat of impending doom galvanized him into action and back toward the orc boarding ramps.

***

The axe dug heavily into Karnon's shield, buckling it in the center with the sheer force of the blow. Seeing the pattern in the fighting style of the vicious orc krudger, Karnon stepped back to narrowly avoid the follow up attack with his adversary's second axe, and then he stabbed forward his with boarding pike, piercing the towering orc's already torn gut. The orc hollered out and brought both of his axes sweeping down, somehow still fighting despite the array of hideous injuries that covered his body.

Karnon dropped a shoulder to dodge the first blow and took the second on the center of his pike, which splintered in half on impact. Sergeant Porphio Aeli appeared at Karnon's side, hacking down with his sword to carve open the orc's shoulder. Bleeding from half a dozen wounds that each would have killed a man, the colossal krudger staggered back again. Karnon tossed aside his bent shield and drew his sword, throwing the remaining half of his pike to his off hand as he continued to advance.

Stepping over the lip of the boarding ramp, Karnon realized that they had finally pushed the krudger and his few remaining warriors back onto their own vessel. He glanced to either side and was surprised to see Basilean sailors hurriedly rushing back to the *Pious's* quarterdeck while Jaymes hacked and kicked apart the orc boarding ramps at the after end of the ships. Looking to his right, he was even more shocked to see Caithlin and her privateers sweeping across the smasher's fo'c'sle, similarly slicing down tangled rigging and kicking boarding ramps away into the sea to sever the physical ties between the *Pious* and the orc flagship.

Whatever was happening, Karnon neither understood nor had time to work out in his head. Sailors at both ends of the two ships were severing the wood and rope that held them together, leaving Karnon and his marines facing the krudger and his warriors on the main boarding ramp in the center. He did not know what the plan was, but he did know he needed to follow it. Karnon quickly checked over his shoulder; he had about twenty marines still standing to face the seemingly unkillable krudger and five huge orc warriors.

"Marines! Advance!" Karnon shouted.

The front rank of his soldiers moved onto the orc ship, tirelessly keeping their line intact as the second rank supported them with pikes at the ready. Another ripple of gunfire from his sharpshooters above tore down into the orcs, sending one of them falling down to the blood-soaked deck. Vastly outnumbered, wounded, and forced back onto their own ship, the orcs finally broke and turned to flee in terror. All except for the krudger. The red-coated orc still stood his ground, blood flowing from one empty eye socket and the huge tear in his side.

"Come on!" he thundered at the advancing marines, "I'll tear you all apart! Come on!"

The last of the sailors on the quarterdeck had now jumped back onto the *Pious*, leaving Jaymes alone on the after end of the orc ship. Up forward, the lines and ramps attaching the *Pious* to the smasher were all cut, leaving a handful of orcs and goblins isolated on the *Pious's* fo'c'sle. Goblins were already leaping off the *Pious* and into the sea below as the survivors of the frigate's crew advanced mercilessly forward. Karnon saw Caithlin and her crew sprinting back for the hatches leading below deck on the smasher, no doubt returning to their own brig.

"Karnon!" Caithlin yelled as she stopped momentarily by the forward hatchway, pointing down at the deck beneath her feet. "The magazines! We've lit the powder magazines!"

Karnon's jaw dropped as the severity of the situation immediately dawned on him.

"Second rank, fall back!" he yelled, desperate to ensure the safety of his marines but cognizant that the krudger still faced them. "Front rank, stand firm!"

Half of his marines immediately turned and ran to the comparative safety of the *Pious*. The orc krudger looked around him at his deserted deck, carpeted with the massacred bodies of his crew. The upper deck of the smasher was now lower than that of the *Pious* as the huge ship slowly sank toward the depths below, the victorious human sailors sprinting for their lives as they retreated. His remaining eye still blazed with spirit and defiance, but in contrast, the orc's body had given up. He dropped down to one knee and both axes fell from his hands.

"Come on," he said again.

The orc's tone was different now, less confrontational. Almost pleading. Karnon knew enough about their warrior culture to realize what the defeated orc was asking for. He wanted a warrior's death, not to be left alone on a sinking ship to drown or burn when the magazines exploded. Then Karnon thought of the sailors from the *Vigil*, struggling in the unforgiving water as two orc ships tilted their guns down to massacre them for nothing more than fun. He thought of Castus Erria, Charn Ferrus, Walt Ganto, and Thaddeus Just – most, men he had barely known, but they were *good* men. He thought of half of his own marines who lay dead on the *Pious's* shattered decks. He thought of all of the men who had died for the orcs' principles; nothing more complex than greed and the childish, pathetic need to prove themselves. He tossed aside his broken pike and held an empty hand to one side.

"Pike," he ordered.

One of his marines obliged by handing him a fresh weapon. Karnon stepped forward and thrust the tip of the weapon through one of the orc's feet, shoving it down through the wood of the deck to pin the krudger in place. The orc let out an agonized howl, no doubt from the realization of the death that awaited him more than the pain.

"Hold onto this for me, would you, pal?" Karnon spat, jeering down at the orc.

He turned his back on the bleeding orc as his marines stared down contemptuously at the helpless monster, some swearing at him, others cursing him, some spitting on him.

"Come on!" Karnon shouted. "Time's up!"

The marines sprinted across the wooden ramps back to the *Pious* and then hurled them overboard as the bows of the frigate eased in toward the smasher, and the quarterdecks drifted apart from each other.

***

Jaymes could already see the first sailors jumping down to the fo'c'sle of the *Martolian Queen* from his vantage point on the smasher's quarterdeck. His sailors had already hacked down the orcs' crude boarding ramps and jumped back across to the *Pious*. A dozen men on the *Pious's* quarterdeck looked up at Jaymes, shouting desperately for him to jump. He looked to the forward end of the ships and saw the lines were all cut, and Caithlin rushing with her last group of sailors back to the hatchway leading below deck and to her escape route. Yet the ships were still held firm together. When the smasher exploded, she would take the *Pious* with her.

Looking up around him, Jaymes quickly identified the problem. There were still tangles in the rigging lines, somehow strong enough to keep a final, tenuous grip that held the two huge vessels together. Jaymes sprinted across to the offending rigging lines, hacking frantically at them with his gold-hilted saber. With twangs and bangs, the lines released in turn as he severed the ropes.

Down on the waist, Karnon led his last marines back to safety. To port, the *Martolian Queen* was already slowly pushing away from the sinking smasher. Jaymes was the only human left onboard. The party of sailors on the fo'c'sle of the *Pious* was double the size now, all yelling and screaming for him to jump. Jaymes severed the last line with his sword.

Finally freed, with a squealing of protesting timbers, the bows of the *Pious* swung in toward the smasher, and the stern pulled quickly away. Jaymes watched in horror as the safety of his own ship rushed away from him, leaving a rapidly opening chasm between the two decks. One word was distinguishable from the shouting and roaring from the sailors on the *Pious's* quarterdeck and waist as fifty men screamed out to him.

"Jump!"

Sheathing his saber, Jaymes ran back a few paces, turned, and then propelled himself across the deck of the smasher. Planting a foot on the taff rail, he pushed himself off the ship with every ounce of strength he had left. The sun sparkled and shone in his eyes, reflecting off the beautiful, green waves below as he jumped frantically across the gap between the two vessels. He reached the apex of his leap quickly and began to fall. He knew he would not make it across. Closing his eyes in defeat, he felt a painful thud as he slammed headlong against the hull of the frigate.

But he did not fall. His armpits hurt intensely from the pressure of hanging, but he did not fall. He opened his eyes and looked up. The edge of the quarterdeck was only two or three feet above, where dozens of sailors stared down at him, crying out joyously. Directly above him, Karnon leaned over from where he held on to Jaymes's wrists.

"Get up here, you stupid bastard!" the marine captain shouted. "This isn't as easy as it looks!"

Swinging his legs forward to plant his feet on the side of the ship, Jaymes slowly climbed up to the quarterdeck as more hands came down to grab him and lift him to safety. A resounding cheer erupted from the crowded quarterdeck of the *Pious* as the wounded frigate pulled away from the sinking smasher, the top men dropping the battered sails to catch the wind and propel the vessel to safety before the orc flagship's magazines exploded.

The *Pious* and the *Martolian Queen* pulled away from the smasher as the *Veneration* chased down the final blood runner, fleeing toward the southern horizon. Then, anti-climactically, a dull boom sounded from within the bowels of the orc warship. There was a stunned silence from the crew as nothing happened. Then a second explosion sounded, and almost immediately afterward, the smasher was torn in half by a cataclysmic fireball that erupted with a sound unlike anything Jaymes had ever heard. A wave of blazing heat shot over the deck of the *Pious* as fire and flames roared up toward the heavens, followed moments later by thick clouds of black, billowing smoke. Another cheer went up from the crowded deck of the frigate.

Jaymes moved across to the stern of the quarterdeck, watching in fascination as the two halves of the smasher blazed and sank into the waves. The *Martolian Queen* altered course to port, hauling herself away from the sinking wreck to swing around northwest and head for home, the two surviving sloops moving in to flank her. To the south, the *Veneration* relentlessly continued the fight, sat off one side of the final blood runner, pummeling the stricken orc ship with broadside after broadside.

"Captain, sir?"

Jaymes took in a deep breath, still fixated on the blazing wreckage of the smasher.

"Captain?" the voice repeated.

Jaymes shook his head. The captain was dead. A hand landed on his shoulder, causing him to jump. He turned around. The quarterdeck was still packed with sailors, chatting excitedly as the euphoria of surviving the battle set in. Francis Turnio looked up at Jaymes.

"What are your orders, Captain?" he asked.

Jaymes's face twisted into an angry scowl. Charn Ferrus was the captain. The *Pious* had no other. Francis took a step back, his face worried. Jaymes took in another breath and forced himself to calm a little before he responded.

"I'm not the captain, Francis," he replied, "I could never replace Captain Ferrus. I doubt anybody ever could."

Adrenaline seeping from his tired, battered body, Jaymes sank down to sit at the after end of the quarterdeck, slumped back against the wood behind him.

"Back to work, please!" Kaeso Innes called politely to the rabble of hardened maritime killers on the quarterdeck. "Back to your stations, gents! Thank you! Come on, back to work!"

The young lieutenant ushered the scores of sailors off the quarterdeck with a polite, unflagging smile.

"North," Jaymes called out wearily to Kaeso. "Bring us around north and head for Keretia. And hoist a signal to the rest of the fleet. Tell them… Shining Ones bless and well done."

The booming of gunfire to the south ceased, and a few cheers on the fo'c'sle was confirmation to Jaymes that the *Veneration* had sunk the last blood runner. It was a resounding victory. They had destroyed a smasher, three blood runners, and three rabbles for the loss of a frigate and a sloop. It had been a massacre. Yet, from his vantage point slumped down at the back of the quarterdeck, looking down at a decimated frigate with over half of its crew dead, it did not feel like a major victory at all.

"You alright?" Karnon asked, sinking down to sit next to Jaymes.

He glanced across at the blood-soaked marine captain.

"Thank you," Jaymes said sincerely, "thank you for catching me. Thank you for everything."

Karnon winced and shrugged.

"Just good at my job. But I do have one question. Why the hell did you jump? Why not just take a quick jog up to the front of the ship and step across where we were still against the smasher? Were you trying to show off?"

Jaymes could not help but grin at the accusation.

"I… I never thought of that," he finally managed. "I feel rather silly now."

"And so you should."

Jaymes looked up again across the deck of the frigate. The blue light on the shredded wooden Elohi figurehead still blazed proudly.

Jaymes hauled himself back to his feet and looked across to see the *Veneration* altering course to follow them home. A ripple of laughter erupted from the crew of the *Pious* as Karnon stood up next to Jaymes. The two officers looked down at the upper deck in confusion.

"Return signal from the *Martolian Queen*, sir!" Francis beamed, one hand still holding the bandage in place on his wounded shoulder.

Jaymes looked across at the privateer brig and saw a long line of signal flags trailing from her halyards. His face cracked into a smile as he read them.

From-Captain-to-Pious-First-Lieutenant-You-Are-Buying-The-First-Round

Chapter Twenty-Two

The four officers marched smartly into the admiral's office, turning in unison to face the desk. The naval officers then slid their feet together across the floorboards to stand to attention, while the two marines each brought a knee up to waist height before slamming it down, standing to attention following the convention of the legion. Admiral Sir Jerias Pattia looked up from behind his desk. A second officer, also middle-aged but with cropped short, iron gray hair and a white tunic, regarded the officers from where he stood, arms folded behind the admiral.

"The formality is appreciated, gentlemen, but quite unnecessary," Jerias smiled. "Please, relax."

The two marines rigidly brought their hands up to clasp together at the smalls of their backs, standing at ease. Jaymes followed Marcellus Dio's lead and stood normally, as normal people do. He noticed the gray-haired man behind the admiral flinch in irritation at the lack of formality. Jaymes felt the scroll inside his jacket pressing against his chest. His lieutenancy certificate, to be surrendered to the admiral. The end was in sight now.

Jerias stood and walked over to his drinks cabinet, producing a decanter of something pungent.

"Anyone for a tipple while we talk?" he smiled across.

"No, thank you, sir," Karnon replied, "I don't drink while on duty."

"Likewise, sir," said Captain Berso, commander of the *Veneration* marine detachment.

"I'll join you for a brief tot, sir!" Marcellus grinned.

"Likewise, thank you, sir," Jaymes nodded eagerly.

He again noticed the irritation of the gray-haired officer as the admiral handed two glasses of rum over to his subordinates.

"Well," Jerias began, standing by the open doors to his office balcony, "you've had quite an eventful few days. Oh, allow me to introduce Dictator Septim Paulus. He's been appointed by the Duma to take over command of the 5th Maritime Legion of Foot."

"Gentlemen," the dictator nodded gruffly.

The admiral took a sip from his rum, glanced out of the window, was momentarily distracted by something in the yard down below, and then returned his attention to the officers gathered before his desk.

"Marcellus, you're initial report indicates that the squadron sank a smasher, three blood runners, and three rabbles."

"That's right, sir," Marcellus nodded, one hand thrust casually in the pocket of his blue breeches while the other idly swilled his rum around its crystal glass.

"For the loss of a single frigate and sloop?" the admiral continued.

"Yes, sir."

"Quite a result," the admiral mused. "Shame about Charn and Alain. Good captains. Both of them. Shame."

Jaymes stepped forward.

"We brought back Captain Ferrus, sir. For a burial at the naval chapel, sir."

The admiral looked up at Jaymes. His features softened.

"He didn't wish to be buried at sea?"

"His records did not indicate either way, sir. The crew felt that a permanent headstone in the yard was more appropriate than a service at sea. Except by those present, those can be very quickly forgotten, sir."

Jerias nodded again.

"I'll ensure that's carried out. Good captain, was Charn. I wasn't surprised to see the *Pious* limp back in in tatters. I was very surprised to hear that it wasn't under Charn's command. Anyway! Dictator Paulus? I believe you wanted a chat with your fellows?"

The stony-faced soldier issued a single nod of his head.

"Yes, I would. Follow me."

Jaymes watched as the dictator led the two marine captains out of the office, leaving him with Marcellus and Jerias. The admiral walked over to his drinks cabinet, retrieved his decanter and wordlessly topped up all three glasses of rum.

"Nice day," he remarked thoughtfully, "shall we take a wander out onto the balcony?"

***

Karnon stood at ease in front of the dictator's desk, remaining motionless next to Berso. Paulus leafed through a collection of loose papers silently. The morning sun shone through the single window behind him, awkwardly focusing directly into Karnon's eyes. Outside, the normal and now familiar sounds of life in the dockyard continued as supplies were taken to ships, small groups of sailors laughed and joked as they made their way frivolously between buildings, senior ratings shouted at small groups of sailors for being frivolous, and halyards pinged against flag poles in the gentle breeze. The only other sound came from the corner of the small office, where the dictator's aide hurriedly scribbled on parchments as he crouched over his own desk.

"It seems that this idea of formalizing a marine organization has gotten off to a reasonable start," Paulus looked up at the two captains.

Neither replied.

"You're both satisfied with the progress made?" the dictator asked directly.

"Aye, sir," Berso replied, "it would be a shame to go round the buoy again if this whole idea is scuppered."

Paulus sat upright and blinked in confusion.

"I beg your pardon, Captain?" he demanded.

"He said it would be a shame to have to start this whole idea again, if it is killed off now, sir," Karnon translated.

"Then why not just say it?" the dictator demanded. "Why talk in riddles like a damn sailor? You're soldiers, aren't you?"

"Marines, sir," Berso corrected. "Maritime Legion of Foot. Attached to the naval service, sir."

The dictator leaned over his desk and tapped one fist lightly into his other hand. He nodded a few times in thought and then looked up at the marine officers again.

"Your results in action speak for themselves," he admitted, "but I'm rather surprised to see legion men so keen to embrace naval customs."

Karnon winced. They were traditions, not customs. He looked across at Berso. The older captain gave a slight shrug. Karnon looked forward again.

"If I may speak freely, sir?"

"Please do, Captain Senne."

Karnon paused for a moment, assembling his thoughts before speaking again.

"I was glad to volunteer for this concept, sir. Proud to be selected. But I will confess to having thought sailors to be rather wet, if you pardon the pun, sir. A bit soft. But having fought alongside them, I've rather changed my mind. You see, for us, we're never helpless. No matter how strong our enemy is, we always have the ability to march at them, sword in hand, and try to kill them."

Paulus listened intently to Karnon's words. He continued.

"A battle at sea involves a lot of sitting around. But for all the time you are sitting around, you can die. Cannonballs are flying, there's wooden splints the size of a man twirling through the air everywhere, ripping people apart. And these sailors have to just ignore it and do their job. Some of them aren't even fighters. There's carpenters, cooks, sail makers, you name it. None of them can escape the battle, and they all have to just carry on, knowing their number could be up at any moment."

"And that's before the boarding, sir," Berso intervened, "because when that starts, the sailors get stuck in just as much as we do. The difference is that we are trained to a much higher level and have better equipment. So the result for them is that more of them die. But they still get stuck in. That's why I'm proud to use their slang, sir. Being a marine isn't just legion. It's a maritime soldier. We're part of this now."

Paulus stood up slowly, pulling down on the hem of his white tunic. He turned to glance out of the window for a moment and then looked back at his officers again.

"What can I do to help you in this new role?" he offered.

Again, Karnon and Berso glanced at each other for a moment.

"Colors, sir," Berso replied, "distinct colors to mark us out as what we are. Colors that show we are marines, so other people don't confuse us for legion. Colors that make soldiers want to earn the right to join us."

"And you, Captain Senne?" the dictator asked, looking across at Karnon.

He hesitated before replying. Part of him considered giving an answer at dutiful as Berso's, but honesty won out.

"Leave, sir," he replied. "I'd like leave from duty so I can go home to see my wife."

The stony-faced dictator's mouth twisted into a smile. He turned to his aide.

"Prepare the requisite paperwork to send Captain Senne home for a couple of weeks. I think he has earned that."

***

Jerias leaned in to shake hands warmly with Marcellus.

"Fantastic work, Marcellus," the admiral said. "Stand your ship down for a couple of days. I'll have a watch sent across from the dockyard to keep an eye on it."

"Thank you, sir," the *Veneration's* captain smiled, walking back into the office and leaving his empty glass by the drinks cabinet.

"And tell your sailors not to ruin it now, would you?" Jerias warned. "It would be a shame for them to return victorious and then throw it away by getting drunk and making a mess of the town. No free passes, Marcellus. If your men are disorderly, I won't have any sympathy."

"Aye, sir," Marcellus said, picking up his hat from the peg on the back of the office door, "I'll make sure they know."

Jaymes leaned back on the balcony rail, his rum glass still half full, the sun beating down on his back. Out of the corner of his eye, he could see *Pious's* masts from where she lay alongside her jetty, the hammering of carpenters beginning the lengthy program of repairs on the stricken frigate was faintly audible even from this distance. The admiral returned from his farewells with Marcellus Dio and met Jaymes out on the balcony. Jaymes smiled awkwardly, very aware of the rolled up scroll tucked into the inside of his blue jacket.

"Well, I should be on my way, sir," Jaymes said quietly, standing up straight again. "Thank you for the rum."

Lieutenants did not spend time idly chit-chatting with admirals on sun-drenched balconies, overlooking palm tree festooned islands. It was not the done thing. But he still needed to hand over the scroll before he left.

"No rush, Jaymes," Jerias said. "I'd rather you stayed for a moment or two. I'd like to talk to you."

"Certainly, sir," Jaymes replied.

The lean admiral finished his rum, placed the glass down on the small, white table on the balcony, and then planted both hands on the rail and looked out across the bay.

"So this is you leaving," he said, "you're done with us."

Jaymes looked down. Only a few hours before, he was relieved to be alive, thanking the Shining Ones above when the blue light on the figurehead of the *Pious* finally faded away and their guardian Elohis returned to Mount Kolosu. Now, merely listening to the admiral's tone, he suddenly felt guilty. As if he was abandoning his duty. No. He shook his head. He had made his mind up. It was time to leave, to go home, to see his parents, his sister, her family. To have a normal life. Jaymes reached into his jacket and placed the scroll on the table next to the empty rum glass.

"My commissioning certificate, sir," he said simply.

Jerias looked down at it briefly.

"People leave the navy," he said, "I understand that. Some officers leave and I shake their hand to wish them all the best. Some leave, and I'm happy to see the back of them! Some go to leave, and I urge them to stay. You're one of those officers."

Jaymes's brow furrowed in confusion.

"Why? I spent my entire career sunning myself on the deck of a sloop, occasionally rescuing a fisherman or two, and then was moved to a desk job which I knew nothing about! Sir, I can't waste any more of my life just treading water. I want to go and do something I can be proud of."

Jerias tutted to himself, swatted at a fly on the back of his hand, and then looked across at Jaymes.

"A month ago, if you'd left the naval service, you would have been one of those fellows who I would have shaken hands with and wished luck to. Not one I'd be glad to see the back of, but one whose decision to leave I would accept and respect. But you're not that man anymore. You stepped up to become second-in-command of a frigate engaged in anti-piracy duties, and Charn said you did the job well. You were then seconded to a privateer brig where, according to the letter I received from Captain Viconti, you were instrumental in preparing the crew for their duties and fought a wanted man in single combat until he and his crew surrendered."

"Sir, I..."

"Furthermore," the admiral interrupted, "you then took part in a major action at sea where you were wounded, your captain was killed, half of your crew was lost, and your ship took significant damage. You took charge of the situation, took command of *Pious*, boarded a larger enemy vessel, and remained onboard while the magazines were lit, ensuring the safety of your crew was guaranteed until you left. The last man off. Jaymes, is any of this untrue?"

Jaymes thought through the past few weeks. He had no idea that Charn had spoken highly of him. He had no idea that Caithlin had taken the time to write to an admiral to commend him.

"It's not how I would describe it all, sir," Jaymes said. "There were hundreds of us working together to achieve what we did. I took command because the regulations dictated that I *had* to, not because I wanted to."

Jerias returned indoors momentarily, grabbing his decanter and taking something from the top draw of his desk. He topped up his own glass, and then Jaymes's, making him wonder how it was at all possible for the admiral to drink as much as he did on a daily basis and still walk in a straight line. Then, the item he had recovered from the desk draw was tossed down onto the table next to the lieutenancy certificate. Jaymes's eyes opened wider.

Captain's epaulettes.

"Forgive the theatrics," Jerias said, "but I wanted to make an impact. If you stay, the *Pious* is yours. You're her captain."

Jaymes stared down at the golden badges of rank. He looked up again.

"I... I couldn't..."

"Say 'yes', and I'll bring in that bloody useless flag-lieutenant of mine and have him sew those epaulettes onto your jacket right now, while we watch. Say 'yes', and you walk out of this building as Captain Ellias."

Jaymes met the admiral's insistent glare but found no words.

"But," the admiral said suddenly, "if you do say 'yes', allow me to be as honest with you as you have been with me. I think this will be as far as you rise. You have every attribute I want in one of my captains. You may even move on to command a larger vessel. But from what others have told me about you, and from what I've seen, you're no admiral. I don't think you ever will be. That's not a sleight on your character, that's plain honesty."

Jerias looked down across the bay again before continuing.

"People tend to look at what others have and be envious, rather than looking at what others don't have and being thankful. It makes us all rather ambitious, always wanting more. Finishing your career as a captain is a fantastic achievement. I really think you should take those epaulettes. But admiral? The day comes... the day comes when you have to look in a mirror and see the face of a man who orders young-er men to sail to their deaths while watching them go from a bayside balcony. And you have to reconcile with that. I don't think you're that man."

Jaymes looked across at the admiral silently as the older officer stared out south to the calm waters of the Infant Sea. He wondered if the last part of his dialogue was meant to help Jaymes at all, or if the aging admiral was soul searching and looking for an outlet for his own insecurities and regrets. The admiral looked back across at him.

"What's the answer, Jaymes?"

***

The Palm Spring tavern in mid-afternoon was all but deserted. Jaymes sat alone at a small table on the open upper floor, one hand clutching a wooden tankard of local juices, the other propping his chin up as he stared out numbly at the horizon. Of the twenty or so tables on the upper floor, only two others were occupied. Jaymes appreciated that. It gave him time to think. Again, clad in the normal, civilian garb of simple breeches and a shirt, he appreciated the simpler things. The simplicity of just being left alone, in a sunny, near empty tavern to listen to the birds sing and be lost in thought.

A clumping of booted feet from the stairs at the end of the floor brought Jaymes attention back from his predicament. He looked across and saw Caithlin, eye-catching in her gold-buttoned greatcoat, saber at her side, and black tricorn hat tilted back on her head. The tavern's few other occupants stared at her as she strode past them, the cocky swagger in her step exuding confidence. She stopped by Jaymes and planted her hands on the table in front of him, leaning over.

"Hello, sailor," she said. "Are you buying me a drink? Excuse my rig, that's what your lot say, isn't it?"

Jaymes smiled and stood to pull the chair out for her. Caithlin tossed her hat on the table and took her jacket off, revealing a red sash wound around her slender waist. She noticed Jaymes looking at it.

"It's made of orc sailcloth," she smiled. "One of my men fished it out of the water before we left the battle. X'And stitched it together for me as a memento. Very kind of him. I'll miss him."

"Oh?" Jaymes queried, catching the eye of one of the tavern workers and pointing at his wooden tankard to indicate a drink order for Caithlin. "What happened?"

"He's gone home for a while," Caithlin said as she sat down, "back to the Three Kings. It's a pilgrimage of sorts that salamanders need to make. A ritual. Hopefully he'll be back in a few weeks."

Jaymes sat opposite Caithlin and looked across at her. The table was silent. She smiled and leaned in closer.

"What's wrong? I know there are plenty of things to be concerned about, but what's troubling you the most?"

Jaymes looked at her again and failed to meet her gaze. With the whirlwind of activity that had surrounded him, he only now remembered that last time they met was on the deck of a sinking ship, where she had kissed him. It would perhaps have been good to enquire about that, and how she felt, but Jaymes knew he had a propensity to look too far into things. In his mind, that was the beginning of an epic romance. He knew the reality was that it was probably nothing more than an impulsive act with no meaning behind it. He dreaded to think what Caithlin would say if she knew he still had that gold coin in his pocket.

"Captain Ferrus," he finally replied. "I'm sat here thinking about his death. I'm sorry to see any of them die. But with the captain... it just confused me."

"In what way?"

"I was with him at the very end. I'd been hit in the head. I... the whole thing was just a blur. I thought I saw the Elohi take him away. His last words were not... he just looked at me and said sorry. I don't know what for."

Caithlin flashed a smile of gratitude as a server brought over a tankard and placed it in front of her. The palm trees outside the tavern rustled gently in the breeze, and colorful birds sang melodic songs.

"Maybe he was sorry for the way he treated you?" Caithlin offered. "Maybe he was sorry because he knew what responsibility he was leaving you with."

That brought Jaymes neatly around to the next concern on his list. After all of the death and derision of the past few days, he also had the future to worry about.

"They offered me the *Pious*," he said to Caithlin wearily. "They offered me a captaincy."

"Well, that's fantastic!" Caithlin exclaimed, smiling broadly. "Congratulations!"

"I said I needed a day to think it over," Jaymes shrugged uncomfortably.

"But... why?"

He looked up at her.

"Because my plan is to go home."

Caithlin's smile faded away. She tapped a finger against her tankard pensively and looked out at the palm trees lining the tavern's gardens.

"You're still intent on that?"

"I think so," Jaymes said. "What would you do?"

Caithlin looked back again.

"I can't tell you what I would do, because I don't know, I haven't walked in your shoes," she admitted and then reached across to take his hand in one of hers. "I can tell you what I want you to do. I want you to stay."

Jaymes looked across the table, a sudden and unexplained nervousness coursing through him.

"When we were last here," Caithlin explained, "sat at this table, you told me about your plan to go home. I wanted to ask you if it would be alright if I visited you there. I wanted to let you know that I want us to be more than friends. But I ran out of courage. I couldn't ask."

Jaymes exhaled, the wind knocked out of his lungs.

"Really?!" he gasped. "Because I feel the same way! I…"

Caithlin held up a hand to save him the trouble.

"I know, Jaymes. You're not a subtle man. You don't hide your feelings well. Look, my path is set now. I'm a privateer, and I'm going to be living by the sword and the gun for a good while. If you go home, I'll sail across to the Golden Horn to see you whenever I can. If you stay, I'll sail alongside you and your frigate every time you leave harbor. And I'll come back in alongside you every time you come home."

Jaymes realized that his hands were shaking. He thought of the peace and safety of a life in the capital, of being able to see his parents and his sister every day, of being his own man and master of his own destiny, with no orders to follow. Then he looked across the table at the woman who smiled at him warmly and the battered frigate out in the bay that was still just about visible from where he sat. Caithlin let go of his hand and stood up. She produced a gold coin from her pocket.

"Is… that the coin I gave to you?" Jaymes asked as he stood up opposite her.

Caithlin smiled and flipped it up into the air with a ping. The shining coin twirled up between them, hovering for a brief moment at eye level before falling back down again to land in Caithlin's hand. She immediately clapped her other hand over the top to hide the result, her eyes fixed on his.

"Crowns says you go home. Dragons says you take the captaincy and stay here."

Jaymes's smile grew as the realization of his decision set in his mind. He placed his hands on her waist and pulled her in.

"I don't need a coin flip to decide," he smiled.

***

TALES OF MANTICA

STEPS TO
DELIVERANCE

By
MARK BARBER
from a story by Mark and Leo Barber

One

As the dry earth gave way beneath his feet and he lurched down toward his death, Orion could not help but wonder at the beauty of the Mountains of Tarkis at sunset. The low, golden sun painted the jagged horizon to the north in shades of orange-gray; the harsh lines of the mountains cascaded down to the foothills to the east overlooking the calm, clear waters of the Low Sea of Suan. The Three Cousins – the islands of Eruks, Kurros, and Ge – sat just offshore, the angular roofs of their little fishing villages just visible even from this distance. The beauty of the surroundings did nothing to calm the sickening fear which shot up through Orion's gut and into his hammering heart as that jagged horizon took on an unnatural aspect while he tumbled over the edge of the treacherous mountain path.

With an audible grunt escaping his lips, he somehow stopped dead in his tracks, dangling over certain death as his thin arms flailed wildly to each side.

"I've got you!" Antoni's reassuring voice called steadily from behind him.

Only now noticing the vice-like grip at the base of his neck, Orion allowed himself to be dragged clear of the edge of the path and flung to the safety of a small plateau to his left. The evening breeze kicked up the pleasant and soothing scent of the lilac, mountainside lavenders as Orion fought to control his breathing. He looked up at Antoni with gratitude.

"Th... th... than..."

"Quite alright," the dashing paladin's lips cracked into a charismatic and contagious smile. "We're here to safeguard each other, after all."

Clad in the distinctive garb of a Basilean paladin, Antoni cut an imposing figure. His highly polished plate armor was lined with a gold trim, while the blue robes of their Order were pinned at his chest by a decorative golden chain. His longsword hung at the hip to one side; to the other was chained his copy of the Eloicon, the sacred text carried by all paladins. Long locks of black hair framed his perfect face; the prerogative of a full paladin in contrast to the obligatory shaven heads of their squires.

"Thank you," Orion finally managed, slowly staggering back to his feet.

"That was...well..."

"What happened?" a concerned voice bawled from the path ahead.

Orion turned to see Jahus carefully picking his way through the rocks to make his way back down to them. Jahus' garb was all but identical to Antoni's, but at nearly twice the age, the veteran paladin's paunch had a slightly ruinous effect on the splendor and nobility of the Order's armor.

"Orion stumbled, that is all," Antoni said. "All is well."

"Yes," Orion nodded, "I am fine, uncle."

A relieved smile emerged from either side of Jahus' broad, black mustache as he clamped his armored hands on Orion's upper arms.

"Take care!" he bellowed, his tone sitting in between admonishment and care. "If I do not bring you home alive, your father will kill me!"

"Yes, uncle," Orion felt blood rush to his cheeks as his gaze fell to the ground.

This was the first time he had ever been allowed to accompany the paladins on an actual task. At sixteen years of age, he was already badly behind schedule for completing his training as a squire – assuming he would ever be successful – and he had spent the last week hampering Jahus and Antoni with various acts of clumsiness and ignorance, without being of any help.

"Go on ahead, Antoni," Jahus nodded. "We shall catch up."

Antoni flashed Orion an encouraging smile. In his mid twenties, Antoni was everything Orion wanted to be – charismatic, respected, proven in battle, and possessing a humility and charm which made it impossible to begrudge him his success. Antoni was already rumored to be considered for promotion to Paladin Defender.

"Keep smiling!" the young paladin winked. "Anything you can walk away from is just a story to impress the ladies when you get home!"

"Enough of that!" Jahus warned. "Go on, up ahead."

Orion watched Antoni vault effortlessly through the gaps in the rocky pathway as he forged ahead. Shifting the strap of the heavy shield on his back so that it cut into a different part of his bony shoulder, Orion set off slowly after him. Although only weighed down by a thick, padded cotton jacket and a coat of mail – less than half the weight of a proper paladin's armor – Orion was already feeling the effects of the hike. Awkwardly, he was already a full head taller than both Jahus and Antoni, but with barely a muscle on his body, he often struggled with the physical aspects of squiredom. Which was pretty much every aspect.

"If you must idolize anybody, you could do worse," Jahus remarked as he followed Orion along the path, their long shadows dancing across the sharp rocks that flanked their path in the late evening sun.

"I don't idolize him, uncle," Orion said honestly.

"He did say one thing which was very sensible."

"What's that?"

"To keep smiling," Jahus said softly. "You'll find in life that there are many things beyond our control. Many things. But what we can always control, with a little discipline, is our outlook. How we react to things we can't control. And for a man to keep smiling no matter what the adversity? That is something special. The ability to keep smiling no matter what is truly a gift from above."

Orion opened his mouth to voice his disagreement but thought better of it.

The sun was half hidden below the jagged, tooth-like horizon now, its fiery orange fading into soft reds and pinks. The chill evening breeze already seemed a little cooler.

"We should stop for..."

Jahus held a hand up to silence his nephew. On the path up ahead, Antoni was stood still and had a hand on his sword. Orion turned to look at his uncle quizzically. Jahus' eyes suddenly widened and he took a quick step forward. An arrow thudded into the aging paladin, slamming against one of his pauldrons before falling harmlessly to the ground.

"Get back, Orion!" Jahus shouted. "Stay clear!"

Orion's jaw dropped open as three armed men sprang from the shadows up ahead to assault Antoni – the paladin firmly stood his ground, and in one rapid motion he unsheathed his sword and hacked down his first assailant. Jahus was already scrambling up the path toward the melee, unsheathing his own sword and grabbing his kite shield from his back.

Orion froze. He stood rooted to the spot as a second trio of bandits leapt out to attack Jahus; he tried to will his legs into action, to force his hand to drop to the sword by his side, but his body seemingly refused to obey his mind's commands.

That was when he saw the third group, another three armed men, scrambling down the rocks to his left toward him. A thousand thoughts danced through his mind as he watched the three men in their battered coats of mail and dented helmets drawing ever closer to him; he wanted to bring his sword up and leap into action, to turn and run for safety, even to shout to his uncle and plead for him to c me back and save him. But in that moment, as the three bandits ran roaring toward him, their axes and hammers held high over their heads, the first time Orion had ever faced a real enemy in his life, he remained completely frozen in place. Completely silent. For the second time in only a few minutes, he was sure he was going to die.

A figure from out of nowhere appeared, no more than a flash of blue and white. With the swing of a heavy flail, the first of the bandits flew back in an arc of crimson spray as the spiked metal ball of the weapon connected with his chin and snapped his head back. The remaining two bandits stopped and took a step back, cautiously pacing around the new arrival. The woman – that much was evident in her lithe form – was tall and powerfully built, her limbs covered in white with a blue gown worn over the top, extending up into a blue hood and mask that covered her features. Battered boots of faded brown leather extended above her knees, and a heavy two handed flail swung menacingly in her grasp as she watched the two bandits.

Both men charged at her, the first swinging a warhammer at her head while the second man swiped at her gut with his axe. The tall woman ducked beneath the hammer blow and swung her flail to wrap it around the wrist of her second assailant.

She dragged him over to bring a knee crashing up into his rotund abdomen before slamming an elbow into his face with an audible crunching of bones. The first, taller bandit swung his heavy hammer around again, but the slim woman was faster, lashing out with her flail to slam the heavy metal ball into the man's ribcage. He dropped to his knees, clutching at his chest and wheezing.

The second bandit saw the fate of his comrades and turned to run. The woman pulled a knife from her belt, slit the throat of the bandit choking helplessly on his knees, and then threw the same blade after his fleeing comrade. The knife thudded into the man's back – his run slowed to a drunken totter as he weakly reached back to try to grab at the blade embedded between his ribs before he fell face down, crying out for help. The woman dashed over, span her flail around to build up momentum, and then brought it crashing down to cave in the man's skull.

Up on the path ahead, two surviving bandits fled as Jahus and Antoni sheathed their weapons. Orion stared down at the three dead bodies by his feet, feeling bile rising rapidly to his throat. Gasping for breath, his body finally obeyed his commands to move and he turned away, desperate to drag his eyes away from the bloodied and broken corpses ahead of him.

"You, boy!" the woman behind him shouted. "You're armed! You shouldn't need me to save you! What were you thinking? Well, boy, speak!"

Orion turned again. The hooded woman paced over to him, her face hidden but her body language betraying her anger.

"I...I..."

"How old are you?" she demanded, standing in front of him and folding her arms.

"Fif... sixteen," Orion managed.

"Sixteen?" She almost spat the word out. "You should be wearing spurs by now, not groveling around as a squire! When I was your age, I'd already fought a full campaign against the orcs!"

"Orion?" Jahus called as he dashed back over. "Are you hurt?"

"Orion?" the woman laughed. "Your parents named you after the patron of courage and hunting? I hope the irony isn't lost on you."

"And your name?" Antoni demanded as he approached, a liberal amount of blood spattered across his gleaming plate armor.

"My name is unimportant, paladin," the woman said, "I'm a sister, you will refer to me as that."

A sister. Orion had of course met nuns from the Basilean Sisterhood's many convents before, but he had never met a fighting sister. While most nun's duties were of spiritual and medical care, there were a few convents scattered across Basilea whose role was to augment the country's legions of men-at-arms and paladin orders. Tales of their prowess in combat were clearly not exaggerated.

"What brings you up this mountain, Sister?" Antoni asked suspiciously.

"My business is my own," the hooded woman said, pacing back down the narrow path to recover a backpack she must have discarded before the fighting began.

She also picked up what looked like a heavy sphere of iron, covered in studs and fitted with a buckled pair of shoulder straps. She slung it over her back, staggering a little under the weight as the metal ball sat painfully across her spine.

"And why are you here?" she demanded as she walked back up the path.

"We are here to serve the Hegemon's authority," Jahus replied coolly. "We are here to bring a criminal in for a hearing."

"Dionne?" the sister exhaled. "So he has finally been declared a criminal? I suppose it was only a matter of time. Don't look so shocked, who else would you possibly be all the way up here to apprehend?"

The hooded woman pushed her way past the three men and carried on up the rapidly darkening mountainside. Antoni shot a quizzical expression at Jahus, the corners of his lips hinting at amusement. Orion saw the butchered bodies by their feet and again felt he would be sick.

"That iron ball she carries," Jahus remarked under his breath, "have either of you ever heard of the Six Steps? The Sisterhood's first three steps are good, positive: the first step is acceptance into a convent, the second is completion of all rights of passage to being confirmed as a full sister, while the third is a little more subjective but is more often than not dying a righteous death."

"And the other steps?" Antoni asked. "Steps four, five and six?"

"Those are a little darker," Jahus said as the three began walking back up the path after the nun. "The fourth step is a formal reprimand, a sign of disgrace for poor performance or violating the Order's rules. The fifth step is a last chance – a penance involving carrying a great weight to a place of spiritual significance. She is carrying out the fifth step."

"And the sixth?" Orion asked.

"Damnation. Expulsion from the Sisterhood."

"Well, well," Antoni nodded, "somebody's been a naughty girl."

"You go on ahead, keep an eye on her," Jahus nodded to Antoni. "We will catch you up soon enough. There is very little light left, and Dionne knows we are here now. This can no longer wait until morning."

Antoni nodded and picked up his pace to close the gap with the woman ahead. Orion let out a sigh and felt his head drop as he realized why Jahus wanted to speak to him alone. He had fallen short of the required standard. Again. He wondered if he would ever become a paladin. Plenty of young men and women failed, so why not he? Perhaps this too was his fifth step. Jahus placed an arm around Orion's shoulders.

"Don't be so despondent," he said warmly. "You have ended up on a long and difficult road, and there will be plenty more obstacles. Any path without obstacles will never lead anywhere exciting."

"I did nothing!" Orion said shakily, fighting hard to keep back the tears of shame. "I stood and did nothing!"

"You didn't run!" Jahus gave a brief laugh.

"All I've done is get in the way! I've been no help, only a burden! You heard that woman; I should be a paladin by now! Instead, I'm barely halfway through my time as a squire!"

"Pay no heed to her, she's clearly not without fault herself," Jahus grimaced.

"And this, all of this, it is what the Shining Ones have chosen for you. There is a plan! Have faith! You are meant to feel this hardship so that one day you can understand how it feels and will be better placed to help others in their time of need."

Jahus stopped and stood in front of Orion, clasping his hands on the taller boy's shoulders.

"Look at me, lad. Your father knew hardship and failure. I've known failure too, many times. I'm forty years old, and I never made it to Lord Paladin! But this was meant to be my lot in life and for that I'm thankful. I think you will be a paladin. I may be wrong, but I have faith in you. But whatever you become, all of this is what is forging you into the man you are meant to be. All of this will give you heart, soul, humility, everything you need to help others. And that's why we are here. To help others."

Orion swallowed and nodded. Jahus smiled broadly.

"Come now, let's catch up with the Antoni. Hopefully we can avoid another altercation, but if we do not, you may yet have your chance to use that sword arm."

*****

A full moon hung high in the clear sky, reflecting the glare of the sun that was now hidden beneath the horizon. It painted the whole sky in shades of dark but vivid orange, giving nearly as much light as that one would see on a bleak, overcast day. It was one of the many things that Dionne loved about Basilea, he reflected as he gazed up at the twinkling starscape above him. It was why Basilea was worth dying for. His eyes drew down to the jagged panorama of mountains that stretched out to the north and the west. The calm seas to the east reminded him of his childhood, his father, and many long days spent battling the elements to bring in a decent catch. His smile faded as he turned to look to the south. There, the mountains petered out into gentle hills where farmers grew olives, grapes, hops, and myriad other crops that were the lifeblood of the nation. And it was these crops that were the final blow in the ever escalating clash between him and the corrupt bureaucrats which lay further south still, in their extravagant mansions and town houses in the twinkling cities of Basilea's heartland.

"Captain?"

Dionne turned to face the familiar voice addressing him. Lourne, his most loyal lieutenant who had fought by his side on a dozen campaigns, stood awkwardly on the rocks a few feet below the mountain precipice that Dionne used to view the world around him. Lourne wore the same mail coat and white tabard as the rest of Dionne's men, but as a unit leader, he was allowed some extravagance. He had three blue feathers emerging from the helmet he carried under one arm, rather than the standard single feather. His cool, gray eyes appeared tired but had lost none of the spark that sustained him through ten years of fighting.

"What is it?" Dionne asked.

"Four armed men, approaching from the south."

"Our own deserters?" Dionne stepped down from the rocky precipice. Lourne shook his head.

"Too well equipped, sir. From this distance, they look to be paladins."

Dionne stopped, a burden of responsibility suddenly falling on his shoulders that was so heavy he could physically feel it.

"It was always inevitable," he whispered, mainly to himself, before glancing across at Lourne. The blond haired soldier fixed him with a defiant glower.

"We all knew the consequences of our action, sir. We stand with you now, as always."

Dionne allowed himself a brief smile as he stepped down from the precipice, patting Lourne on the shoulder as he passed. The two made their way awkwardly through the rocks back to the main encampment on the mountainside below. A ring of wooden stakes, taller than a man, had been driven in between the rocks to form an uneven defensive palisade that acted as the encampment's perimeter. A rickety guard tower stood over the one gateway leading into the camp, where a motley assortment of tents and wooden huts acted as accommodation and storage. Some forty soldiers had chosen to side with Dionne after he had struck out and began to act on his own initiative following a series of disagreements with his seniors in the Basilean Legion; but while many of his men had chosen their loyalty to their senior commanders over their own captain, some locals who had heard of Dionne's exploits and choices had thrown down the tools of their trades to join his cause.

The buzz of conversation immediately died down as Dionne and Lourne approached, replaced by the calm crackle of torch flames and the distant chattering of mountain bats rising from their slumber for the night. Dionne's forty soldiers stood in a loose semi-circle ahead of him, looking at him expectantly. Some stood rigidly to attention, while others pulled on their mail hauberks and strapped their sword belts to their waists.

"You've no doubt already heard that armed men are only moments away,"

Continue this in "Steps to Deliverance" from Zmok books